THE HOUSE OF HALE
RETURN OF THE ELEMENTALS

Stephanie A. Hamlin

This book is a work of fiction. Names, characters, places, and incidents are products of the author's imagination or are used fictitiously and are not to be considered as real. Any resemblance to actual events, locales, organizations, or persons, living or dead, is coincidental.

The House of Hale: Return of the Elementals
Copyright © 2025 Stephanie A. Hamlin
All rights reserved.
Cover by @GetCovers
ISBN: 9798270062835

DEDICATION

To Amira, for reminding me of how much joy I truly find in writing.

To my family, for their endless encouragements. And for always recognizing when it was needed.

To my readers, for sticking with both me and Amira through this journey. I hope it's worth the wait.

Prologue

Long before the rise of the House of Hale, there lived a mortal man named Horatius Croatoan. Born to a minor noble house in Zarandore, Horatius was gifted—some said cursed—with a rare affinity for alchemy. Yet, for all his talent, he yearned for power. He hated the nature spellcasters for their abilities, and when they succeeded in opening the first Standing Portal, he grew enraged.

Soon though, Horatius's envy turned to ambition. He stole the Elemental Staff, and guided by visions only he could see, journeyed north to the wild, unclaimed lands of Zarandore. There, he began the ritual that would change the fate of Hekagia forever.

In that moment, the balance of magic in Hekagia shifted. The Northern Portal became a beacon, drawing astral magic to itself and severing the subtle threads that once connected Hekagia to the other realms. Only the link to Earth remained, tenuous and fragile. Only able to be opened by the deep magic of Royal blood. The other pathways were lost in the storm of astral energy unleashed by Horatius's spell.

Horatius was thrilled at first, but astral magic is a hungry force. It does not blend with the elements—it consumes them. As Horatius's spell reached its climax, he realized that the portal he'd created was not like the others. It was a tear in the world itself, a swirling vortex that bled into a world made of shadow and despair. The Northern Portal was born, but at a terrible cost.

CHAPTER ONE

LET THE CHAOS BEGIN

The day you turn eighteen is supposed to be exciting. Unless, of course, you're the future queen of a magical realm and are about to be married off to someone you barely know in order to claim your throne. As first in line to the throne of Hekagia, that's exactly what was in store for me in less than a month.

I sighed, crossing off yesterday's date on my makeshift wooden calendar.

One day closer to my impending doom…

A sharp knock rattled my bedchamber door, jolting me from my melancholy.

"Amira! Get your royal butt out here—these snot-nosed brats are getting restless," Kira barked, pounding on the door like she was trying to break it down.

I groaned, dragging my feet. With Kira, "restless" usually meant someone was on fire… Again.

I had seriously underestimated how much work it would be to run a school when I'd suggested it six months ago. Sure, we had our headmaster—Master Frederick—but the ancient alchemist was no match for thirty preteens who all seemed determined to obliterate each other.

The whole point of opening the academy had been to bring the next generation of Hekagians together, but so far, it had been an absolute disaster.

The astral spellcasters and nature spellcasters couldn't be in the same classroom without a fight breaking out, and the alchemy students had immediately barricaded themselves in their own wing, refusing to interact with anyone else.

My days were now spent breaking up petty arguments and putting out fires—sometimes literally. I didn't mind most of the time; the chaos served as a welcome distraction from my coronation. But today was not like other days. Today, my mother was coming for her monthly visit, and she expected everything to be perfect—me included.

Kira burst into my bedchamber without warning, the door banging against the stone wall with a deafening *crack*. Her long blonde hair had come half-undone from its braid, wild strands framing her flushed face. Her eyes—usually green—glowed a vivid purple, the telltale sign that her patience had been worn dangerously thin.

"Amira! Seriously, what's taking you so long?" she snapped, her voice tight. "If you don't get out here in the next ten seconds, I'm dragging you out in your pajamas."

I hesitated, glancing at the scattered papers on my desk, the half-crossed calendar, the mess of my own thoughts. "Is it safe to come out, or should I just barricade myself in here until the coronation?" I asked, dreading her answer.

Kira kicked at a loose floorboard. "It's the Kilburn twins. Again." She spat the words like they tasted bad. "Those little monsters blew up the alchemy lab and now Master Frederick's hiding in the broom closet. I've got half an eyebrow, Amira. *Half.*" She pointed at her burned brow for emphasis.

"Maybe they'll get bored and take up knitting instead," I muttered, trying to lighten the mood.

"Doubtful," Kira grumbled.

The Kilburn twins—Calix and Cassandra—were more than just the school troublemakers. As the niece and nephew of Lord Adley, the Zarandorian representative and perpetual thorn in my side on the Golden Council, the twins took pride in the chaos they sowed. Their flaming red hair and matching devilish grins were a warning sign to every teacher and student in the academy to stay on their good side.

All the students knew that my mother was coming for her visit, and while most of them understood how important it was that things went smoothly while she was around, the Kilburn twins took it as a personal challenge to cause the most mayhem possible. So I wasn't at all surprised to find Kira standing in my doorway, one eyebrow singed off and—remarkably—still smoldering.

"Maybe you should go to the infirmary before you lose the other half. Madame Galena can probably fix you up before my mother gets here."

Kira shot me a withering glare. "I'm fine. But if I catch those two, they'll wish they'd never heard of potassium." She shrugged off her black leather jacket and tossed it onto my nightstand, revealing a thin line of blood soaking through the collar of her shirt.

"You're bleeding," I pointed out.

She rolled her eyes, yanking the collar down to inspect the wound herself. "It's nothing. Just a scratch." But I could see the tension in her jaw as she revealed a shallow cut running up the side of her neck.

"Madame Galena is a good healer," I coaxed, trying to keep my tone light. "She fixed up my toe last month when Calix 'accidentally' dropped a battle-ax on it. Put it back on, right as new."

Kira shot me an icy glare.

"Seriously, she's basically a miracle worker. I mean, you can't even tell which toe it was anymore!" I said with a bright smile.

Kira rolled her eyes, but I could tell she was wavering. She hated showing weakness, even in front of me, but the blood soaking through her shirt was starting to drip onto the wood planks of my floor— a sight that was likely to send my chambermaid Aria into a frenzy.

I ushered Kira into the corridor. "Come on, I'll go with you."

As we stepped into the hallway, the distant sounds of chaos drifted toward us—shouts, laughter, and the unmistakable crash of glass. I glanced at Kira, who was doing her best to look unfazed, but her hand hovered near the cut on her neck.

"I'll survive. And you don't fool me. You just want an excuse to go see Treander." Kira smirked.

My cheeks flushed. "I—I don't know what you're talking about." I tucked a stray curl behind my ear, refusing to meet her quizzical eye.

"So this has nothing to do with Treander?" Kira asked, waggling her singed eyebrow at me, lips twitching in amusement.

"No! I mean—of course not. Why would it?" I started walking faster, hoping she'd drop it.

Kira gave a low whistle, shaking her head as if to say, 'sure, whatever you say, big sis.'

"If I wanted to see how Treander was doing, I'd go see him myself. I wouldn't send my little sister," I shot back.

But as usual, Kira was right. Treander had been on my mind all morning.

Kira's gaze shifted to a painting on the corridor wall, like she didn't want to make eye contact with me. Her voice dropped, almost sounding gentle. "He'll pull through, Amira. He always does."

I wished I could be so sure…

Even after Treander had woken from the Timeless One's magical coma, it was like he hadn't really come out of it. At first, things had felt almost normal. We'd stay up late talking about everything and nothing, and once he was cleared to leave the infirmary, we were basically glued at the hip. But even then, I could see it—the way his hands shook when he tried to string his bow, the haunted look in his eyes when he thought I wasn't watching. I couldn't pinpoint when it started, but it was like his spark just… started to fade.

That's when I hired Madame Galena, hoping her healing magic could reach the places medicine couldn't. But nothing had worked. Most days now, Treander didn't leave the infirmary. When he did, he was quiet, moody, and so far away from the boy I'd met in the ravine—the one who used to make me laugh so hard I'd snort water out my nose, who'd face down monsters with nothing but a crooked grin and a battered bow.

Now, every time I saw him, I wondered if that boy was gone for good, or if somewhere under all the scars and silence, he was still fighting to find his way back.

Kira broke the silence, her voice unusually quiet. "He just needs time," she said, her words softer than I was used to. "You have no idea what he's been through. Being used by Raideron like that…" Her eyes darkened, and for a moment, I saw the shadow of old memories flicker across her face—memories of her time trapped at Shadowfell Castle.

"I know," I replied, my voice just as soft.

Kira's jaw tightened, a flash of anger spreading across her face. "And your mom isn't helping any," she said, her words edged with frustration. "She never shuts up about Ajay."

"I know that too," I admitted.

On paper, a match with Ajay made perfect sense—politically,

it would unite two of the most powerful houses in the realm. And Ajay was a great guy: kind, thoughtful, and everything a future queen was supposed to want.

But he wasn't Treander.

The royal trumpet sounded from the courtyard, its brassy notes slicing through my thoughts. Kira and I groaned in unison.

After six months of my mother's inspections, the students had learned exactly what was expected of them. By the time Kira and I reached the entrance, they were lined up on either side of the massive mahogany doors, standing in perfect, almost unnatural silence. Their uniforms were crisp and spotless; even the Kilburn twins looked acceptable for once.

The marble floors gleamed so brightly I could see my own anxious reflection in them, and the air was thick with the scent of fresh wax and wildflowers—someone's last-ditch effort to make the place seem less like a war zone and more like a school.

Master Frederick came bustling into the entrance hall, his shoes squeaking with every step, cheeks flushed and hair sticking up like he'd just lost a duel with a cauldron. The Kilburn twins snickered, and I shot them my best "don't even think about it" glare.

"Has Princess Lilliana arrived?" Master Frederick asked, his voice pitched somewhere between panic and a plea for mercy. He scanned the room like he expected my mother to materialize out of thin air and start pointing out dust.

"Her carriage just pulled up," I said, trying to sound calm, but my stomach was doing somersaults.

He frowned, his eyes darting to the empty spaces in the line of students. "Is this everyone?"

I grimaced. "It is. Seven more went home yesterday… It's been a rough week."

Kira snorted beside me, arms folded. "Rough? Try catastrophic. I'm surprised anyone's left."

I bit my tongue, but she wasn't wrong.

Raideron's army hadn't taken long to regroup after the Battle of Shadowfell Castle. I'd finally managed to convince the Golden Council he was alive—just in time for his first attack. The war had started in earnest two months ago. Spellcasters and alchemists from all over Hekagia had banded together to stand against Raideron's forces, but some had defected to his army too. Hekagians—and even families— were suddenly pitted against each other, even here at the academy. The halls now echoed with whispered suspicion and fear.

Master Frederick let out a long, weary sigh, his shoulders slumping. "Well, at least the academy remains open…for now."

The front doors swung open and my mother swept in, flanked by two elite members of the Golden Guard and looking every inch the Royal. Her platinum hair was pinned up tightly and her long green dress looked like it belonged in a ballroom rather than a school.

But then I caught a look at her face. Her eyes were rimmed red, like she hadn't slept in days, and her skin, usually sun-kissed, had faded to a sickly yellow. The sight sent a jolt of worry through me.

I hugged her, trying to make it look casual, like I wasn't searching her face for answers. "What's wrong?" I whispered.

She pulled away, lips pursed in that familiar, regal way that meant she was about to dodge the question. "Is that any way to greet your mother?"

I rolled my eyes—she never made this easy—and asked again, a little louder this time. But she just waved me off, already scanning the room for imperfections. "Everything is fine. Now, how are things going here?"

"Everything is fine," I echoed. But the words had barely left my mouth when, of course, chaos erupted behind me.

Calix Kilburn, eyes practically glowing with mischief, stepped out of line like he was about to accept an award. "For Zarandore!" he bellowed, hiking up his uniform robe just enough to reveal a suspiciously large jar clutched between his knees.

I barely had time to groan before he twisted off the lid and dumped the contents onto the gleaming floor. Dozens of magical green frogs tumbled out, hitting the polished stone with a chorus of wet plops.

Instantly, the frogs began to burp—loud, echoing belches that released clouds of green gas so foul it made my eyes water. Within seconds, the hall dissolved into pandemonium.

The students shrieked and scattered, some ducking for cover, others chasing after the frogs like it was the best day of their lives.

One little girl, whose magic chose that exact moment to awaken, let out a terrified wail and accidentally astral projected herself onto the second-story balcony—her attempt to escape a group of boys brandishing handfuls of the slimy amphibians.

I glared at Calix, who grinned back at me with infuriating pride, then high-fived his twin sister before the two of them darted off toward the dormitories—leaving mayhem, and the lingering stench of frog gas, in their wake.

Some days, I wondered if being queen could really be any harder than this…

"What is going on here?" my mother snapped. She didn't even raise her voice—she didn't have to. The whole hall froze, except for the frogs, which kept burping up clouds of toxic green gas.

"Just your average Tuesday," Kira called, sarcasm dripping from every word. "We're running a magical zoo now. Didn't you get the memo?" She snatched a frog, yelped as it belched in her face, and glared at Master Frederick. "You want to help, or are you just going to stand there?"

Master Frederick, cheeks flushed and robes askew, tried to herd a cluster of frogs toward the door, but only succeeded in tripping over his own feet. "I—I'm doing my best, Princess Kira!" he stammered.

My mother tsked, her hands trembling as she smoothed her dress. Then, as if the weight of the morning finally caught up to her, she sat down hard on a nearby bench.

"What's going on with you?" I asked, hoping she'd actually answer me this time.

I could see the hesitancy in her eyes, but also how tired she was. The stress lines on her face deepened and her brows pinched together. "Fine," she said at last. "There's trouble at the castle. Raideron's army is getting closer every day, and the villagers are restless. Food supplies are… not what they should be."

I felt a pang of guilt at her words.

"I didn't realize things had gotten that bad," I admitted, my voice small. "The council's reports never really say much. I wish someone had told me sooner."

Kira, who'd been wrangling frogs with a scowl, shot a look at me over her shoulder. "Yeah, well, the council thinks we're too young to handle the truth. Like age has anything to do with it."

My mother pressed her lips together, her regal composure flickering. "I didn't want to worry you. You have enough on your plate here."

"I want to help, Mom. This is my kingdom and people are suffering. I should do something."

"There's nothing you can do for the villagers," she said, giving a little shrug, like my concern was just another thing to brush aside. "The best way you can help is to focus on your own responsibilities."

I clenched my fists, feeling my face grow hot.

"You don't know that. There must be something I can do—"

"The best way you can help Nithandore is to marry Ajay and become queen," she said abruptly, her tone sharp. She beckoned for one of the guards to help her stand, like the matter was settled.

"Are you serious right now?" I snapped.

Kira cleared her throat, stepping up beside me, her presence solid and reassuring. "This isn't the time or place," she said, her voice steady as she addressed my mother. "We've got enough crazy happening without adding more."

But my mother wasn't one to back down. She turned on Kira, her eyes flashing with a mix of exhaustion and stubborn determination. "And when would you suggest *is* the right time, Kira?"

"The coronation is a month away. She has time," Kira said. "You need to let Amira figure this out for herself."

"And if she doesn't?"

I couldn't take it anymore. "Excuse me," I cut in, my voice sharp. "Can you two stop talking about me like I'm not standing right here?" My magic hummed under my skin, but I forced myself to keep it in check.

"Then stop acting like a child, Amira!" my mother hissed.

Kira's eyebrows shot up, surprise flickering across her face at my mother's harshness. She glanced at me, her eyes asking if I wanted her to step in. I shook my head and turned back to my mother, determined not to let her see how much her words stung.

"You can't be serious," I said through gritted teeth, struggling to keep my voice steady. "After everything I've been through?"

"You are being selfish, Amira," my mother's snapped at me. "Marrying Ajay and uniting our families is what's best for Hekagia. Not carrying on with some common thief."

Something inside me snapped at the mention of Treander. Sparks flickered at my fingertips. "Don't call him a thief," I growled.

"Why not? That's what he is."

"You don't even know Treander," I shot back, my voice trembling with anger. "You don't know anything about him, or what he's been through. He's risked everything for me—for all of us."

She scoffed at that. "I do know that he's been locked away in the infirmary for weeks, barely alive and entirely unfit to rule the realm. What is it about the boy that has you so enamored that you would risk everything for him?" Her words were sharp, each one landing like a blow.

The truth was, I couldn't explain why I felt so strongly for Treander—I just knew that I did. Maybe not strongly enough to marry him at eighteen, but I knew that I didn't want to marry anyone else, either.

"And what if I refuse to marry either of them?" I said, dodging her question, my voice tight. "What will you do then?"

Master Frederick, who'd been lurking near the front door, let out a scandalized gasp. "But you must get married before your coronation!" he exclaimed, his voice rising in alarm.

"Why? I'm going to be queen. I can do whatever I want then," I shot back, my frustration boiling over.

"But…" Master Frederick stammered. "It is the law!"

"Some laws should be broken," I said hotly.

The startled look on Master Frederick's face told me I'd pushed him too far. He looked helplessly to my mother for support, his hands fluttering at his sides.

My mother grabbed me by the arm and pulled me into one of the empty classrooms. "Enough of this spectacle. You're sending Master Frederick into a fit," she said, glancing back at our weathered old headmaster.

"Why are you forcing me to do this?" I asked her as I slammed the door shut with a loud *bang*.

"Amira, I know that this isn't easy, and I wouldn't ask it of you if there was any other way—"

"There is another way," I cut in, my voice rising. "Screw your old-school traditions. I shouldn't have to marry someone just because I'm a woman!"

"It has nothing to do with your gender," she replied, her tone weary but unyielding. "The monarchy must be strong. You cannot rule alone. That is the law."

"Says who?" I countered.

She sat down heavily on a wooden stool, her eyes flickering to the window, and Vail Castle way off in the distance. She suddenly looked very tired—and, if I was being honest, a bit sad. Guilt pricked at me for adding to her stress, but that guilt was quickly extinguished by what she said next.

"Amira, I understand that you care for Treander, but we both know that he is unstable. Ajay will be a good leader. For once in your life, just do what you are told."

"Are you serious right now?" I said, my voice shaking with disbelief and anger.

"Hush now," my mother soothed, her tone softening as if she could smooth over the sting of her words. The change in her demeanor gave me whiplash.

"I didn't mean to upset you," she said. "I'm just trying to do what is best for Hekagia."

"How about, for once, you just be my mother!" The words burst out of me before I could stop them.

My mother's eyes widened and her mouth fell open.

"What is that supposed to mean?" she demanded.

"It means you care more about keeping the crown than you do about me. Do you even care whether or not I have feelings for Ajay?"

She drew herself up, shoulders straightening. "Of course I care," she bristled. "But you are a royal. Love is a luxury for us."

I stared at the floor, my anger cooling into something heavier. "What if I don't want to be a royal, then?" The words slipped out, sharp and brittle, echoing in the quiet room.

My mother rolled her eyes, exasperated. "Enough of this childish nonsense. Being queen is your destiny. There is no escaping it. Not for you."

Her words sent me spiraling back to the last time I'd seen my grandma. She'd said the same thing: that being queen of a united Hekagia was my destiny. I could still remember the way her voice had trembled—not with weakness, but conviction—and how I had almost believed I could be the person she saw in me.

I looked up at my mother then, her face set in lines of worry and exhaustion, and wondered if she'd ever really seen me—not as a princess, not as a future queen, but as her daughter.

I wasn't sure I wanted to know the answer.

"I can't do this right now." My voice cracked as I fought back tears. "We can talk about this later."

"You are running out of laters," my mother replied, her words heavy with warning.

"You don't have to remind me."

For once, my mother's eyes were sympathetic as she laid her hand on my shoulder. "I'm sorry for being so harsh, but I truly do want what's best for you."

"And if I don't want to marry Ajay?" I asked, skepticism thick in my voice.

"That is for you to decide."

"Really?"

"I'm not a heartless monster, Amira." She sighed. "If you don't want to marry Ajay, I won't force you."

My heart sped up as I looked at my mother. Not only was she pale and sweating, but she didn't even sound like herself. She was flip-flopping more than a sandal.

"Seriously, Mom, is everything okay with you?" I asked, unable to keep the worry from my voice.

"I've been… under the weather, but I'll be fine," she replied.

I was far from convinced of that, given the way her hand trembled as she brushed a stray strand of hair from her face. But before I could press her on it, she switched gears again.

"Have you heard from Caleb recently?" she asked.

I shook my head, trying to match her matter-of-factness. "Not in a few weeks. Last I heard, he was somewhere in Alkrimia, chasing down the Elemental Scrolls with Master Sadiki."

The Elemental Scrolls supposedly held the history of the first spellcasters—maybe even the secret to stopping Raideron. But even after months of relentless searching, we hadn't found them. The search dragged on, getting more desperate by the day.

"I'm sure they'll find the scrolls soon," my mother said as she stood, leaning against a bookshelf for support. "I must return to Vail Castle. It is hard to be away right now, with more refugees arriving by the hour."

I was almost a little disappointed that my mother had to leave. That had been the most civil conversation we'd had in a long time, and it reminded me how much I missed her—when she wasn't being an overbearing control freak, that is.

"Are you sure you have to go?"

She managed a small smile and nodded. "I need to get back, and it seems like you have everything well in hand here."

No sooner had she said it, the hallway exploded with noise—Savannah and Kira's voices rising in a full-blown shouting match. I sighed. "Here we go again."

I opened the door just in time to duck behind a statue of a unicorn as a streak of astral magic shot past my head. It slammed into the wall, leaving a dent the size of my face in the stone.

"What the heck is going on out here?" I demanded.

Kira stood in the middle of the corridor, wisps of astral magic curling around her fists as she glared daggers at Savannah. "Maybe you should ask her," she snapped, jabbing a finger at Savannah like she was ready to launch another magical assault.

Savannah's short hair stuck up in every direction, and a thin trickle of blood ran from the corner of her mouth. Her eyes darted from Kira to me, wide and urgent. "We need to talk," she said without missing a beat.

CHAPTER TWO

THE TIES THAT BIND

Aunt Lilliana hauled Amira into the classroom and slammed the door in my face. But that was fine with me. No way did I want to get between those two when they were heated.

Besides, it wasn't my place to tell Amira how to live her life. That was Lilliana's job.

Master Frederick shuffled up beside me, his cane tapping out a slow rhythm on the stone floor. "Princess Kira, do you think you can convince your sister to marry the Alkrimian boy?"

I snorted. "Not a chance."

He shot me a disapproving look. "She is your sister. She will listen to you."

"Unlikely," I said dryly. "Amira has a mind of her own. And besides, I'm on her side with this one."

"Why do you say that, Princess?"

I shrugged, shoving my hands in my jacket pockets. "Who in their right mind would get married that young? I wouldn't, not even for Ravenna."

Master Frederick shook his head, the lines around his eyes deepening. "Princess Amira is not just anybody, she is the—"

"The future queen," I grumbled, cutting him off. "The Savior of Hekagia. Trust me, I've heard it all before."

"So you do not want the throne then, I take it?" His bushy eyebrow quirked in question.

"Not even a little," I said, deadpan.

He leaned in, lowering his voice as if sharing a secret. "Well, you'd better talk some sense into your sister then. The law is clear. If Amira refuses to marry, she forfeits her right to the throne."

I stopped short, making Master Frederick run into me.

"Wait, what?"

Master Frederick steadied himself against the wall, fixing me with a classic teacher glare as he readjusted his robes. "If Princess Amira will not marry, the crown passes to the next in line."

"But that's me!" I blurted, my voice shooting up an octave.

"Precisely," Master Frederick huffed, as if this was all perfectly reasonable. "If you do not wish to bear the responsibility of ruling the realm, you had better convince your sister to do what is expected of her."

I just stood there, stunned, as Master Frederick shuffled off toward the headmaster's office, probably to file some ancient paperwork or whatever it is he does. Did he really expect me to pressure Amira into marrying some guy she barely knows, just so I wouldn't have to be queen?

The thought of sitting on the throne, listening to villagers complain about stolen cows and whose fence was on whose land, sounded like pure torture. But as much as I dreaded the idea, I couldn't bring myself to manipulate Amira just to avoid it. That would make me no better than our grandpa Alastair—a man so obsessed with power he once tried to sacrifice Amira to Raideron just so I could take the throne in her place. I'd sworn I would never become like him.

Ribbit Ribbit

Of course. One of the Kilburn twins' magical frogs had escaped the hall. It landed right on my boot, nearly giving me a heart attack. I kicked it away on reflex—then, feeling guilty, knelt down to make sure the little troublemaker was okay.

Ribbit Ribbit

"Sorry, buddy." I opened a small portal and sent it hopping through, watching it disappear into the grassy front lawn of the academy. Then I straightened up and headed for the Armory. I needed to find Ravenna. If anyone could help me make sense of what Master Frederick had just dumped on me, it was her.

The academy was way too quiet. After the Kilburn twins' little "frogpocalypse" in the entrance hall, most of the students had gone into hiding. The place felt like a ghost town. But I didn't mind the silence. It gave me time to plot my revenge on those two little monsters.

First idea: fill their dorm with a hundred magic frogs and let the stink drive them up the walls. Classic, but too easy. The more I thought about it, the more I realized the twins deserved something way worse. And if I had anything to say about it, they'd be begging for frog stench by the time I was done.

I gingerly poked at the burned patch of skin where my eyebrow used to be, wincing at the sting. With a sigh, I changed direction and headed for the infirmary. The last thing I wanted was for Ravenna to see me like this—half an eyebrow was not a good look on anyone. Besides, that gave me an excuse to check up on Treander, my sister's addlebrained boy toy.

Don't get me wrong, I liked Treander well enough. But lately, all he did was mope around the place. Whatever the Timeless One had done to him had really scrambled his brains. Just last week, I'd found him wandering around the astronomy tower in the middle of the night in nothing but his underwear. That had been awkward...

"Good morning, Princess Kira." Madame Galena, our raven-haired healer, greeted me with a bright smile as I stepped into the infirmary.

"Can you do something about this?" I asked, pointing to the spot where my eyebrow used to be.

Madame Galena motioned for me to sit on the empty cot next to Treander, who was staring absently out the window like he was waiting for a sign from the universe.

"Hey," I said, giving him a nod as I sat down.

Treander barely noticed me. He looked straight past me towards the door —clearly hoping for someone else.

"Amira's not with me." I shot him an apologetic look, but he just nodded and drifted back to his window, lost in whatever fog he lived in these days.

I lowered my voice, leaning toward Madame Galena as she dabbed cooling cream onto my burned eyebrow. "Is he doing any better?"

Madame Galena grimaced as she glanced over at Treander. "Not as much as I had hoped," she admitted quietly. "Whatever that foul creature did to him, it's left a deep mark on his mind. Some days are better than others, but today..." She shook her head, setting down the applicator stick on a metal tray table.

She looked at me, her gaze gentle but firm. "It does him good to see familiar faces. Do you think Princess Amira might be able to visit him today?"

"I wouldn't count on it," I said quietly so Treander wouldn't overhear.

Honestly, for as much as I knew Amira cared about Treander, she hadn't really been there for him lately—probably because her mom was piling on the pressure for her to ditch him for Ajay. Amira hardly ever visited Treander anymore, and when she did, she didn't stay long. Which was too bad, because Treander really did seem better whenever she was around.

Madame Galena handed me a small mirror and I used it to inspect my new eyebrow, which had already grown back, thanks to her magical balm. "Please tell Princess Amira to visit as soon as she can," she pleaded.

"I'll see what I can do, but no promises."

The infirmary was freezing, and the whole place reeked of that sharp, sour potion smell—like someone had tried to mask a crime scene with lemon and failed. I couldn't get out of there fast enough. I hesitated, then gave Treander a quick pat on the shoulder—meant to be reassuring, I guess, but he jerked away like I'd zapped him with a live wire.

"See you around, Treander," I muttered, trying to keep it light, but my words just bounced off the silence. He didn't even blink, just kept watching the rain streak down the glass. I left him to his staring contest with the storm.

I slipped out into the corridor, my thoughts turning to Ravenna. I hadn't seen her in days—she'd been off with Gnash and the archers, prepping for whatever disaster was coming next. She'd only got back that morning.

Being apart from her sucked. I couldn't imagine being stuck in the infirmary and not wanting to spend every second with her. Still, even if I didn't agree with how she was handling things with Treander, I got where Amira was coming from. Why get closer to someone if you're just going to have to let them go?

A voice, low and suspicious, yanked me out of my thoughts and made me freeze mid-step. "Be quiet or someone will hear me." Savannah's voice, but not her usual chirpy nonsense— this was tight, urgent, and way too serious for her.

I followed the sound to the broom closet. Weird enough on its own, but the purple glow leaking out from under the door? That was a whole new level of suspicious. Savannah couldn't conjure portals. And everyone knew Raideron was watching them anyways. Only a total bonehead would risk opening one here at the academy. Or a spy.

I didn't hesitate. I yanked the door open, ready for anything. Savannah yelped, tumbling backwards into a mop bucket with a crash that echoed down the hall. The portal fizzled out, leaving nothing but a curl of purple smoke.

"What are you doing in here?" I demanded, my voice sharp.

Savannah scrambled upright, cheeks blazing, eyes wide like I'd caught her robbing the place. "Nothing... what are you doing here?" she shot back defensively, like she was the one with the right to be mad.

I planted myself in the doorway, arms crossed, making it clear she wasn't getting past me. "I heard voices. Who were you talking to?" Savannah's eyes darted around the cramped closet—over the mop bucket, the stack of rags, anywhere but at me—like she was searching for an escape hatch.

She opened her mouth, closed it, then tried again. "I—I was just looking for cleaning supplies. You know how messy the hallways get after the Kilburn twins—"

I cut her off with a glare. "Don't insult me. I saw the portal, Savannah. Who was it?"

"Why do you always assume the worst of me, Kira? Maybe if you spent less time spying on me and more time minding your own business—"

"Maybe if you weren't always sneaking around, I wouldn't have to," I shot back, my voice low and dangerous. "So, who was it? Or should I just go get Amira and let her sort this out?"

Savannah eyes flashed. "What exactly are you going to tell her? That you caught me in the act... of looking for a mop?" Her voice was all mock innocence, but there was a bite underneath.

I stormed back to the entrance hall, the echo bouncing off the stone walls. I stopped outside the classroom where Amira and Aunt Lilliana had disappeared, pressing my ear to the door. No shouting—just the low murmur of voices. Good. Lilliana was still here. She'd believe me, even if Amira kept falling for Savannah's "poor me" routine.

No one but Amira had been fooled by Savannah's innocent act when she'd shown up, claiming to have escaped from Shadowfell Castle. I knew better. No one escaped Raideron. Not really.

And Savannah? She was always too quick with her stories, too smooth for her own good. I'd seen enough liars to know one when I heard it.

Savannah's voice rang out, sharp and defensive as she followed me. "You're just going to upset Amira for no reason. Don't you think she's got more important things to worry about right now?" Her words dripped with accusation, like I was the problem. Typical. Always flipping the script, always making herself the victim.

I clenched my fists, fighting the urge to whirl around and let Savannah have it right there in the hall.

"You might have Amira fooled, but not me," I said, my voice low and steady. "I know you're working for Raideron." I let the words hang between us, daring her to deny it.

"I am *not*," she snapped. "And besides, Amira would never believe you even if I was. I'm her best friend."

"Yeah, well, I'm her sister," I hissed, stepping closer, refusing to back down.

"A sister she's known for what…barely three years? She's known me practically her whole life."

"And you lied to her the entire time," I countered.

"Amira already forgave me for that," Savannah said, but her voice shook a little. "Not that you'd understand forgiveness."

I rolled my eyes at that. "Just make this easier on everyone and admit you're working for Raideron," I replied, my frustration boiling over. "You've always been good at playing the victim, Savannah. But I see right through you."

She clutched her chest, eyebrows shooting up in a perfect imitation of innocence. "How could you even suggest such a thing?" she cried, her voice ringing out loud enough to wake the dead. "Amira is my best friend. I would never do anything to hurt her." She glared at me, all wide-eyed and wounded, like I was the villain in her tragic little story.

Please. I'd seen better acting from the Kilburn twins when they tried to fake sick to get out of magical history class.

The more she played the victim, the hotter my anger burned—my magic itching to break loose. "You're a liar!" I shouted. Before

I could even think, a pulse of astral energy shot from my palm, crackling through the air toward Savannah. She yelped and dove aside—just as the classroom door behind her banged open.

Amira stepped out, curls wild, eyes wide, right as the magical blast zipped past her ear.

"What's going on out here?" she demanded.

I jabbed a finger at Savannah. "Maybe you should ask her."

"I'm asking you, Kira."

I folded my arms, planted my boots, and refused to budge. "I caught Savannah talking to Raideron." My words came out flat, but I made sure Savannah could hear every syllable—no way was I letting her squirm her way out of this one.

Amira's eyes went huge, disbelief written all over her face. "What are you talking about?"

"I was on my way back from the infirmary when I overheard Savannah talking to someone through a portal. Who else could it have been?"

Savannah shrank back, her voice suddenly meek. "It's not what you think," she mumbled, refusing to meet Amira's eye.

"Then what is it?"

Savannah's shoulders slumped. "Raideron...he told me to spy on you or he'd make me pay. But I swear I didn't tell him anything!"

"Why didn't you tell me this sooner?" Amira's voice trembled, full of hurt.

Savannah stared at the floor, her shoes scuffing the flagstones. "I don't know. I guess I didn't think you'd believe that I'm not really working for him." She looked up, eyes wide and pleading, like a kicked puppy. "But you believe me, don't you?"

Amira hesitated—just for a second. But then she nodded.

"Of course I believe you."

My jaw clenched so hard it hurt but I couldn't keep it in.

"You're really going to believe her… just like that?" I shot Savannah a glare, daring her to smirk, to gloat, to do anything but look guilty. She just looked away, lips pressed tight, like she'd already won and didn't even need to rub it in.

Aunt Lily coughed, the sound sharp, probably trying to break the tension. I spun, ready to snap at her for butting in, but the words died in my mouth. She was slumped against a statue, her breath coming in shallow gasps. For the first time ever, Aunt Lily didn't look like she could take on the world and win. She looked small. Breakable.

"My mom needs to get back to the castle," Amira said in a worried tone. "Savannah, why don't you help her out to her carriage?"

Savannah hesitated, shooting me a look—uncertainty flickering in her eyes. She clearly didn't want to leave me alone with Amira, not after all that.

"We'll talk more later," Amira said, her tone final.

Aunt Lily gave me a solemn nod before following Savannah out the front door.

The second the door slammed, I spun on Amira, my anger practically buzzing under my skin. "Seriously? You're taking Savannah's side. Again. Why am I even surprised?" I threw my hands up. "You always pick her over me. Every. Single. Time."

"I'm not taking anyone's side, Kira."

"Sure seems like you are," I snapped.

Amira's gaze narrowed, irritation flashing in her eyes. "What makes you so sure that Savannah's up to no good?"

"I can't explain it. It's just… every time she talks, it feels like she's hiding something." The words sounded weak, even to me, but it was the truth. My gut had never steered me wrong before.

Amira pinched the bridge of her nose and let out a long sigh. "Kira, I know you're worried. And I get it—really, I do. But I can't just accuse Savannah without something more. If you really think she's hiding something, bring me proof. But I need more than a feeling to go on."

I crossed my arms, voice rising. "I'm your sister. Doesn't that count for something?"

"Of course it counts. I love you, Kira. But I care about Savannah too!" Amira reached for me, but I backed out of her reach.

"Sort of like how you feel about Treander and Ajay?"

The words slipped out before I could stop them, but whatever—I was too angry to care. "You're stringing them along just like me and Savannah."

Hurt flickered across Amira's face. "That's not fair, Kira."

"Seriously, do you even like either of them? Or do you just get a kick out of it?" I snapped.

Amira looked like she might melt right into the floor, but I wasn't about to let her off the hook.

"I just came from the infirmary, you know. Treander's a wreck. You're treating him just as badly as you treat me." My words came out sharp—too sharp—but I couldn't stop. "You act like you're the only one who has to make hard choices, but you're not. You're not the only one who gets hurt, Amira."

She reached for me, her eyes glassy with tears, but I jerked away, putting a good three feet between us before I did something stupid—like blast her with astral magic.

"Where is all this coming from?" she asked, her voice soft and confused, like she couldn't believe I'd actually call her out.

"You're going to be a great queen, Amira," I spat, the words tasting like poison, "but you suck as a big sister."

I didn't wait for her to answer. I spun on my heel and stomped off, boots echoing down the corridor. My anger burned in my chest, hot and wild. I needed Ravenna—someone who'd actually listen, someone who'd take my side for once.

The armory was packed—apparently every student in the academy had decided it was the safest place to hide out. Not that I blamed them. The stench of frog gas still filled the halls, thick enough to make your eyes water. But here, the air was different—tense, buzzing with excited energy.

Ravenna and Gnash were in the center arena, putting on a show with the battle axes. Probably because of the whole Calix dropping one on Amira's toe thing. Most of the students were spellcasters—like Calix, who'd rather set something on fire than pick up a sword. Give them a weapon and they looked like they were holding a dead fish.

Ravenna, of course, made it look easy. She swung the axe at Gnash, missing him by an inch, and he just grinned, dodging like it was nothing. For a guy built like a tank, he moved with the kind of grace that made you wonder if he'd been a dancer in another life. The two of them together? Unstoppable.

After a few more rounds, Ravenna set down her axe. The students burst into applause, some of them looking at her like she'd just invented magic itself. Not a single strand of her long hair was out of place. She hadn't even broken a sweat.

She turned, caught my eye, and flashed that wide, beautiful smile—the one that made me forget about the frogs, the drama, and even Amira. It was just Ravenna, looking at me like I was the only person in the room.

I tried to play it cool, leaning against the wall and crossing my arms like I wasn't dying to run over and hug her. "Show-off," I called out, keeping my face neutral.

Ravenna just grinned, tossing her hair over her shoulder like she knew exactly how distracting it was. "You're next, Kira. Think you can handle an axe without losing a limb?"

"No promises," I said, trying to hold back a smile. "But at least if I lose a toe, I know Madame Galena's got me covered."

Gnash let out a booming laugh that echoed through the room.

Ravenna crossed the room in three long strides. She wrapped me in a hug that was all warmth and muscle.

"I missed you," I admitted, the words slipping out before I could stop them.

Ravenna kissed me on the lips, and the students erupted—half of them making obnoxious "ooh" noises, the rest gawking like they'd never seen two girls kiss before. I shot them a glare that sent them all scattering like cockroaches.

"Has something happened?" Ravenna asked me, her voice low and steady. Her eyes searched my face like she could see every thought I was trying to hide.

I tried to shrug it off, but my shoulders sagged. "Rough morning," I said, and before I knew it, everything just spilled out: the school falling apart, my fight with Amira, Savannah sneaking around, and how nobody seemed to believe me—not even my own sister. The words tumbled out, messy and desperate, like if I didn't get them out now, I'd explode.

Ravenna's eyes went wide, but she didn't cut me off or try to fix it. She just squeezed my hand, grounding me. "That's a lot."

"Amira didn't think so," I muttered, stalking over to one of the practice dummies. I yanked my dagger from my boot and drove it into the dummy's chest again and again, imagining it was Savannah's smug face. "She never believes me when it comes to Savannah. Never."

Ravenna crossed the room and pried the dagger from my hand. "I believe you," she said, her voice soft but steady.

I shot her an appreciative smile, but my fingers still twitched, itching to break something. "Yeah, well, you're the only one," I grumbled. "I can't even stand to be around Amira right now." My voice came out rough. "She just—she never listens. Not when it actually matters."

Ravenna's eyes searched mine with a steady, unflinching intensity. "I have a proposal," she said, her lips curving into a small, hopeful smile. "Don't worry, it's not a marriage proposal."

I snorted, rolling my eyes. "Good, because I left my white dress at home," I shot back, trying to keep things light, even though my stomach was tying itself in knots.

Ravenna's mouth twitched, but her eyes stayed serious. She reached into her battered satchel and pulled out a folded piece of parchment, the edges frayed and stained like it had been through a war. She handed it to me, her fingers brushing mine—warm and callused from years of training with her taiaha.

"What's this?" I asked.

"It's a summons," Ravenna said quietly, her tone heavy. "I am to return to my village the day after tomorrow."

A cold wave crashed over me. "Wait, what? You're leaving? Now?" My voice cracked, and I hated how desperate I sounded. "Ravenna, Raideron's army could show up any second. We need you here. I need you here."

She shook her head, her dark hair falling into her eyes. "I know. But my village… they're scared, Kira. Even the old ones. I can't ignore that. My people need me."

"You said you had a proposal?" I managed, my voice rough, trying to keep it together.

"Come with me," she said, her voice soft but unshakable. "I want you by my side, Kira. My home… it's wild, and it's not easy, but you'd be welcome there."

I just stared at her, my brain short-circuiting as the hope in Ravenna's eyes flickered, then fizzled out.

Awesome. Way to go, Kira—break the heart of the only person who'll actually put up with you.

"I'm sorry," I said, reaching for her hands, guilt twisting in my gut. "You surprised me, that's all."

Ravenna squeezed my fingers. "Will you come with me?" she asked again.

A lump the size of a boulder lodged in my throat.

"I… I can't," my words faltered as I tried to get them out.

The devastated look on her face nearly broke me.

Realizing that we had an audience again, I grabbed Ravenna's hand and led her out into the corridor. "I'm sorry," I said once we were out of earshot of the gremlins.

"Kira, look at me." Her voice was low and steady as she tilted my chin up to meet her eyes. "Tell me the truth. Why won't you come with me?"

I tried to come up with the right words, but they rushed out of me in a tangled mess. "Because if I go with you, I'm leaving Amira and the academy to fend for themselves. I can't just bail when everything's falling apart. That's not who I am."

Ravenna's gaze didn't budge—dark, deep, and way too honest. "And what am I, then?" she asked. "Am I not your whānau too?"

My chest tightened. "Of course you're my family! You're the only person who actually gets me."

She stepped in, close enough that I could smell the wildflowers in her hair. Her hands found mine. "Come with me," she said, her voice soft but insistent, like she was offering me the whole world and daring me to say no.

Gods, she made it sound easy. Just drop everything and run away. For a second, I actually let myself picture it—me and Ravenna, somewhere nobody could find us, no council meetings, no family drama, just… peace.

Yeah, right. Like I'd ever get off that easy.

"I can't," I choked out, shaking my head. "If Raideron attacks and I'm not here…"

Ravenna's face fell, her hands slipping from mine. But she didn't turn away. She just nodded, her jaw set, eyes shining with that stubborn, unbreakable loyalty that made me fall for her in the first place. "I hear you," she said quietly. "I'll go because I must. But my heart stays here, with you. Remember that."

I pulled her into a fierce hug. "I know you have to go," I muttered into her shoulder, "but can't you just… I dunno, stall for a couple days?"

Ravenna buried her face in my neck, her breath warm. "Kira," she murmured. "My family needs me. I must begin the journey home in two days. But until then, I am yours."

I grabbed her hand and didn't let go, like maybe if I just clung tight enough, she'd forget about her whole "duty" thing and stay. (Delusional? Maybe. Worth a shot? Definitely.)

"Come on then," I said, forcing a crooked smile. "Let's run away for a while. Just you and me."

CHAPTER THREE

TROUBLES OF THE HEART

My mother's carriage rattled its way down the muddy road, wheels splashing through puddles as it headed toward Middlehaven. The village looked so small from here—just a handful of rooftops huddled together, as if they were bracing for a storm. Beyond, the Aether Woods stretched out, burnt and twisted. In the other direction, Vail Castle rose up, looking like something out of a legend. My legend, apparently. No pressure…

I should've been excited, right? Future queen, magical realm, all that. But mostly, I kept thinking about the whole "marry before you're crowned" thing, and it made me want to crawl under my bed and never come out. Everyone expected me to just go along with it, like deciding to marry someone was as easy as picking out a new dress. And then there was the guilt. It twisted inside me, especially after Kira's little speech about how I'd been treating Treander.

It's not like I'd stopped caring about him. I hadn't. But he'd gone so quiet, so far away. Every conversation felt like walking a tightrope over a pit of spikes. I never knew what to say, especially if Ajay's name came up. The easy smiles, the inside jokes, they'd all been replaced by awkward silences.

But Kira was right. I couldn't keep dodging Treander forever. He deserved the truth, even if it meant ripping off the world's biggest, most painful bandage. It was time to stop hiding. Time to finally say everything I'd been too afraid to say.

The corridors were quiet—too quiet. Most of the students had retreated to the dorms, or at least had the good sense to steer clear of me after this morning's disaster. The silence was actually kind of nice, though. It gave me space to untangle the mess in my head.

I stopped outside the infirmary, heart pounding. For a second, I just stood there, staring at the door. Then I sucked in a shaky breath, squared my shoulders, and slid it open.

Madame Galena was there, as always—her hair pulled back, her robes spotless, not a single thing out of place. She dipped into a gentle curtsey, her smile warm and soft. "It is good to see you, Your Highness," she said.

I tried to smile back, but my lips just twitched awkwardly. "How is he?" I asked, trying not to show how nervous I was.

Her smile faded, sadness flickering in her eyes. "No change, I'm afraid. He perked up a little when Princess Kira visited earlier, but only for a moment. He hasn't spoken in days."

My heart sank. I glanced over at Treander, sitting on his cot, completely still. He had his back to the room, staring out the stained-glass window at the empty training arena below. For a second, I wondered if he even knew I was there.

I hovered in the doorway, not sure if I should say something or just…leave. But I couldn't. Not after everything. Not after all the times he'd been there for me.

"Hey," I said, my voice barely above a whisper. "It's me."

He didn't move. Not even a twitch.

I shot Madame Galena a helpless look. She just gave me that gentle, patient smile—the one that said, "Give it time." So I did. I crossed the room and sat down on the edge of his cot.

For a long moment, neither of us said anything. The silence pressed in, thick and heavy.

Finally, I tried again. "I, um… I missed you at breakfast. Kira says the porridge was extra lumpy today. You'd have hated it."

Still nothing.

I swallowed hard, fighting the urge to bolt. "I know things have been…weird. And I know I haven't exactly been the best at, you know, talking about stuff. But I'm here now. And I'm not leaving until you say something. Even if it's just to tell me to go away."

He didn't answer. But I thought—maybe—I saw his shoulders tense, just a little.

I glanced back at Madame Galena, who gave me a tiny nod, like she was rooting for me. Or maybe for both of us.

Treander didn't say a word. He just reached out and slipped his hand into mine, his fingers curling around my knuckles like he'd never let go again. My heart fluttered, and I managed a shaky, lopsided smile. I leaned my head against his shoulder, letting out a breath I didn't realize I'd been holding. "I've missed you," I whispered, because it was true, and because I needed him to hear it.

He lifted my chin with gentle fingers, familiar but hesitant. Then he kissed me, soft and slow. It was the kind of kiss that felt like a promise. "I've been right here," he murmured, his voice rougher than usual from not being used in so long.

Guilt crashed over me. "I'm sorry," I said softly.

Treander's brows knit together, confusion flickering in his eyes. "What are you sorry for?" he asked.

"For being so distant. For… not being here. Not really." My words tumbled out, awkward and raw.

He shook his head, a small, crooked smile tugging at his lips. "I understand, Amira. You've got a whole kingdom to look after. I'm just glad you're here now."

That surprised me. I searched his eyes, looking for any sign he was just saying it to make me feel better. "You really understand?" I asked.

He didn't answer right away. Instead, he shifted closer, wrapping his arm around my waist. The move was so natural, so him, that it sent my heart into a tailspin. I shivered as his fingers brushed the bare skin at the small of my back where my shirt had ridden up, and for the first time in ages, I let myself lean into him—just for a moment, or so I told myself.

"I do," he said quietly, his voice steady. "I can only imagine the weight you carry every day. I never want to be another burden for you."

His words wrapped around me, softening the guilt and easing the distance that had grown between us. I let my head rest against his shoulder, gazing out the window with him. But then a knot twisted in my stomach. I knew I couldn't keep putting it off.

"I need to tell you something," I said suddenly, turning to face Treander. I searched his eyes for the boy I'd met in the ravine—the one who'd made me believe in hope. But now, all I saw was a man worn down by sorrow and scars.

He gave me a small, tired smile. "You can tell me anything. You know that."

I swallowed, my throat suddenly dry. "In order to become queen, I have to be married." The words felt heavy as I said them.

Treander didn't even blink. "I know. It's the law." His voice was gentle, but there was a sadness in it, like he'd already made peace with it.

"My parents… they want me to marry Ajay." I tried to keep my voice steady, but it wobbled anyway.

He looked at me, steady as ever. "And what do you want?"

I stared down at my hands, twisting my fingers together. "I… don't know," I whispered.

The truth sat between us, thick and awkward. I wanted to say more, but the words just wouldn't come. The silence stretched, full of everything I was too scared to admit.

Treander nodded slowly before turning back to the window. He didn't say anything. Just stared out at the world, like maybe the answer was out there somewhere.

I waited, hoping he'd say something—anything—to break the tension. But he just looked away, and the silence started to sting. Finally, I couldn't take it anymore. "You're not going to say anything?"

He shrugged but kept silent.

"You're just okay with this? With me being married off to someone else?" I hated how desperate I sounded, but I couldn't help it. I wanted him to fight for me—for us.

Treander's shoulders went rigid. "What do you want me to say? Ajay is a nobleman. He'll make a fine king. I'm just…me. I have nothing to offer you, Amira. Your path ahead is clear."

I reached for him, but he pulled away, folding into himself like he was bracing for a storm.

"But what if I don't want to marry Ajay?" I whispered.

Treander's jaw tightened. "You must do what is best for Hekagia," he said like he was reciting a lesson he'd learned by heart.

I swallowed hard, blinking back tears. "If that's how you feel, maybe I should just marry Ajay,"

"That settles it, then." Treander's voice was final. He turned away, shoulders hunched. "You should go, Your Highness. I need to rest."

The way he said it—so formal, so far away—hurt worse than any argument ever could.

I stumbled out of the infirmary, doing my best to avoid Madame Galena's worried stare. As soon as I was outside, I collapsed against the cold stone wall, trying to catch my breath and keep the tears from spilling over. My chest felt tight, like I'd swallowed a thunderstorm.

That's when Ajay appeared—so quiet I hadn't even heard him coming. He always moved like he was afraid to disturb the air, hands folded, gaze lowered. In the chaos of the school, he looked like he belonged somewhere peaceful, maybe a sunlit garden, not these drafty halls full of drama.

He stopped a few paces away, his voice soft and careful. "Amira… forgive me, but—are you well?" His accent curled around the words, gentle and precise, and I could hear the worry tucked between each syllable.

I blinked, swiping at my cheeks, but there was no hiding the tears. Ajay's eyes met mine—dark, kind, and impossibly patient. He reached into his robe and offered me a handkerchief, holding it out with both hands like it was something precious.

"Thank you," I whispered, taking it. I tried to dab away the mess on my face, but the tears just kept coming. "I'm fine," I lied.

Ajay knelt beside me. "If I may say so, Princess… you do not look fine." His lips twitched in a shy, almost apologetic smile. "But it is no shame to grieve. Even the bravest hearts must rest."

I almost laughed at that—the future queen of Hekagia, crying in a hallway over a boy. How cliché. If Kira saw me now, she'd never let me live it down.

I handed Ajay back his handkerchief, trying to pull myself together. "Sorry. I'm just… it's been a long day."

He shook his head, earnest and bashful. "There is no need for apology. My mother always says, 'A sorrow shared is a sorrow halved.' If you wish to talk, I am here. If you wish for silence, I will sit with you until you are ready."

His words were so gentle, so sincere, I felt the ache in my chest loosen just a little. I pushed myself to my feet, drawing in a shaky breath. "I'll be alright," I said, and this time I almost believed it.

Ajay's gaze flickered past me, toward the clear doors of the infirmary. I didn't dare look back—I knew he could see Treander, and I hated how obvious my feelings must have been.

Ajay cleared his throat, the sound soft and careful. "There is something I would like to ask you, if I may?" His eyes met mine, and for a second, I saw a spark of determination beneath all that quiet. "Though... I realize my timing could be better."

My stomach twisted. I knew what was coming, and suddenly I felt like I was standing on the edge of a cliff. I nodded, not trusting myself to speak.

Ajay stepped closer, moving with that gentle, deliberate grace of his. He took my hands—his palms warm, stained faintly yellow with turmeric from the spice cakes he'd made for me so many times over the summer. The familiar scent drifted between us, grounding me, and for a moment, the world seemed to slow as I looked into his gentle, earnest eyes.

"It is no secret that our families wish for us to be wed," Ajay began, his voice soft but steady. He raised his eyebrows in a silent question, and I nodded, unable to find my voice.

He continued, his voice honest, almost painfully so. "It is also no secret that your heart... may be elsewhere." He looked down, a faint blush coloring his cheeks. "I would never wish to cause you pain, Amira. My family's honor is important to me, but so is your happiness. If there is hope for us, I would be honored to try. But if not, I will step aside, with no anger in my heart."

For a moment, I just stared at him, caught between gratitude and guilt. Ajay was so good—so careful with my feelings, so bound by duty and kindness. I wished I could give him an easy answer, but nothing about my life felt easy anymore.

Ajay's eyes met mine—deep, dark, and so full of questions I could barely stand it. He always looked so composed, but I could see the nerves flickering beneath the surface, like candlelight in a drafty hall. My words caught somewhere between my heart and my mouth.

He nodded, slow and careful, a shadow of sadness passing over his face. "I see," he said, his voice soft, almost formal. "That is all I needed to know." He cleared his throat, the sound awkward in the quiet corridor, and turned as if to leave, his shoulders just a little slumped.

"Wait—" The word tumbled out before I could stop it, surprising both of us. "I know what you've heard, but I haven't... I haven't decided anything yet."

Ajay paused, turning back. He hesitated, then reached for my hands, his touch gentle and warm. "Does that mean," he asked, his accent curling softly around the words, "there is hope for us?"

I nodded, ducking my head to hide the ridiculous, shy smile tugging at my lips. "Maybe," I said, my voice barely above a whisper.

He let out a breath, relief flickering in his eyes. "Then… may I court you?"

I couldn't help it—I grinned, the tension breaking. "You mean, like, ask me on a date?" I teased, my voice lighter than it had been in days.

Ajay's lips curved into a real smile, the kind that crept up to his eyes. "I suppose that would be the Earth equivalent, yes," he said, a little bashful. He looked down, like he was embarrassed by his own boldness.

"Then you may," I said, my voice soft but certain.

Ajay lifted my hand and brushed his lips across my knuckles. The gesture was so old-fashioned, so Ajay, it sent a warm ache spiraling through my chest. I let myself lean into the comfort of it—the familiar scent of his skin, the memory of summer afternoons by the lake, when everything felt simple and safe.

Ajay had been a steady presence at my side all summer. When Treander withdrew from me, Ajay and I wandered the school grounds, talking about everything and nothing—sometimes about the future, sometimes just about the shape of the clouds. He made me laugh when I thought I'd forgotten how, and listened without judgment when I needed to talk about the war, my fears, or even about Treander. There were mornings when his quiet encouragement was the only thing that got me out of bed.

Somewhere along the way, as much as I didn't want to admit it, our easy friendship had shifted, deepening into something more complicated. With Ajay, I felt safe—seen in a way that was gentle and patient. I wasn't sure if it was love, definitely not the wild, breathless kind I felt for Treander, but it was real, and it mattered. And that was what made everything so confusing.

Out of the corner of my eye, I caught a flicker of movement at the glass-paned door. My breath caught.

Treander stood there, watching us. Our eyes locked—just for a moment—and in that silent exchange, I felt the full weight of everything I stood to lose. His gaze was raw, wounded, and then he turned away, shoulders hunched, disappearing back to his cot.

A sharp pain twisted inside me. I knew I had to do what was best for Hekagia, but in that moment, I wasn't sure what that even meant. I owed it to myself, and to my kingdom, to see if there was a future with Ajay.

But the hurt in Treander's eyes pierced me to my core, leaving me feeling like I'd betrayed him in the worst possible way. Even as Ajay's arms wrapped around me, steady and reassuring, all I wanted was to run to Treander and take away the pain I'd caused him. I wanted to tell him that he was the one I truly wanted, that I couldn't imagine my life without him. But the weight of an entire realm pressed down on my shoulders, and I knew that it could never be that simple.

So I shut my eyes and let my head rest on Ajay's shoulder, hoping he wouldn't notice the tears leaking down my cheeks and soaking into his perfectly pressed robes. Great. Future queen of Hekagia, reduced to a soggy mess in the hallway. If the Golden Council could see me now, they'd probably faint.

Ajay didn't say anything for a moment, he just let me breathe. Then, gentle as ever, he murmured, "I must go now. But I hope we can meet again soon." His voice was soft, but there was urgency in it.

I wiped my face with the back of my hand, trying to pull myself together. It wasn't fair to Ajay for my thoughts to keep drifting back to Treander. I'd told Ajay there was a chance for us, and now I had to try to mean it. Ajay was steady and kind, and with him, I never felt like the ground was about to fall out from under me. I had to believe that could be enough.

"I hope so too," I managed, forcing a smile that probably looked as fake as it felt.

And then—because the universe has a twisted sense of humor—the warning bell blared through the corridor, shrill and jarring, like a banshee with a grudge. For a second, I just stood there, heart pounding, wishing I could crawl under the nearest tapestry and disappear. Raideron's troops had arrived.

Ajay's eyes went wide as worry flickered across his face. "I must find my sister. She was in the training arena with the other students." He gave me a quick, respectful bow—always the gentleman, even in a crisis—and then he was gone, sprinting down the corridor, his robes flapping gracefully behind him.

I pressed my back against the cold stone wall, trying to steady myself. I'd known this moment would come, but I'd hoped—just for once—that we'd have more time. But being a Hale had taught me that the world never waits for you to be ready, it just barrels ahead, dragging you with it.

I was about to leave when the infirmary door slid open. Treander stepped out, looking like he'd seen a ghost. His face was pale, eyes shadowed, and before I could even say his name, he grabbed my shoulders, fingers digging in like I might disappear if he let go. "You must stay here, Amira," he said, voice tight and urgent.

I blinked at him, thrown by the intensity in his eyes. "Why?"

"It's safer for you here." He sounded so sure, like he could actually protect me from the world outside.

I shook my head, pulling away. "You know I can't stay. Come with me. Gather the archers—help us."

Treander's hands dropped to his sides, his body sagging. "I cannot," he whispered, barely loud enough to hear over the pounding of my own heart.

"Why not?" I demanded, anger flaring up to cover the fear. "What happened to you, Treander? The boy I knew would never abandon his men. He'd never let them fight a battle without him."

He slumped against the infirmary door; pain etched deep in every line of his face. "Please, Amira," he moaned, voice cracking. "You don't understand."

"You're right, I don't!" My voice trembled, but I didn't care. "So help me. Make me understand."

He just shook his head. "I don't know how…"

He reached for me, but I stepped back, putting as much space between us as I could. I squared my shoulders, forcing my voice to go cold. "You should go back to bed. You need rest."

I sounded like my mother—formal, distant, like I could just order my feelings away.

I waved Madame Galena over, and in no time, she had Treander tucked beneath the crisp white sheets, looking so breakable it made my chest ache.

"Find Darreon. He'll know what to do," Treander murmured, sweeping a trembling hand through his russet hair.

I turned to leave, telling myself I'd done my duty, that he was safe for now. But before I could make it two steps, Treander's hand grabbed my wrist. His grip was desperate, almost frantic, and suddenly I was tumbling into his lap, my knees knocking awkwardly against the bedframe.

There was nothing gentle about the way he held me—his fingers tangled in my hair, anchoring me to him like he was afraid I'd vanish if he let go. Then he kissed me. Fiercely, hungrily, like he was pouring every word he couldn't say into that single, breathless moment. My heart stuttered, and for a second, the world shrank to just the two of us—no war, no crown, no impossible choices. Just us.

When he finally pulled away, his voice was low and raw, barely more than a whisper. "Be careful," he said, the words trembling between us.

I wanted to tell him I would. I wanted to promise him everything would be okay. But all I could do was nod, because in that moment, I wasn't sure I believed it myself.

CHAPTER FOUR

A FRIEND IS LOST

It didn't take long to find Darreon—Treander's right-hand man. He moved through the corridor with a quiet, coiled energy that always made me think of a panther: calm, but you knew he could tear through a battlefield if he had to. Henrick—his ever-present shadow—trailed close behind him. I greeted them both with a quick nod.

"Treander needs you in the infirmary," I said, my voice low and urgent.

Darreon nodded, his voice iron-strong when he spoke. "I'll see to him, Princess. You have my word."

"Come on, Henrick," I said, leading him away, but he pulled out of my grip.

"No way! I'm not going back to the dorms," he cried out, his voice cracking. "I'm twelve now. I can fight. I'm not a little kid anymore!"

Darreon crouched down, his broad shoulders blocking out the chaos behind us. His voice dropped, low and gentle. "Henrick, the young ones need a protector. We are counting on you to be there in our stead."

"Fine," Henrick muttered. His jaw was set, and I knew he'd do it, if for nothing else than to make Darreon proud.

Darreon straightened, towering over Henrick. "Good man," he said in a voice like velvet. "I'll check on you when I can. Hold the line for us, yeah?"

Henrick puffed up chest and squared his shoulders. "I will, sir. Promise." He marched off, chin high, and for a second, I saw the man he was trying so hard to become. But to me, he'd always be the soot-streaked kid from the ravine—the one who'd once tried to fight a grown man with nothing but a stick and a stubborn streak.

Darreon watched Henrick disappear, shaking his head with a wry, affectionate sigh. "That boy's got fire. Too much fire." His lips twitched, but the humor faded fast, replaced by a shadow that seemed to settle over his features.

He turned to me, his voice dropping even lower. "I didn't want to say it in front of the kid, but I got word from the outpost. Middlehaven is gone. Burned. No survivors reported."

The words seemed to smack into me. My knees buckled and I slid down the wall, the world spinning. My breath came in short, panicked bursts, and for a moment, I couldn't see anything but the memory of my mother's carriage rattling down the muddy road. Had she made it out? Or was she…

Darreon's hand hovered, not quite touching my shoulder. "What is it, Your Highness?"

I forced the words out. "My mother's carriage left for Vail Castle not an hour ago. She would've passed right through Middlehaven."

Darreon tried to offer comfort. "I'm sure she made it out in time," he said. But we both knew how quickly Raideron's army moved.

Before I could even wrap my head around the idea that my mother might be gone, the academy shuddered as the first volley from Raideron's army slammed into the outer walls, rattling the stained-glass windows and sending a rain of dust from the ceiling.

"Go—" I barked at Darreon, my voice coming out raw. "Get the archers. We need everyone. Now!"

My boots pounded the stone as I sprinted for the courtyard, the air thick with the scent of burning oil and fear. Kira and a dozen students were already there, their faces pale but set, like they'd all aged a year in the last five minutes.

Outside the academy gates, Raideron's army had stopped just fifty yards away. Hundreds of spellcasters in blood-red armor shifted restlessly, their eyes locked on us.

Kira stepped forward, jaw clenched, every inch the warrior princess. Yasmine was right beside her, and together they started weaving a protection spell—hands moving in perfect sync, magic sparking between their fingers. I watched the barrier shimmer to life. I had no idea how long it would hold, but for now, it was all that stood between us and total annihilation.

Kira stumbled back into line, sweat pouring down her face. "Oof," she groaned.

I moved closer, worry thick in my voice. "Are you okay?"

"I'm fine."

Translation: she was still mad at me about this morning.

I hesitated, searching her face for any sign that she might forgive me—assuming we survived the next hour.

"Can we just... not fight for five minutes?" I asked her.

"Fine," Kira grumbled. "But if Savannah's hiding again, I swear—"

My stomach twisted. "I... I don't know where she is."

Kira's eyes narrowed. "Of course you don't. And that's not suspicious at all?"

Ravenna cleared her throat, shooting Kira a warning look, but I shook my head. "Kira's right. It is weird. Savannah wouldn't just disappear—not with Raideron's army literally at our gates."

Kira folded her arms, scanning the looming army. "You know what's weird? These guys. Look at them—they're just standing there, like they're waiting for something. Gives me the creeps."

I followed Kira's gaze, my eyes snagging on the silent, red-armored wall of Raideron's army and then drifting to the ruins of Middlehaven. Smoke curled up in lazy, mocking spirals—like the world was reminding me just how outmatched we were.

"My mom's out there somewhere," I said, my voice barely more than a squeak. The words tasted like ash.

Kira suddenly snapped her fingers. "Wait—I almost forgot." She dug through her jacket, hands moving fast, and pulled out a scorched scrap of papyrus. "A message from her Ladyship," she said, waving it like a flag. I recognized my mother's handwriting instantly. The note was short—but it said she was safe, and that the Golden Army was on its way.

Good thing, too, because as much as I wanted to believe in the ragtag army of teenagers at my back, we were about as ready for this as a flock of chickens facing a pack of wolves.

As if on cue, Raideron's army surged forward, a tidal wave of crimson and steel. For a second, I was frozen—future queen, paralyzed by fear.

Then the academy doors crashed open behind me. Ajay and his twin sister Shani burst out, a whole squad of alchemy students trailing after them, faces pale but determined. Shani dipped into a bow so fast her braid nearly smacked her brother in the face. "Your Highness, good to see you."

I managed a quick smile. "You too. Perfect timing, as usual."

Shani's eyes sparkled with mischief as she leaned in, voice pitched just loud enough for everyone to hear. "I heard my brother finally worked up the nerve to ask you out."

Kira's eyebrows shot up so high I thought they might fly off her face. She shot me a look—equal parts surprise and "are you kidding me?"—but, for once, she kept her mouth shut. Miracles do happen, apparently.

Ajay cleared his throat. "This is not the time, Shani," he said. "If you haven't noticed, we're about to go to battle."

Shani just rolled her eyes and flashed a wicked grin. "Oh, relax, brother. I'm only teasing. Besides, you're adorable when you're flustered. I bet Amira thinks so too." She winked at me conspiratorially.

Despite the spellcasters heading straight for us, I couldn't help but return Shani's smile. Shani's humor had become a lifeline for me over the summer—a welcome break from the endless, exhausting Golden Council meetings and the general doom-and-gloom of being the future queen. But Shani was more than just comic relief. She was a force in her own right—a formidable alchemist who'd been working with Earl on some top-secret project for months.

"What are you up to, Shani?" I asked, eyeing her as two students staggered forward, struggling to carry a large wooden barrel between them.

Shani shrugged, a sly smile tugging at her lips. "Just trying to even the odds a little." She pried open the barrel, and a wave of stench—rotten eggs and iron—rolled out, making my eyes water.

Kira recoiled, pinching her nose. "What in the name of the ancestors is that?"

Shani held up a small black sphere, no bigger than an egg, and flashed a grin that promised trouble. "A blend of sulfuric powder, magnesium, and a few other surprises. Let's just say Raideron's army won't know what hit them."

I shot Shani a look, one eyebrow raised, hope flickering in my chest. "Wait—this is what you and Earl have been cooking up in the alchemy wing all summer, isn't it?"

Shani's grin was pure mischief, her eyes practically glowing. "It is indeed, Your Highness. All we need now is a little spark." She tossed me a look that said, come on, princess, show us what you've got.

I grinned, flexing my fingers as fire magic danced across my palm. "I think I can handle that."

Raideron's army surged closer, a wall of red armor and snarling faces. Shani hurled the first handful of black spheres into the air—alchemy bombs, each one reeking of sulfur. I flicked my wrist, sending a ribbon of fire arcing through the sky. The spheres ignited midair, exploding in a rain of blazing shrapnel that tore through the enemy's front lines.

The courtyard erupted in cheers. For that one moment, hope felt real. But it didn't last. Raideron's spellcasters rallied, and suddenly the sky was full of astral orbs the size of boulders, crackling with deadly energy. One hit would have flattened the academy like a house of cards. But the barrier shimmered to life, a dome of light that caught the first orb with a thunderous crack. The ground shook, dust raining down from the eaves, but the shield held—for now.

"Nice work, my love!" Ravenna called, darting over to plant a quick kiss on Kira's cheek, like this was just another day at the training ring.

Kira turned beet red. She cleared her throat, trying to sound cool and unbothered. "Yeah, well, don't get too excited. We're not out of this yet—not by a long shot."

Shani was already on the move, tossing another handful of black spheres toward the enemy. "I can fix that!" she crowed, her voice ringing with fierce, almost reckless triumph. The barrage sent Raideron's forces scattering, their neat lines breaking apart under the onslaught. "We're winning!" she shouted, grabbing another fistful of explosives, ready to go again.

And then—ROAARRR.

"What was that?" I asked Kira.

If anyone knew monsters, it was her.

Kira's eyes darted around the courtyard. "No idea. But I really don't like it."

From the chaos, something emerged—a creature straight out of my worst nightmares. Jet-black, its body shimmered with an oily, unnatural sheen as it barreled toward us, covered head to toe in vicious porcupine spikes. It let out another roar, even more blood-curdling than the first, then raised its claws and hurled a ginormous astral orb right at us.

The orb slammed into Kira's barrier. The shield shuddered, groaned, but—miraculously—held. For now.

"That's not good." Kira muttered nervously.

The creature didn't even pause. It hurled another barrage of astral orbs, each one exploding against the barrier like it was made of paper. Kira had tied the shield straight to her own magic—brilliant, but now every hit landed on her, too. I could see her flinch with each impact, her knuckles white. When the barrier finally collapsed, so did Kira.

I dropped to my knees next to her. "Kira! Are you okay?"

She gritted her teeth, sweat streaming down her face. "No," she snapped, her voice raw and furious. "And now I'm really pissed off."

The courtyard went dead silent—every eye fixed on the monster. Then it let out a piercing cry that rallied Raideron's troops.

"Bring it on," Kira snarled, her hands crackling with astral energy as she squared off against the beast. Ravenna stood next to her, taiaha at the ready.

I wished I could match their confidence, but despite years of training, I'd never felt like a real fighter. My magic had only just come back, and it still fizzled at my fingertips like it was deciding whether or not to show up for work. As the first wave of Raideron's army surged toward us, I gripped my sword tighter, forced a battle cry from my lungs, and charged into the fray—because if I was going down, I was going down swinging.

Steel clanged and spells exploded all around me. I found myself face-to-face with an enemy spellcaster—he couldn't have been much older than me, but his eyes were cold, empty, like he'd already decided who would win. I fought to hold my ground, but I kept glancing over my shoulder, tracking the astral monster as it tore through friend and foe alike, leaving nothing but destruction in its wake.

Then the creature's soulless eyes locked onto mine. Without

warning, it curled itself into a ball—like some kind of nightmarish hedgehog—and launched straight at me, rolling so fast I barely had time to blink. A trail of poisonous slime hissed in its wake, eating through stone and armor like it was nothing.

Kira threw herself in front of me, shielding me from the monster's charge. "Stay behind me!" she barked, hurling an astral orb at the creature. The monster dodged with unnatural agility, spikes bristling, and for a second, I wondered if we were all about to become monster chow.

Kira let out a frustrated growl—her signature sound when things went sideways. She yanked her dagger free and charged, reckless as always. "Come on, ugly!" she shouted, slashing at the beast. Her blade found its mark, but as she pulled back, one of the monster's spikes raked across her arm, slicing from wrist to elbow. Blood welled up, bright and shocking against her sleeve.

The creature didn't waste a second. Its spiked tail whipped around, catching Kira square in the chest. She flew backward, crashing into a boulder. Her head snapped back, and then—nothing. She sprawled on the ground, terrifyingly still. The monster unfurled, stretching to its full, nightmare height, looming over Kira's limp body like a shadow that wanted to swallow her whole.

Ravenna's cry rang out across the courtyard. "No!" she roared, sprinting toward us, her taiaha raised. But she was too far away. The beast opened its mouth, rows of jagged, shark-like teeth glinting, ready to strike.

"Kira!" I screamed as panic clawed up my throat. I tried to run to her, but Shani's hand clamped around my arm, surprisingly strong for someone so small.

"Amira, don't!" she snapped, her voice fierce. "You can't help her if you're dead!"

Before I could even argue, Ajay stepped in, his grip like iron as he seized my wrist. "Let go of me!" I shouted, twisting and kicking, but Ajay didn't budge.

"I will not let you go to your death," he said, eyes blazing with a kind of desperate protectiveness. "You are too important to the people of Hekagia... and to me."

My brain short-circuited.

"I... you... what?" I stammered, completely thrown by the intensity in his eyes.

Shani called out, fierce and unafraid. "Stand down, monster!" she yelled, planting herself between Kira's crumpled form and the beast. Her grip tightened on the last black explosive, eyes blazing with wild, stubborn fire. "You want a fight? Try me."

The monster's tail whipped out, a blur of spikes. Shani dodged, but her boot snagged on a fallen spellcaster's arm. She hit the ground hard, the explosive skittering out of reach.

Ajay was there in a heartbeat, sword drawn, his face set with quiet, desperate courage. "Get away from her!" he shouted, swinging with everything he had. The blade bounced off the monster's armored hide with a dull clang. He tried again—wilder, more desperate—but the sword barely left a scratch.

I sprinted toward them, heart in my throat, but I was too slow. The creature's claws closed around Ajay, tossing him aside like he weighed nothing. He crashed to the ground, unmoving, and my stomach dropped.

With Ajay down, the monster turned back to Shani. She was already dragging herself up, blood streaking her leg, black hair plastered to her face. But she didn't back down. She limped forward, chin high, clutching the explosive like it was her last hope.

"Throw it now!" I shouted, my voice raw with fear.

With a snarl, Shani hurled the explosive, every ounce of her stubborn will behind it. The monster's claw shot out, snatching the black sphere from the air. It paused, eyes narrowing, suspicion flickering across its twisted face.

With no time to think, I flung out my hand, magic burning through my veins. "Please work," I whispered.

A fireball shot out from my palm, streaking straight for the monster's claw. It hit the sphere and the world detonated around me—white-hot light, heat like a furnace blast, and a roar that rattled my insides.

The monster howled so loudly it felt like the ground itself was screaming. Flames raced across its spiked body and all I could see was a writhing shadow thrashing inside the inferno.

But even dying, the monster wasn't done. With a guttural, furious roar, it unleashed a storm of thick, black poisoned spikes in every direction. The air turned deadly—I dove behind one of Shani's barrels just as the spikes tore through the courtyard, splintering wood, shattering stone, sending up choking clouds of dust and debris. Screams and shouts echoed everywhere.

When the screams finally faded, I crawled out from behind the shattered barrel, my heart pounding so hard I thought it might crack my ribs.

The courtyard was a wasteland—scorched earth, splintered stone, bodies everywhere. Some people were moving, dragging themselves upright. Others weren't.

My eyes darted, searching for Kira. For one awful second, I couldn't find her. But then I spotted her, battered but breathing under Ravenna's shield.

Ajay was sprawled nearby, groaning as he pushed himself up, somehow untouched by the monster's final attack. For a split second, hope flickered. Maybe, just maybe, we'd made it through.

But then I saw Shani.

She was lying just a few feet away, so still it didn't seem real. One of the monster's black spikes was buried in her chest, right where her heart should have been. Her hand was outstretched toward Ajay, like she'd been reaching for him, even at the end. Her eyes stared up at the sky, wide and unblinking—her fierce, stubborn spirit gone in an instant.

Ajay's scream tore through the courtyard, raw and shattering. He stumbled through the debris, collapsing beside Shani. "No, no, no—Shani!" His voice cracked as he yanked the spike from her chest, blood welling up, staining his hands, the ground, everything. He sobbed, clutching her, his grief so loud it drowned out the rest of the world.

I stood frozen, tears streaming down my cheeks as I stared at my friend's lifeless body. Her dark hair was tangled and matted with blood, her face still. My hands shook uncontrollably and I choked back a sob.

Around us, the sounds of fighting faded. Raideron's army had been beaten back, and the battered survivors began to gather in the courtyard. Students drifted toward us, their faces streaked with sweat, soot, and tears.

Ravenna knelt down beside Ajay. Tears glimmered in her eyes as she placed a gentle hand on his shoulder. "We should move her," she said softly.

"No!" Ajay's voice cracked, raw and desperate. He clung to Shani's body as if he could anchor her soul with his own. "Don't touch her! Please—just—don't."

Ravenna bowed her head and began to whisper a Māori blessing over Shani, her words weaving through the silence. The crowd stilled, many bowing their heads in respect. When she finished, Ravenna looked back at Ajay, her voice soft but insistent. "Raideron's army will regroup. We need to move her, Ajay. Let us help."

Ajay's shoulders shook, but he nodded, silent tears cutting tracks through the dirt on his face. He didn't let go until Gnash—massive, gentle Gnash—knelt beside him. With surprising tenderness, Gnash lifted Shani's broken body into his arms. Ajay stumbled after them, Ravenna at his side, as they carried Shani through the shattered doors of the academy

Nearby, the Kilburn twins huddled together on the cracked flagstones, knees drawn up, their faces streaked with grime. They looked impossibly small—just two kids in uniforms several sizes too big, blood spattered on their sleeves.

Calix's jaw was set, his freckles standing out stark against his pale skin. His eyes, usually full of mischief, were huge and glassy. Cassandra's hands shook as she wiped at her nose, leaving a smear of dirt across her cheek.

She tried to look brave, but her lower lip trembled, and she pressed closer to her brother, clutching his arm like it was the only solid thing left in the world. I didn't have the heart to scold them for sneaking into the fight. Whatever punishment they deserved, they'd already paid it a hundred times over.

It didn't take long for Raideron's army to regroup. We barely had time to drag the wounded inside before a sharp war horn blew from somewhere within the smoldering ruins of Middlehaven. The sound echoed across the battered academy grounds, sending a chill down my spine.

Within minutes, Raideron's army started to materialize from the haze—first a handful, then a flood, their blood-red armor catching the last of the sunlight and turning the courtyard into a nightmare painting. Without Kira and Yasmine's barrier, we were sitting ducks. We pressed together near the front steps, every face pale but determined. I could feel the fear in the air—sharp, electric—but nobody ran. We stood our ground, braced for the onslaught.

Just as the horde of enemy spellcasters reached us, a portal whirled to life above the front steps. In a brilliant flash, the Golden Army appeared—armor shining, banners unfurling, their arrival as sudden as it was miraculous. The dimming sunlight caught on their polished breastplates, casting dazzling reflections across the courtyard. Behind them, Darreon and the archers joined the fray, arrows already nocked and ready.

"You took your sweet time," Kira called, trying for her usual sass, but her voice shook with relief.

Darreon just shot her a look—half exasperation, half a crooked grin. "Archers, with me!" he barked.

Bolstered by their arrival, we surged forward, meeting Raideron's army with renewed strength and fury. The Golden Army crashed into Raideron's forces with a precision that was almost beautiful—swords flashing, shields locked, every movement practiced and sure. The archers loosed a volley of arrows, picking off spellcasters before they could regroup. The students fought with a wild, desperate courage, their magic sparking in the dusk.

When the dust finally settled, the hillside was littered with the bodies of Raideron's defeated army. The acrid smell of smoke hung heavily in the air, but the academy stood —battered, but unbroken.

Ajay never rejoined the fight—not that I'd expected him to. After a long moment of hesitation (and more than a little nudging from Kira— "Go on, Amira, he needs you"), I finally made my way to the infirmary. The room was thick with silence, the kind that presses on your chest. Ajay sat beside Shani's body, his posture rigid, grief carved into every line of his face. He didn't look up as I entered, just kept his gaze locked on his sister's still form.

Treander did look up, though. His dark blue eyes met mine, and for a second, I saw everything—pain, exhaustion, maybe even a flicker of accusation. I cleared my throat, suddenly feeling like an intruder in my own story. I looked away, but I could feel his eyes on me as I crossed the room.

I sat down quietly, not trusting myself to speak. Ajay's shoulders shook with silent sobs, his hands clenched tightly in his lap. I wanted to say something—anything—but every word felt useless, too small for the weight of what he'd lost.

My hands trembled as I reached out to say goodbye, but I hesitated, half-expecting Ajay to flinch, to tell me I had no right— that I'd failed her, failed them both. But he didn't move. He just watched, hollow-eyed and shattered, as I set my hand gently on top of Shani's.

Ajay's voice, when it finally came, was rough and raw. "I must take her home, to Alkrimia." He stood, every muscle rigid, his eyes locking onto mine.

"I understand," I said quietly.

Just then, the infirmary doors banged open and Kira rushed in with Yasmine right behind her, both of them supporting a dazed-looking boy. I recognized him as one of the new alchemy students, barely a week into his first term. They eased him onto a cot, and Madame Galena swooped over, her face pinched with worry.

"What happened?" Madame Galena demanded, already reaching for her vials.

Kira grimaced, brushing soot from her sleeve. "He got a little too close to one of the explosives. Kid's lucky to be alive."

"Oh dear me," Madame Galena muttered, her hands moving fast as she checked the boy's pulse and started dabbing at a burn on his arm.

Yasmine's jaw tightened as her gaze landed on Shani's body. She didn't say a word, but the way her hands curled into fists and her shoulders stiffened, spoke volumes.

I remembered Eden then, and the sting of her betrayal. I couldn't say that I was sad she was gone, but it pained be to see Yasmine suffer alone. I wanted to reach out to her, to say something that would make it better, but words felt clumsy and useless.

Instead, I caught her eye. She looked away, blinking hard, her jaw set in a stubborn line. Yasmine never asked for comfort, never let herself fall apart in front of anyone. But I saw the grief simmering beneath her calm, the way she stood a little straighter than necessary.

I stepped closer, lowering my voice so only she could hear. "Yasmine," I said, careful not to crowd her, "would you… would you go with Ajay and the students back to Alkrimia? I think they'll need you."

She didn't answer right away. Her eyes flicked to the students— lost, frightened, looking for someone to follow.

Yasmine's lips pressed into a thin line, and then she nodded, just once, sharp and decisive. She was already moving before I could thank her, her grief tucked away. But as she passed me, her hand brushed my arm—a fleeting gesture, gone in an instant, but enough to say what neither of us could put into words.

Then she turned to Ajay, her voice softer than I'd ever heard it. "I don't know if it helps, but… I lost my family too. Not long ago."

"Ajay looked up at Yasmine as if seeing her for the first time. His voice was barely more than a whisper. "I'm sorry. I would not wish this pain on anyone."

Yasmine's lips quirked in a sad, understanding smile. "Come then. Let's bring Shani home."

CHAPTER FIVE

THE TOURNAMENT

The clang of swords echoed across the training grounds and I couldn't help but grin as I watched the chaos unfold. Dozens of would-be knights were going at it like their lives depended on it—which, to be fair, they kind of did. Losers got stuck mucking out the griffin stables for a week, and trust me, nothing motivates a guy like the threat of shoveling griffin poop before breakfast.

Every swing, every block, every wild-eyed charge, was delivered with the kind of determination you only see when pride and clean boots were on the line. I leaned against the fence, patu in hand, and tried to look casual, like I wasn't itching to jump in and show them how it was done.

Even though the tournament was meant to be a free for all, I'd promised Josiah I'd wait a while before unleashing my awesomeness. He'd said something about "letting the others have a chance," but I knew he just wanted all the glory for himself.

"Hey, Caleb!" Josiah called from the sidelines, flashing that cocky grin of his. "You planning to join the tournament, or just stand there looking pretty?"

I shot him a smirk. "Why not both? Besides, I'm just giving everyone else a fighting chance."

Josiah rolled his eyes, but I could see the challenge in them. That's the thing about Josiah—he never lets me get too comfortable. Which, honestly, is probably good for me.

The crowd's energy was infectious. Every clang of steel, every cheer, every groan from a particularly nasty hit made my blood sing. This was my element—competition, camaraderie, and just a hint of chaos. I thrived on it. And yeah, maybe I was a little too cocky for my own good, but hey, someone had to keep things interesting.

As the next pair of knights squared off, I twirled my patu and called out, "Loser has to clean my boots, too!" That got a round of laughter—and a few groans from the unlucky ones who'd already lost. I winked at Josiah, who just shook his head, grinning.

Let the others chase glory and honor. Me? I was here for the thrill—and, okay, maybe to remind everyone that Prince Caleb was more than just a pretty face. I was here to win. And if I had to muck out a few griffin stables along the way, well… at least I'd do it with style.

Finally, my turn came. I bounced on my toes, grinning as I sized up my opponent—a mountain of a guy swinging a club that looked like it belonged in a siege, not a tournament. He grunted and took a wild swing at my head. I darted left, heart pounding, and dropped into a roll just as the club whooshed past my ear.

"You'll never win like that, Caleb!" Josiah called from somewhere to my left, flashing that infuriatingly cocky grin before turning back to his own opponent—a nature spellcaster who was trying (and failing) to wrap him up in vines like a badly-mummified scarecrow.

"Maybe you should worry less about me and more about yourself!" I shot back, weaving through the chaos. But Josiah—three years older, annoyingly talented, and the best fighter at camp—just shredded the vines like they were made of tissue paper.

"Show off!" I yelled, ducking and weaving as the battle raged around us.

Josiah didn't even break a sweat. He disarmed his opponent with a flick of his wrist, pressed his sword to the poor kid's throat, and growled, "Do you yield?"

"I yield," the boy moaned, sounding like he'd rather be anywhere else.

With my competition thinning out, I knew it was time to take charge. I hefted my patu, feeling the familiar weight in my hand, and brought it down on the club-wielding brute's head before he even realized what was happening. He toppled like a felled tree, and I couldn't help but flash a grin at the cheering crowd.

Josiah grinned and shook his head at me, that "you're impossible" look on his face.

"What?" I said, putting on my best innocent act.

"Cheater," he teased. But we both knew there were no rules in this tournament. Anything went—magic, weapons, whatever you could get your hands on, as long as nobody got seriously hurt. Honestly, that was half the fun.

I flashed him a cocky smile. "You're just jealous of my awesomeness."

"You wish," Josiah shot back, but I could see the glint in his eyes. He loved this as much as I did.

By then, only a handful of us were left standing. I scanned the field, sizing up my next opponent. Damon—a seven-foot-tall behemoth—caught my eye. He had one of the new recruits pinned to the ground, strangling the poor kid with his own whip.

Typical Damon. Subtle as a brick to the face.

I gripped my patu, feeling a familiar rush of adrenaline, and marched straight toward what looked like certain doom.

(Hey, if you're going to go down, might as well do it with style.)

"Need some help?" Josiah called, raising an eyebrow, probably hoping I'd say yes so he could swoop in and play hero.

"Nope, he's all mine," I called back, rolling my shoulders. Six months of training with the Golden Guard in Mistral had prepared me for moments just like this. Besides, I wasn't about to let Josiah steal my thunder.

"Hey Damon, why don't you let the kid go?" I called out, trying to sound casual, like I wasn't already plotting three different ways to take him down.

Damon didn't even glance up. He just kept pummeling the kid, who looked like he was about to pass out.

"Come on, man, he's had enough," I tried again, a little more serious this time.

"Wait your turn, Caleb. You're next." Damon grunted, hoisting the kid up by his feet like a sack of potatoes. "Yield yet, pipsqueak?"

The kid let out a pitiful whimper, his face turning a shade of purple I'd only ever seen on overripe plums. He nodded frantically, gasping, "I yield!" like his life depended on it.

Damon dropped him onto the grass without a second thought, then turned his attention to me, cracking his knuckles like he was about to break a tree in half.

I grinned, patu at the ready. "Guess I'm up. Let the games begin…"

"You going to fight me without that magical club of yours this time?" he sneered.

My patu practically hummed in my hand, eager for a rematch. But honestly? I didn't need it to beat Damon. I'd already wiped the floor with him twice, and I was ready to make it a hat trick.

"I'll beat you however you want," I shot back, grinning as I set my patu down in the grass—just to prove a point.

I took a quick scan of the arena, just like the Masters drilled into us. Only four of us left now; the rest had gathered around, hungry for a show. Josiah was still locked in hand-to-hand with Millicent, the alchemist with a mean right hook and a hidden dagger up her sleeve. She flashed steel at him, but I couldn't worry about Josiah—he could handle himself. I had my own mountain to climb.

Damon stalked toward me, the other recruits forming a ring, laughing and placing bets. Most of them were rooting for Damon, convinced I was puppy chow without my patu. That's just because they hadn't seen what I could do with my magic yet.

I knew better than to let Damon get close—those hands were like bear traps. So I backed up a few steps, keeping just enough distance that he couldn't grab me like he did Kieran.

"Come on Caleb, get on with it," someone shouted from the crowd.

Damon laughed, rubbing his hands together like a villain in a bad play. "Oh, the things I'm going to do to you, you little punk."

"Still holding a grudge, I take it?" I shot back.

Last tournament, I'd swept Damon's feet out from under him with my patu in the first thirty seconds. He'd thrown a giant-sized tantrum and complained to the Masters. But hey, anything goes in love and war —and especially in tournaments.

Damon gnashed his teeth and glared at me, all bluster and bruised ego. "You're a cheating little pretty boy, and I'm going to teach you a lesson you'll never forget."

He lunged, swinging for my head, but I was already moving—leaping out of the way, heart pounding, adrenaline singing in my veins. I countered with a burst of nature magic, conjuring a dust cloud and flinging it straight into his face. (Hey, if you're not cheating, you're not trying hard enough.)

As Damon sputtered and wiped at his eyes, I seized the opportunity. With a flick of my wrist, I sent a vine lasso snaking around him. I yanked hard, and Damon crashed onto his back with a thud that shook the ground. He howled in outrage, but I wasn't done yet—I made tiny pink flowers blossom all over the vines, just to rub it in.

"What is this nonsense?" Damon shouted, struggling against the vines.

"Do you yield?"

Damon's face turned even pinker than the flowers that covered him from head to toe. "Never!" he roared.

"You sure about that?" I asked, tightening the vines.

Damon fought to break free, but I knew the vines would hold—and so did he.

"We both know you'd never beat me without magic," Damon growled.

I rolled my eyes. "Just yield already."

He glared at me, then finally muttered, "Fine... I yield."

The crowd erupted into cheers—though a few kids who'd lost their bets on Damon booed in protest. I held my patu high, grinning as the chant rose up: "Prince Caleb! Prince Caleb! Prince Caleb!"

I used to hate being called a prince. Here in Hekagia, it meant something—responsibility, expectations, and a kingdom watching my every move. It had taken years for this place to feel like home. Sometimes, I still missed the old farmhouse. But Mistral had grown on me. For the first time, I actually felt like I belonged.

And, hey, being a prince definitely didn't hurt my chances with the ladies. Not that I'd ever admit it out loud, but I'd noticed the way Naomi—Amira's old chambermaid—looked at me. She handed me a jug of water, her smile bright enough to outshine the sun. "Well done, Prince Caleb," she said, her eyes sparkling.

I tried to play it cool, but I could feel my ears turning red. "It was nothing," I said, a little bashful, taking a long swig before handing the jug back. Naomi bowed and slipped into the crowd, but I caught her sneaking another glance my way. I grinned, feeling a little bolder than usual.

I swung my patu in a wide arc, challenging the crowd. "Who's next?" I called, letting my voice carry across the field.

"How about me?" called a cocky voice.

I spun around, heart thumping, to see Josiah standing in the center of the training field. He had a smile on his face and a bloody gash running down his left cheek—proof he'd managed to best Millicent. "Looks like it's just you and me," he said, raising his hands in challenge.

I shot him a grin, trying to look braver than I felt. Josiah was good-hearted, the kind of guy who'd befriend the new kid on day one—even if that new kid happened to be a prince. He never treated me any differently than the other recruits, which I appreciated more than he knew. But Josiah was also a beast in the ring. He never went easy on me when we sparred—and, annoyingly, he always won.

My heart was pounding so hard I was sure everyone on the tournament field could hear it. Losing to Josiah during practice was one thing—he was older, faster, and pretty much good at everything—but out here, with the whole camp watching? No way was I going down without a fight.

Josiah grinned at me, all easy confidence. "Come now, Caleb, there's nothing to worry about," he teased, like we were just two buddies about to toss a ball around, not duel in front of half the kingdom.

Yeah, right. I snorted, rolling my eyes as I reached for my patu. "Sure, Josiah. Just a friendly duel," I shot back, my voice dripping with sarcasm. I knew better than to trust that innocent act—he was already sizing me up, waiting for me to make the first move.

His green eyes flashed, a hint of purple swirling in them as astral magic curled from his hands. He cocked his head, daring me to try something. Well, if he wanted a show, I'd give him one.

Without a second thought, I dropped to the ground and plunged my hands deep into the dirt. I could feel the earth's heartbeat, the thrum of roots and rocks far below. I gritted my teeth, sweat beading on my brow, and summoned one of the biggest boulders I could sense. The ground shook as it rose, and I flung it at Josiah with everything I had. He dove aside, landing in a smooth crouch.

"No causing serious injuries," he called, shaking his head at me. "You could have killed me with that thing."

"We both know you're too good for that, Josiah!"

"True, but stranger things have happened," he quipped.

I snorted, already spinning my vine lasso in one hand.

"How about we do this without magic?" Josiah suggested, all innocence.

"How about not," I shot back, flashing him a cocky grin. If he thought I was going to give up my edge, he was dreaming.

Josiah was a great spellcaster, but he was an even better swordsman. I wasn't about to let him show me up in front of Naomi and everyone else.

I raised my vine lasso, feeling the magic hum at my fingertips. Josiah, ever the show-off, readied an astral orb in his palm. Sweat dripped down my forehead and stung my eyes, but I didn't dare look away from him for even a second. One wrong move and he'd have me flat on my back.

"Prince Caleb!"

A loud shout drew my attention to the other side of the tournament field. Someone in long yellow robes was barreling across the field, dodging soldiers left and right. Only one person could look that ridiculous and important at the same time—Master Sadiki.

"Oh man," I grumbled, lowering my lasso as he skidded to a stop in front of me, gasping for breath.

"Prince Caleb," Master Sadiki wheezed, "I… am glad… I found you. There is something I must show you."

"Can't it wait? I'm kind of in the middle of something," I said, waving a hand at Josiah and the crowd, who were all watching with bated breath.

"No, it cannot."

I sighed, half annoyed, half relieved that I wouldn't have to face Josiah in front of everyone. "Sorry guys, the show's over!" I called, trying to sound disappointed, but honestly, I was grateful for the interruption.

The crowd booed and groaned, but Master Sadiki glared at them so fiercely that they scattered like a flock of terrified chickens. I couldn't help but smirk—he might be old, but the man had presence.

"That means I win then," Josiah called out, grinning like he'd just been crowned king of the world.

"Only by default," I grumbled.

Josiah just grinned wider. "We both know I would have won."

"Maybe…maybe not. I've been getting a lot stronger," I shot back, nudging him with my elbow as he passed.

"Sure, but I taught you everything you know." Josiah nudged me back, then headed off toward the citadel, probably already planning his next "friendly" duel.

Master Sadiki, clearly done with all the tournament drama, pulled a weathered scroll from beneath his robes and thrust it into my hands. The thing looked like it belonged in a museum, not in the middle of a muddy training field. "What's this?" I asked, eyeing the scroll with a mix of curiosity and suspicion.

"It's what we have been searching for," he replied, practically bouncing with excitement. For a guy who usually looked like he'd rather be napping, he was suddenly wide awake.

"Are you sure?" I asked, raising an eyebrow. I'd learned to be skeptical whenever Sadiki got that gleam in his eye.

Master Sadiki nodded, urging me to unroll it. I did, careful not to tear the ancient papyrus. The writing was so faded and weird I couldn't make out a single word. Not that it mattered—I was more of a "show me, don't tell me" kind of guy anyway.

"What am I looking at here?" I asked Master Sadiki.

He pointed to the bottom of the scroll, where a rough map was sketched in black and red ink. It showed a tall stone temple surrounded by endless desert.

"That is the lost temple of the Elementals," Master Sadiki said, his voice brimming with excitement. "If we want answers about what happened to them, that's where we'll find them."

Great... I thought, fighting the urge to groan.

The last time Master Sadiki and I went on an "adventure," it had been a disaster—bugs, rain, and way too many desert pirates for my taste. The only good thing to come out of it was finding Hercules, my griffin. And now, apparently, we were heading back into the wild.

Just another day in the life of Prince Caleb Hale: tournament champion, adventurer, and, apparently, professional bug magnet.

I eyed Master Sadiki warily, already bracing myself for whatever wild quest he was about to propose. "I'm assuming you want me to go find this temple."

He nodded. "Yes, we must leave at once."

I let out a dramatic sigh. "Of course we must. But you're going to have to break the news to the Masters. They're not going to be thrilled about me leaving in the middle of my training." I could already picture their faces—equal parts horror and exasperation.

"You know they're probably still mad about the last time you 'borrowed' me for an adventure." That trip had involved a runaway griffin, a flooded alchemy lab, and a week's worth of extra chores. Good times.

He grunted. "That's their problem, not mine."

"Master Sadiki, is it okay if Josiah comes with us?" I asked as he tucked the ancient scroll back into his robes. If I was going to trek across the desert, I wanted backup—and Josiah was the best there was.

He shot me a look over the rim of his glasses. "What use could a recruit possibly be to us?"

"I'm a recruit," I reminded him.

"That different…" he huffed, but I could tell he was already caving.

I shrugged, playing it cool. "Josiah is quick on his feet, and honestly, he's saved my skin more than once. Plus, he's not bad in a fight."

Sadiki rubbed his beard, clearly annoyed but considering it. "You're vouching for him?"

"Absolutely," I said. "Besides, you always say we need all the help we can get."

He sighed, relenting. "Fine. But if he slows us down, he's your responsibility."

I grinned, feeling that familiar rush of excitement. "Deal. You won't regret it."

And if he did, well, at least it wouldn't be boring.

CHAPTER SIX

ATTACK OF THE DESERT PIRATES

I stuffed the last of my gear into my pack, not bothering to fold anything, and ran out of the barracks with Josiah at my heels. He'd jumped at the chance to join me on this "no doubt perilous quest"—his words, not mine. All that was left was the hardest part: saying goodbye to Naomi.

I found her in the library, sunlight catching in her golden hair as she waited by the door. I tried to play it cool, flashing her my trademark crooked grin. "Sorry, babe," I said, trying to keep things light even though my stomach was in knots. "Looks like I have to go save the world again."

Naomi's smile faltered, and for a second, I hated myself for leaving. "I understand, Prince Caleb," she said softly. She leaned in, pressed a kiss to my cheek, and then—just like that—she was gone.

Josiah, who'd been quietly checking his gear nearby, caught my eye and grinned.

"Such the lady's man," he teased.

I shot him a glare, trying to mask the ache Naomi's departure left behind. "Jealous much?" I fired back.

Josiah just laughed, shaking his head. "Not even a little," he said, slinging his shield over his back. He had Kendra—his girlfriend of two years—who had already stopped by to say her goodbyes.

Master Sadiki, ever the traditionalist, shook his head at me in disapproval. "Perhaps you should find another young lady to pursue," he said, his voice stern. "Naomi is your sisters' Lady in Waiting, after all."

I shrugged, feigning indifference. "Amira won't mind," I said, though we all knew that wasn't true. Amira would definitely have an opinion about it, but I didn't care. Naomi treated me like a person, not just a prince or a pawn in someone else's game. Her kindness and honesty had been a lifeline since I'd come to Hekagia, and I wasn't about to let anyone—royal protocol included—ruin that for me.

Josiah changed the subject. "Will Hercules be joining us?" he asked.

"Yeah, why wouldn't he be?" I replied. Hercules, my loyal griffin companion, had been with me through every trial and triumph. I couldn't imagine facing what was ahead without him.

Josiah shrugged. "I haven't seen him around much lately."

He wasn't wrong. Hercules had grown restless over the past few weeks, wandering farther and farther from Mistral, exploring the wilds beyond. Sometimes, I'd catch a glimpse of his massive wings soaring in the distance, but more often than not, he just disappeared for days at a time. I never really knew what he was up to anymore, but I liked to think he was out there having his own adventures—just like me.

As soon as we left the library, I stopped smack in the middle of the courtyard and let out a long, sharp whistle—one of those that echoes off the castle walls and makes everyone look up. Josiah rolled his eyes, but I just grinned and scanned the sky for any sign of Hercules. We waited. And waited. Fifteen minutes ticked by, and all we got for our trouble were a couple of crows circling the towers and a lot of impatient sighs from Master Sadiki.

"We cannot wait any longer," Sadiki finally said, glancing at the sun like it was personally offending him. "Every minute we waste, Raideron grows stronger. We must make haste."

I crossed my arms and shook my head. "I'm not leaving without Hercules." My voice came out firmer than I meant, but I didn't care.

I whistled again, louder this time—loud enough to make Josiah wince.

Just when I was starting to worry that I'd have to go on this quest without my best friend, a massive shadow swept across the garden. There he was—Hercules, my griffin, golden-brown fur gleaming, wings beating the air like thunder. He landed with a heavy thud, claws digging into the earth, sending up a cloud of dust and startling the gardeners.

"See?" I said, shooting Josiah a smug look. "Told you he'd come."

Hercules folded his wings and flopped down, letting out a groan that sounded way too dramatic, even for him. My magic had gotten good enough that I could actually understand animal speech now, but honestly, I didn't need magic to see he was in a mood. He looked about as cheerful as a wet cat.

"What's wrong, big guy?" I asked, crouching down to scratch behind his ears.

"*Hercules met girl*," he rumbled, sounding like he'd just lost his last gold coin.

"Oh... well, that's good, isn't it?" I said, trying to sound encouraging. I mean, who doesn't love a little griffin romance?

Hercules shook his head, feathers drooping. "*Griffins mate for life. My mate died...I cannot take another.*"

I frowned, patting his thick fur. "That's a rough rule, buddy. Seems kind of unfair."

"*Now I will be alone forever*," he moaned, laying his head down with a sigh that could have wilted the castle roses.

"You'll always have me," I pointed out.

He lifted his head and nuzzled me affectionately.

"Look, if you like this girl, you should go for it. Who cares about some old griffin rule?" I said, trying to sound practical, even though I knew griffin society was about as stubborn as the Golden Council.

"*If I do, I will be banished by the other griffins,*" Hercules replied, all doom and gloom. "*That is our way.*"

I patted him again, glancing at Josiah and Sadiki, who were both pretending not to listen but totally were. "Well, I can't help you with your love life, but I can offer a distraction. We're going on another quest—want to come with?"

Hercules looked up, his ears twitching, and gave me a look that said he was weighing his options. "*Will it involve more swamps?*" he grumbled.

I shuddered, the memory of our last mud-soaked adventure still fresh. "I really hope not," I said, shooting Josiah a look. "If it does, I'm blaming Sadiki this time."

Josiah just snorted, and Sadiki pretended to be very interested in the clouds. Hercules let out a low, resigned groan, but I could tell he was in. No matter what, we were in this together—mud, monsters, and all.

Two days into our trek, I still couldn't decide which was worse: last year's endless slog through the swamps, or the desert of Alkrimia we were stuck in now. At least in the swamp, you could pretend you weren't being slow-roasted alive. The desert was relentless—hot, dry, and the wind blew sand into every possible crevice. Boots, packs, even my teeth. By nightfall, the sun was still hanging around like it owned the place, baking the landscape in harsh, golden light.

"This sucks," I grumbled, yanking my scarf tighter around my face. The sand was everywhere. I was pretty sure I'd be coughing up grit for a week.

"What?" Master Sadiki called out through the wind.

"I said this sucks!" I shouted back, not caring if the whole desert heard me.

Hercules, who'd been trudging along beside us with his wings tucked in tight, squawked in agreement. He looked about as miserable as I felt—head low, feathers full of sand.

"I'm pretty sure I've eaten at least a pound of sand," I muttered to Josiah, who was walking next to me. "We need to stop." My mouth felt like I'd been chewing on a sandcastle, and my eyes stung from the dust.

Josiah nodded, looking just as done with the desert as I was. "I'd like nothing more, but we're in the middle of nowhere. What do you propose we do for shelter?" He glanced around, but there was nothing but dunes and cracked earth in every direction. No trees, no rocks, not even a single sad bush.

I pulled down the strip of cloth I'd tied around my face and looked around. Josiah was right; there was nothing but sand as far as the eye could see. It seemed impossible that anything could survive out here.

But then, I paused. I could feel something—a faint vibration under my boots, a subtle pulse of life, way down deep. Even here, life found a way. I crouched down and pressed my hands into the hot sand, reaching as deep as I could. I focused, channeling my nature magic, drawing water upward and coaxing roots to grow. I willed the energy to spread, infusing the ground with magic.

Almost immediately, the ground began to rumble. In rapid succession, rows of palm trees shot up from the sand, their trunks tall and straight. Grass spread out in a thick carpet, and clusters of desert flowers bloomed in bursts of color. In moments, we were surrounded by a small oasis, the new growth forming a natural barrier against the wind and blowing sand.

Josiah stared around in disbelief. "Caleb, this is remarkable," he said, turning in a slow circle to take it all in.

I couldn't help but grin, pride swelling in my chest. "Told you—I'm the best nature spellcaster there is." And for once, I didn't even feel like I was bragging.

Josiah scoffed, but there was a hint of a smile on his face. "As impressive as this is, it's far from the best nature magic I've ever seen. You've still got a ways to go."

I shot him a look, grinning. "We'll see about that." I dug my hands into the sand again, determined to show off a little more. Thick green vines erupted from the earth and wove themselves between two of the palm trees, forming a sturdy hammock. I hopped in and stretched out, hands behind my head, feeling pretty pleased with myself.

Josiah shook his head and dropped his pack down at the base of a palm tree, leaning against the trunk. "Show off…" he muttered, but he looked relieved to finally have a place to rest.

Hercules curled up under my hammock and was out like a light, wings tucked in tight. The oasis I'd conjured was already proving useful—shelter from the wind, a patch of grass for Hercules, and a hammock for yours truly.

Master Sadiki, though, didn't look impressed. He stood at the edge of the oasis, his weathered face creased with concern as he scanned the dunes. "I'm not sure this was wise, Caleb," he said, his tone all doom and gloom.

I tried to flick a thorn out from between my shoulder blades and nearly fell out of the hammock. "What are you on about now?" I grumbled.

"Do you not recall the last time we traversed this desert?" Master Sadiki asked, sounding way too serious for my taste.

"Yeah, I remember. We got attacked by desert pirates and it royally sucked. But the Golden Guard took care of them," I said, waving it off like it was no big deal.

Josiah, who'd been scanning the horizon, suddenly sounded grim. "I wouldn't be so sure about that."

I followed his gaze. Off in the distance, a sandstorm was building, the sky darkening as the wind picked up. The wall of swirling sand was moving steadily in our direction. If I hadn't already had a run-in with the band of pirates that roamed the Alkrimian desert, I might've thought it was just another storm. But I knew better—this was a sign that trouble was coming: a horde of bloodthirsty pirates using the storm as cover. And just my luck, I'd conjured us a perfect little oasis right in their path.

"Not again," I groaned, rolling out of my hammock and grabbing my pack. Of course it had to be pirates—because why wouldn't it be? I swear, if there's trouble in a hundred-mile radius, it's got my name on it.

Master Sadiki grimaced. "I won't say I told you so, but..." He gestured toward the sandstorm barreling our way, and I could just make out the silhouettes of pirates and their monstrous camels riding the edge of the storm.

I shot him a look right back. "You can scold me later, let's just get out of here."

"And go where?" Master Sadiki replied. "The sun will be setting soon. If we stray from the path, we'll surely be lost to the desert."

He had a point. The sun was already sinking, and the desert at night was no place for amateurs—or for a prince with a knack for getting into trouble.

"Then we'll have to fight," I said, trying to sound braver than I felt as I searched for my patu. I really didn't want to tangle with desert pirates again, but I wasn't seeing a better option.

Josiah, always ready for a scrap, unsheathed his sword and flashed me a grin. "About time things got interesting."

Meanwhile, Master Sadiki started rummaging through his endless pockets and pulled out a handful of vials filled with some thick, green sludge. "What's in those?" I asked, eyeing them warily. With Sadiki, you never knew if you were about to get a healing potion or a face full of frog slime.

"With any luck, you won't have to find out," he replied, which was not at all reassuring.

The pirates descended on us in a swirling cloud of sand. They were riding the biggest camels I'd ever seen—seriously, these things looked like they could eat a horse for breakfast. The pirates quickly surrounded us, cutting off any chance of escape.

Hercules let out an indignant squawk and lunged at the nearest camel, pecking it right on the rump. The poor beast nearly tossed its rider, who yanked the reins and shouted, "Halt!" like he actually thought he was in charge of this circus.

"What do you want?" I demanded.

The lead pirate, all wrapped up in desert rags and a black scarf, fixed me with a stare that I supposed was meant to be intimidating. His voice was gravelly, like he'd swallowed a handful of rocks for breakfast. "Do you not remember me?"

I gave him a once-over, unimpressed. "Should I?" I shot back, raising an eyebrow. He looked like every other bandit I'd ever seen—dusty, cranky, and in desperate need of a bath.

He growled, tightening his grip on his sword. "My crew was slaughtered by the Golden Guard thanks to you. I ought to take your head right here and now, but there's a price on it, so says Lord Raideron."

My hands curled into fists, my patu itching for action. "I dare you to try," I growled, meeting his glare with one of my own.

The pirate just laughed—a nasty, rotten-toothed cackle that made my stomach turn. "You've got spirit, boy, but it won't save you." He started to draw his sword, but he was way too slow. I swung my patu with everything I had, catching him square in the chest and sending him sprawling into the sand.

The rest of the pirates didn't waste a second—they closed in on me, weapons drawn and eyes wild. But Josiah was already at my side, his sword flashing as he parried a blow from another pirate—all tan skinned with seashells braided into his hair. The dude looked like he'd stepped straight out of a pirate legend.

Josiah shot me a look, dodging the pirate's blade with way too much ease. "You just can't go anywhere without picking a fight, can you?"

I couldn't help but smirk, even as I ducked a wild swing. "I can't help it. I just have this effect on people for some reason."

Honestly, it was like trouble had me on speed dial.

Not that Josiah needed my help—he was handling his guy just fine—but I circled behind the pirate anyway and clocked him on the back of the head with my patu. He dropped like a sack of potatoes. One down.

Josiah and I fell into our usual rhythm, moving together like we'd been fighting side by side our whole lives. His sword flashed, parrying and striking, while I used my patu to knock opponents off balance. We took down three more pirates in quick succession, barely breaking a sweat. For a second, I actually thought we had things under control.

Then, out of nowhere, a sharp, piercing whistle cut through the chaos. The sound was so intense it felt like someone was drilling straight into my skull. I dropped to my knees, clutching my ears, the world spinning around me.

I looked up, desperate to find the source of the horrible noise. Josiah and Master Sadiki didn't seem fazed at all—just my luck. The leader of the pirates limped toward me, clutching his chest with one hand and blowing into a blackened piece of wood with the other. Whatever that thing was, it was pure torture. I doubled over, sick from the pain, wishing I could just magic the sound away—or at least punch the guy in the face.

Josiah knelt down and tried to help me up. "Are you okay, Caleb?" he asked, concern etched on his face.

I could barely hear him over the screech in my head. "Can't you hear that?" I managed, still clutching my ears like that would somehow block out the pain.

Josiah shook his head. "Hear what?"

The pirate leader stalked forward, grinning like he'd already won. Josiah stepped in front of me, his sword raised. "Stay back!" he shouted.

Hercules swooped in, pecking at any pirate dumb enough to get close. Good griffin.

The pirate leader sneered, "Fight all you want, Lord Raideron is already on his way. I'll collect the bounty and, if I'm lucky, he'll let me take your heads for my personal collection."

"You're sick," I spat, shuddering at the thought of my head sitting in a jar on some pirate's mantle. Not exactly how I pictured my legacy.

Master Sadiki stepped up, uncorking one of his vials with a flourish. The pirate's eyes narrowed.

"What trickery is this?" he growled.

"You are about to find out!" Master Sadiki shouted, and with a grunt, he hurled the vial at the ground.

The vial shattered, and a plume of green smoke exploded everywhere. My eyes burned, my throat felt like it was on fire, and I dropped to my knees again, coughing and trying to crawl away from the worst of it. I called out for Josiah and Master Sadiki, but the only answer was the sound of panicked screams—pirates or friends, I couldn't tell.

When the gas finally cleared, I blinked through watery eyes and found Josiah and Master Sadiki a few feet away, curled up in the sand, coughing and rubbing their eyes. The oasis was eerily quiet. The pirates, who'd surrounded us only moments before, were nowhere to be seen.

I let out a shaky laugh, still coughing. "Well, that's one way to clear a room."

I pushed myself to my feet, still blinking away tears from the stinging gas. "Where did they all go?" I asked Master Sadiki, squinting around the oasis for any sign of the pirates. For all I knew, they'd just vanished into thin air.

He nodded toward the pond. I shuffled over, half-expecting to see a bunch of pirates hiding behind the reeds. Instead, I found a group of giant toads—each one bigger than my fist—hopping around the water's edge. Their mottled green and brown skin looked almost comical as they croaked and leapt from rock to rock, sending ripples across the pond.

"You turned them into toads?" I asked, glancing back at Master Sadiki. I had to admit that was a new one—even for him.

"It was the best solution I could think of in the moment," he replied like it was just another day at the office. "The transformation spell was quick and effective. At least they won't be a threat now."

"Impressive," I said, watching as one of the toads tried to climb onto a lily pad and promptly slid off into the water. I couldn't help but grin. "Bet they didn't see that coming."

"Hmph," Sadiki grumbled, clearly not as pleased with the outcome as I was.

Josiah, still catching his breath, looked over at the camels that had been left behind. The animals stood in a loose cluster near the edge of the oasis, stamping their feet and snorting, clearly agitated by the sudden disappearance of their riders.

"What about the camels? We can't keep them. They are vile creatures that only obey their masters," Josiah said, eyeing the beasts warily.

"Can't we set them free?" I suggested. Not that I loved the idea of getting too close to those massive, shaggy monsters with their yellowed teeth, but I couldn't just leave them to their fate.

Master Sadiki frowned, rubbing his beard like he always does when he's about to say something wise and inconvenient. "I suppose we'll have to. If Raideron truly has been summoned, we'll need to throw him off our trail. The camels might wander off and confuse anyone tracking us."

We got to work untying the camels, shooing them away from the oasis. Most of them just stomped their feet and glared at us, like we'd interrupted their beauty sleep. But one particularly massive camel—let's call him King Spit—waited until I got close, then swung his head around and let loose a glob of half-digested, foul-smelling goo right down the front of my shirt. The stench hit me like a punch to the face. I gagged, ripped off my shirt, and chucked it into the sand, wishing I could throw my dignity in after it.

Josiah, of course, doubled over with laughter.

"Thanks a lot," I grumbled, giving King Spit a gentle kick in the rear. He snorted and lumbered off after the others, leaving a trail of deep tracks in the dust.

With the camels gone, I turned my attention back to my oasis. I pressed my hands into the ground, focusing hard, and drew the magic back into myself. The palm trees, grass, and flowers withered and sank beneath the sand. I could feel my magic reserves draining, like running a marathon after having nothing but camel spit for breakfast.

By the time I finished, it was close to midnight. The desert air had cooled, but exhaustion pressed down on me like a sandbag. All I wanted was to collapse and sleep for a week, but Master Sadiki was already lighting a torch and waving us onward.

"Come, we must leave this place," he said, his voice all urgent and mysterious.

"Are you sure we have to go right this minute?" I asked, barely able to keep my eyes open. "I could really do with some shut eye."

"That depends," he replied, glancing at the dark horizon.

"On what?" I asked.

"On how much you enjoy being alive."

Josiah chuckled and fell in behind Master Sadiki as he started down the winding path that led away from the oasis and into the dunes. I made a face at Josiah as he passed, but he just shook his head and kept walking.

As we left the oasis behind, the desert seemed even bigger and emptier. Off in the distance, I caught a glimpse of a dark shadow moving along the edge of the dunes. It was gone as soon as I blinked, but a cold shiver ran down my spine. I quickened my pace, closing the gap between me and Josiah as the night pressed in around us. I wasn't about to let anything—camel, monster, or otherwise—catch me lagging behind.

CHAPTER SEVEN

THE TEMPLE OF THE ELEMENTALS

The night dragged on, every hour stretching longer than the last, my nerves wound tight as a bowstring. I kept expecting Raideron to leap out from behind a sand dune, cackling like the villain he is, but he never showed. Maybe he had better things to do than chase two half-dead teenagers and a cranky old alchemist through the desert. Or maybe—just maybe—he'd finally realized we weren't as easy to pick off as he thought. I'll admit, the idea gave me a little flicker of pride.

By the time dawn started creeping up, my legs felt like they'd been replaced with lead pipes. Every step was a battle: sleep versus stubbornness, and stubbornness was barely winning. Master Sadiki was up ahead, trudging along in that silent, mysterious way of his, when suddenly he threw out a hand to stop us.

I nearly walked right into him. "What's wrong?" I croaked. Honestly, I was so tired I probably would've kept walking straight into a pit of scorpions if he hadn't stopped me.

He didn't answer right away. Instead, he pointed down the slope we'd just crested. I followed his gaze—and my exhaustion vanished in an instant.

Spread out below us, glowing in the golden sunrise, was a temple straight out of a history book. I'm talking ancient Egypt vibes: limestone walls stretching forever, two massive obelisks with gold caps flanking the entrance, the whole place shimmering like it was showing off for us. For a second, I forgot about my aching feet, the sand in my boots, and the fact that I probably smelled like camel spit.

I let out a low whistle. "That's... incredible."

Master Sadiki actually smiled. "Welcome," he said, "to the Temple of the Elementals."

For a moment, all the fear and exhaustion melted away, replaced by awe. This wasn't just some old ruin. It was a promise. A mystery. Maybe even a sign that we weren't completely doomed after all. As the sun climbed higher, lighting up every ancient stone, I felt hope stirring in my chest for the first time since we'd set foot in this blasted desert. And let me tell you, it felt pretty good.

"Why would the Elementals ever abandon this place?" I asked, glancing at Master Sadiki. "Seriously, it looks perfect! If I had a place like that, you'd have to drag me out kicking and screaming."

He paused at the edge of the slope, his expression shadowed. "It was perfect—once. But that was a long time ago."

I shot him a look. "You're really going to leave it at that? Come on, you can't just drop a cryptic bomb and expect me not to ask questions."

He didn't even crack a smile. His eyes lingered on the temple below, all gleaming and golden in the morning light. "You'll see soon enough," he said, voice heavy. Which, let's be honest, did nothing to calm my nerves.

The temple was at the bottom of a steep, winding valley, and getting there was about as fun as wrestling a porcupine. The path was a nightmare—thorny shrubs clawed at my legs, snagging my woolskin trousers. At one point, a fat scorpion darted across the trail and I yelped, almost face-planting into the sand. Josiah, of course, snorted with laughter behind me.

Glad I could provide the entertainment...

Sometime during the night, the landscape had transformed. The endless sand dunes gave way to a limestone plateau, dotted with rolling hills and jagged cliffs. The wind that had battered us all night finally died, leaving the air crisp and dry. I tugged down my scarf and took a long drink from my canteen, savoring the cool water.

"We must keep moving," Master Sadiki urged, glancing back at us like we were a couple of slowpokes. "There's no time to waste."

"Proper hydration isn't a waste of time," I shot back, but I fell in behind him anyway. Priorities, right?

As we got closer, the temple's true condition became apparent. The stones near the entrance were blackened with old burn marks, deep scars I hadn't seen from the top of the valley. Up close, the place looked like it had survived a war and lost. Sections of the walls had collapsed, leaving piles of rubble and gaping holes where windows should've been. What wasn't charred was crumbling, the stonework pitted and worn by time and violence. Even the towering obelisks flanking the entrance hadn't escaped, it's ancient inscriptions smeared with what looked disturbingly like dried blood.

"Who did this?" I asked Master Sadiki.

Sadiki scowled, his eyes darkening like a brewing storm. "The Magni Nostrum," he spat. "In their endless hunger for power, they came here to destroy the Elementals and steal their secrets. Let us hope they failed."

I let out a low whistle. "Figures. Leave it to a bunch of power-hungry spellcasters to ruin the coolest place I've ever seen."

As we crossed the threshold into the temple grounds, a weird energy prickled along my skin—like the air itself was buzzing with secrets. The obelisks flanking the entrance practically hummed with ancient power.

I couldn't help myself; I stopped and pressed my palm to a swirling koru carved deep into one of the stones. Instantly, a jolt of energy shot through me—warm, electric, and so alive it made my hair stand on end. I gasped, breath catching in my throat. "Whoa. That's... new."

"What was this place?" I asked, shaking out my tingling hand. "And why is the royal symbol carved into this obelisk? Not that I'm complaining, but it's a little on the nose."

For once, Master Sadiki's expression softened, just a little. "This was the home of the Elementals," he said. "They lived and trained their disciples here for thousands of years. Their power was beyond imagining. It doesn't surprise me to find the koru here—they knew your bloodline would be important, even then."

I reached out again, unable to resist the pull of the carving, but Sadiki caught my wrist in a grip that was way stronger than it looked. "Best not to touch anything," he warned, his voice suddenly sharp. "This place is riddled with traps. The Elementals were wise—they protected their secrets well. Keep your hands to yourself, unless you want to lose them."

I swallowed, stepping back from the obelisk, the weight of history pressing in all around me. "Noted. No touching. Got it."

Beside me, Hercules let out a low, anxious mewl and pawed at the ground with his talons. I knelt down, scratching behind his ears. "What's wrong, big guy?"

"*I can go no further,*" Hercules replied.

"Why not?" I asked.

"*Magical wardings. They're too strong for me to pass through. I will wait here and guard the entrance.*"

I ruffled his feathers, trying to sound braver than I felt. "Be safe, big guy. Don't let any sand monsters sneak up on you." Hercules bowed his head in solemn respect, then nudged me gently toward the temple doors with his beak, like he was telling me to get on with it already.

"Alright, alright, I'm going," I muttered, shooting him a grin. "But if you see anything weird, squawk twice."

I followed Master Sadiki inside, and—wow. The air was thick with the musty stench of a fire that had burned itself out ages ago, but somehow still managed to cling to everything. Charred human bones were stacked in a grim pile in one corner. Every piece of furniture had been trashed—bookshelves toppled, tables smashed to splinters, paintings ripped from the walls and left in sad, tattered heaps. It looked like a tornado had come through, then decided to stick around for a barbecue.

"What happened here?" I asked, my voice echoing off the ruined walls. I tried to sound casual, but honestly, I was just trying not to gag.

Master Sadiki's face was grim. "No one knows for certain. The Elementals vanished after the Magni Nostrum attacked this temple. The few scrolls we've recovered suggest they hid themselves away, hoping to keep their powers out of the Magni Nostrum's hands. Presumably, they sealed themselves in the tomb we found in the swamps, until Raideron found them, at least."

A shiver ran down my spine at the memory of that bug-infested nightmare. The only good thing to come out of that swamp was finding Hercules. Everything else had been a disaster. Now, with Raideron holding the Elementals captive at Shadowfell Castle, ready to use them for his own dark purposes, the urgency of our mission pressed in on me. We had to find a way to free them.

Anger simmered under my skin as we ventured deeper into the ruined temple. Each step left a trail in the thick soot and ash, the silence broken only by the crunch of debris beneath our boots. The darkness grew heavier the farther we went—no windows, just endless shadows. I squinted, straining to make out shapes in the gloom, hands outstretched so I wouldn't faceplant into some ancient, cursed statue.

"I can't see a thing in here," I grumbled, squinting into the pitch-black corridor.

Master Sadiki reached into his robe and pulled out a glass orb. He muttered something under his breath—probably something fancy in Ancient Alchemist—and the orb flared to life, nearly blinding me.

I blinked, holding up a hand. "Warn a guy next time, would you?" But I took the glowing sphere anyway, grateful for the light (not that I'd admit it out loud). Sadiki handed another orb to Josiah, who grinned like he'd just won the lottery.

The orbs lit up a circular chamber at the heart of the temple. In the center stood a massive stone pedestal, and on top of it, a jade gemstone the size of my fist. It glowed like it was holding a secret, pulsing with power. Around it were five smaller pedestals, most of them scorched and cracked, blackened by fire. Only one was still standing, and on it sat a half-burned scroll, its edges curled and brittle—like it had survived a really bad day.

Master Sadiki's voice dropped to a reverent hush. "This must be the inner sanctum..." He tilted his head back, eyes going wide. I followed his gaze and, would you look at that—there was a window in this place after all.

High above us, a domed skylight let in the faintest trace of light. Through the glass, I could just make out the moonless sky. On any other night, the rays would've landed right on the jade gemstone, like a spotlight on the main event.

Josiah nudged me in the shoulder, snapping me out of my awe. I shook myself and turned my attention back to the sanctum, where Master Sadiki was already hunched over the scroll, brow furrowed like he was trying to solve the world's hardest riddle.

I leaned in, lowering my voice. "Is it the one we need?" I asked, trying to sound cool and collected. If it was, maybe—just maybe—this whole crazy quest was about to pay off.

"That is what I am trying to determine," Master Sadiki muttered, not even glancing up from the scroll, like he was defusing a bomb and I was just background noise.

I eyed the scroll—edges blackened, looking like it would crumble if you so much as sneezed on it. "How are you going to do that? It looks like it's about to fall apart."

"Carefully," he grumbled, lips pressed so tight I thought they might disappear. His hands shook just a little as he started untying the ancient leather cord, as if he was trying to unwrap the world's most dangerous birthday present.

"Are you sure that's a good idea?" I asked, because someone had to be the voice of reason here.

He shot me a glare. "Do shut up, please. I am attempting to open a thousand-year-old scroll that could very well determine the fate of the world, if you hadn't noticed."

Josiah snickered, and I shot him a look. "I was just asking…" I muttered, but Sadiki was already back to his scroll surgery.

Sadiki sucked in a breath as the last knot came loose. The scroll unraveled—and immediately snapped into three pieces, thin as onion skin and twice as fragile.

"Oh no!" I yelped, reaching out on instinct, but Sadiki just let out this weird sigh of relief, like this was somehow the best-case scenario.

"That could have gone worse," he said, way too calm for someone who'd just broken Hekagia's most important piece of paper.

I stared at the ruined, half-burned scroll, totally baffled. "How could it be worse? The scroll is indecipherable in this condition." I mean, seriously—was I the only one seeing the problem here?

Master Sadiki smiled confidently. "Then it's a good thing you brought along a master alchemist," he said, like he'd been waiting his whole life for this moment.

He reached into his robe and pulled out a little rectangular vial filled with some mysterious dark blue liquid. As he unscrewed the lid—eyedropper and all—Josiah leaned in, eyes wide with curiosity. "A restoration potion?" he asked.

Master Sadiki nodded, then squeezed a few drops onto the brittle parchment. The liquid hissed as it hit the scroll, and right before my eyes, the three torn pieces started knitting themselves back together. The burned edges smoothed out, the faded ink darkened, and suddenly the scroll looked almost brand new. Magic, right? Sometimes it actually works.

"Well done!" Josiah exclaimed in relief.

I wanted to feel relieved too—really, I did. This scroll was supposed to be our golden ticket to figuring out what happened to the Elementals.

But there was this pit in my stomach that wouldn't go away. Something about this whole thing felt off.

Why would the Magni Nostrum torch every other scroll, but leave this one behind? Why make it so easy to find, knowing any halfway decent alchemist could fix it up?

Unless... unless they wanted us to find it.

A chill crept up my spine. "I think this is a trap," I said, keeping my voice low.

Master Sadiki looked up from the scroll, his eyes suddenly sharp. "What do you mean?"

"Just think about it... this was all way too easy."

Master Sadiki straightened, his gaze sweeping the room, suddenly on high alert. Josiah, ever the optimist, piped up, "Maybe the Magni Nostrum were interrupted. The Elementals surely would have fought back."

"But why leave the scroll out in the open like this?" I pointed out. "It doesn't make sense."

Master Sadiki's jaw tightened. "Someone wanted us to find it," he agreed, his voice grim.

Suddenly, a surge of magic shot through me—like when I'd touched that obelisk outside, only this time it was less "cool artifact" and more "oh crap, something's about to go down." The hairs on the back of my neck stood up, every instinct screaming that we were being watched.

From the shadows, Raideron slithered out, looking like he'd just crawled out of a grave. His face was all sharp bones and evil grins, and when he pulled back his hood, his eyes glinted with the kind of malice that made my stomach twist.

"Well done," he rasped, his voice like a cheese grater on stone. "I was wondering how long it would take you to figure it out."

I tensed, patu ready, every muscle screaming for a fight. But Raideron didn't look like he was here to throw down—at least, not yet. His weird cat eyes flicked to the pedestal, where the Elemental

Scroll we'd just fixed sat, practically glowing with "steal me" energy.

Josiah lunged for the scroll, but Raideron just flicked his wrist like he was shooing a fly. Josiah froze mid-leap, hand inches from the parchment, looking like someone had hit pause on him.

"Not so fast," Raideron chided, his tone so smug I wanted to punch him right in his bony face.

"What are you doing here?" I growled.

He smiled, giving me a look of pure malice. "Those foolish pirates were finally good for something. Once I realized what you three were up to, it was easy enough to follow you here. You've actually saved me a lot of trouble."

Of course. Master Sadiki had been right—Raideron had been on our tail the entire time. Though, judging by the sour look on his face, he wasn't happy about being right. Master Sadiki slid one hand into his robe pocket, the other held out protectively in front of the scroll.

"Thank you for fixing the scroll, by the way..." Raideron drawled. "There was a spell on it that kept me from touching it—until now."

I squared my shoulders, not taking my eyes off him. "Why do you want the scroll so badly?"

Raideron smirked. "And why would I tell you that?"

"Because you're not all that smart," I shot back, gripping my patu tighter. If he wanted a fight, I was more than ready to give him one.

Raideron cackled, the sound crawling up my spine. "Ah, the gallant young prince. I've heard stories about your bravery, but you don't seem that impressive to me. Perhaps we should test your mettle?"

"Perhaps we should." I took a step forward, ready to smash his ugly mug in with my patu.

Something flickered in Raideron's expression—not quite fear, but a flash of uncertainty. For a second, he looked like he might actually be rethinking his whole "evil overlord" routine.

Then he pulled himself together, straightening his cloak like he hadn't just flinched. "Give me the scroll and perhaps I'll let you all live," he said, switching tactics.

"Not a chance."

I stepped in front of the pedestal, shoulder to shoulder with Master Sadiki. No way was I letting this creep get his hands on the scroll. Not while I was still breathing.

Raideron's gaze slid over to Master Sadiki. "I do not wish to harm you," he said, all casual, like he hadn't just threatened to kill us all a second ago.

Master Sadiki narrowed his eyes. "Is that so?"

"It's true. I find your alchemy skills to be most impressive... I don't suppose you'd consider joining my side?"

Master Sadiki's voice turned colder than the Alkrimian desert at midnight. "I will never join you," he replied.

Raideron's lips curled into a cruel smile. "I was afraid you would say that. Oh well though."

Before I could even blink, Raideron cocked his head to the side, his eyes blazing with astral magic. Master Sadiki was hurled across the room like a rag doll, slamming into the pedestal with a sickening thud. He crumpled to the floor, blood pooling beneath his head from a deep gash.

Rage exploded inside me. I didn't even think—I just swung my patu at Raideron with everything I had, aiming to wipe that smug grin off his face for good. But he caught my weapon mid-swing, yanking it right out of my hands like it was nothing.

"Careful now, boy." Raideron's eyes glowed with a sinister purple light as astral magic seeped into my patu.

With a devilish grin, he snapped my patu in half with his bare hands. The pieces clattered to the ground at my feet.

For a moment, the world just... stopped. I stared at the broken remains, numb with shock. My patu wasn't just a weapon—it was a part of me. I'd trained with it for years, learned to trust its weight, to channel my magic through its polished wood. It had saved my life more times than I could count. Now, it was nothing but splinters.

Josiah, having come free of Raideron's magical freezing trick, tried to hold me back, but I tore free, dropping to my knees to gather the shattered pieces. Splinters dug into my palms, but I barely felt it.

"Caleb, we have to go!" Josiah hissed, grabbing my arm. I barely heard him over the roar in my ears—rage, grief, and a stubborn refusal to let Raideron win.

Then I saw it: Josiah had conjured a portal, swirling open right there in the middle of the chaos. Through it, I could see the golden hills and towers of Mistral Castle—home. Safety.

But I wasn't ready to leave. Not without my patu. Not with this defeat burning in my chest like acid.

"Take Master Sadiki and the scroll. I'm going to finish this," I said, my voice raw and shaky. I meant it, too. I was ready to go down swinging if it meant making Raideron pay.

"No, Caleb. You're not." Josiah shoved me towards the portal.

For a split second, I was weightless—caught between worlds, the roar of magic in my ears, the broken pieces of my patu still clutched in my hands. Behind us, Raideron's furious cry echoed, sharp and desperate. I almost smiled.

At least I'd gotten under his skin.

CHAPTER EIGHT

SECRETS OF THE SCROLL

I woke up in my bed at Mistral Castle, feeling like I'd been trampled by a herd of stampeding griffins. The room was quiet, curtains drawn against the sun. Then I spotted Naomi perched on the edge of my mattress, her face scrunched up with worry. I tried to sit up, but Naomi pressed a gentle hand to my shoulder, like I was some fragile artifact she needed to protect.

"You should rest, Prince Caleb," she said in a soft voice.

"How long have I been out?" My voice sounded like I'd swallowed a bucket of sand.

"Three days…"

"Three days?" I cried, trying to wrap my head around it. "Why did you let me sleep that long? I could've missed a whole war!"

Naomi's eyes went wide. "I'm sorry!" she stammered. "I was under strict orders not to wake you."

"Whose orders?" I demanded, still feeling like my brain was stuck in a fog.

"The Masters," Naomi said, pouring me a glass of water from the tray on the bedside table. "You could hardly move when you arrived through the portal."

I took the glass, gulping down the water like it was the best thing I'd ever tasted. "What about Josiah and Master Sadiki?" I asked, my mind racing. I needed to know they were okay—and that the Elemental Scroll hadn't ended up as kindling. The last time I'd seen Master Sadiki, he'd looked like he'd gone a few rounds with a mountain troll, and Josiah… well, I just hoped he was still in one piece.

Naomi shook her head. "I don't know," she admitted quietly.

"I've been here, by your side, since you arrived."

That hit me with a weird mix of relief and dread. On the one hand, I was grateful—seriously, Naomi had been a rock, sticking by me through whatever magical coma I'd landed myself in. On the other, not knowing what happened to Josiah and Master Sadiki gnawed at me. I flopped back against the pillows, my body still heavy as lead, and tried to piece together what might've happened after Josiah shoved me through that portal. My brain felt like it was stuffed with cotton.

The silence stretched between us, and suddenly I realized—I was alone in my room with a girl. Not just any girl, but Naomi. In my bed. Well, technically I was in the bed, and she was perched on the edge, but still. The realization that someone had undressed me down to my underwear hit me like a bucket of cold water. My face went hot. Naomi's cheeks turned pink too, and she quickly looked away, which pretty much confirmed what I already suspected—it had been her.

I wanted to crawl under the covers and disappear, but I couldn't ignore how kind she'd been. Naomi had seen me at my absolute worst—out cold, drooling on the pillow, probably snoring like a dying walrus—and she hadn't run for the hills. That meant more than I could say. I reached for her hands, a little awkward, but I managed to draw her gently toward me.

"Hey," I said, my voice a lot softer than usual, "thanks for being here for me. Seriously. I don't know what I'd do without you." I tried to give Naomi a smile, but it probably looked more like a grimace. My head was still spinning, and my body felt like it had been used for target practice by a bunch of angry trolls.

"Of course, Your Highness," she whispered.

"You know you can call me Caleb," I said, trying to lighten the mood with a tired grin, but before Naomi could answer, a sharp knock rattled my bedchamber door.

A guy in the royal army's uniform poked his head in, muttered something to Naomi that I couldn't catch, and then disappeared as quickly as he'd come. Naomi let out a sigh that sounded like she'd been holding her breath for three days straight, and closed the door behind him.

"What's going on?" I croaked, my throat still scratchy.

"Master Sadiki is awake," she said, and I could see the relief and worry fighting for space in her eyes.

Master Sadiki—right. The last time I'd seen him, things had gone sideways at the temple, and I'd barely made it out with my skin intact. Relief washed over me, but it was quickly replaced by a sharp ache in my chest as I remembered my patu.

I sat up, ignoring the way my head spun, and scanned the room, hoping—praying—that my patu had somehow survived the trip through the portal. Naomi bit her lip, worry flickering in her eyes, then knelt beside me. She reached under my bed and pulled out a bundle of fractured wood, setting it gently in my lap with a heavy sigh.

"My patu!" I wailed, clutching the broken pieces like they were the last slice of cake at a royal banquet.

Naomi's voice was soft, almost apologetic. "The Masters tried to fix it…but it is beyond repair."

I stared down at the splintered wood in my lap, my heart sinking all the way to my toes. Of course. Just my luck. First I get knocked out for three days, and now my patu is toast. Some hero I turned out to be. I tried to blink away the sting in my eyes, running my fingers over the jagged edges. The Masters would have to be miracle workers to put this thing back together.

"Perhaps the Hakuturi could fix it?" Naomi suggested.

I shook my head, letting out a sigh. "No. I don't think even the Hakuturi could fix this mess."

Naomi's voice dropped to a whisper. "I'm so sorry."

I swallowed hard, forcing myself to focus on something—anything—other than the ruined club in my hands. "What about the scroll?" I asked, my voice barely steady. "Did we at least manage to keep it from Raideron?"

Naomi nodded, her expression gentle. "Yes, the Masters are working on deciphering it now."

Right on cue, a sharp knock sounded at the door. Josiah burst in, not even waiting for permission. He slapped a hand over his eyes in this ridiculous show of modesty, a crooked grin plastered on his face. "I hope you two are decent in here," he teased, like he hadn't just barged in on the most awkward moment of my life.

Naomi's face went beet red. She curtsied so fast she nearly tripped, then bolted out of the room, leaving me alone with Josiah and a fresh wave of embarrassment.

I glared at him, trying to mask my own awkwardness with irritation. "What did you have to go and do that for?"

He shrugged in apology, but his excitement was barely contained. "Sorry, Caleb. The Masters have finished their translation of the scroll. You are definitely going to want to hear what it says."

He ducked out into the hallway, leaving me alone to pull myself together. My muscles still ached, but I managed to haul myself out of bed. I grabbed the first pair of wool trousers I could find—probably inside out, but who cared—and yanked on a plain tunic. My hands moved on autopilot, lacing up my boots while my brain tried to catch up.

Josiah knocked again, impatience leaking through his usually chill voice. "Are you almost done in there?"

"Just about," I called back, trying to sound less like a guy who'd just spent three days in a coma.

My hand went straight for my patu—old habits die hard—but all I found was the pile of broken wood on the bedside table. The ache in my chest was sharper than I expected. I hesitated, then grabbed the silver dagger instead, tucking it into my waistband with a sigh. Not the same, but it would have to do.

When Josiah and I finally made it to the library, the place was buzzing with tension. The Masters were huddled around a table, their voices overlapping in a storm of anxious debate—like a flock of crows fighting over the last scrap of bread. The second we stepped inside, the noise cut off. Every head turned our way, and suddenly it felt like I'd walked into the middle of a tribunal instead of a study session. My skin prickled under the weight of their stares.

"What's going on?" I tried to play it cool, but my voice caught.

Nobody answered right away. But then Earl stepped forward, and just like that, the tension in my shoulders eased a notch. If something was wrong, he'd tell me straight.

"Prince Caleb, it is good to see you," Earl said, giving me a nod that was equal parts greeting and reassurance. "Though I wish the circumstances were better…"

My stomach tightened. "What do you mean?" I asked, bracing for bad news.

Earl grimaced and handed me the scroll I'd risked my neck for. His hands lingered on the parchment, like he wasn't quite ready to let it go. That alone told me this was something big.

"The scroll contains the information we'd hoped for," he said quietly. "It tells us what Raideron did to corrupt the Elementals—and how to fix it."

I stared at the scroll, my mind racing. "That's good news... isn't it?" I asked, searching Earl's face for any sign that this was finally the break we needed.

But Earl's expression didn't budge. If anything, he looked even more grim. "Indeed," he said, "but we will need the Elemental Staff to reverse Raideron's curse."

He looked at me like I was supposed to know why that was a big deal. I felt my ears go hot—apparently, I'd skipped one too many history lessons in favor of combat training.

I tried to play it cool. "Then let's go get it," I said with a shrug.

Earl's jaw tightened. "The staff is on Roanoke Island. It was stolen and used by a dark spellcaster named Horatius Croatoan to create the Northern Portal."

Now that sounded familiar...

Suddenly, I was back at Amira's sixteenth birthday, Kira bursting into our lives, all those stories about the Standing Portals and the hot mess Horatius had made on Roanoke Island. Supposedly, the place was still crawling with the leftovers of his dark magic.

I flashed Earl my best crooked grin—the one I always saved for when I was about to do something reckless. "Great! Sounds like my kind of quest."

Josiah snorted, barely holding back a laugh. "Of course it does," he muttered, just loud enough for me to hear.

I shot him a look, already knowing what he'd say but needing to hear it anyway. "You wanna come with?"

Josiah's grin stretched even wider, his eyes practically glowing with the thrill of it all. "When do we leave?"

Earl's voice cut through our excitement, low and grave. "This quest will be dangerous. The Northern Portal is located in the heart of Zarandore. Raideron will most definitely have it heavily guarded."

I couldn't help but smirk, waving off his concern. "I've snuck into Zarandore plenty of times. I'd like to see them try to stop me from getting to the Northern Portal."

One of the Masters—this guy was younger, sharp cheekbones,

skin like polished mahogany, and a stare that could cut glass—cleared his throat so loud it made me jump. He shot Earl a look that said, "Get on with it, old man."

The whole room went dead quiet. Earl's jaw clenched, and he glared right back at the youngster.

I leaned back in my chair, raised an eyebrow, and tried to lighten the mood. "Let me guess, there's more to it?" I said, putting on my best "I'm totally not worried" face.

If there's one thing I've learned, it's that when adults get that serious, it's never good news.

Earl nodded, looking like he'd just swallowed a lemon. "The staff alone will not be enough to undo the stronghold that Raideron has on the Elementals. We'll also need the Obsidian Firestone, an ancient stone imbued with alchemical properties."

"And let me guess... we have no idea where that is?"

Typical.

There was always some lost magical doodad we had to chase down.

Earl shook his head. "The council does not," he said, sounding way too calm for my taste. "But Ravenna may. It has long been rumored to be guarded by her village."

I perked up a little at that.

"Great. I'll send a message to her about it." At least that was something I could actually do.

I was already thinking about how fast I could get Hercules saddled up if it came to it. But Earl hesitated, and I felt my stomach drop. Here it comes. The real kicker.

"There can't seriously be more..." I said.

Earl's face went all grim, and I knew we were about to get to the part that had everyone in the council so freaked out. "If we take the staff from the island, the Northern Portal will close—permanently."

He let that hang in the air, and for a second, nobody said a word. Even I didn't have a joke for that one. The weight of it settled over us, heavy as a mountain. And just like that, the adventure got a whole lot more complicated. But hey, that's kind of my thing, right?

The old stories about the Northern Portal's creation had always made it sound like a disaster waiting to happen, but I hadn't wanted to be the one to say it out loud. There were only three portals left that let you travel between Hekagia and Earth. The idea of losing one—of cutting off the only way back to the place where I'd grown up—made my stomach sick. But if we didn't get the Elemental Staff, Raideron would wipe out Hekagia. No contest. I couldn't let that happen, not for anything.

"Well, that settles it," I said, keeping my voice steady.

Earl gave me a look, puzzled. "It does?"

"Yep. We need Amira," I

If there was one thing I'd learned, it was that when things got this complicated, you needed your family. Especially when they are as powerful as mine.

CHAPTER NINE

THE AFTERMATH

Despite everything Raideron had thrown at us, the academy still stood—battered, bruised, but stubbornly alive. He hadn't even shown his face, just sent some astral monster to do his dirty work. We'd won, but the cost was devasting.

Kira and I moved through the courtyard, smoke curling around us, the air thick with the smell of burnt grass and magic. We worked side by side, dragging enemy bodies into rows. Darreon tried to stop me with, "Your Highness, this isn't for you", but I shook him off. I needed to see what this war had done, I needed to feel it in my bones.

But even in the wreckage, something unexpected was growing. Raideron's attack had forced everyone—nature spellcasters, astral kids, even the alchemists—to work together. I watched them patching up walls and gardens, sweat and soot streaking their faces, and for the first time, I felt a flicker of hope. Maybe, just maybe, something good could come out of all this pain.

As we worked, I glanced at Kira. She was quiet, her jaw set, but I could see the storm in her eyes. I didn't know what it was like to have a twin, but I knew what it meant to have a sister—and a brother. The thought of losing either of them made my chest ache. In that moment, surrounded by ruins and survivors, I understood just how fragile those bonds were. I promised myself I'd make things right with Kira, no matter what.

The royal trumpet blared, and I looked up just in time to see a line of carriages winding toward the academy gates. With everything that had happened, we'd made the call to send the students home. I hated it—hated admitting that the academy wasn't safe anymore. But after today, pretending otherwise felt like a lie.

We said our goodbyes—some tearful, some just stunned silence—and then they were gone. I stood at the edge of the road, watching the caravan disappear in a cloud of dust, my heart sinking with every turn of the wheels. I couldn't shake the feeling that I'd failed them all. Failed to keep them safe. Failed to teach them how to fight. Failed to save Shani…

My eyes found Ajay at the back of the last carriage, his face hollow with grief, and the memory of Shani's laughter echoed in the emptiness she'd left behind. Tears slipped down my cheeks, hot and silent, but I forced myself to stand tall and wave until the last wagon vanished from sight.

A warm hand slipped into mine, and for a split second, hope fluttered in my chest.

"Treander?" I whispered, but when I turned, it was Kira. Her eyes—usually full of mischief—were clouded with worry.

"Hey," she said softly. "You holding up?"

I wiped my eyes, trying to muster a smile. "I'll be fine," I lied, my voice barely steady. "Are we okay?"

Kira's hand slipped from mine, her expression shifting—like maybe she'd forgotten about our fight, but my question brought it all rushing back.

"No, we aren't okay," she said, her voice tight. "If Savannah really did tip off Raideron, then she's just as much to blame for Shani's death as he is. How can you be okay with that?"

Her words hit me hard. I opened my mouth, but nothing came out. I wasn't sure what hurt more—her anger, or the truth in it.

Still, it wasn't fair for Kira to throw out accusations like that, especially without a shred of real proof.

I squared my shoulders, my voice coming out sharp. "We don't know Savannah had anything to do with it," I shot back, heat rising in my cheeks. "You can't just blame her because you're angry."

Kira let out a bitter laugh, folding her arms tight across her chest. "How much proof do you need, Amira? Seriously. Why don't we just go ask her? Actually, where is she? Because I haven't seen Savannah since before Raideron's attack. Have you?"

"No, I haven't," I admitted, biting my lower lip in concern.

Kira's eyes flashed, disappointment and anger flickering across her face. "Unbelievable," she muttered, then turned on her heel and stormed off, leaving me standing alone in the ruins of the courtyard.

I'd known Savannah practically my whole life. I wanted so badly to trust her, to believe that our friendship actually meant something, but Kira's words wouldn't leave me be. Savannah had lied to me for years: about Hekagia, about my birth parents, about who I really was. That was a hard thing to overlook.

And then there were the rumors about her parents. Savannah always insisted they'd been kidnapped by Raideron, but we'd gotten report after report that they were actually working for him willingly. Every time I tried to bring it up, Savannah would dodge the question, like if she ignored it long enough, it would disappear.

As night settled over the academy and Savannah still hadn't shown up, a gnawing worry took root in my chest. I found myself replaying Kira's accusations, wondering if she might be right.

I wanted to talk to Kira, to admit my doubts, but she kept her distance all evening, sticking close to Ravenna and Gnash. The space between us felt wider than ever.

After dinner, I collapsed into my bed, desperate for sleep. My body ached in places I didn't even know could hurt, and my mind was a tangled mess of grief, suspicion, and regret, all knotted together. I knew I'd have to face Savannah—and Kira—in the morning, but right then, all I wanted was to disappear.

I'd barely let my eyelids flutter shut, the exhaustion of the day finally pulling me under, when a sharp, icy wind sliced through the stillness of my room. It wasn't the gentle draft that sometimes slipped beneath the door, but a wild, unnatural gust—one that whipped my hair across my face and sent the candle flames sputtering in protest.

The shadows on the ceiling twisted and danced, swirling into a vortex of shimmering purple light. My blanket tangled around my legs as I bolted upright, adrenaline flooding my veins.

From the heart of the portal, a tightly rolled piece of papyrus shot out, spinning end over end like a wayward comet. I barely had time to throw out my hands before it smacked into my chest and bounced onto the tangled sheets.

My hands trembled as I reached for it, the parchment still warm from its journey through the portal. The familiar, chaotic scrawl on the outside made my heart skip a beat—Caleb's handwriting.

TOP SECRET INFORMATION INSIDE!!!

We found the Tomb of the Elementals! We ran into Raideron along the way, but everyone is fine. We also turned a bunch of desert pirates into toads, but that's a long story.

We have to go get this magic staff (of course, right), but It's on Roanoke Island. I bet there will be zombies!!! Are you up for one last adventure? Meet me at the Northern Portal, if you aren't too busy with your princess stuff.

Oh yeah…the purification spell requires an obsidian fire stone. I have no idea what that is, but Master Sadiki said that Ravenna will know where we can get one.

See ya,
Caleb

I barely slept after that. My brain was a hamster wheel of doubts and what-ifs. The idea of going back to Earth—cursed island and all—was both electrifying and terrifying. I kept picturing the Golden Council's faces. They'd see every risk, every reason to say no to my request to go. But I had to try.

As soon as the first sliver of sunlight crept through my window, I was up—still in my nightgown, hair a disaster, Caleb's letter clutched in my fist. Aria, my lady's maids, would faint if she caught me roaming the halls looking like this, but I didn't care. Etiquette could wait—this couldn't.

Kira's door was closed, and when I knocked, all I got was a muffled groan. I tried again, knocking harder.

"Whoever you are, go away!" Kira's voice was pure grump—raspy, exhausted, and 100% done with the world.

"It's me. Open up!" I whispered through the door.

A few seconds later, the door swung open. Kira stood there, her hair a wild mess, dark circles under her eyes. She looked like she hadn't slept at all. "Do you have any idea what time it is?" she grumbled.

I didn't bother with an apology. Instead, I shoved Caleb's letter into her hands. I watched her eyes widen, sleepiness vanishing as she read. "Now do you see why this couldn't wait?" I whispered.

Kira blinked, then let out a long, dramatic sigh. "You're lucky this is actually important," she muttered, but her voice had lost its edge. She shut the door in my face, reappearing a moment later, robe cinched tight, fuzzy slippers on.

She marched off, and I scrambled to keep up, my heart thudding with excitement. "Where are we going?

Kira rubbed her eyes, yawning so hard I thought her jaw might unhinge. "To get Ravenna. Obviously."

I hesitated, falling a step behind. "Do you think she really knows where to find an Obsidian Firestone?" I asked.

Kira shrugged. "No idea. But if anyone does, it's Ravenna."

When I knocked on Ravenna's door, she was already awake, which wasn't really a surprise. Ravenna was the kind of person who woke up before dawn to hit the training room.

She stood before us in all black, taiaha strapped across her back, looking like she was ready to take on Raideron's army single-handed.

Kira's voice changed, gentler than I'd heard in days. "Going somewhere?" she asked.

Ravenna nodded, her voice steady. "Just making preparations for my journey home."

I stepped forward, suddenly feeling awkward. "That... might have to wait," I said, my voice apologetic as I handed her Caleb's letter. She read it, her eyes growing wide and eager.

"Caleb is correct," she said, her eyes landing on Kira. "I know where the Obsidian Firestone is."

Kira perked up, curiosity sharpening her features. "Where?"

"My village," Ravenna replied, her voice low, almost bashful. "Wahiao has kept it safe for generations."

Kira and Ravenna exchanged a look—a silent, loaded conversation that made me feel like I was missing something important.

I cleared my throat awkwardly. "Do you think you could portal there and get it?" I asked.

Ravenna shook her head, a wry smile tugging at her lips. "The closest a portal will get us is twenty miles out. The land itself keeps strangers at bay."

Kira's lips quirked into a determined smile. "Then we walk. I'm not afraid of a little mud."

Ravenna's eyes shimmered, emotion flickering beneath her steady exterior. "Are you sure?" she asked.

"Definitely," Kira said, her tone fierce with loyalty. She leaned in and kissed Ravenna on the cheek. "There's no way I'm letting you go alone."

Ravenna managed a watery laugh. "I wouldn't be alone; I've asked Gnash to come as well. But you do smell a lot better than he does."

"Depending on the day," I teased, unable to resist a jab at my little sister, even as my heart ached at the thought of us going separate ways.

But I knew there wasn't enough time for me to join them on the journey to Ravenna's village and also still meet Caleb at the Northern Portal. We'd have to split up.

A lump formed in my throat. "I'm going to miss you both," I said, my voice thick.

Kira rolled her eyes. "It'll only be a few days...a week tops. No need to be a big baby about it."

Ravenna, who'd been quiet, stepped closer. Her voice was low and steady. "You know, in my village, we say goodbyes with a promise: 'I'll see you on the wind, or in the fire, or wherever the world needs us most.'" She squeezed my hand, her grip strong and grounding. "We'll be back before the moon changes, Amira. I promise."

We stood there for a moment, the three of us tangled up in nerves and hope. Outside, the sky was just starting to lighten, painting the world in soft gold. I watched them go, their laughter echoing down the corridor, and hugged myself tight.

"I'll hold you to that," I murmured after them.

CHAPTER TEN

THE WEIGHT OF SECRETS

Convincing the Golden Council to let me go to Roanoke Island had been every bit as difficult as I'd expected. Lord Adley in particular wasted no time in voicing his doubts.

"So, the future ruler of Hekagia wants to abandon her duties before she's even crowned?" he sneered, his words sharp as a blade. "How unsurprising." He stared me down, waiting for me to flinch.

But I didn't. I stood my ground—explaining that the fate of the Elementals, and maybe all of Hekagia, depended on this trip. I wasn't asking for a vacation. I was asking for a chance to save our realm.

After what felt like hours of arguing (and resisting the urge to set Lord Adley's wig on fire), the council finally caved, as long as I promised to be back in time for my coronation. Two weeks was plenty of time to find the staff on Roanoke Island, cure the Elementals, and, if the universe was feeling generous, stop Raideron once and for all... Right?

Of course, the council couldn't just let me have this one thing. "You're not going alone," Lord Adley declared, like he was bestowing some great wisdom. "And your brother is still in training. He's hardly qualified to protect the heir to the throne."

I wanted to fight back, but I bit my tongue. I needed their approval more than I needed to win an argument.

In the end, they insisted on sending a knight from the Golden Army—handpicked by them, naturally. I pictured some grumpy old veteran with more scars than patience, watching my every move. Not ideal, but I'd survived worse than a cranky chaperone.

And at least Earl would be coming.

He'd shown up the day before, to the council's dismay. He might not have been the council's favorite alchemist, but he was definitely mine. Just knowing he'd be there made the whole ordeal feel a little less impossible.

After the council meeting, I wandered the echoing halls of Vail Castle, my mind spinning with thoughts. I'd meant to find my mother—maybe get some advice, or just a motherly hug. Instead, my feet dragged me to the Hall of Memories. This long, echoey gallery where all the old monarchs stare down from their portraits, judging you (or maybe just waiting for you to mess up).

I drifted past them, one by one. Some looked like they'd bite your head off for sneezing in their presence; others seemed kind. But every single one of them had that same look: the heavy, quiet weight of being the one everyone expects to have all the answers.

I stopped in front of the portrait of one queen—a woman with fierce eyes and a crown that gleamed, even in oil paint. She looked like she'd never doubted herself a day in her life. But I couldn't help wondering: did she ever feel like I do now? Did she ever want to run away, or wish someone else could carry the burden for a while?

A familiar voice interrupted my spiraling. "Careful, that one's been known to blink when you're not looking," Earl said with a smile as he stopped in front of the painting, giving it a mock critical eye. "Or so the kitchen staff say. I suspect it's just the draft, but you never know with old queens."

I couldn't help it—I laughed, the tension in my shoulders easing just a little.

"Coin for your thoughts, Your Highness?" Earl asked me.

I managed a wry smile. "I was just thinking how strange it is to be going on my last big adventure."

He clapped a hand on my shoulder, nearly knocking me off balance. "Last adventure? Pah! You sound like Master Frederick after a single glass of wine—full of doom and gloom. The universe has a way of throwing new quests at you the moment you think you're done. Just you wait and see."

He spun on his heels, gesturing grandly at the row of monarchs. "You see that one?" He pointed at a surly old king with a crown so big it looked like it might tip off his head. "Legend says he once tried to outlaw laughter in the throne room. It lasted all of two days before his own council staged a pie fight. The point is, you might be surprised what changes and what doesn't, even with a crown on your head."

I shook my head, grinning despite myself.

"You're ridiculous, Earl."

He puffed out his chest, eyes twinkling. "Thank you, I do try. Now, come on. Let's go find some trouble before the council ties you to a throne and throws away the key. I've got a new batch of exploding ink I'm dying to test, and you look like you could use a distraction."

And just like that, the weight of all those painted eyes felt a little lighter. Earl was right—about the universe, about adventure, and about the strange, stubborn magic of not giving up, no matter how heavy the crown felt.

As we stepped out of the gallery, I hesitated. "Shouldn't we wait for the council's knight?" I asked Earl.

Earl's eyebrows shot up, and he flashed me that wild, mischievous grin of his—the one that always made me wonder if he was about to hand me a potion or set something on fire.

"Wait for him? Pfft! If this knight is half as legendary as the council claims, he'll find us. Besides, I'd wager a week's worth of my best elixirs he's already lost his way in the kitchens."

But the knight did find us. Just as our wagon rolled to a stop at the front gates of the academy, a man stepped out in front of the horses, forcing them to halt. He looked to be about fifty, with a thick beard and a jagged scar that ran from his right ear to the corner of his eye. His hand hovered near his sword like he expected someone to leap out and attack him at any moment.

He didn't bother with a bow. "Your Highness," he said, voice low and gravelly, "I am Sir Gallahan. You were meant to wait for me at Vail Castle." His gaze flicked over me, then landed on Earl with a look that could curdle milk.

Before I could even open my mouth, Earl hopped down from the wagon, landing with a flourish that sent his golden robes swirling. "That was my fault, Gallahan!" he boomed, as if he were greeting an old friend at a tavern instead of a knight with a stick up his armor. "You know how it is—adventure waits for no one, not even council knights."

Sir Gallahan's scowl deepened, and he squared his shoulders, making it clear he wasn't here for jokes. "The council told me you'd be joining us. I'll have no trouble from you, understand? I've got enough to manage without minding a—" He cut himself off, but the look he gave Earl said the rest. "And as for you, Princess, you'll do as you're told. This isn't a pleasure trip."

I bristled, but Earl just grinned, waving off the insult like it was a stray fly. "Trouble? Me? Never! Unless you count the time that I accidentally turned the council's tea set into mice. But don't worry, Gallahan, I'll be on my best behavior. Wouldn't want to upstage your heroics."

Gallahan grunted. "Just keep your tricks to yourself. I don't have time for nonsense. My job's to keep the princess safe, not to babysit council pets or—" He shot me a look, "—deal with royal whims."

"What instructions?" I asked, glancing between them, but Sir Gallahan ignored me, clearing his throat so loudly it sounded like he was trying to swallow a toad.

"Right," he barked, "Let's get the princess inside. It isn't secure out here."

"I'm right here," I grumbled, unable to keep the irritation from my voice. "You don't have to talk about me like I'm not."

But Gallahan was already shouting orders at the stable hands, acting as if I was invisible. My dislike for the knight grew by the second.

If this was the council's idea of protection, I had a feeling this journey was going to be even longer than I'd thought.

I left Earl and Sir Gallahan in the stables, grateful for a moment to myself as I made my way through the academy. My mind was a storm—plans, worries, the weight of what was coming all swirling together. I was so deep in thought that I nearly collided with Savannah as she rounded the corner.

She froze, her mouth forming a silent "oh," and for a second, we just stared at each other awkwardly. Her boots were caked in mud, and her short blonde hair was streaked with soot, like she'd recently been outside.

"Where have you been?" I asked, unable to keep the edge of concern—and suspicion—out of my voice.

Savannah shifted, her fingers twisting the hem of her dirty

dress. "Out walking the grounds," she said, her voice thin but stubborn. "I wanted to help wherever I could, after… missing the battle." She wouldn't meet my eyes, and the guilt in her tone was unmistakable.

I studied her, searching for the friend I used to trust with everything. "I was wondering about that…" I said, letting the words hang between us. I wanted to believe her, but the old certainty was gone, replaced by a gnawing doubt I hated.

Savannah's jaw tightened. "My nature magic has been all over the place lately. I figured I was better off inside, watching after the students." Her voice was small, almost apologetic.

"I didn't see you afterwards either, though." I tried to keep my tone light, but the question slipped out with a sharp edge.

She looked up at me, her face pinched with guilt. "I couldn't stand the smell…" she admitted. "The courtyard was… awful."

I nodded, letting the silence stretch. The aftermath of the battle had been a nightmare—blood, smoke, the acrid stench of burnt magic clinging to everything. Kira probably would have called it cowardice, but I recognized it for what it was: self-preservation.

Finally, Savannah looked up, her eyes searching mine for something—absolution, maybe, or just a sign I still believed in her. "Where have you been? I haven't seen you all day. Is everything okay?"

I hesitated. There were just too many secrets Savannah couldn't (or wouldn't) explain.

"I was at Vail Castle, visiting my mom," I lied.

Savannah's eyes widened, her worry so genuine it nearly undid me. "Is she okay?" she asked, her voice trembling with concern. For a moment, I almost told her the truth—almost let myself believe we could go back to the way things were. But the moment passed, and I just nodded, the lie settling between us like a stone.

I reached for my door handle, hoping the gesture would be enough—a silent plea for space, for a moment to breathe.

Evidently, it wasn't.

"Are you going somewhere?" Savannah asked, her voice tentative.

My hand froze on the doorknob. "Why do you ask?"

She shrugged, trying for casual but not quite landing it. "I heard some of the kitchen staff talking about packing food for a journey."

Her eyes flicked up to meet mine, searching.

I stared back, looking for any crack—any sign of betrayal, or just the truth. But Savannah had always been a good liar when she needed to be, and I was starting to realize that I might be too blinded by years of friendship to see her clearly.

"I'm going to stay at Vail Castle for a while," I said, forcing my voice into something light, almost breezy. "I want to be closer to my mom. Help look after her." The deception tasted bitter, but I smiled anyway, hoping it would be enough.

"I could come with you, if you want?" she offered, her voice soft and unsure.

I shook my head, maybe a little too quickly. "No, you should stay here and help Darreon keep the academy running."

"The students have all gone home, Amira. There's not much to do," she said in a flat tone.

"You could help with repairs," I suggested, reaching for something—anything—that would end the conversation.

"If that's what you want…"

"It is. There isn't anyone else I trust more to look after the school while I'm away," I said, the words tumbling out. I wasn't sure if I was trying to reassure her, or myself.

That seemed to do the trick, at least on the surface. Savannah nodded, but her eyes were still clouded with something I couldn't quite name. Then, with a reluctant nod, she headed off toward her bedchamber.

I watched as Savannah reached a fork in the corridor. She paused, glancing back at me with her usual half-grin—a smile that, tonight, didn't quite reach her eyes. For a moment, I saw something flicker across her face: guilt, maybe.

Acting on instinct, I waved back, then opened the door to my room, stepping halfway inside so it would look like I'd gone in for the night. But curiosity—or maybe something deeper—kept me rooted to the spot. I waited, breath held, and peeked back out into the corridor just in time to see Savannah hesitate, then turn and head in the opposite direction. It was late, well past midnight. Unless she was sneaking off to the kitchens for a late-night snack, I couldn't imagine where else she'd be going at this hour.

My stomach plummeted.

Quietly, I slipped out of my room and followed her. Whatever

Savannah was up to, I needed to know.

I trailed her down the dark corridor, careful to keep a few paces behind. I didn't want to believe Savannah could be up to no good, but I couldn't shake the sense that she wasn't being entirely truthful. And my instincts proved to be right.

Savannah rounded the corner and came to a stop in front of a nondescript door. I had no idea where it led, but I knew that we were near the infirmary—close enough that Kira's story seemed more likely to be true by the minute.

With a quick knock on the door, Savannah slipped into what I assumed was the broom closet. Within seconds, a purple glow emanated from underneath the door. I'd been through enough portals to recognize the telltale traces of astral energy.

I didn't stick around to confirm what I already knew in my gut. Savannah had somehow summoned a portal.

But I wasn't able to solve the mystery of who she was talking to, because she came out of the closet as quickly as she'd gone in, nearly spotting spotted me. I pressed myself into the shadows, heart pounding in disbelief.

I watched her slip away, her silhouette swallowed by the darkness. The ache in my chest sharpened. I wanted to believe in her, to trust her the way I always had. But tonight, trust felt like a luxury I couldn't afford.

I made my way back to my chambers, every step heavy with exhaustion and the bitter taste of doubt. The memory of Savannah's silhouette in the corridor haunted me, looping in my mind like a curse. I wanted so badly to believe she was innocent, to cling to the friend I'd always known, but the evidence gnawed at me.

By the time I reached my door, dawn was just beginning to paint the hills in pale gold. I barely managed to close the door behind me before I collapsed onto my bed, dragging the covers over my head as if I could hide from the world—and myself.

But sleep was a distant hope. A soft, persistent knock sounded at my door just minutes later.

Aria's voice, thin and precise, slipped through the wood: "Your Highness? Forgive me, but Master Earl is insisting that you must wake."

I groaned, burrowing deeper into my pillow. "Go away, Aria,"

There was a pause—a tiny, indignant huff, almost too quiet to hear. "I'm sorry, Your Highness, but Master Earl was most insistent," she replied, her tone clipped and proper, as if she were reciting a rule from a dusty etiquette book. I could almost picture her on the other side of the door, wringing her hands, torn between duty and the scandal of disturbing the future queen at this hour.

A moment later, the door creaked open. Aria entered, balancing a heavy tray with the rigid grace of someone who'd spent her life serving others. She was small and neat, her hair pulled back so tightly it looked painful, her uniform starched to perfection. She set the tray down beside me with a soft clatter, then stood back, hands folded, eyes averted.

"I brought you some coffee, Your Highness," she said, her voice barely above a whisper. "It's not as strong as you like, but the kitchens are short on beans again." There was a hint of apology in her words, as if the state of the pantry was a personal failing.

I sat up, accepting the mug. The warmth seeped into my hands, but did nothing for the chill inside me. The thought of food made me nauseous. When Aria offered a muffin, I shook my head.

"You must eat something, Your Highness," Aria chided gently. "It will be a long journey; you'll need your strength."

I managed a weak smile, grateful for her care even as I felt hollow. "Thank you, Aria. But what I really need right now is Darreon."

Aria's eyes widened, scandalized. "Shall I ask him to meet you in the training room?" she asked, her voice dropping to a whisper, as if the very idea of a man in my bedchamber might summon the wrath of every ancestor in the Hale line.

"No," I said, shaking my head. "Bring him here."

Her brows shot up so high I thought they might disappear into her hairline. "To your bedchambers?" she repeated, aghast.

"It's not like that," I assured her, my voice weary. "I just need to talk to him somewhere we won't be overheard."

Aria hesitated, torn between the ironclad rules of propriety and her duty to obey. "But... your bedchambers?" she echoed again, her voice barely more than a squeak.

"Yes, my bedchambers. Right now, please," I insisted, letting a note of command slip into my tone.

She pressed her lips together, gave a tiny, old-fashioned curtsy, and hurried from the room, her slippers whispering against the stone. I felt a pang of guilt for being to short with her, but I didn't have time for protocol or decorum.

Ten minutes later, a hesitant knock sounded at my door. I was halfway through pulling a thick woolen tunic over my head, the fabric catching on a snarl of hair at the nape of my neck. The tunic wasn't exactly flattering—definitely not the sort of thing Aria would have chosen for me—but it was warm and practical, and right now, that was all I cared about.

"Come in," I called, my voice muffled as I yanked the tunic into place. I glanced down at myself: sleeves bunched at my wrists, leather leggings clinging a little too tightly, and my bare feet pressed against the chilled stone floor. Not exactly regal, but at least I wouldn't freeze to death on the road to Zarandore.

The door creaked open, and Darreon stepped inside, his posture as stiff as a fencepost. His eyes flickered over me, then quickly darted away.

"Your Highness," he said, his voice wavering just a little. "Would you like me to come back later… once you're dressed?"

I blinked, momentarily thrown. Was I not dressed? I looked down again—no, definitely clothed, just not in the silk-and-lace Aria would have insisted on.

"I am dressed," I replied, amusement slipping into my tone. "Or at least, as dressed as I'm going to be today."

Darreon's lips twitched in a nervous half-smile, and for a moment, the tension in the room eased.

"Come in," I said, softening my voice. "There's something important I need to talk with you about."

He nodded, stepping further into the room, careful to keep his gaze politely averted from my bare feet. "Of course," he replied, his tone respectful but tinged with uncertainty. "What can I do for you, Your Highness?"

Just then, Aria's voice drifted from the doorway, thin and precise as ever: "If you need anything warmer, Your Highness, I've set your boots by the hearth." I caught a glimpse of her—small, neat, her hands folded primly on her apron. Looking at her, I almost forgot she was only sixteen, the way she was always hovering nearby like a ghost. But I was grateful for her, for the way she fussed over the little things, as if keeping my boots warm could somehow keep the world from falling apart.

I nodded at Aria and then turned back to Darreon, squaring my shoulders. "Sorry about the state of things," I said, gesturing vaguely at my rumpled clothes and half-packed bag. "It's been one of those days."

"It is not a problem, Your Highness," Darreon replied, his eyes landing on the open bag on my bed. "You said you wanted to speak to me about something?"

I hesitated, searching his face for any sign that he might balk at what I was about to say. Darreon had always been loyal—steady as bedrock—but this was different. "I'm leaving the academy," I said quietly, the words heavier than I'd expected. "And I'm not sure how long I'll be gone."

His hazel eyes widened, his composure slipping for just a heartbeat. "You're... leaving?" he echoed.

I nodded, feeling the weight of the decision settle on my shoulders. "I'm leaving you in charge," I added.

His eyes went even wider, and for a moment, he looked almost comically shocked—mouth open, brows high. But then, as if a switch had flipped, he straightened, pride and responsibility overtaking his nerves. "That is a great honor, Your Highness," he said, his voice steadying. "I will serve you proudly."

A genuine smile tugged at my lips. "I know you will," I replied, meaning it. Darreon had always been dependable, and I trusted him more than anyone to keep things running in my absence.

He hesitated, then asked, "May I ask where you are going?" His tone was careful, respectful, but I could hear the worry beneath it.

I shook my head, my expression turning grim. "It's better that you don't know," I said quietly. "For your sake, and for everyone else's."

Darreon nodded in acceptance, but I could see the disappointment flicker in his eyes. He wanted to help, but he understood the necessity of secrets, especially in times like these.

"Honestly, I would tell you if I could," I said, my voice softening. "You've been a huge help these past few months. Well, years, really. I don't know what I would do without you." The admission slipped out before I could stop it.

Darreon's face flushed crimson and he cleared his throat, clearly uncomfortable with such direct praise, especially in my bedchamber.

He looked away, searching for something else to focus on. "Will you visit Treander before you leave?" he asked, his tone respectful but quietly probing, as if he was testing the boundaries of what he was allowed to ask.

The question caught me off guard, and for a moment, I couldn't find my voice. "No," I said finally. "I think it's for the best if I don't."

Darreon's gaze sharpened, a note of gentle challenge in his voice. "The best for whom, if you don't mind me asking?"

His comment stung—more than I wanted to admit. I looked away, unable to meet his eyes. Of course I wanted to see Treander—how could I not? But with the way we'd left things before Raideron's attack, I couldn't risk letting my emotions cloud my judgment. There was too much at stake now, and the drama between us would have to wait. I needed to be focused, not worrying about my mess of a love life.

Trying to regain my composure, I cleared my throat and forced myself to move on. "I have another favor to ask of you, Darreon," I said, my voice steadier than I felt.

"Anything, Your Highness." He bowed his head respectfully, but I could sense the questions he was holding back in the way his hands fidgeted at his sides.

"I need you to keep an eye on Savannah," I said, making sure my tone left no room for misunderstanding. I couldn't risk telling him more, but I hoped he understood the weight behind my words. My gaze lingered on his face, searching for any sign of doubt or hesitation.

Darreon's expression flickering with surprise and confusion. For a moment, I thought he might ask why, but he caught himself. He simply nodded, his jaw set with determination.

"And take care of yourself," I added, crossing the room to give him a quick, fierce hug. The gesture surprised us both—Darreon stiffened at first, clearly unaccustomed to such displays of affection. But then he relaxed, his arms coming up in a hesitant but genuine embrace.

"Things are more dangerous than ever," I whispered, my voice thick with emotion. "Promise me you'll be careful."

He pulled back, his eyes meeting mine with quiet resolve. "I will, ma'am," he replied softly.

As I watched Darreon straighten his shoulders and accept the weight of responsibility, a knot of anxiety twisted in my stomach. I knew he would do everything in his power to keep the academy safe—he always had—but letting go was harder than I'd imagined. The halls I'd worked so hard to fill with hope and unity suddenly felt distant, as if they belonged to someone else now.

I tried to reassure myself that I'd left things in capable hands, but the truth was, the uncertainty of what lay ahead on Roanoke Island gnawed at me. Legends and warnings about that place echoed in my mind, and I couldn't shake the fear that I was walking straight into the unknown, leaving behind the fragile peace I'd managed to build.

As I turned away from Darreon, the weight of both the academy and the journey pressed down on me, and I wondered if I was truly ready for what was coming next.

CHAPTER ELEVEN

THE NORTHERN PORTAL

As we rode north, Middlehaven's ruins crept out of the fog—burned beams jutting up like broken ribs, rooftops caved in, the whole place smelling like wet ash. Even though the villagers had escaped, the emptiness pressed in on me, heavy and cold.

Earl rode beside me, his golden robes looking way too cheerful for the landscape. He sat tall on his mare, Maisy, but I could tell he was watching me out of the corner of his eye.

He cleared his throat, gentle but not pushy. "Is everything alright, Your Highness?" he asked.

I managed a wry smile. "Oh, you know. Just the usual—impending doom, existential dread, and the tiny detail that the fate of Hekagia might rest on whether or not we find a thousand-year-old staff." I tried to sound lighthearted, but the words fell flat, heavy with the weight of truth.

Earl's lips twitched, but his eyes were serious. "Well, if it's any comfort, destiny has a habit of working out for those who don't run from it." He nudged Maisy closer, his tone turning conspiratorial. "Besides, I've always found that a little doom keeps the mind sharp. And if all else fails, I have a flask of something strong tucked away for emergencies."

I rolled my eyes but couldn't suppress a grin. "Everything is just such a mess. I don't know what to do or who to trust."

He gave me a gentle smile. "Then trust yourself."

A bitter laugh slipped out before I could stop it. "You make it sound like that's such an easy thing to do."

Earl's smile deepened, the lines at the corners of his eyes crinkling. "I never said it was easy. But it's worth it."

He nudged Maisy ahead, golden robes fluttering behind him as he caught up to Sir Gallahan. I watched him go, his words settling over me like a heavy, weirdly comforting blanket. Earl always seemed to know who he was, even when the world was falling apart. Maybe I could figure that out too somehow.

Just before we left, I'd found myself reaching for the battered old copy of *Because of Winn Dixie* that my grandma Ana had given me years ago. The book was soft and worn from countless readings, its corners bent and its pages yellowed with age. It still smelled faintly of her lavender perfume and the sunlit farmhouse where she used to read to me on rainy afternoons. The edges were frayed, the ink faded, but her words were still there, looping and familiar, like a promise I wasn't ready to let go of.

My precious Amira,
I miss you so much! I know it's hard to understand why I had to leave, but we'll be together again someday, and I promise that everything will make sense then. Until that day comes, remember my stories, and if we do not meet before you must make your choice, listen to your heart. Those who love you will understand.
~Grandma Ana

As I read, the world faded until it was just the steady clop of hooves, the crinkle of paper in my hands, and my grandma's voice echoing in my head—soft, warm, the way she used to sound when she read to me on rainy afternoons. I pressed the page to my chest, squeezing my eyes shut, letting her memory wrap around me like a blanket. But the words she'd written still made no sense. Not now, not any more than the day Savannah had handed the book back to me. It was like trying to solve a riddle with half the clues missing—close, but never quite enough. I wanted her message to be some kind of answer, a map to the future, but it hovered just out of reach, taunting me.

"Come on, Princess! We haven't got all day!" Sir Gallahan's voice cut through the fog, sharp and impatient. He and Earl waited up ahead, their horses stamping in the mud.

Gallahan looked like he was about start riding back to take control of my reigns; Earl just gave me that gentle, lopsided smile of his, like he knew a secret and was dying to share it.

I let out a sigh and tucked the worn page back into my tunic, fingers lingering on the soft, frayed edges. Grandma's words still buzzed in my head, but there was no time to figure them out now. I nudged my mare forward, trying not to think about it.

As I caught up, Gallahan scowled at me. "Roanoke Island awaits. I hope you're prepared." Doubt was clear in his voice.

"Yeah, well, I hope so too," I muttered, mostly to myself.

The journey to Zarandore felt like it would never end. Every mile was a new test—of my patience, my endurance, and my ability not to scream at the sky. If Raideron hadn't locked down the portals, we could've been there in a blink. Instead, we slogged along the old-fashioned way: on horseback, soaked to the bone, with the wild spring weather of Hekagia doing its best to drown us.

The world around us was bleak—rolling hills shrouded in mist, forests dripping with rain, and the ever-present threat of Raideron's patrols forcing us to take long, exhausting detours. My cloak was plastered to my skin, my cheeks stung from the wind, and I couldn't feel my feet anymore. I was pretty sure my boots had become their own ecosystem.

Earl, who was usually the first to crack a joke, looked like a grumpy wizard under his soggy hood. "This weather is abominable," he muttered, barely loud enough to hear over the wind. "What do you say, Princess? Shall we stop and light a fire? I promise I've got a trick or two left."

I shook my head, teeth chattering so hard I could barely get the words out. "Unless your tricks include a portable sun, I think we're out of luck. Let's just keep moving." I tried to sound brave, but my voice was as tight as my frozen fingers.

Sir Gallahan, riding ahead, didn't even look back. "We're almost to the Zarandian border," he called, his voice all business. "The weather's only going to get worse."

That's just great.

The rain never did let up, but at least nothing tried to eat us, I guess. We skirted the shadow of Shadowfell Castle, its towers black smudges behind the sheets of rain. Every so often, we'd come across a small patrol, but Sir Gallahan and Earl handled them with the kind of efficiency that made me glad they were on my side.

I hunched lower in the saddle, wishing I could just disappear into my cloak. The only thing keeping me going was the thought that, eventually, this road had to end. Right?

Two days, just before sunset, we finally made it to the Northern Portal. The forest was so thick it felt like the world was holding its breath—branches arching overhead, ancient and gnarled, like the ribs of some long-dead beast.

Then the trees opened up into a clearing, and there it was: a stone tower, half-eaten by moss and brambles, runes crawling up its sides and pulsing with a weird, purple light. The whole place looked like it had been ripped straight out of a nightmare—or maybe one of Earl's more dramatic stories.

"Took you guys long enough," Caleb called out once we got close, his smirk practically audible. He was sprawled against the trunk of a massive oak, looking way too pleased with himself. Hercules, his griffin, lounged beside him, golden-brown feathers catching the purple glow. The griffin's eyes tracked us, sharp and curious, like he was sizing up whether we were friend or snack.

Next to Caleb sat a boy I didn't recognize—about my age, with close-cropped blond hair and a look that said he noticed everything. I shot Caleb a questioning look.

"Oh, right," Caleb said, waving a hand like he'd just remembered we were all standing there. "This is Josiah. He's coming with us." Caleb's tone was breezy, but there was a mischievous glint in his eyes—like he was secretly hoping for a little chaos.

Josiah scrambled to his feet, brushing dirt from his trousers with quick, nervous hands. "It is an honor to meet you, Your Highness," he said, and then, to my horror, he dropped into the kind of deep, formal bow you only ever see in history books.

I shot Caleb a look, but he just rolled his eyes, looking more like an exasperated little brother than a prince. "You really don't have to do that," he muttered, sounding half-annoyed, half-amused.

Josiah straightened, his jaw set. "Princess Amira is the future queen. It's only right," he insisted.

Before I could even process that, Earl shuffled forward, his golden robes looking even more tragic than usual after days on the road. Caleb's face lit up. "Hey, Earl! You survived the mud bath, huh?"

Earl managed a tired smile, but his eyes sparkled with that familiar, secretive energy. "Barely, Prince Caleb. I'd say I'm about one puddle away from turning into a frog myself."

Caleb grinned, then jerked his chin toward the last member of our group, who stood a little apart, hand never straying far from his sword. "And who's the guy with the 'touch my sword and die' vibe?" he asked, nodding at the knight.

I shot a sideways glance at Sir Gallahan, still not sure what to make of him. His eyes were sharp and calculating, and he looked Josiah and Caleb up and down like he was sizing up a pair of mismatched boots. If he was impressed, he hid it well.

Josiah's eyes went huge. "That's Sir Gallahan!" he exclaimed, his voice practically tripping over itself with excitement. "He's one of the most famous knights to ever live."

Caleb's eyebrows shot up. "Wait, seriously?"

Josiah nodded, vibrating with awe. "Yes! He's defeated more astral creatures than I could ever hope to!"

Sir Gallahan harrumphed, his cheeks going a little pink at the unexpected praise. "We don't have time for idle chatter," he barked gruffly. "Let's get a move on. Raideron could be here any moment."

Josiah straightened. "You're right," he said, scanning the shadows like he expected trouble to leap out at any second. "We should get inside as soon as possible."

The tower loomed over us, its stone walls crawling with runes and magic.

"And how exactly do we do that?" I asked.

Josiah motioned for me to follow, his expression all business. As we crept closer to the tower, the air buzzed—magic pressing against my skin, sharp and electric. I took a cautious step toward the door, but something invisible shoved me back, hard. I stumbled, heart pounding.

Josiah shot me a quick, reassuring look and started circling the tower, boots squelching in the moss. "This way," he whispered, like he'd done this a hundred times before. We ducked around the right side, to where the brambles were thick enough to snag my cloak. The pressure in the air faded, the magic thinning out until it was just a tingle at my fingertips.

I reached out, half-expecting to get zapped again, but my fingers brushed rough, damp stone. No barrier. No warning. Either the protection spell had faded with age, or someone had left this spot open on purpose.

I glanced at Josiah, my nerves jangling. "Guess this is our invitation inside," I muttered, trying to sound braver than I felt.

Caleb knelt beside Hercules, scratching the griffin behind his ears. Hercules leaned in, nearly bowling Caleb over with his giant, feathery head. "Alright, big guy," Caleb said. "Time for you to head home. Try not to eat anyone on the way, okay?"

Josiah looked between Caleb and Hercules with confusion. "Can't we bring him with? He's rather handy in a fight."

Caleb snorted, shaking his head. "Yeah, if we want to cause a mass panic. There aren't any griffins on Earth, Josiah. People would lose their minds."

Josiah blinked. "Really? No griffins at all?" He sounded genuinely shocked, like he'd just learned the sky was green.

"Have you ever even been to Earth, Josiah?" I asked.

Josiah's cheeks went pink. "No," he admitted. "I'd never even left Alkrimia before I met Caleb."

Caleb's eyebrows shot up. "Seriously? Man, you're in for a wild ride."

Josiah smiled, but his eyes shifted to the ground. "I have to admit, I'm a bit nervous about it."

Caleb nudged him with his elbow. "You'll be fine. Earth's weird, but it's got its perks. Like pizza. And movies. And, you know, not being chased by astral monsters every other week."

Earl, who'd been listening with a faraway look, suddenly piped up, his voice warm and wistful. "Earth is wonderful," he said. "I do miss my little beach house. The sea air, the sound of the waves... and my flamingos."

I grinned, remembering the chaos of Earl's old shack. "Do you think your plastic flamingos are even still there?" I teased.

Earl's eyes twinkled with mischief. "Oh, I wouldn't count on them being plastic anymore."

I narrowed my eyes, suspicious. "Earl... what did you do?"

He gave me a sly, utterly unrepentant smile. "Turned them all into real flamingos, of course."

"Why would you do that?" Caleb asked.

Earl just shrugged, his grin growing wider. "Why not? Life's too short for boring lawn ornaments."

I snorted, shaking my head. "You're impossible, Earl."

But I couldn't help smiling as he strode into the tower like he owned the place. The rest of us followed him inside, the door creaking shut behind us.

Inside, the tower was all stone and shadows, except for a massive portal in the center of the spiral room—a whirlpool of purple magic, bright enough to make my eyes water. Through the shimmer, I could just make out the outline of a forest, dark and unfamiliar: Roanoke Island.

"Well that was easy," I said, my eyebrows pinching together in confusion. "We didn't even have to open the standing portal."

"Just take the win, sis," Caleb quipped.

Even Earl looked unbothered. "The Northern Portal is different than the other two," he said with a shrug. "Horatious used vile magic to create it, and it's that magic which sustains it now."

Caleb turned to me, his eyes bright with excitement. "You ready for this?"

I took a deep breath, heart pounding. "I guess so. You?"

"Always," he said with a lopsided grin.

I rolled my eyes. "Don't you ever get tired of almost dying?"

"Never," Caleb said with a wink as he stepped into the portal like he'd never been afraid of anything in his life.

CHAPTER TWELVE

WAHIAO VILLAGE

I'd only seen the ocean twice before—once on a freezing, foggy day in California (overrated), and once on the wild coast of New Zealand. But nothing, and I mean nothing, could have prepared me for the Eastern Sea of Alkrimia.

The water was so blue it looked fake, like someone had cranked the saturation up just to mess with me. Every so often, glowing ribbons of color would break the surface—nature spirits darting around like they owned the place. Show-offs.

I stood next to Ravenna on a jagged chunk of black rock, the wind whipping my hair into my face and making my eyes water. The village was half a mile away; a bunch of thatched roofs huddled together beyond the curve of the bay. We could have made it there before dark, but Ravenna had insisted we stop for the night. "It's tradition," she said, all mysterious like.

Personally, I think she just wanted an excuse to watch the sunset with me. Not that I was complaining.

"Seriously, I can't believe this place is real," I said as I reached for her hand.

Ravenna squeezed my hand, her grip warm and steady. She leaned in and pressed a kiss to my cheek, soft and gentle, and for a second, I almost forgot how much I hated being sappy.

"Believe it," she whispered, her voice low and soothing. "This is my home... maybe someday it'll be ours."

I looked over at Ravenna, trying to read her face for any sign that she was even a little bit nervous. Of course, she wasn't.

Ravenna just stood there, soaking up the last bit of sunlight—calm, steady, totally unbothered by the fact that we were about to waltz into her village and meet her entire family. She caught me staring and flashed that perfect smile, the one that says she knows exactly what's going on in my head.

"You're going to do great, Kira," she said, all warm and reassuring, like she actually believed it.

I tried for a smirk, but my nerves got the better of me. "Yeah, sure. If you say so."

"I do say so," she insisted, squeezing my hand. She had this quiet confidence that made me want to believe her, even though my brain was already running through every possible way I could embarrass myself in front of her parents.

I nudged her, trying to lighten the mood. "You have to say that; you're my girlfriend. It's in the contract."

Ravenna grinned, her eyes softening in that way that always makes my heart race. "I love you, so how could they not?"

I snorted, rolling my eyes and looking out toward the village lights flickering in the distance. "Please. I can think of at least a dozen reasons."

We sat together on the rocks, legs dangling over the edge, watching as the sky turned into a watercolor painting. For a second, I actually let myself breathe. No awkward "meet the parents" looming, no "what if they hate me" panic. Just me, Ravenna, and the kind of magic you don't get in Nithandore—or anywhere, really.

As the sky turned to black, Ravenna stood and stretched. She gave a wave at the village, where a lone figure—probably a sentry—stood watch near the flickering lights. Even from half a mile away, the glow of Wahiao was unmistakable, like fallen stars scattered at the base of the volcano.

And that volcano? It was just sitting there in the dark, looming over everything. It hadn't erupted in a thousand years, but had left the soil black and rich, the rocks jagged and dramatic. The plateau gave you a view of everything. No sneaking up on these people. I was pretty sure the sentries had already spotted us, and I couldn't help but wonder if they were thinking, "Hey, look, Ravenna brought home a stray."

Behind us, Gnash shifted his weight, the ground crunching under his boots. The guy's basically a walking bulldozer—broad shoulders, arms like tree trunks, and a face that looks like it's never lost a fight. He doesn't talk much, but when he does, you listen. He grunted, low and deep, and I glanced back just in time to catch the warning in his eyes.

"Trouble," he said in a voice like gravel.

A burst of high-pitched chittering cut through the air, and the brush behind us rustled like something big—or a lot of little somethings—was about to break through. My heart sped up, but Gnash just squared his stance, fists clenched, ready to take on whatever came at us. The guy's idea of a good time is punching first and asking questions never.

Ravenna, of course, was already on it. She tightened her grip on my hand, her voice low and steady. "Be on your guard. The spirits here are wild and dangerous."

Gnash grunted again, eyeing the bushes with a grim look on his face. "We build fire now?"

Ravenna nodded, moving quickly to gather dry twigs and driftwood. "Hopefully the light will keep them from causing any mischief," she said.

But I wasn't worried. If anything tried to mess with us, it was going to have to get through Gnash first—and good luck to them.

I kept my eyes peeled, collecting twigs and whatever else I could scrounge up for the fire, every muscle tense. The land spirits weren't exactly friendly—they wouldn't kill you (usually), but they had a reputation for being viciously territorial. If you let your guard down, you'd end up limping home with a few less appendages.

Gnash got the fire going in record time. In no time, we had a solid blaze going, the kind that pushed back the darkness and made the shadows think twice about creeping any closer. I rolled out my sleeping pad right next to the fire. No way was I crawling into a tent with the air this thick and sticky. Besides, if anything did come for us, I wanted to be ready.

Ravenna tossed a stack of twigs onto the fire. "You should try and get some sleep," she said, her voice gentle.

"So should you," I replied, managing a tired smile.

She knelt down next to me, and just having her there made everything feel a little better. She smelled like wildflowers and rain—probably from scouting the plateau—and I let myself lean into her touch when she planted a kiss on my forehead. Without thinking,

I pulled her down to me, needing her closeness.

Gnash averted his eyes and suddenly got really interested in the fire, giving us as much privacy as he could manage with wild nature spirits lurking everywhere.

Ravenna pulled back, her eyes teasing. "What did I just say? You need to rest," she said, trying to sound stern, but I could see the smile tugging at her lips.

"But I'm not tired…" I protested, even though my voice sounded as worn out as I felt.

Ravenna's playful smile faded into something softer. "You're still thinking about tomorrow, aren't you?"

"I'm terrified," I admitted. The idea of meeting her family—of being sized up by the people who mattered most to her—made me more scared than any astral monster I'd ever faced.

Ravenna reached out, her hand warm and solid as it cupped my cheek. "My family isn't like the nature spirits that surround our village, Kira," she said, her voice full of quiet reassurance. They'll see you for who you are—if you let them. You don't have to prove anything. Just be you."

"That's a terrible idea," I teased, pulling her close.

Ravenna smacked my hand away with a playful grin. "You really should get some rest now. We both should."

I let her go, even though I didn't want to. Ravenna pushed herself up, her attention snapping to a high-pitched whine somewhere out in the dark.

"The spirits are restless tonight," she murmured, her voice edged with caution. "Perhaps you should retire to your tent."

"I'll be fine… better than fine if you join me," I said.

Ravenna laughed, shaking her head. "That would not be proper behavior for a princess of Hekagia and you know it."

"I do know that—I just don't care," I said, grinning up at her.

"Rest easy, Kira." Her tone was gentle but final as she opened the flap to her tent and disappeared inside.

I did not, in fact, rest easy. The nature spirits didn't try to kill us, but they sure didn't care about letting me sleep. All night, it was chittering, giggling, and what sounded suspiciously like a full-on rave in the bushes. By the time dawn came, I felt like I'd been run over by a herd of wild goats. My eyes burned, my head ached, and I had twigs stuck in places twigs should never be stuck.

Ravenna emerged from her tent looking infuriatingly well-rested, her long black hair already half-tied back as she slipped on her boots. She took one look at me and suppressed a smile. "You look beautiful this morning," she said.

"Liar," I grumbled.

Ravenna just laughed, warm and unbothered. "Are you ready?" she asked, her eyes bright with anticipation.

"Not even remotely."

Gnash shoved a stone mug into my hands—full of Hekagia's version of coffee, which was basically mud with a caffeine kick. It tasted like burnt earth and regret, but I drank it anyway. Gnash grunted, then nodded once, like he approved of my suffering.

Ravenna draped a thick wool blanket over my shoulders. "You should've slept in your tent last night," she said, her voice gentle but with that hint of teasing she reserved just for me.

"It was like a sauna in there," I muttered, pulling the blanket tighter. "I'd rather risk the spirits than suffocate."

"Was it worth it?"

I shot her a tired grin. "What do you think?"

My hair was a disaster, and she made a show of pulling a twig out of it, her lips quirking in amusement. I hadn't packed a mirror, let alone a hairbrush—priorities, right?

"Don't worry, my parents aren't going to care what you look like," Ravenna said, her gaze soft and steady.

"Let's just get this over with," I said, a little sharper than I meant, staring out at the rooftops beyond the plateau. "The longer we wait, the more I feel like bolting."

It didn't take us long to break down camp. Gnash moved around camp like a one-man cleanup crew—rolling up sleeping mats, stamping out the last embers, and grunting at anyone who got in his way. The guy didn't say much, but you could always count on him to get things done.

Before I knew it, we were heading down the rocky path. The air was thick with dew, but all I could focus on was the way my stomach twisted tighter with every step toward the village gates.

A pair of sentries stepped forward as we neared, faces stone-cold but eyes sharp. They wore cloaks with feathers and intricate patterns woven in. I clocked the way they looked at Ravenna, then at me and Gnash.

As the daughter of the village leaders, Ravenna was basically royalty in Wahiao, even if she'd never admit it. The sentries didn't hesitate. They stepped aside, eyes lowered, as she approached. Suddenly, I felt every bit the outsider, standing there with my nerves jangling and my pack digging into my shoulder.

Chief Rawiri was impossible to miss—broad-shouldered, towering over everyone, his presence filling the village gate like a living wall. His cloak was heavy with feathers and bones, each one telling a story, and his eyes were sharp as obsidian, missing nothing. But when he saw Ravenna, his whole face changed. The stern lines softened, and a proud, almost goofy smile tugged at the corners of his mouth.

He stepped forward, placing a massive hand on Ravenna's shoulder, his grip gentle despite the size of it. "There you are, my girl," he rumbled, his deep voice carrying the warmth of a bonfire.

"You've kept your old man waiting." He pressed his nose to hers in the hongi, their foreheads touching—a gesture that was both greeting and blessing.

Then he turned his gaze on me and Gnash, sizing us up with a single look. I felt like I was about to be squashed like a bug. But then he grinned, wide and genuine, and clapped me on the back so hard I stumbled. "Welcome to Wahiao," he said, his voice booming across the plateau.

Ravenna's mother was a force of nature. She practically bowled over Chief Rawiri to get to her daughter.

"You were gone far too long, *taku kairangi*…my treasure," she murmured. Her deep voice was thick with emotion as she wrapped Ravenna in a hug that looked strong enough to crack ribs.

Still holding tight to her mom, Ravenna turned to her father, her voice small for once. "Do you know why we have come?"

Chief Rawiri's whole demeanor shifted. He straightened, his eyes going serious. "You seek the Obsidian Firestone," he said, his voice rumbling like distant thunder.

"Yeah, what is that anyway?" I asked.

Chief Rawiri reached beneath his feathered cloak and pulled out a scroll, handling it with the kind of care that said this was no ordinary piece of paper. He handed it to me with a solemn nod.

I unrolled the papyrus, revealing a charcoal drawing of a round, polished stone with big, wild swirls of red, black, and yellow, like it was alive on the page. I let out a low whistle.

"What does it do?" I asked after a moment.

Chief Rawiri's gaze lingered on the drawing, his massive hands steady as boulders. "The Obsidian Firestone is no ordinary stone," he said, his deep voice rumbling through the morning air. "The stone has kept our rivers clean, protected our children from spirits that would do them harm, and it can even cleanse a soul that's lost its way."

He glanced at me, then back at Ravenna, pride and sorrow mingling in his expression. "But you must understand, in the wrong hands, the Firestone could destroy everything we've built here."

Ravenna's voice was hopeful but tense as she asked, "Will you entrust the stone to us, Papa?"

Chief Rawiri's jaw tightened. "Ah, my girl, I wish I could. But we failed to protect it. The sirens took it from us not a month past—stole it right out from under our noses. Raideron's shadow stretches even to the sea."

"Stupid sirens," I muttered, bitterness scraping my throat. "I bet it was Olivia. She's probably still salty about what happened at the pier."

Ravenna and her parents traded a look—her mother's eyebrow arched and Rawiri's lips twitching like he wanted to ask what I meant, but he stayed silent.

"It's a long story," I said, waving a hand. "Let's just say the sirens aren't lining up to braid my hair."

Chief Rawiri's face turned serious, the warmth in his eyes cooling to stone. "That's going to make things difficult, Kira. If we want to avoid a war, we'll have to bargain for the Firestone's return. There's no other way." His voice was deep, steady—the kind that made you want to listen, even if you didn't like what he was saying.

Ravenna squared her shoulders, her jaw set. "What do you propose, Papa?"

"I've sent word to their emissary—a siren named Klerope—to arrange a meeting with their queen."

I couldn't help myself, a sharp snort escaped. "Queen? That she-monster is no queen."

Rawiri's eyes narrowed, his tone suddenly steel. "That's the kind of thinking that's kept this feud burning for generations. The sirens have every reason to resent the way humans have treated them."

I bristled, crossing my arms. "Well, they do have a habit of luring people to their deaths. It's not like they're innocent."

He fixed me with a look that could pin a hawk to the ground. "And which do you think came first, Kira? The violence, or the vengeance?"

"Does it really matter anymore?"

Ravenna stepped in, trying to change the subject. "This Klerope—can we trust her, Papa?"

Rawiri's sternness faded, replaced by a thoughtful frown. "She's been reasonable before. But with the Firestone at stake, we'd be fools not to be careful."

Chief Rawiri led us through the village, his stride slow and commanding. People peeked out from their doorways and shop as we passed, curiosity in their eyes. I tried not to stare back, but the attention frazzled my nerves.

"So... when do we find out if the queen's actually going to meet with us?" I asked Chief Rawiri, trying not to let my anxiety show.

"Klerope will deliver the queen's answer tomorrow."

Ravenna's mother, Nyrah, interjected with a decisive look. "Which leaves us tonight." Her tone was brisk. "I want to hear about your journey. War can wait until morning."

Rawiri gave her a look—half challenge, half resignation. "Nyrah, we can't just ignore what's coming."

Nyrah didn't even blink. "We can for one night." She turned to me, her eyes sharp but not unfriendly. "Come. You look like you've been dragged through a bush backwards. Let's get you cleaned up." Nyrah took my hand—her grip strong, no-nonsense—and led me deeper into the village.

We followed the main path through Wahiao. Kids darted between the houses, elders wove baskets in the shade, and everyone seemed to pause just long enough to size us up before getting back to work. I kept my chin up, but inside, my nerves were a tangled knot. I kept thinking, don't trip, don't say anything stupid, don't embarrass Ravenna in front of her whole world...

Eventually, we reached a wide grassy clearing at the village's heart. At the far end stood a massive meeting house, its steep roof topped with carved figures and painted patterns that looked like they could tell a hundred stories. I tried not to stare, but honestly, it was impossible not to. The place was stunning—fierce and welcoming all at once, like Ravenna herself.

Chief Rawiri stopped in front of the building, his voice filled with pride. "This is the meeting house. Tonight, we'll feast here in your honor."

Nyrah shot her husband a look and then turned to me and Ravenna. "First things first—rest and a bath. You two smell like wet feet." She didn't even bother to sugarcoat it.

"Yes, Mama," Ravenna muttered, sounding half-annoyed, half-amused. I could tell she was happy to be home.

I started to follow Ravenna, but Nyrah blocked my path with a single, outstretched arm. She was taller than I'd realized, her presence as sharp as a drawn blade. "You are our guest, so you'll stay in the guesthouse." Her tone made it clear there was no point in arguing.

I glanced at Ravenna, who just shrugged, her eyes saying, "Don't bother."

Nyrah led me to the guesthouse herself, her stride purposeful and unhurried. I tried to keep up, but my legs felt like jelly. The hut was simple but comfortable—a thick mat of leaves and feathers, everything in its place. I dropped my pack and sat down on the ma, letting out a sigh of relief. My feet ached from all the walking we'd done over the past couple of days.

"You'll rest here until nightfall," Nyrah said, her voice clipped but not unkind. "I'll come for you when it's time." And just like that, she was gone.

I slumped back, staring at the ceiling, my mind racing. I was exhausted, but sleep felt impossible. All I could think was: Don't mess this up, Kira. Not for Ravenna. Not for yourself.

CHAPTER THIRTEEN

THE SIREN QUEEN'S OFFER

Nyrah's knock rattled the washhouse door just as I was finally starting to relax. Figures. I'd barely had five minutes to myself in the giant stone tub—water hot, blossoms floating on top, the whole thing smelling like a garden exploded. For once, I was actually enjoying the quiet.

"Are you almost ready, Princess Kira?" Nyrah called through the door. "The welcome ceremony is about to begin."

"Five more minutes!" I yelled back, sinking deeper into the water and letting the steam clear my head.

But then the chanting started—soft at first, then louder, drifting through the open window like a not-so-subtle reminder that the whole village was waiting on me. I groaned, splashed water on my face, and forced myself to get up.

I grabbed a towel, muttering under my breath about "welcome ceremonies" and "tradition," and got ready to face the crowd. If I was going to be paraded around like some prized sheep, I'd at least do it on my own terms. And no way was I letting anyone shove me into some ridiculous outfit without a battle, either.

But then I spotted it: a hand-woven cloak draped over the chair. I paused, running my fingers over the animal skin lining—soft, warm, way nicer than anything I'd ever had before.

"Do I get to keep this?" I asked Nyrah, already pulling it on.

"It is a gift from our people," she confirmed with a nod.

"Sweet." I grinned, hugging the cloak tighter.

Okay, maybe I was a sucker for a good cloak. Sue me.

Nyrah gave me that look—half 'hurry up,' half 'don't embarrass me in front of the ancestors'—and picked up the pace. I rolled my eyes but followed, the evening air biting at my ankles.

And then there was Ravenna, waiting for me on the steps of the meeting house. She looked incredible: hair twisted up with some fancy jade comb, that tan dress hugging her in all the right ways. The second she saw me, her whole face lit up, and—yeah, I'll admit it—my heart did a traitorous flip.

The second I stepped inside the meeting house, the air changed. It was warm and thick with woodsmoke. Every inch of timber was alive with stories, and the rafters overhead were painted in bold reds, blacks, and ochre, koru patterns twisting up to the ceiling. Ancestors glared down from the beams, daring anyone to mess with their descendants. I kinda liked their style.

Chief Rawiri gave the guy standing next to him a nod, and suddenly the whole place erupted in low chanting. I had no clue what they were saying—my ancient Alkrimian is about as good as my patience—but I could feel it. The sound just rolled over me, warm and wild. It was… a lot.

Ravenna squeezed my hand, her thumb tracing circles on my skin. "Are you okay?" she whispered, her eyes searching mine.

I wiped at my face before anyone could see. "Yeah, I'm fine. Never better," I said, forcing a grin. No way was I going to start bawling in front of a room full of strangers.

But I'd never felt so welcome anywhere else. Wahiao was different. It wasn't just that Ravenna was there; it was the whole village. For once, I didn't feel like I was running or waiting for the next disaster. I couldn't explain it, but it didn't feel like being in a new place. It felt like… coming home.

The chanting faded, and Chief Rawiri waved everyone to sit at this massive table that seriously looked like it could seat an army. I dropped into a chair next to Ravenna, my nerves finally shutting up for once. For the first time in forever, I wasn't looking for the exit. I was exactly where I was supposed to be.

The table was loaded with food—all of it fresh and colorful. Roasted meats, yams, corn on the cob straight from the gardens. I didn't bother pretending to be polite. I loaded up my plate, ignoring the amused look Chief Rawiri shot me.

Let him laugh. I was starving.

"Are you ready for tomorrow?" Chief Rawiri asked Ravenna, trying to sound casual, but he was about as subtle as a war horn.

Ravenna froze, her fork dripping lamb grease onto her plate. "Papa, can't we talk about this later?" Her voice was gentle, but I could see the tension in her shoulders.

He shrugged. "It was only a question—"

Nyrah cut him off, her tone sharp. "We agreed there'd be no talk of war tonight." She shot him a look that could've set all the mats in the meeting house on fire.

Chief Rawiri let out a deep, rumbling laugh and raised his hands in defeat. "I yield," he said. Then he turned to me with a glint in his eye. "Let's get to know our guest better instead."

I nearly choked on my slice of pork. Ravenna hid her smile in a cup of berry juice, clearly entertained by my discomfort.

I managed to swallow and took a long sip from my own cup, feeling their eyes on me. "There's not much to know," I said, trying to sound casual, but my cheeks were burning. I wasn't about to start spilling my sad, disaster of a life story, no matter how much Ravenna's family wanted to play twenty questions.

Chief Rawiri arched an eyebrow, not buying it for a second. "Somehow, I doubt that. Everyone has a story."

"True," I said with a shrug, "but I'd rather hear about Wahiao." I was eager to change the subject, but also genuinely curious. The village had this energy, like everyone was part of something bigger, and nobody got left out.

The chief's face softened, pride flickering in his eyes. "Our village has stood at the base of the volcano for generations. The ash gives us rich soil for our gardens, and when the land cannot provide, we look to the sea. Everything you see on this table comes from our own hands."

I snorted, glancing at the massive platters. "Well, you all must be part fish, then."

Chief Rawiri let out another rumbling laugh, the kind that vibrated through the whole room. "Here, every child learns to swim, even before they can walk. The ocean is as much a part of us as the earth beneath our feet."

"Yeah, well, I can barely dogpaddle. Guess I'd be the village embarrassment." I stabbed a chunk of roasted yam with my fork, trying not to let my embarrassment show.

Ravenna grinned. "You'd catch up. Or I'd save you," she whispered, squeezing my knee under the table. That made my heart do a flip, but I covered it with a smirk.

Curiosity got the better of me. "So, does anyone here actually have magic? Or is it all just good vibes and swimming lessons?"

Chief Rawiri shook his head, his expression turning thoughtful. "No spellcasters here. We don't need magic when we live in harmony with the spirits."

That threw me. I'd grown up hearing that nature spirits were dangerous, unpredictable, and not to be trusted.

Ravenna leaned in, her voice low. "Things aren't the same here as everywhere else. The spirits here are... different. They are mostly willing to coexist."

Chief Rawiri drummed his fingers on his cup, thinking. "Or maybe it's the people who are different," he said. "We respect the spirits, and they respect us. We don't hunt them out of fear, like some do. That fear has caused more harm than the spirits ever have."

Given that a water spirit had nearly drowned me last year, I had a hard time buying Rawiri's whole "spirits are our friends" speech. But it was my first day in Wahiao and I wasn't about to start a fight with Ravenna's dad.

"Ravenna says some of the villagers can actually talk to the spirits. Is that true?" I asked instead.

Chief Rawiri nodded. "A few in our village can speak with the spirits. It is a skill that has been passed down through many generations. It requires patience and a willingness to listen."

I clicked my tongue. "Patience isn't exactly my strong suit, but that's... actually kind of cool."

I tried to picture myself chatting with a wild water spirit—probably would end with me getting dunked in a river again.

"It is also lucky," Chief Rawiri added, his voice dropping a notch. "We will need the spirits on our side, if we are granted a meeting with the siren queen. Without their blessing, the sea can be as dangerous as any enemy."

Nyrah shot him a look so sharp I thought she might actually combust. Her eye twitched, and for a second, I wondered if I should duck. "That's all I'll say for now," Rawiri finished, looking like he'd rather face a sea monster than an angry wife.

But I wasn't about to let that go. "Wait—what does that mean?" I pressed, leaning forward, impatience prickling under my skin. I hated being left in the dark, especially when it sounded like my life might be on the line.

Rawiri glanced at Nyrah, like he was asking for permission to spill the family secrets. She gave him a tight, reluctant nod. "The siren queen dwells at the bottom of a deep trench, far beneath the waves, in the very heart of the water spirits' realm."

A chill ran down my spine, but I covered it with a smirk. "Oh, cool. So, just a casual swim to the bottom of the ocean. No big deal," I said, trying to sound like I wasn't already picturing myself drowning. "I kinda figured she'd come here, since, you know, we can't breathe underwater."

Chief Rawiri shook his head. "That is unlikely. The siren queen is proud—some might say arrogant—but she is no fool. She will not leave the safety of her stronghold beneath the sea."

I tried to picture it—crushing darkness, freezing water, pressure that could snap bones, and a whole army of spirits who might not be thrilled to see us. My stomach twisted. I shot Ravenna a look, hoping she'd have some brilliant plan, but all I got was her steady hand squeezing mine under the table.

Still, there was one thing I had to know.

I looked from Rawiri to Nyrah, my voice dropping. "But... how exactly are we supposed to breathe down there? Or is that just another one of those 'figure it out as you go' kinda things?"

"That's a discussion for tomorrow," Nyrah cut in, her jaw tight. "If the queen even agrees to see us, we'll bargain the terms then." Her words had that final, don't-push-me edge, but I could see the worry flicker behind her eyes.

Chief Rawiri, who clearly knew when to back off, cleared his throat and switched gears like a pro. "So, Kira—are you enjoying the meal?" His tone went all light and casual, like he hadn't just been talking about possible doom at the bottom of the ocean.

I was too busy stuffing my face with bread to answer. It was still warm, the butter melting all over my fingers. I just nodded, cheeks full, hoping he'd get the message: food first, awkward small talk later.

The conversation faded out after that, everyone turning their attention to the mountain of food still on the table. The earlier buzz of laughter settled into a comfortable quiet, broken only by the clink of cups and the scrape of plates. One by one, villagers drifted off to bed, their welcomes paid in full.

I was picking sweet yam out of my teeth, thinking about sneaking off to bed, when the doors to the meeting house burst open so hard half the oil lamps flickered. One of the village sentry ran in, cheeks red, his breath coming in sharp gasps. His eyes darted around until they landed on Chief Rawiri.

"The siren queen has sent her reply," he announced, not bothering with the usual bow or any of that formal stuff. "Her emissary is here to deliver the message."

"Already?" Rawiri's voice was tight, and I caught the flicker of irritation in his eyes. He straightened up, folding those massive arms across his chest. The whole room went dead quiet, the warmth of the feast sucked out and replaced by heavy, electric tension. Even the ancestors seemed to lean in, waiting.

Rawiri fixed the sentry with a stare that could've stopped a charging bull. "Send Klerope in," he said, nodding once.

But the sentry just stood there, shifting from foot to foot, staring down at the woven mats like he wished he could disappear into them.

"What is it?" Chief Rawiri asked, his voice sharp.

The sentry swallowed hard. "It isn't Klerope who has come."

Chief Rawiri's eyes narrowed, all business. "Then who is it?"

The sentry hesitated, but I didn't need him to say it anyway. The second the air shifted, I knew.

"Olivia," I said flatly.

She didn't just walk in—she made an entrance, hips swaying, red hair gleaming like she'd spent an hour brushing it just to annoy me. "The one and only," Olivia purred, her voice all honey and venom. She flashed a dazzling smile, the kind that made half the room stare and the other half (me) want to throw something.

I had to grip the table to keep from launching myself at her. Ravenna squeezed my knee under the table, a silent warning: don't start a fight. Not yet at least.

"What are you doing here, Olivia?" I growled.

Olivia smirked, eyes glinting. "Oh, Kira, you look so tense. Relax. I'm here on royal business."

If looks could kill, Olivia would be a pile of seaweed on the floor. But she just winked, like she knew exactly how much she was getting under my skin—and loved every second of it.

Chief Rawiri rose. "Where is Klerope?" he asked, his voice rumbling with suspicion.

"The queen thinks Klerope's gone soft for your little village," Olivia said, her tone all fake sweetness. "So she sent me instead."

"But why you?" I asked.

Olivia's lips curled into a wicked smile. "Because I asked," she said in a smug tone. "I thought it'd be fun to deliver the message myself. Besides, I do love an audience." She let her gaze sweep the room, making sure everyone was watching her, which they were.

"Well?" I snapped, clutching my fork so tightly that my hand started to go numb.

Olivia's expression turned icy. "The answer is no. The queen won't see you." She said it like she was announcing the winner of a beauty contest.

"Why not?" I demanded.

Olivia rolled her eyes. "Seriously? You're not that clueless, are you? It's obvious you want the Obsidian Firestone. The queen has no intention of giving it up."

"It isn't yours," I growled, my anger flaring.

She shrugged. "It is now," she said, her tone so casual it made me want to throw something at her. "Maybe if you'd gotten here quicker, you could've kept it. But I guess you're just not that good after all."

My astral magic thrummed in my veins, every muscle in my body itching for a fight. Ravenna squeezed my leg under the table—a silent "don't you dare"—and I forced myself to stay put, even though I was shaking with rage.

"There must be some bargain we can strike," Chief Rawiri said, his voice tight as he tried to keep his own temper in check.

But Olivia just laughed, a high, mocking sound that made my skin crawl. "You have nothing we want," she said.

I clenched my jaw. "Then why bother coming at all?" I shot back, my voice sharp. "You didn't swim all this way just to show off your hair, Olivia."

She let out another laugh, this one even higher, and turned just enough so everyone could see her profile—like she was posing for a portrait. "You know me so well, Kira," she purred, her eyes glinting with mean delight. "I almost feel bad about that time I tried to drown you."

I glared at her, refusing to give her the satisfaction of a reaction. "No, you don't," I said flatly.

"You're right, I don't. But I do have another message for you." She paused, letting the silence stretch, loving every second of the attention.

"Then get on with it," I snapped.

Olivia's eyes glittered, her voice dropping to a taunt. "If you want the stone so badly, you're welcome to come and get it... if you dare."

Chief Rawiri's voice rumbled from the end of the table, low and dangerous. "Speak plainly, siren."

Olivia turned to him, her expression that of a shark circling its prey. "Gladly," she purred, her voice syrupy-sweet. "The Queen has challenged you to a duel. Winner gets the Obsidian Firestone."

For a second, I could only stare at her, my brain scrambling to catch up. Was she serious? A duel? On the siren queen's turf? That was basically asking to get eaten alive.

"Seriously?" I said, my voice coming out way calmer than I felt. "That's your big message? A duel?" I shot Ravenna a look, but she was just watching Olivia with that calm, unreadable face of hers. Typical.

Olivia's eyes sparkled, and she leaned in, lowering her voice so only I could hear. "What's wrong, Kira? Scared you'll mess up your pretty new cloak?" I could see the challenge in her eyes. She wanted a reaction. She always did.

I settled for shooting her a death glare. "You wish," I said, my tone even. "Tell your queen we accept her offer. If you're lucky, maybe you'll get to watch me win."

Chief Rawiri slammed his palm on the table. "Absolutely not," he shouted, the sound echoing through the rafters. "The queen has dishonored us by stealing the Firestone. If there's to be a fight, it will be between our armies."

Olivia leaned in, her eyes glinting like she'd just won a prize. "Is that your final answer?"

Before Rawiri could answer, Ravenna shot to her feet, her chair scraping back so hard it nearly toppled. "Wait!" she called, her voice slicing through the tension.

Every head in the meeting house snapped to her. "Papa, think this through. Why risk a war with the sirens when Kira and I can just go get the stone ourselves?"

I nodded, but bit my tongue. It wasn't my place to challenge the chief, especially not in front of the whole village, but Ravenna was right. It wasn't worth risking the whole village when we could get the job done, no problem.

But Rawiri wasn't convinced. "I won't risk losing you, or Kira," he said, shaking his head.

Ravenna crossed the space between them and grabbed his arm respectfully, her gaze fierce and steady. "Have faith in us, Papa," she said, her voice low but unshakeable. "We can do this."

Chief Rawiri let out a heavy, reluctant sigh and turned to Nyrah, searching her face for answers. Nyrah's face was unreadable, but her eyes darted between her husband and Ravenna. She knew exactly what was at stake.

She gave the tiniest nod, barely more than a twitch, and then stood up so fast her chair fell over. Without a word, she swept out of the meeting house, a single tear sliding down her cheek.

Ravenna straightened, her voice strong and steady as she faced Olivia. "We accept your offer."

Olivia reached into her satchel, pulling out a folded map, waving it like she was handing out party invites. "I'll leave you with this then, but only because the queen insisted." She tossed the map onto the table, her eyes locked on me, daring me to flinch.

I raised an eyebrow, refusing to let her rattle me. "What's that for?" I asked.

"It's a map to Palaesar, our capital city," she said in a bored voice. You're expected to show up there in three days. If you're late, or if you chicken out, we'll use the Obsidian Firestone to torch this village."

"Don't worry. We'll be there," I growled.

Olivia smirked. "Good luck getting past the water spirits. They are going to eat you alive. Literally."

Then, with a dramatic twirl—because of course she couldn't just leave like a normal person—Olivia vanished in a puff of smoke. The magic in the air felt wrong, oily. It confirmed what we'd all been dreading: the sirens were working for Raideron.

It had taken every ounce of self-control not to lunge at Olivia the moment she entered the meeting hall. My hatred for her was a storm that I'd been carrying around ever since she'd poisoned

Caleb with her siren song. I could still see the way his eyes had gone glassy and empty, like she'd flipped a switch and turned him into her own personal puppet. I'd never felt so useless or so furious in my life.

Now, seeing Olivia's smug little smirk, all that rage I'd been bottling up begged to be released. I bolted out of the meeting house, straight into the freezing night, not caring who saw or what they thought. I ran hard, past the village gates, out into the wild dark, my breath burning in my chest.

"Kira!" Ravenna's voice chased after me.

But I couldn't stop. All I could think about was how much I hated Olivia. All I wanted was to burn something down, to make the world feel as raw as I did.

So I let go. I threw my hands up and screamed, pouring every ounce of fury into my magic. The night lit up with a blinding flash of purple—pure, white-hot rage exploding out of me. And for a second, it felt good. Powerful. Like maybe I could burn away everything that hurt.

But when the light faded, I was left shaking, soaked in sweat, my legs barely holding me up. I dropped to my knees in the grass, the anger draining out of me until there was nothing left but exhaustion.

When I finally managed to look up, the world was quiet—too quiet. The darkness pressed in, heavy and cold. And that's when I saw her: Ravenna, lying in the grass, completely still.

And just like that, nothing mattered. Not Olivia, not the sirens, not even Raideron. The only thing that mattered was Ravenna. And I was pretty sure I'd just killed her.

CHAPTER FOURTEEN

ROANOKE ISLAND

The portal landed us deep in the woods, moonlight barely slipping through the thick canopy overhead. The air was heavy with the scent of moss and old leaves, and every shadow seemed to lean in, curious and a little too close. I tried to steady my breathing, but my heart was already racing, tightening my chest.

Not far from where we stood, I spotted a battered metal plaque, its edges dulled by years of rain and neglect. I squinted, trying to make out the faded words: "Fort Raleigh National Historic Site." The Lost Colony of Roanoke. Even the name felt haunted, like a warning whispered through the trees.

It was well past midnight, and the world felt suspended—caught in that strange time just before dawn. But it wasn't the darkness that made my skin prickle. It was the howling.

The cries weren't like the distant yips of coyotes I remembered from Michigan. These were deeper, and so much closer. Each howl seemed to wind its way through the trees, making the hairs on the back of my neck stand up. I hugged my arms around myself, wishing I could disappear into the shadows instead of feeling like they were closing in on me.

Josiah and Sir Gallahan flanked me, swords drawn, their faces set and determined. I knew I should have felt safer with them there, but I just felt smaller. The woods felt alive, restless, and I couldn't shake the sense that we were being watched.

I edged closer to Earl, matching my steps to his along the old, warped boardwalk. "What's that howling?" I asked him, glancing over my shoulder, hoping he'd have an answer that would make the fear in my chest loosen its grip.

Earl's face was unreadable in the dark. "That," he said, "is a long story. Best we just keep moving." He led the way, his golden robe flapping and his flashlight beam zigzagging like he was searching for buried treasure instead of a haunted staff.

He hummed under his breath—something that sounded suspiciously like the theme from Ghostbusters—until Caleb finally broke the silence.

"Okay, Earl, you're seriously creeping me out. What's actually out there?" Caleb's voice was half-joke, half-nervous.

Earl spun around, his eyes wide behind those ridiculous spectacles. "Oh, just the usual: ghosts, curses, possibly a raccoon with a vendetta. But what you're hearing? Those are Wendigos. Nasty business, that…"

"What the heck is a wendigo?" Caleb asked.

Earl's voice turned serious. "It's Horatious Croatoan's fault, really. The man had the magical sense of a turnip."

"The spellcaster who made the Northern Portal?" I asked.

Earl nodded "Horatious stole the Elemental Staff from their temple. He twisted its magic to create the portal, but in doing so, he poisoned the land itself. The dingbat."

"Poisoned it how?" I asked, unsure I really wanted to know.

Earl pulled his robe tighter around him as the wind picked up, but I didn't think that it was the cold he was trying to keep away.

"Horatious poured all his worst feelings into the spell—jealousy, rage, the works. When he forced open the portal, all that anger spilled out. The land soaked it up like a sponge. And then…well, the people changed. The survivors, anyway. They became wendigos. Not the friendly kind, either. The kind that'll eat your face for no reason."

"That's… awful," I whispered.

"Where was the Golden Council for all this?" Caleb asked.

"Ah, the Council," Earl said, pushing his glasses up his nose with a finger that was stained purple from some long-ago potion. "They tried, bless their bureaucratic little hearts. But Horatious and his merry band of monsters were a bit much for them. In the end, they decided to—how do the kids say it—let the chips fall where they may."

Caleb snorted. "Typical for the council."

Earl's mouth twisted into a wry smile. "Perhaps. But don't be too quick to judge. The wendigos—ghastly as they are—do serve a purpose. They guard the Elemental Staff. If not for them, Raideron would've snatched it up ages ago and we'd all be living in a much less charming story."

His words made me think of all the stories I'd heard about Roanoke—the endless documentaries, the archaeologists combing every inch of the island, the mysteries that never seemed to unravel. "But… how is it that nobody's ever found the staff by accident?" I asked. "People have been searching the island for the lost settlers for centuries."

Caleb nodded, his tone lighter but still edged with nerves. "Yeah, seriously. This place has been the focus of more TV specials than Bigfoot."

Earl's face grew thoughtful. "A strong protection spell surrounds the staff—Horatius' last hurrah before he went the way of all reckless spellcasters. The spell keeps even the most intrepid adventurers away, though several have come close."

Josiah, who'd been quiet until now, shot Earl a wary look. "And what happened to those unlucky souls?"

Earl's voice went flat, all the humor gone. "They all met a grisly fate at the hands of the wendigos. Not a pleasant way to go, I'm afraid."

I shivered, glancing at the shadows shifting between the trees. "That's… comforting," I said, my voice barely above a whisper.

Sir Gallahan's grip tightened on his sword. "So we're walking straight into a nest of monsters, then? Brilliant plan, Earl," he muttered, sarcasm dripping from every word.

Caleb shot Earl a nervous glance. "Sorry, but I'm with Sir Gallahan on this one. This seems like a bad idea. How are we supposed to find the staff without getting ourselves eaten?"

Earl grinned, his spectacles glinting in the moonlight. "With magic, of course!" he declared, as if it were the most obvious thing in the world.

Josiah frowned, his voice low and uncertain. "You mean the same magic that'll make us a beacon for those… things?"

"That is correct!" Earl chirped, not missing a beat. "Like moths to a very unfortunate flame."

And they'll eat us if they find us…" Caleb said.

"Undoubtedly," Earl agreed.

Sir Gallahan let out a low, irritated growl. "I didn't sign up to be monster bait, Earl."

Trying to break the tension, I mustered a shaky smile. "Maybe we could just ask the wendigos nicely to hand over the staff?" My voice sounded scared, even to me, but I hoped someone would at least crack a smile.

Sir Gallahan sure didn't. He just shot me a look so dry it could have started a fire. "I think that would be unwise—unless your intent is to die a painful death."

Josiah, though, gave a nervous chuckle. "I don't know, maybe they're just misunderstood… or maybe they'll eat us first and ask questions later. Only one way to find out I suppose."

I smiled gratefully in his direction. At least I wasn't the only one trying to keep things from falling apart.

Meanwhile, Earl just shrugged, completely unfazed. "We'll just have to search quickly then, won't we?" he said as if we were looking for a lost sock instead of a legendary artifact guarded by monsters.

Earl dug in his robe pocket, producing a small golden compass. I didn't recognize it, but Caleb surely did.

He threw up his hands, exasperated. "You've got to be kidding me! We're going to rely on that piece of junk to find the staff?"

Earl arched an eyebrow, looking almost offended. "May I remind you that this 'piece of junk' helped you lot find the Elemental Scroll? It was rather generous of Master Sadiki to let us borrow it, you know."

Caleb just huffed, crossing his arms. "If you say so…"

He didn't sound convinced, but I could tell he was too tired to argue.

Earl peeked over his spectacles at Caleb. "Unless you've got a better plan, Prince Caleb, I suggest we trust the compass. Or would you rather wander around until the wendigos get bored and eat us?"

Sir Gallahan stepped forward, his voice firm and commanding as he surveyed the woods. "Then it's settled. We stick together, move fast, and if anything comes for us, we fight as one. Understood?" His voice was so steady, I almost believed we could do this. The rest of us murmured our agreement, though I could hear the uncertainty in everyone's voices—including my own.

We walked on in silence, every step heavy with tension. I could feel the wendigos out there, somewhere in the trees, and the hairs on the back of my neck tingled. I kept telling myself to be brave, to act like the queen I was supposed to become, but that was easier said than done.

Up ahead, the battered sign for the visitor center glowed faintly in the dark. Earl slowed, holding out the golden compass like it was some kind of magical dowsing rod. The needle pointed straight ahead, unwavering.

Caleb let out a disbelieving snort. "You're telling me the Almighty Elemental Staff is hidden in a visitor's center? That's... anticlimactic."

Earl pursed his lips, peering at the compass as he turned it in slow circles. The needle didn't budge.

"It appears so..." he said, but even he sounded a little doubtful.

"Told you that thing doesn't work," Caleb muttered.

The visitor center looked almost comical in the gloom—just a squat, wood-sided building with flickering floodlights. Gravel crunched under our boots, each step sounding way too loud.

As soon as we set foot in the empty parking lot, I felt it. Somehow, I knew, deep down, that we were in the right place. Then a strangled howl ripped through the night, confirming it.

My heart jumped into my throat as more howls followed, a chorus of angry, guttural growls that made my blood run cold.

Shapes emerged from the shadows—grotesque, twisted, nothing like any animal I'd ever seen, which was saying something after the year I'd had. Their eyes gleamed with a hunger that felt ancient, and they moved with a kind of predatory grace that made it clear we were the intruders here.

Their leader stepped out of the gloom, antlers sharp and glistening, his long tail lashing the air. He stopped just a few feet away, massive and terrifying under the flickering floodlights. When he spoke, his voice was a guttural rumble that vibrated in my bones. "What do you want?"

I swallowed, trying to find my voice. I'd expected a monster, not a question. And suddenly, I wasn't sure which was scarier.

Earl, being the quickest to recover, stepped forward. His voice was cautious, but there was a spark of curiosity in it too. "You can talk?" he asked, peering at the wendigo like he was trying to figure out what made it tick.

"When I must." The wendigo's black eyes narrowed. "Why have you come?" he snarled.

"We are here for the Elemental staff," Earl said, his tone respectful but steady. "We don't mean you—or the staff—any harm." He even gave a little bow, which might have been funny if the situation wasn't so terrifying.

The wendigo leader let out a deep, angry huff that vibrated in my chest. "Wrong answer."

Everything happened so fast after that. The wendigos charged, their limbs impossibly long and fast, shadows twisting in the floodlights.

"Run!" Sir Gallahan barked, stepping in front of us, sword gleaming.

Josiah drew his blade and shot Gallahan a defiant look. "I'm staying," he said firmly.

Gallahan shook his head, jaw set. "No! Go with the others. I will not be responsible for your death."

Josiah grinned, wild and reckless, his eyes shining with a kind of thrill I'd never understand. "Then I guess I'll try not to die."

Gallahan let out a grunt—half frustration, half something like respect. He gave Josiah a look that said more than words ever could. Then, side by side, the two of them charged into the chaos, weapons raised, meeting the wendigos head-on.

Earl grabbed my arm, dragging me toward the visitor's center as chaos erupted behind us. Caleb followed, but I could see the conflict in his eyes—he wanted to stay, to fight with Josiah and Sir Gallahan, but he forced himself to keep moving. For me. I knew it, even if he didn't say it.

"They'll be fine," I said to him, breathlessly, as we reached the front doors, though I wasn't sure even I believed it.

Caleb nodded. "Yeah. They'll be fine," he echoed.

I reached for the handle, my hands shaking, and pulled—but it was locked.

Of course the door was locked. It was the middle of the night!

"Now what?" I asked Earl, my voice rising in panic.

"Step aside," Earl said, his voice cutting through my fear.

He fished a small vial from his satchel and poured its inky contents over the handle. Instantly, the metal hissed and bubbled, dissolving in a plume of acrid steam. The door swung open with a groan, and Earl shoved us inside, slamming it shut behind us as the sounds of battle raged on.

And then we waited, the silence inside almost as terrifying as the mayhem we'd left behind.

CHAPTER FIFTEEN

A KNIGHT'S GAMBIT

The visitor center felt surreal—just one big space cluttered with dusty dioramas and a gift shop that suddenly seemed ridiculous. I reached for the light switch out of habit, but Earl caught my wrist, his voice low and oddly serious. "Leave them off."

So we waited. Every second stretched out, heavy and endless. The sounds of fighting faded, replaced by a silence so thick it felt like it might smother us. My heart hammered in my chest, and I kept counting the seconds, wishing I could do something—anything—but wait.

Finally, Caleb broke the silence, his voice tight with worry. "Where are they? Do you think they're…"

As if in answer, a sharp, desperate knock echoed through the room, making us all jump. We exchanged tense glances, every muscle in my body wound tight, bracing for whatever was on the other side.

"It's me. Let me in!" Josiah called, sounding ragged and desperate.

Caleb rushed to the door and flung it open. Josiah stumbled inside, barely upright. His face and shirt were smeared with blood, and his breath came in harsh, uneven gasps.

And he was alone.

Earl's voice was tight with dread, all the usual humor gone. "Where is Sir Gallahan?" he asked Josiah.

Josiah collapsed to the floor, clutching his side, blood seeping through his shirt.

Earl didn't hesitate, he was at Josiah's side in a heartbeat, hands steady as he uncorked a tiny glass vial. "Drink this, lad. It's not tea, but it'll do." The sharp, herbal scent filled the air as Josiah gulped it down, shuddering.

For a few agonizing minutes, we waited, the silence in the visitor center thick and suffocating. Finally, Josiah's breathing slowed, and he managed to speak, his voice barely more than a whisper. "The creatures... they tore Gallahan to shreds. I just barely managed to escape."

I hadn't liked Sir Gallahan much—he was gruff, old-fashioned, and honestly, kind of a jerk. But he was also a knight of the Golden Army, and he'd volunteered for this mission when others would have run. In the end, for all his flaws, he'd given his life to protect us. That mattered. That would always matter.

Josiah's voice shook. "I can't believe he's gone." He looked so much younger in that moment, grief written all over his face.

Earl's tone turned brisk, but I could see the sadness in his eyes. "There's no time to mourn now. The wendigos are regrouping as we speak. We must find the staff." He helped Josiah to his feet, his movements gentle despite his words.

For once, nobody argued. We just went on—because that's what Sir Gallahan would have wanted.

"What do we do now?" I asked the others.

"Use your fire magic to light the room," Earl replied. "Just for a moment. I need to get my bearings."

I bit my lip nervously. "Are you sure that's a good idea?"

"Now," Earl said as he held up the compass.

I took a steadying breath and a small orb of fire flickered to life in my palm, casting a shaky glow across the room. The flames lasted only a few seconds, but it was enough.

Outside, heavy footsteps thudded across the gravel, circling the building. The visitor center's thin walls did nothing to muffle the guttural snarls and the scrape of claws against concrete. Something massive brushed against the door, rattling it.

A chorus of howls erupted outside. Shadows darted past the window, and for a split second, I caught the glint of yellow eyes peering in from the darkness.

"Earl..." My voice was barely more than a whisper, thick with dread. "We need to get out of here."

He nodded, his eyes darting to a black door on the far side of the room, half-hidden in the shadows. I hadn't noticed it before, but a battered sign above it said 'basement' in bold neon letters.

Another crash rattled the visitor center's front doors. The hinges shrieked under the assault, and for a moment, I wondered if we were about to be torn apart.

We hurried after Earl, down a narrow, creaking staircase into the basement. Above us, the sounds of the wendigos tearing through the visitor reached us—snarls, claws scraping, the splintering of wood and metal.

I summoned my nature magic, weaving a barrier of spiky vines across the doorway. The vines writhed and thickened until they completely blocked the stairwell.

"Come, help us search," Earl called to me.

"What exactly are we looking for?" I asked.

Earl's eyes darted across the room, his brow furrowed in concentration. "I'm not sure," he murmured, his voice tense.

He ran his fingers along the stone walls, searching for any sign—any clue—that might point us in the right direction. "The staff has been hidden for centuries. It won't be easy to find."

Josiah hovered just behind Earl, his eyes darting anxiously toward the stairs, one hand never leaving the hilt of his sword. "We need to hurry," he whispered, his voice tight with urgency.

Caleb paced in tight circles, the beam of his flashlight jittering across the walls. "This is insane," he muttered. "Why would the staff be buried in a dusty old basement? We're wasting time—the wendigos will be here any second."

Earl paced the perimeter of the cramped basement, boots crunching on loose gravel as he held out the compass, its needle stubbornly refusing to move.

"I told you it was broken," Caleb snapped, frustration and fear heavy in his voice. "And now we're going to be eaten by angry mutants!"

Earl spun on his heel. "Do be quiet now," he snapped, glaring at Caleb with a look that could have frozen fire. Caleb opened his mouth to protest, but the words died before they could escape.

Then, suddenly, the compass in Earl's hand began to glow an eerie blue. The needle spun wildly, then snapped to a stop, pointing straight at a wall on the far side of the room.

Earl's breath caught, and for a moment, he looked almost delighted. "Aha! There we are!" His voice was low, but there was a spark of excitement. "There must be a secret passageway. Come, help me look—now!"

Josiah was already at the wall, his hands moving quickly over the slick stones. He was so focused, so precise—nothing like the way I fumbled through moments like these. "There's something here," he murmured. "A seam—like a door. I think I can—"

Before he could finish, a thunderous crash split the air as the basement door was ripped clean off its hinges. The wendigos poured into the stairwell, snarling and yelping as they slammed into my barrier of vines. Sweat beaded my brow as I forced more energy into the vines, but my strength draining away as they slashed and bit at the vines.

Caleb abandoned his search for the staff and rushed to my side. He slashed at the nearest wendigo with a small knife. "Josiah, any luck over there?" he called, ducking as a taloned hand swiped at his face.

Josiah's voice rang out, urgent and triumphant. "I've found it!" There was a frantic scrape as he pressed on a false stone in the wall. It gave way beneath his hand, revealing a jagged opening—barely big enough for any of us to squeeze through.

"Let's go!" Caleb's voice was raw with adrenaline as he grabbed my arm, yanking me away from the stairs just as the wendigos succeeded at breaking down the barrier.

The wendigos barreled after us, their howls echoing in the cramped basement. Caleb shoved me through the false wall just as the creatures caught up to us. He'd barely made it through when the wall snapped back into place with a grinding thud. I pressed my back to the cold stone, gasping for breath, the sound of my own heartbeat thundering in my ears.

"That was close," I whispered to Caleb, my breath still shaky.

"We aren't done yet," he whispered back, his eyes darting to the far side of the small chamber we'd been plunged into.

Dread pooled in my stomach like molten lead as I followed Caleb's outstretched hand. There, floating above a stone dais, was the Elemental Staff. It looked impossibly untouched by time, its surface gleaming in the dim light.

I almost believed it would be easy—just walk up and take it. But the longer I stared, the more the air around it seemed to pulse, like the staff itself was warning us to stay away.

Still, I took a cautious step forward to see what would happen. A wave of angry magic rippled out from the dais, filling the air with a sharp, electric current that made all the little hairs on my arms stand on end. A shimmering, translucent wall sprang up between us and the staff.

"What do we do now?" I asked, turning to Earl. He had the Elemental Scroll unrolled, his eyes scanning the ancient script.

"The scroll doesn't say how to get past the barrier," he said after a moment. "We'll have to figure this one out ourselves."

Caleb edged closer to the staff. "Maybe we should just grab it and see what happens," he suggested.

Josiah shot him a look. "That's reckless, even for you. We have no idea what kind of magic is protecting it. For all we know, it could kill whoever touches it."

Caleb just shrugged. "You're the expert on spells and potions, Earl. Got any brilliant ideas?"

Earl tugged at his beard, his usual quirky spark dulled by frustration. "I wish I did," he said, his words clipped but honest. "But I've never come across a protection spell quite like this."

I glanced back at the staff, anxiety gnawing at me. "Horatious wouldn't have hidden the staff here without a way to retrieve it… would he?" My voice echoed, the question hanging unanswered. I needed someone to say it wasn't hopeless. That we hadn't come all this way for nothing.

Out of the corner of my eye, I noticed that Josiah had gone strangely still, his hand still outstretched like he'd been reaching for the staff. He locked eyes with me from the other side of the magical wall.

"Looks like there is a way across," he said, his voice tight.

The air between us rippled with a faint, silvery haze, distorting his outline.

Caleb's eyes went wide. "What did you go and do that for?"

Josiah shook his head, looking down at his boots. "I didn't do it on purpose, Caleb. One second, I was standing near the barrier, the next… I was here. I don't even remember crossing over."

Earl's eyes lit with excitement. "Curious! Perhaps the barrier responds to intent, rather than blood or magic. Josiah, what were you thinking right before you crossed over?"

Josiah hesitated, his voice dropping low. "I was thinking of Sir

Gallahan and his sacrifice. And how I would do the same if called upon."

Earl hummed thoughtfully, running a hand through his beard. "Intent then. That's very old magic. Very dangerous, too."

I looked at Josiah, my chest tight with worry. "You didn't have to risk yourself for us," I said softly.

He met my eyes, steady and sure. "I know. But I wanted to." His words were simple, but the conviction in them made my throat ache.

Josiah's eyes widened. "Wait—something's changed. Two brass goblets just appeared on the dais."

I squinted, but saw nothing—just the empty, dust-choked altar. The goblets must have been hidden by the protection spell, visible only to whoever crossed the barrier.

Earl's whole demeanor shifted. The exhaustion in his face vanished, replaced by a flicker of hope. "Good," he said, his voice suddenly alive with possibility as he studied the dais.

"Why is that good?" I asked.

Earl drew a slow, steady breath, the torchlight glinting off his spectacles. "Because it means the spell is responding. It's giving us a choice." Without another word, he stepped forward—right through the shimmering wall.

My heart lurched. "Earl, what are you doing?" I called, my voice trembling as the magical barrier shimmered between us. I wanted to reach for them, to pull them back to safety, but all I could do was stand there—helpless, watching.

Earl's voice was eerily calm, almost distant. "I know what we must do," he said, his gaze fixed on Josiah. "I trust you've figured it out as well?"

Josiah straightened. "I have," he replied, and even though there was fear in his eyes, his voice didn't waver.

Caleb's fists clenched at his sides, his frustration boiling over. "Would one of you care to fill the rest of us in?" he growled.

Earl turned, his expression grave, all his usual oddball humor gone. "It's an alchemical spell," he explained. "One goblet contains the elixir that will allow its drinker to retrieve the Elemental Staff from the dais."

"And the other?" I asked, my mouth suddenly dry.

Earl's eyes darkened. "The other will turn its drinker to stone."

"No, absolutely not!" Caleb shouted, his voice cracking as it echoed off the walls. "There's no way I'm letting either of you be turned into stone!"

Josiah gave a brave smile, meeting Caleb's eyes. "This is what I am meant to do, Caleb. Protecting the House of Hale—it's my duty and my honor. Don't try to talk me out of it."

Josiah grabbed one of the brass goblets, tipped it back, and drank. His hands were steady even as the rest of us held our breath.

"Well, how do you feel?" Caleb asked him.

Josiah let out a shaky sigh of relief. "I feel fine, I—"

His words cut off as his eyes went wide with shock. The goblet slipped from his fingers, clattering to the stone floor. I watched helplessly as a gray sheen crept up from his boots, crawling over his legs, his chest, his arms—turning him to stone, inch by inch.

Josiah stood frozen—transformed into a perfect statue, his final expression a mix of surprise and courage.

"Josiah!" Caleb lunged forward, but I caught the back of his cloak before he could throw himself across the barrier.

"Are you out of your mind?" I shouted, tightening my grip as Caleb struggled against me. "We don't know what that thing will do if you cross over now!"

Caleb twisted in my grasp, his voice raw. "We have to help him, Amira! He did this for us!" I held onto him, even though my own heart was about to explode.

"If you go in there now, you'll just make it worse. Josiah did this to protect us. Don't throw that away!"

Caleb fell to his knees, his shoulders shaking with grief.

Earl grabbed the second goblet. There was a new fire in his eyes. "For Josiah," he said, and downed the potion in one gulp. Then he walked to the dais and wrapped his fingers around the Elemental Staff. The instant he lifted it, the barrier shattered, its magic exploding around us like shards of glass.

"It's time to go," Earl said, his voice low but urgent. He glanced at Josiah's statue, and something flickered in his eyes—grief or guilt, maybe both.

"I won't leave him!" Caleb's voice cracked.

"You must," Earl said as he hauled Caleb to his feet. "The magic holding this place together is falling apart. If we stay, we're all dead."

Tears streaked down Caleb's cheeks as he stared at Josiah—his best friend, now frozen in stone. I felt my own throat close up, but there was no time to fall apart. We ran, boots pounding through the collapsing tunnel, until we burst out into the basement—and straight into a pack of ravenous wendigos.

The leader stepped forward, his black eyes boring into Earl. "What have you done?" he snarled.

Earl didn't back down. He stood tall, the staff glowing in his grip. "Your job is done. Go now. I'll make sure the staff never falls into the wrong hands again." He raised the staff and pointed it at the wendigos. Instantly, every single one of them collapsed.

"What did you do?" I gasped, my hand flying to my mouth.

"I set them free."

White wisps of smoke curled up from the wendigos' bodies, swirling higher and higher until they shimmered into the shapes of people—pilgrims, maybe, from some other time. Their faces were peaceful, finally at rest after who knows how long trapped in those monstrous forms.

"Thank you," the leader of the wendigos whispered, his voice echoing like a memory. "But you must go now. Without the Elemental Staff in place, the portal will soon close forever."

A deep rumble shook the visitor center, dust raining down from the ceiling. "Go, go, go!" Caleb shouted, grabbing my arm as we bolted for the stairs. I could barely see, but I could hear Earl's wheezing breath right behind me, and Caleb's curses as we stumbled up the narrow steps.

We burst into the main room, coughing and blinking through the haze. The air buzzed with magic. Purple light pulsed everywhere, swirling in through the shattered window, where a jagged beam of violet shot into the night sky.

"What the—?" I gasped, pointing. My heart was pounding so hard I thought it might crack my ribs.

Earl's face was grim, his knuckles white on the Elemental Staff. "The Northern Portal is failing. We must reach it before it closes for good."

We sprinted for the door, the beam of magic lighting up the woods outside like it was daylight. The portal itself was a mess—swirling, flickering, nothing but darkness on the other side. The wind whipped at our faces, yanking at our hair and clothes.

"Is it safe?" I yelled against the roar.

"We must take our chances!" Earl shouted back.

We grabbed hands—me, Caleb, Earl—and on the count of three, threw ourselves into the portal.

For a split second, I felt weightless, the roar of magic in my ears. Then, with a jolt, we were gone—uncertain if we would ever see the other side.

CHAPTER SIXTEEN

TEST OF THE TIDES

Every time I closed my eyes, I saw Ravenna lying there in the dark, so still it made my stomach clench tight in panic. My hands wouldn't stop shaking, and my brain kept replaying the moment I'd lost control—my astral magic exploding out of me.

I'd always thought I could handle it, that I was strong enough to keep my powers in check. But it turns out I was wrong.

All of Wahiao buzzed with energy. I could hear people whispering outside my hut, torches flickering in the dark. They were all waiting to see if the chief's daughter, my Ravenna, would make it through the night. And it was my fault.

I'd give anything—my magic, my title, my whole stupid future—if it meant Ravenna would just open her eyes and tell me I was being dramatic. But I couldn't fix this. I couldn't do anything except wait and hope. I hated it.

For the first time, I actually understood why Yasmine wanted to get rid of her astral powers so badly. I would have traded mine in a heartbeat if it meant Ravenna would be okay.

The door to my hut opened with a quiet knock. I spun around, heart pounding like I'd just run a marathon, and there was Tane, the village healer.

"Is she okay?" I asked him breathlessly.

His dark eyes searched mine for a long moment, and I swear I almost yelled at him to spit it out.

"Ravenna will live," Tane finally said, his voice strained from exhaustion. "But she is still very weak. It will take time for her strength to return."

Relief hit me so hard my knees almost gave out. The thought of losing Ravenna—not knowing if she'd ever wake up—had been eating me alive.

"She'll need plenty of rest," Tane added, like he was already planning to body-block anyone who tried to bug her. Me included.

"Yeah. I get it," I said, even though I didn't like it.

Tane studied me for a second, then said, "Chief Rawiri wants to know if you intend to face the siren queen."

I straightened, forcing myself to look him in the eye. "I have to. We need the Obsidian Firestone and the queen's not just going to hand it over because we ask nicely. Sending Olivia was proof enough of that."

Tane nodded, and for a split second, I thought I saw something like respect in his eyes. "I will tell the chief of your intentions," he said, then turned and left.

"Yeah, you do that," I muttered, not caring if he heard me as the door clicked shut behind him.

The second I was alone, I just deflated. I dropped onto my sleeping mat, elbows on my knees, and let my head fall into my hands. I thought I was actually making progress with Chief Rawiri—earning his trust, maybe even his approval. But when I'd stumbled back into Wahiao, Ravenna limp in my arms and her blood staining my shirt, all that goodwill had gone up in smoke. If Nyrah hadn't stepped in, I'm pretty sure the chief would've tossed me out on my butt right then and there.

Now I was stuck here, basically a prisoner while Tane tried to fix what I'd broken. They wouldn't even let me see Ravenna, like I was some kind of curse. I got it, I really did—but that didn't make it suck any less.

I'd tried to send a portal message to Amira, desperate to explain, to do something, but my magic fizzled out before I could even finish the spell. Maybe I was too drained, or maybe she was already off on her own quest and out of reach. Either way, the portal just sputtered and died, leaving me alone with nothing but my own frustration and a mountain of regret.

The night dragged on forever. I paced the hut like a caged animal, sleep impossible. My eyes burning from exhaustion and the tears I couldn't hold back, but every time I sat down, my brain just replayed everything that had happened, over and over, until I thought I'd lose my mind.

When I couldn't take it anymore, I grabbed my travel sack and made for the door, desperate for air, for movement, for anything that wasn't just sitting around doing nothing.

I opened the door and crashed into a wall of muscle. A guard, broad-shouldered and stone-faced, blocked my way.

"Going somewhere, princess?" he asked, and there was this annoying little glint in his eyes, like he thought this was funny.

"I'm leaving. Get out of my way," I snapped.

His face went hard. "I cannot let you do that."

"Says who?" I shot back, folding my arms.

"Says the chief. He gave me orders to bring you to him." The guard's grip was firm as he caught my arm—not rough, but definitely not letting go.

The guard steered me toward Chief Rawiri's longhouse. As we walked, I could feel eyes on me—villagers peeking out from behind curtains, candles flickering in the dawn. Yesterday, these same people had smiled at me, waved, even called out greetings. Now they wouldn't even meet my eye. The ones who did just stared, their faces hard and cold, like I was something they'd scraped off the bottom of their shoes.

"Did the chief say what he wanted?" I asked the guard. He didn't even bother answering my question—just kept his jaw locked and his eyes straight ahead, like he was marching me to my own execution.

"Great," I muttered, loud enough for him to hear but not loud enough to get myself in more trouble.

The guard stopped at the front door of the chief's house and announced us, all formal like. I tried to act like I wasn't about to puke, but inside my guts were churning.

"You may enter," Chief Rawiri's voice boomed from inside, all deep and dramatic.

I stepped inside, hands shaking, breath coming in short, panicky bursts. The heat hit me like a wall. There was a massive fire blazing in the middle of the hut, sweat instantly prickling at the back of my neck. Chief Rawiri sat at the far end, looking every inch the judge, jury, and executioner in his giant chair. Nyrah sat next to him, her face totally unreadable. I stood there, wishing I could melt into the floor, but knowing I'd have to face whatever was coming next, alone.

"Chief, please, just let me explain—" I started, desperate to defend myself, but Chief Rawiri raised his hand, and the words died in my throat.

"Enough," he said, his voice booming through the smoky air. "You will not speak. You will listen."

Nyrah glanced at him, concern flickering in her eyes, but she stayed silent, her posture rigid beside his.

Rawiri's gaze locked on me, cold and unyielding. "You are not of Wahiao, yet we welcomed you, even though your bloodline has brought nothing but trouble to our door. Now you have harmed my daughter—the future of this village. That cannot go unanswered."

His words landed like blows. Shame settle in my chest, heavy and suffocating, pressing down until I could barely breathe.

"I would never hurt Ravenna on purpose. I love her!" The words burst out of me, but Rawiri's face didn't even twitch.

"If you truly loved her, you would have learned to control yourself, and your infernal powers, long ago."

That one cut deep.

My knees buckled and I fell to the ground. "You're right," I choked out. "I would do anything to fix this."

Chief Rawiri's eyes narrowed, and I swear he was sizing me up like a wild animal he wasn't sure if he should let loose or put down. "Anything?" he asked. It was a challenge, not a question.

"Yeah. Anything," I shot back, chin up, even though my insides felt like they were turning to water.

Chief Rawiri stood, and suddenly the whole room felt smaller. He was huge—block-out-the-sun huge—and when he stepped closer, his shadow swallowed me up. "There is a path to redemption," he said in a grave voice. "But it will not be easy. You must face the siren queen. Bring back the Obsidian Firestone and save Wahiao from destruction. Only then will you have proven yourself worthy of forgiveness—and of my daughter."

I swallowed hard, forcing myself to nod, even though my voice came out way shakier than I wanted. "Fine. I'll do it. Whatever it takes."

Chief Rawiri crossed his arms across his chest and narrowed his eyes. "There is more," he said in a deep voice.

Of course there was.

"You must complete this task without your powers."

Wait. What? My brain short-circuited.

"Chief, you can't be serious!" I croaked out, panic spiking in my chest. "You want me to go up against the siren queen with nothing but—what, my winning personality?"

He shut me down with a stern look. "You have leaned on your astral magic for too long, Kira. It has become wild and dangerous. You must learn to stand on your own feet, for your sake and for those you claim to love."

No magic. Just... me?

My powers were my shield, my sword, my backup plan for every disaster. Without them, I felt helpless. How was I supposed to face the siren queen with nothing but stubbornness and a bad attitude? What if I failed? What if I lost the Firestone—or worse, Ravenna?

I turned to Nyrah, hoping for some backup. "You're really okay with this?" I asked, searching her face for any sign of mercy.

But Nyrah's gaze was steady. "For once, my husband and I are in agreement. This is the only way."

I let out a shaky breath, trying to keep my chin up even as my insides twisted. "Okay," I said, my voice unsteady.

No magic. No shortcuts. Just Kira Hale, about to do something incredibly stupid for love.

Chief Rawiri reached into his belt pouch and pulled out a chunk of violet amethyst, holding it up so the firelight made it glow like something out of a nightmare. "Do you know what this is?" he asked me.

I nodded. Of course I did. Grandma Ana had shown me one. Her face had been serious as she'd explained how amethyst could rip the magic out of a spellcaster's body, leaving them just a regular human. Amira and Caleb had both gone through it, but their magic had been barely more than a spark at the time. For me? This was going to be a whole different level of pain.

"When you are ready, I will place the amethyst into the fire," Chief Rawiri said, his eyes intent on mine.

"Let's just get this over with," I muttered.

Chief Rawiri grimaced, his face turning sympathetic. "Prepare yourself, Kira. Your astral magic will not leave you willingly."

I sucked in a breath, bracing myself as he tossed the amethyst into the fire.

And then... BAM.

Agony exploded through me, white-hot and merciless, like I was being burned alive from the inside out. I tried to scream, but couldn't. Time stopped making sense. I was lost in it—the pain, fire, everything spinning out of control.

When it finally ended, I woke sprawled in the dirt, drenched in sweat and shaking so hard I could barely move. My body felt hollow, like the amethyst had burned everything out of me and left nothing but a shell.

Chief Rawiri knelt down, his massive shadow falling over me. His eyes were dark and unreadable, but for a second, I thought I saw regret—or maybe hope—flicker before he looked away.

"I hope you survive, child. For all our sakes," he said, his voice low and grave.

I wanted to snap back with something defiant, but I could barely breathe, let alone yell. The chief nodded at one of the guards, who scooped me up and hauled me back to my hut. He set me down on my mat, shoved a water jug next to my head, and left me alone with the world spinning around me.

When the dizziness finally faded and I was sure I wasn't going to puke, I forced myself to sit up and took a tiny sip of water, my hands still shaking. Instinctively, I stretched out my palm, trying to summon even a flicker of astral magic—just a spark, a whisper, anything. But there was nothing left. I felt completely defenseless, stripped bare, like someone had taken a part of me.

A wave of frustration crashed over me. I picked up the water jug and hurled it at the wall. The noise brought the guard back, his scarred face peering into the hut with a frown.

"You may visit Ravenna once you've calmed down," he said, his tone clipped.

"I am calm," I snapped through gritted teeth.

Nyrah entered the hut then. She didn't waste time with soft words or pity. "Come now," she said, her voice calm but with a no-nonsense edge. "Don't waste the time you have left here being angry. Let's go see my daughter. I hear she is doing much better."

I nodded, swallowing the last of my pride. I was powerless, but I still had something left to fight for. I practically leapt up from my mat, only to remember, too late, the toll the Severing Ceremony had taken. My legs wobbled beneath me, and I nearly faceplanted, but Nyrah caught my arm with surprising strength. She didn't say anything, just steadied me and steered me out the door, like she'd done this a hundred times before.

She guided me quietly toward the healer's hut, not letting go until we were inside. No pep talks, no coddling—just solid, silent support that made me feel like just maybe, I'd be okay.

Inside, Ravenna was propped up on her cot, talking quietly with Tane. She was pale, her long dark hair tangled around her shoulders, but she was alive. I rushed over and hugged her, careful not to squeeze too tight. She buried her face in my shoulder, and for a moment, everything was perfect.

But then Ravenna pulled back, her eyes wild and searching. "Kira, what did you do?"

I told her about the chief's ultimatum, the whole "prove yourself or else" deal. Ravenna's face went stormy, and she turned on her mom, her voice sharp. "How could you let him do this to her?" she demanded.

Nyrah only shrugged, her face unreadable. "Kira chose this, we forced nothing on her."

"But she could die!"

I cleared my throat, trying to sound braver than I felt. "Hey, I'm not planning on dying, okay? I can handle myself—even without magic." I tried to smirk, but it felt weak.

Ravenna squeezed my hand. "I know you can," she whispered, her voice thick with worry. "But doing this alone, without your powers...." She tried to hide it, but I could see the fear in her eyes, and for once, I didn't have a joke to make it better.

"It's going to suck, I'm not gonna lie. But I've been through worse," I said, forcing a crooked grin even though my insides felt like they'd been scooped out. "Besides, the chief never said I had to go solo. Just that I couldn't use my powers."

Right then, Gnash stomped into the healer's hut, already geared up for battle, his giant axe slung over his shoulder like it weighed nothing. The sight of him—solid, loyal, basically a walking tank—made something in my chest unclench. "You up for another adventure?" I asked, trying to keep my voice light.

Gnash gave me a toothy grin and nodded, all in.

"See?" I said to Ravenna, nudging her with my elbow and managing a real smile. "I'm not going in alone."

Ravenna's face unclenched slightly, but I could still see the worry in her eyes. "You still need to convince the water spirits to help you, and that won't be easy."

"No, it won't be," Nyrah cut in, stepping forward with calm, unshakeable energy. "You'll need to offer them something they cannot refuse. Fortunately, I have just the thing." She didn't smile, didn't soften—just handed me the next impossible task like it was a loaf of bread. Typical.

A while later, Gnash and I headed down to the rocky beach. Ravenna was still stuck in bed, so we'd already done the whole emotional goodbye thing. The villagers hadn't thrown a party for me, but at least they weren't throwing rocks at me, either.

Plus, I didn't need a crowd watching me try to negotiate with a bunch of bad-tempered water spirits. If I was going to make a fool of myself, I'd rather do it with just Gnash as my witness.

The tide was low, so we carefully picked our way across the slick stones, the wind whipping salt in my face. Nyrah's voice kept echoing in my head: *Don't touch the water until the spirits have accepted your offering.*

I rolled my eyes, but clutched the pearl tightly anyway—the thing was huge, practically begging to get stolen again. Apparently, one of the villagers had swiped it from the water spirits forever ago, and they'd been holding a grudge ever since.

I knelt at the edge of the waves and lowered the pearl into the water. It didn't take long for the first water spirit to show up—pale, floaty, and looking like it wanted to bite my head off.

More followed, shifty and see-through, their eyes black as the bottom of the sea. One of them rose up, its voice shrill and accusing: "You dare to mock us, human?"

I crossed my arms, making sure the pearl was still visible. "Yeah, because coming all the way out here just to mess with you is my idea of a good time." My voice was steady, but my pulse raced. "I'm here to return the pearl."

The spirit just stared, those bottomless eyes boring into me. I stared right back, refusing to flinch. If there's one thing I'm good at, it's not backing down—even when I probably should.

"Why would you do this?" the spirit demanded.

"The pearl's yours. I'm just here to give it back," I said, keeping my tone even. "But I need something in return."

They didn't seem to like that.

The water spirits—still looking like a pack of creepy, blank-faced kids—erupted in outrage. Their voices echoed across the water. For a second, I wondered if I was about to get dragged under and eaten alive.

Whatever. I'd faced worse.

"Who are you to bargain with us!" one of them shouted, its voice ancient sounding even though it looked like it should have been asking me for a bedtime story.

I shrugged. "I'm nobody special. Just someone with a deadline. I need to reach the siren queen by tomorrow night or Hekagia's toast. I'll give you the pearl, but you have to let me and my friend through. That's the deal."

The spirits closed in, eyes like black stones, the air going cold. Gnash shifted beside me, his grip tightening on his axe, but I didn't budge.

"It would be easier to just take the pearl from you," the first water spirit sneered.

"Yeah, probably," I shot back. "But then Raideron wipes out Hekagia, and trust me, he won't stop at the land. You think he'll spare the ocean? Not a chance."

The spirits went quiet, just the waves slapping rocks and a bunch of blank, creepy kid faces staring me down. One of them snickered, all sly, and said, "Even if we agree, how will you breathe under the waves, land dweller?"

I snorted. "Please. I came prepared." I dug into my satchel and pulled out two vials of Gill Draught—Chief Rawiri's idea of a party favor. The stuff looked like it belonged in a witch's cauldron, but whatever.

I tossed one to Gnash, who caught it like it might explode.

He eyed it, nose wrinkling. "Do I have to?"

"Kinda. Unless you don't want to come after all?" I said.

Gnash glared at me like I'd insulted his honor. He uncorked the vial and drank the Gill Draught, his face twisting like he'd just swallowed a bucket of swamp water.

"Tastes worse than it looks," he grumbled.

The spirits watched, fascinated, as Gnash lurched forward and face-planted into the surf. I braced myself for a full-on disaster—maybe he'd sprout a second head or something—but nope.

Nash's legs fused together, scales rippled up his skin, and gills popped out along his neck. He thrashed around, all elbows.

The spirits lost it, cackling like a pack of hyenas.

"Alright, you've had your fun," I called out. "Do we have a deal or not?"

They stared at me, their blank faces giving nothing away. For a second, I thought they might just snatch the pearl and vanish, but after a long, tense pause, the lead spirit finally spoke. "Give us the pearl and you may pass."

I let out a shaky breath and handed over the pearl, watching as it vanished into the spirit's translucent hands. They faded away, slipping back into the deep like they'd never been there at all. Guess I'd just have to trust they'd keep their end of the bargain—because if not, well, I was out of backup plans.

I uncorked the second vial of Gill Draught and tossed it back. The taste was pure ocean garbage—like licking the bottom of a bait bucket. I shuddered, then dove face-first into the water, because what else was I going to do—back out now?

The change hit fast. My legs fused together, skin tingling like I'd rolled in stinging nettles, and suddenly I was gasping—until I realized, oh, right, gills. Breathing water felt wrong, but I forced myself to get over it. No time for a meltdown. After a minute of flailing (and maybe kicking Gnash by accident), I figured out how to move. Not graceful, but it worked.

Gnash was already ahead, looking like a mutant sea monster, but at least he was still with me. We were headed straight for the Queen of the Sirens—me, magicless, but not alone. And that was enough. I'd figure out the rest as I went.

CHAPTER SEVENTEEN

CITY OF THE SIRENS

The ocean was a whole circus. Schools of neon fish zipped around like they were late for something, weird glowing jelly-things pulsing in the shadows, and armored critters flashing like underwater lanterns. It was wild, and kind of awesome. If I hadn't been on a mission to maybe die, I might've actually enjoyed it.

Gnash was beside me, "swimming" if you could call it that. The guy flailed so much he looked like he was wrestling an invisible octopus. Every few strokes he'd spin out, kicking up sand and nearly taking out a passing fish. Meanwhile, the water spirits, those see-through show-offs, glided around us. They kept shooting us these looks, half pity, half "are you kidding me?" Their laughter echoed through the water, and I could practically hear the bets they were placing on how long we'd last.

We'd only asked for safe passage, but the spirits seemed to think we were their new favorite entertainment. They led us through kelp forests and coral canyons, deeper and deeper toward Palaesar—the siren city. The farther we went, the more spirits joined in, trailing behind us like a pack of giggling ghosts. Judging by the way they snickered every time I got tangled in seaweed, I was pretty sure none of them were betting on me to win my showdown with Queen Narissa. But hey, let them laugh. I'd get the last word—one way or another.

Even with a tail, swimming across the Eastern Sea took forever, and the deeper we went, the weirder and bigger everything got. We passed shipwrecks tangled in coral, guarded by octopi the size of wagons. At one point, a shadow the size of a house glided underneath us. I didn't look twice. If it wanted a fight, it could get in line. But none of the sea monsters came close to us. The water spirits drifted along with us, all ghostly and smug. Even the scariest predators gave them a wide berth. I guess having a pack of supernatural babysitters has its perks.

"You good?" I called out to Gnash, trying not to laugh as he spun in a slow circle, kicking up a cloud of sand.

Gnash grunted, spitting out a bubble. "Swimming... hard."

"You look like a walrus with a cramp," I shot back, smirking. "But at least you're not shark bait."

He flashed a toothy grin. "Shark try, I smash."

I snorted. "That's the spirit. Just don't drop that axe, or I'm leaving you for the mermaids."

Gnash just shrugged, unbothered. "Mermaids not scary."

I rolled my eyes, but couldn't help the smirk tugging at my lips. Typical Gnash—nothing fazed him. I kept my tail moving, trying not to think about how weird it felt to swim without legs

Down here, time meant nothing. It felt like we'd been swimming forever, muscles aching, the water pressing in from all sides. Every so often, I'd catch Gnash flailing in my peripheral vision, but at least he wasn't complaining. Not that he ever did.

Out of nowhere, one of the water spirits let out a shriek that made my skin crawl. In a blink, the whole ghostly crowd scattered, vanishing into the gloom and leaving us alone in the dark. Great. Just what I needed—creepy silence.

I scanned the shadows, hand drifting to my dagger. "Guess we're not the main attraction anymore," I muttered, more to myself than to Gnash. He didn't answer, just tensed up, eyes narrowed, axe ready. That was all I needed to know. Something was coming.

Quick as lightening, a dozen figures slid out of the darkness, circling us. Sirens. Tall, sharp-toothed, and not looking for a chat. Their tridents glinted in the dim light, aimed right at our chests.

I didn't flinch. I squared my shoulders and glared right back. "If you're here to threaten us, get in line. I've had worse things than you try to kill me before breakfast."

The nearest siren bared her teeth in a grin that was all predator, no charm. "You will follow us, land-scum. Try anything clever, and I'll gut you myself."

Gnash growled and reached for his axe, but I shook my head at him, staying his hand... for now.

"Name's Kira. Who are you?" I asked the siren.

She sneered, her black hair swirling around her like a shadow. "Nyx. Remember it, human. It'll be the last name you hear if you step out of line." She didn't even bother to hide the disgust in her voice. "The only reason you're still breathing is because the queen wants you alive. If it were up to me, I'd let you roast in the Scalding Labyrinth."

I snorted. "Scalding Labyrinth? Sounds like a spa day. Lead the way, Nyx. But don't think for a second I'm scared of you or your queen."

Nyx's eyes narrowed, her voice dropping to a hiss. "You should be. Humans never last long in our waters."

I fell in line, but not because I was afraid. I just wanted to see what this so-called labyrinth looked like—and if Nyx tried anything, she'd find out real quick that I wasn't the easy prey she thought I was.

Nyx gestured ahead, and I got my first real look at the mess we were about to swim through. The seafloor was a disaster—cracked wide open, with black water billowing out of a hundred gaping fissures. The whole place was a maze of boiling vents, the water shimmering with heat and bubbles so thick you couldn't see more than a few feet ahead.

"What's that?" Gnash asked, his eyes wide with fear.

"They're hydrothermal vents," Nyx snapped, her voice dripping with impatience, like she couldn't believe she had to explain this to a bunch of clueless land-dwellers. "Try not to touch the bubbles. Unless you like third degree burns, that is."

"So what, we just go around them?" I asked, scanning the labyrinth. There was no obvious path, just a whole lot of ways to die.

Nyx flashed a grin of pure malice. "We go through. If you can keep up, land-girl. But don't expect me to fish you out if you fall behind."

Nyx and her pack of sirens slipped through the Scalding Labyrinth like it was their own private garden, slipping between the boiling plumes with a smug, effortless grace that only a lifelong sea monster could pull off. Meanwhile, I tried not to fry my tail off every time a jet of scalding water hissed past me. The heat simmered around us, warping the water and making it impossible to see more than a few feet ahead.

"Hurry up, land dwellers! We haven't got all day!" Nyx's voice sliced through the swirling currents, sharp and impatient, echoing off the jagged walls of the undersea labyrinth. She sounded like she'd be just as happy leaving us here to become seafood stew.

Every time I glanced back, the shadows of the vent fields twisted around us, and we fell farther behind with every stroke. Gnash let out a nervous whimper as he barely dodged a plume of superheated bubbles erupting from a fissure. "I don't like this," he muttered, tail flailing. "We almost there now?"

I gritted my teeth, fighting the drag of the current. "Let me find out." I surged forward, refusing to let Nyx think I was scared, and called out, "Hey, Nyx! Are we almost to Palaesar, or are you just trying to roast us for fun?"

Nyx glanced back at me. "Almost," she called, her lips curling into a sneer. "But the hardest part of the vent fields is coming up. Pay attention neanderthal… or maybe I should just leave you here—one less problem for the queen."

"Don't even think about it," I growled. "Or you'll see what happens when this 'neanderthal' gets mad."

Nyx shrugged, her tail flicking with that infuriating, effortless grace. "Why not?" she purred. "Might be a kinder fate than what's waiting for you in Palaesar." She flashed a row of needle-sharp teeth, clearly enjoying herself.

If I'd had my astral magic, I would've shown her exactly what a 'neanderthal' could do. But stripped of my powers and literally out of my depth, all I could do was grit my teeth and keep swimming, cursing her out in my head with every tail stroke.

Gnash drifted closer, his eyes narrowed. "You want me to hurt her?" he rumbled, flexing his massive hands as if he was itching for his axe.

I couldn't help but snort, patting his broad shoulder. "Probably not the best idea. The siren queen wouldn't like it—and I'm not in the mood to start an underwater war. Yet."

Gnash let out a dissatisfied grunt and fell back in line, his tail sending up a cloud of silt as we pressed on—deeper into the labyrinth, and closer to whatever fate was waiting for us in the city of sirens.

It wasn't long before the city of Palaesar emerged from the gloom—a vision so unreal it almost made me forget the danger.

The whole place shimmered like a giant, luminous pearl, domes and spiraling towers crafted from iridescent nacre, all nestled inside the gaping maw of an enormous clam shell. It looked ready to snap shut at the first sign of trouble. For a second, the sheer absurdity of it almost distracted me from the threat waiting just beyond the gates—but only for a second.

Queen Narissa waited for us, floating at the head of her little army like she owned the ocean. Her crown was sharp obsidian, perched on a head of blonde hair so perfect it looked fake. Olivia, her favorite attack dog, hovered at her side—blue-skinned, tail flicking, eyes full of smug. The rest of the sirens fanned out, forming a living barricade. As soon as we got close, the circle snapped shut, trapping us like prey.

"What's this, the welcoming committee?" I called out to Narissa, my voice echoing through the water.

Nyx darted forward. She jabbed the butt of her trident into the backs of my knees, sending me sprawling onto the shell-strewn seabed, pain radiating up my legs. "Do not speak to the Queen unless spoken to, you filthy land parasite!" she spat.

Gnash reached for his axe, but the siren guards were faster. In a blur, they pinned him, tridents digging into his chest until blood drifted in the current. He gritted his teeth, but didn't make a sound. I could tell he wanted to fight, but I shook my head—no point getting us both skewered.

Queen Narissa drifted closer, her eyes cold and bored, like she was already over this whole scene. "Did you really think I'd fight you fairly?" she drawled, her lips curling in a lazy, predatory smile. "You landfolk are always so naïve. The Obsidian Firestone is ours now. It was laughable to think I'd ever let it fall back into your grubby hands."

It was then that I realized just how screwed we were. Palaesar might look like a pearl, but it was a fortress—and we were trapped at the gates, surrounded by an enemy who didn't give a damn about rules.

I forced a smirk, even as my mind raced for a way out. "Then why bother sending Olivia to make a deal? Or is this just your idea of entertainment?"

Olivia answered with a sneer. "Lord Raideron has promised more gold than you could ever dream of for your capture. He wants you out of the way for what comes next."

I rolled my eyes. "Oh yeah? And what exactly is that, Olivia? Do you even know? Or are you just running your mouth?"

She scoffed, tossing her hair. "Like I'd tell you. How dumb do you think I am?"

I gave her a slow, unimpressed once-over. "Well—"

She lunged, teeth bared, but I was already reaching for my dagger. "Bring it on!" I snarled, but before either of us could make a move, Queen Narissa threw her arm out in front of Oliva.

"Enough, Olivia," Narissa drawled, her voice slicing through the water like a knife made of boredom and disdain. "Klerope!"

A tall, slender siren woman with short brown hair threaded with seashells drifted forward, eyes glued to the sand, shoulders hunched like she wished she could disappear. "Yes, my queen?" Klerope's voice was barely a whisper, trembling at the edges.

Narissa didn't even bother to look at her. She just waved a lazy hand, her tone dripping with contempt. "Take our prisoners to their cells. And make sure they're actually guarded this time. I'm not interested in another embarrassing escape."

I watched Klerope, sizing her up. I'd heard the rumors—she was Narissa's cousin, next in line for the throne, and apparently the only one in the room with a conscience. Not that Narissa cared. She looked at Klerope like she was a stain on her crown, then turned away.

Klerope nodded quickly, not daring to meet the queen's gaze. "At once, Your Majesty," she murmured, her hands shaking as she gestured for the guards. In an instant, sirens closed in—two on either side of me and three more on Gnash.

If I'd had my magic, I would've blasted a hole straight through Narissa's smug little court. But for now, all I could do was glare and let them drag us away, promising myself that the next time I saw that crown, it'd be at my feet.

As far as dungeons went, this one wasn't all that bad—if you ignored the whole "underwater prison" thing. At least the sirens had the decency to give us a private bathroom. Raideron's dungeon? All filth and misery. I smirked, thinking of Amira's legendary escape from Shadowfell Castle by dumping a chamber pot over her ogre guard's head. It was a classic Hale story now.

But my amusement faded the moment Olivia swam into the dungeon, her movements theatrical as ever, even with webbed hands and an iridescent fishtail.

She stopped just an inch from the bars of my cell, careful not to get too close. They'd already confiscated my dagger, but if I could have reached her, I'd have gladly strangled her with my bare hands.

"What do you want?" I snapped.

She spun in a slow, mocking circle, her red hair swirling like she thought she was in a shampoo commercial. "Nothing much. Just here to gloat." She drifted over to Gnash's cell, flashing him a grin sharp enough to cut kelp.

"Go away," Gnash rumbled, fists clenched, looking like he'd love to snap her in half.

Olivia laughed. "No, I think I'll stay. Watching you two stew in here is the most fun I've had all week."

Klerope stood silent, her expression tight with discomfort. From the way she watched Olivia, it was clear the two weren't exactly besties.

"You already won," I said, glaring at Olivia as she flitted around the dungeon. "No need to rub it in."

"Oh, there's every need," Olivia shot back, her eyes glittering with spite. "After what you and your little gang put me through last summer? I'm going to enjoy every second of this."

Klerope's hands tightened around her ring of keys. Her voice was quiet, but there was an edge to it. "That's enough, Olivia. These humans are under my care."

Olivia pouted, all fake innocence. "Come on, Klerope, lighten up. I'm just having a little fun. Besides, the queen doesn't care what happens to them as long as we keep them breathing… for now."

Klerope's eyes narrowed, worry flickering across her face. "What's that supposed to mean, Olivia?"

Olivia just shrugged, flicking her tail with a bored flourish as she drifted toward the dungeon door. She leaned against it, sighing like she was the one suffering here. "Let's just say these two don't have much time left."

Klerope's jaw tightened. "You shouldn't talk like that. We're not monsters, Olivia. We have rules."

Olivia let out a dramatic, exasperated sigh. "You three are so painfully dull. I'm going to find some real entertainment." She huffed and stormed out, slamming the door behind her.

I couldn't help myself—I muttered, "Don't let the door hit you on the way out."

As the echo faded, Klerope lingered by my cell, her face still tense. She hesitated, then squared her shoulders and unlocked the door with a sharp, decisive click. "How much longer will your Gill Draught last?" she asked, her voice suddenly sharp.

I stared at Klerope, caught off guard. The meek, anxious girl from the city gates was gone. In her place was someone fierce, eyes burning with purpose. For the first time since we'd been thrown into the dungeon, I felt a flicker of hope.

"Quickly!" Klerope urged, glancing over her shoulder like she expected Olivia to slither back in at any second.

I tried to keep my voice steady, but my heart was pounding. "I don't know, maybe a couple hours if we're lucky."

Klerope's lips twitched into a smile, softening the sharp lines of her face. She looked older than me—mid-twenties, maybe—but right then, she seemed almost younger, her pale skin glowing and her hair drifting around her cheeks like a halo of kelp.

She squared her shoulders, the nervous energy gone, and her eyes—dark and determined—locked on mine. "That's more than enough time to get you out of here and take down the queen," she said, her voice steady and fierce, like she'd just made up her mind to change the world.

I narrowed my eyes, not sure if I was hallucinating or if the Gill Draught was just messing with my head. "Why would you want me to do that?" I asked.

Klerope's gaze darted to the door, her voice dropping to a whisper. "Because Narissa isn't our queen anymore. Raideron's poisoned her mind—she's forgotten what it means to protect our people. I can't just watch her destroy everything."

The dungeon door creaked open and a squad of sirens swept in, their faces set and determined. I jerked my chin toward them, keeping my voice low but sharp. "Friend or foe?" I asked Klerope, ready to fight if needed.

"Friend," Klerope said, her voice sure as stone.

She darted forward and threw her arms around one of them, a tall guy with gold hair and a tail like polished onyx. He kissed her cheek and she flushed a deep violet.

"Care to introduce us?" I asked Klerope.

"I am Thalior, betrothed of Klerope," the man said, his voice deep and formal. "And Protector of Palaesar. I take both duties equally as serious."

"Yeah, I can tell. Thanks for the rescue, by the way," I said.

Thalior barely spared me a glance, waving a webbed hand like he was shooing away a fly. "I don't care about you human. My loyalty is to Klerope and to Palaesar. I will see her on the throne, as our people deserve."

Klerope's blush deepened, but she stood a little taller.

"Still," I said, glancing at the growing crowd of sirens, "I appreciate the help."

Thalior gave a curt nod, then let out a low, trilling whistle. Instantly, more sirens poured into the dungeon—at least two dozen, all armed to the teeth with tridents. Normally, that would have been my cue to panic, but right now, it felt like the tide was finally turning in my favor.

Klerope took a deep breath, her shoulders straightening as she faced the crowd of sirens. Her voice rang out clear and strong—no trace of the timid girl I'd seen earlier. "Listen to me, all of you!" she called. "Today is about Palaesar, about our future. Narissa's let Raideron poison her mind, and now she's dragging us toward a war we never wanted."

"She's right!" I shouted, my voice echoing weirdly in the water. "Humans aren't your enemies. Let us fight with you to take back your city and show Narissa what real strength looks like!"

The dungeon erupted—cheers, shouts, the slap of tails against stone. Klerope shot me a look, fierce and grateful. It was then that I saw what she could be: a real leader.

"To the throne room!" Klerope commanded, her voice carrying like a battle cry. The sirens surged forward, united and wild, and for the first time since I'd set foot in Palaesar, I actually believed we might be able to win this thing.

CHAPTER EIGHTEEN

A VISITOR IN THE NIGHT

I woke up the way I always did after a portal jump—like I'd been spun in a washing machine and then dumped out on the wrong side of reality. My head throbbed, and sunlight stabbed through my eyelids, painting shifting patterns across my face.

Then Caleb's voice cut through the haze, sharp and urgent. "Amira, wake up!" He sounded exhausted, but there was an edge to his tone—like he was trying to hold the world together with sheer stubbornness.

I forced my eyes open. Caleb was a few feet away, slumped in the grass. His curls were plastered to his forehead with sweat and dirt, and his shirt was torn at the sleeve. He looked like he'd gone three rounds with a tornado and lost. But his eyes—haunted, wild, and so tired—were fixed on me.

"Caleb, are you okay?" My voice came out scratchy, like I'd swallowed a bonfire.

He shrugged, trying for casual but not even coming close. "I'm fine," he muttered, but his jaw was clenched so tight I could practically hear his teeth grinding.

I sat up, every muscle screaming in protest, and scanned the clearing. "Where's Earl?" I asked, panic flickering in my chest.

Caleb jerked his chin toward the edge of the meadow. "Over there. With Hercules."

I followed his gaze and spotted Earl. He was crouched down next to Hercules, murmuring something to him, his hand moving in slow, soothing circles. I wasn't sure if he was calming the griffin or himself.

Relief washed over me, so fierce it almost hurt. We'd made it.

Somehow, against all odds, we'd actually made it.

But as I looked at Caleb—at the bruises blooming on his arms, the way his hands shook—I realized that "making it" didn't mean we were okay. Not even close.

"Hercules was here waiting for us," Caleb said, his voice going soft as he watched the griffin. There was this flicker of pain in his eyes and I knew he was thinking about Josiah.

The ache in my chest tightened.

"He's a good friend," I said with a small smile.

Caleb nodded, but his gaze was somewhere far away. "Yeah. He is." His voice was quiet and mournful.

I took a shaky breath, trying to get my bearings. The air was sharp and clean, with the scent of pine and rain. "Where are we?" I asked, my voice small. "Did we make it back to Hekagia?" The last thing I remembered was chaos—Roanoke, the portal, the wendigos…

"Hercules says we're in Eastern Alkrimia, not far from a place called Iron Mountain Village."

A surge of excitement broke through my exhaustion. "No way!" I couldn't help grinning at the thought of seeing the little mountainside village again.

Tucked high in the misty peaks, its people were tough as old boots and twice as stubborn, but they were kind, too. The village felt like a crossroads—where old magic and new dreams met, where every stone had a story if you listened close enough.

Caleb shot me a look. "Alright, what's up with you?" he asked, eyebrow raised.

I shrugged, brushing a clump of dirt off my tunic. "I've been to Iron Mountain Village before." There was an ache in my chest as I said it—nostalgia, maybe.

Caleb blinked, skepticism written all over his face. "You have? Seriously? What are the odds?" He sounded like he didn't believe me, but I could tell he was curious, too.

"It was a while ago," I said, glancing away. "Remember when I told you about the whole Becky the Bat Lady fiasco?" That had been one of those moments where Hekagia stopped feeling like a storybook and started feeling real—and dangerous. It was also when I realized how much I depended on the people around me.

Caleb just shrugged, all innocent, like he'd never heard the story in his life—even though I knew I'd told it at least three times. Typical little brother move.

I rolled my eyes, letting it go. "Whatever. Doesn't matter." I started walking, the grass cold and wet against my boots.

"Ah! Your Highness!" Earl boomed, pausing mid–belly rub to Hercules and nearly toppling over as he scrambled to his feet. He swept off his battered hat with a flourish, scattering a few stray feathers. "Marvelous to see you among the living!" He dropped into a ridiculously formal bow.

I groaned, cheeks burning. "Earl, seriously, you don't have to bow. Not to me." I'd never gotten used to the whole royalty thing—especially not from someone who'd once taught me how to make stink bombs in the castle kitchens. Behind me, Caleb snickered, clearly loving every second of my embarrassment.

Earl straightened, his eyes twinkling behind his crooked spectacles. "Nonsense! It's tradition, and besides, I rather enjoy it. Keeps the joints limber." He winked.

To my utter shock, Hercules dipped his massive head in a slow, solemn nod. The griffin's golden eyes met mine—wise, steady, and just a little bit intimidating.

Caleb grinned. "You're not still scared of him, are you?" he teased, eyebrows waggling. He knew exactly how I felt about his overgrown housecat and never missed a chance to rub it in.

"Of course not!" I lied, trying to sound indignant, but my voice came out a little too high. Caleb's grin only got wider.

"Good, since he's our ride back to Nithandore." He shot me a look that was pure mischief. "And you know how much Hercules loves a nervous passenger."

I groaned, looking around as if a carriage might magically appear if wished hard enough for one. "There's got to be another way," I muttered, mostly to myself.

Earl popped up beside us. "No alternatives, I'm afraid," he boomed, voice echoing like he was announcing the start of a royal banquet. "The roads are crawling with Raideron's goons and he's still watching the portals."

Caleb chimed in. "Yeah, and we're kind of on a time crunch here." He was already scanning the skies, his hand shading his eyes, alert for trouble.

I was groggy from the portal jump and my limbs felt heavy. For a second, I forgot why we were even there, until a jolt of remembrance shot through me.

"The Elemental Staff!" I spun around, heart pounding. If we'd lost it, all our sacrifices would have been for nothing.

"No need to panic, Your Highness!" Earl declared, winking at me as he patted a small leather bag tied securely to his belt. "I've got it right here. Shrunk it down with a pinch of moonwort and a dash of wishful thinking."

"Glad that's cleared up. Let's get going now." Caleb tried to sound casual, but I caught the way his fingers drummed against his patu and his eyes kept darting to the sky.

The wind was picking up, sharp with the promise of rain—and maybe something worse.

"What do you sense?" I asked him, my voice low.

He shook his head, his brow furrowed. "I don't know, but something's off." He glanced at Hercules, who was stamping his massive paws and letting out a low, anxious whine.

The griffin's wings twitched like he was ready to bolt at the first sign of trouble. Caleb reached up, murmuring to him, "Easy, big guy. We're leaving soon, promise."

We'd already lingered too long, and the tension in the air was thick enough to taste. Still, I couldn't let the moment pass.

Earl, who'd been rummaging through his satchel and humming some off-key tune about pickled newts (seriously, only Earl), caught my eye. He fixed me with that wild, twinkling gaze of his. "What is it, Your Highness?" he asked. "If you're in need of a tonic to calm the nerves, I've got just the thing—though it might turn your hair blue."

I almost laughed, but my nerves got the better of me. "Actually, can we stop at Iron Mountain Village? Just for a little while?" My words sounded small, almost childish, but the thought of that sturdy little village with its stone houses tucked into the mountainside, was the only thing that made my heart stop racing.

Earl glanced up at the sky, squinting as if he could read the weather like a potion recipe. "Hmm. I don't know if that's wise," he said, suddenly thoughtful. "But I also fear we may not have a choice." There was a note of resignation in his voice, like he understood the pull of fate—or maybe he just liked a good detour as much as I did.

Hercules, picking up on the shift, kneeled down in a low, graceful crouch, his wings folding tight against his sides. Caleb hopped onto his back with the kind of ease that comes from years of griffin-riding. Earl followed, swinging himself up with surprising agility for someone who claimed to have "bad knees and worse luck." He patted Hercules' flank and muttered something about "never trusting a griffin with your lunch."

I hovered awkwardly at Hercules' side, my boots sinking into the grass. The griffin looked at me like I'd just insulted his entire family line.

Caleb rolled his eyes, but there was a quiet encouragement in his voice. "Come on, Amira. He won't hurt you."

Hercules cocked his massive head, fixing me with those deep, intelligent eyes—like he was trying to decide if I was worth the trouble. His tail swished, stirring up the grass, and he let out a low, rumbling sound that was equal parts "hurry up" and "I'm not scary, you know."

"Alright, alright," I muttered, letting out a breath. "I'm coming." I reached out a shaky hand, and Hercules leaned in, giving my palm a rough, sandpapery lick—more giant cat than mythical beast. Then, with a huff that sounded suspiciously like a sigh, he crouched even lower, making it impossible for me to refuse.

I scrambled up, my fingers sinking into his thick, golden fur. Not that I would ever admit it to Caleb, but my hands were shaking with nerves, and I was certain Hercules could feel my fear.

To his credit, Hercules didn't show off or try to spook me. He launched into the sky with careful, deliberate beats of his wings, gliding low over the hills and patchwork fields. Even as the wind picked up and the first hints of a storm gathered, he seemed to know exactly how to find the smoothest path, like he'd done this a thousand times before and I was just along for the ride.

I wouldn't say it was a comfortable ride, but it wasn't nearly as terrifying as I'd feared. By the time we reached Iron Mountain Village, my pulse had slowed and my hands had stopped trembling. I even managed to dismount without making a total fool of myself, which felt like a small miracle.

I patted Hercules on the neck, feeling the heat of his skin through his feathers. He nudged me gently, letting out a low, rumbling purr—like a giant cat who was content with the world.

"See, told you he wasn't so bad," Caleb teased, coming up beside me and ruffling Hercules' wing feathers like they were old pals. He shot me a smug grin.

Hercules let out a playful roar. Then, with a dramatic sweep of his wings, launched himself back into the sky, circling above us in wide, lazy loops, like he was keeping watch.

I glanced up at the clouds, which had thickened into a bruised, swirling mess. "Do you think he'll be alright?" I asked, nodding toward Hercules. "There's some nasty weather coming…"

"Oh yeah, he'll be fine," Caleb replied, his tone confident. "If it gets too bad, he'll find somewhere to hunker down."

Earl, who was busy dusting off his golden robes, turned to me with a twinkle in his eye. "We won't be long though, correct?" he asked, as if he was already plotting his next experiment—or maybe just thinking about lunch.

"Right. I just want to say a quick hello," I promised, though I couldn't help but linger, taking in the view.

From up here, Iron Mountain Village looked like something out of a fairytale. It was twice as big as I remembered, with new stone cottages huddled around the old square and a shiny new sentry tower keeping watch over the road. Smoke curled from a dozen chimneys, and the sound of laughter and hammers drifted up the hillside, warm and alive.

As we made our way down into the heart of the village, people started pouring out of their houses and shops, waving and calling out. Their faces were bright with excitement, and their voices rose in a chorus of cheers that made my cheeks flush. I'd never get used to being the center of attention, but there was something about Iron Mountain that made it feel less overwhelming.

Near the inn, I spotted Caeli, the little girl we'd saved from Raideron last summer, standing with her little brother Sam and their mom. Caeli's eyes went huge when she saw me, and before her mother could even blink, she and Sam barreled straight at me, arms wide. They crashed into me with a hug so fierce it nearly knocked me over, both of them laughing and shouting my name.

Their mother hurried after them, her face a mix of worry and pride. "Caeli, Sam, mind your manners!" she called, but she was smiling too. For a second, I just let myself be hugged, soaking in the warmth and the wild, unselfconscious joy of it all.

Earl leaned in. "You see, Your Highness? This is the real magic—no potions required." he whispered, as if he was letting me in on some ancient alchemist's secret.

Then, with a dramatic flourish, he pulled a handful of candied nuts from the depths of his robe (where did he even keep those?) and offered them to Sam. The little boy grinned, snatched a few, and gave Earl a sticky-fingered salute.

Their mother dipped into a quick curtsy, her smile warm and a little shy. "We're so glad you're here, Princess," she said, and then—almost as if she'd been practicing—she pulled a small box from her apron and held it out. Caeli gasped, her hands flying to her mouth, eyes huge with excitement.

"Can I give it to her, pretty please?" Caeli begged, bouncing on her toes like she might actually take flight.

"That's not fair!" Sam protested, his lower lip jutting out in an adorable pout. "I wanted to give it to her!"

Their mom just laughed, patient but firm. "Hush now. You can both give the princess her gift." She gently guided their hands, and together they thrust the little paper-wrapped box into mine, their faces shining with pride.

"Thank you," I said, my voice thick with emotion. I had received many gifts since coming to Hekagia, but few had been delivered with such earnestness.

"Open it, please!" Caeli urged, her voice sweet and insistent. Her mother chided her again to behave, but I smiled, touched by her excitement.

I peeled back the wrapping paper, careful not to tear the delicate patterns pressed into it. "Did you make this paper yourself?" I asked, glancing between Caeli and Sam, genuinely amazed by the care in every detail. Their proud nods made my heart squeeze.

Inside the wrapping was a plain wooden box, its surface polished smooth by careful hands. I slid the top open, and my breath caught. A gold-plated brooch was nestled inside, its surface adorned with diamonds clustered in the shape of an oak tree: the ancient symbol of the House of Hale. Every stone was set with such care, it was like someone had poured all their hope and gratitude into this one small thing.

"It's beautiful!" I gasped, my voice coming out higher than I meant. I looked up, blinking fast, and caught Caeli's wide-eyed grin and Sam's proud, fidgety shuffle.

Their mother dipped into another curtsy, her cheeks flushed with pride. "We're glad you like it, Your Highness. It's from the whole town, for saving us from Raideron's creature. Without you, Iron Mountain might not have survived."

"You didn't have to do anything for me," I said, my voice soft and awkward. I could feel my cheeks heating up. "I only did what anyone would have done."

Caeli's mom shook her head, her eyes shining with that fierce, stubborn pride I'd come to recognize in Iron Mountain. "Maybe so, but we wanted to," she said. "Thanks to you, the village is thriving again. People have come back, and the mountain's open for mining. The diamonds in your brooch? They're from deep inside Iron Mountain."

I turned the brooch over in my palm, feeling the weight of it. "It's… incredible. Thank you so much," I said, my voice thick.

I meant it. This wasn't just a gift. It was a piece of their story, and now it was part of mine.

Caeli, who'd been bouncing on her toes the whole time, suddenly blurted, "I wonder—"

"Hush, not now!" her mother scolded, but there was no real bite to it.

I grinned at Caeli, nodding for her to go on. "What is it?"

"There had been talk in the village of us making your coronation crown, but the castle said no…" Her eyes were wide with hope as she peered up at me through thick lashes.

"Oh," I said, surprised and genuinely touched. "Well, I'm not sure who you spoke to at the castle, but I would be honored for Iron Mountain Village to make my crown. But only if you'll present it to me at the coronation."

Caeli's whole face lit up, her joy so bright it was contagious. "Really?" she squeaked.

Sam, not to be outdone, puffed up his chest. "Hey, what about me?" he demanded, his voice full of indignation.

"Of course, I meant both of you," I said, laughing. "As long as it's alright with your mom."

"We couldn't possibly, Your Highness," she said. "That's too great an honor for simple folk like us."

I shook my head, giving her my best "future-queen" smile. "It's definitely not. I'd love to have you all there."

"At your coronation?" she whispered, like she was afraid to believe it.

"Front row seats," I promised. "If you're lucky, you'll get to see me trip over my dress."

"But..." Her cheeks went bright red as she glanced down at her patched dress and the kids' scuffed boots. "We don't have anything nearly fancy enough to wear for a coronation."

I hadn't even thought of that. In all likelihood, the family had little more than the simple, homespun clothes on their backs—a badge of their hard work and resilience, but not what the court would expect.

"That's easy," I said, my smile going full sunshine. "Come to Vail Castle before the coronation. We'll get you all fitted for new clothes—whatever you want. You'll be my honored guests."

Sam's jaw dropped, Caeli squealed loudly, and their mom just stared at me like I'd handed her the moon. I felt lighter than I had in weeks—like maybe, just maybe, I was doing something right for once.

Caeli's mother swiped at her cheek with the back of her hand, beaming brightly. "The least we can do is see you well fed and rested, if you'll allow us?"

I glanced over my shoulder at Caleb and Earl. Caleb just shook his head, giving me that "we really need to move" look, and Earl offered a sympathetic shrug, already eyeing the sky like he was calculating the odds of us getting struck by lightning.

"I'm really sorry, but we should get going before the weather gets worse," I said with a grimace.

As if the world itself was listening, a bolt of lightning split the sky, so close it made my teeth rattle. Thunder crashed right after, shaking the ground under our boots. Hercules, who'd been circling above, swooped down in a flurry of rain-soaked feathers, landing with a dramatic spray of leaves.

Earl pulled his cloak tighter, his usual cheer gone. "I fear it may be too late," he said, just as fat raindrops started to fall.

"Then please, let us shelter you for the evening," Caeli's mom insisted, her voice fierce in that way only moms can manage. Around us, villagers nodded, some already ushering us toward the inn like they'd made up their minds for us.

We followed Caeli and Sam through the winding, cobbled streets. The inn was sturdier than I remembered—timber-framed, patched with fresh thatch, windows glowing like a promise. The sign above the door—a mountain and a golden griffin—swung wildly in the wind, creaking like it was laughing at us.

Inside, the place was nothing like the last time I'd seen it. Back then, the common room had been filled with sheep, the villagers desperate to keep their flock safe from Becky the Bat Lady's rampage. The smell had been… memorable, to say the least.

Now, the air was thick with the scent of roasting meat and fresh bread. Music floated through the room as a guy with a flute danced between tables, his tune so lively even the grumpiest farmer was tapping his foot.

The innkeeper—grumpy as ever, with eyebrows that could have swept the floor—met us at the door. For a second, he looked like he might shoo us off the porch, but then his eyes landed on me and softened. "Well, if it isn't the princess herself," he said, his voice still gravelly but with a smile hiding underneath. "Didn't expect to see you back here so soon."

I grinned, taking in the packed common room. The place was buzzing—villagers everywhere, some faces I recognized, others brand new. It was wild to think how much Iron Mountain had changed since last summer.

"Looks a bit different than the last time I was here," I said, unable to hide my amazement.

The innkeeper's chest puffed up with pride. "Aye, the village has come back strong. And we've got you to thank for that, whether you'll admit it or not."

I felt my cheeks go hot. "I didn't really do anything special," I mumbled, wishing I could melt into the floorboards.

He waved me off with a snort. "Don't be daft. That monster would've flattened us if you hadn't shown up. And then you sent all that coin—enough to fix the roofs and feed the whole town through winter. We owe you more than you know."

"I just did what I could."

The innkeeper just grinned, his eyes crinkling. "Well, we couldn't be more excited to see you crowned queen soon enough," he said, his voice booming over the chatter.

"That makes one of us," I muttered.

The innkeeper clapped his hands, already signaling to the kitchen. "You'll be wanting a hot meal, I expect?"

"Honestly?" I said, rubbing my eyes, "I think I just want to collapse somewhere and sleep for a week."

The innkeeper gave a sharp whistle, and an elderly woman—her gray hair pulled back in a neat bun, her hands still clutching a damp rag—looked up from where she was wiping down tables.

"Claudette, come show the royal family to their rooms," the innkeeper called, his voice carrying over the music and chatter.

Claudette snapped her rag over one shoulder, fixed me with a sharp look, and marched over. "Well, don't just stand there gawking, Your Highness," she said, her voice surprisingly loud for someone who barely reached my shoulder. "I won't have you tracking mud all over my clean floors. Follow me, and mind your boots!"

The room went silent at the innkeeper's mention of our arrival. Even the flute player froze, his cheeks puffed mid-note. Every eye in the inn was on Caleb and me. Then the silence shattered into cheers and applause.

The flute player grinned and launched into a wild, celebratory tune, and the inn was suddenly alive again—music, laughter, and the unmistakable sound of Claudette muttering about "royals and their muddy boots".

But out of the corner of my eye, I caught a figure moving against the tide of villagers. He was tall, wrapped in black robes that seemed to swallow the candlelight, and he moved with eerie, practiced smoothness. He kept his head down, hood pulled low, and before I could blink, he'd slipped out the door and vanished into the storm. The sight sent a jolt of unease through me, like a cold hand on the back of my neck.

I nudged the innkeeper, nodding toward the door. "Who was that?" I asked, trying to sound casual.

He followed my gaze, his bushy brows knitting together. "I'm not sure," he said, his voice low and wary. "Never seen him around here before." There was a note of concern in his tone, as if he too sensed that the stranger's presence was out of place.

Claudette, who'd been waiting at the foot of the stairs, gave me a gentle (but insistent) nudge. "Up you go, Your Highness. No use fretting over shadows when there's a warm bed waiting for you."

As we climbed, the music and laughter faded behind us, replaced by the creak of old wood and the cozy scent of lavender and hearth smoke. I tried to let myself relax, grateful for the shelter and the kindness of these people. But even as Claudette fussed over the turn-down service and Caleb cracked a joke about "royal treatment," I couldn't shake the image of that stranger slipping away into the rain. It was a reminder that the world outside was still watching, and not everyone wanted me here.

The room smelled like pine resin and old dust, just like I remembered. I barely managed to kick off my boots before faceplanting onto the feather bed, too tired to care about anything except the thick wool blanket at my feet. I yanked it over me, letting its weight press me down, and for a moment, I just listened to the muffled laughter and music drifting up from the commons. It was almost enough to make me forget about mysterious strangers and looming destinies.

I must've been asleep for all of five seconds when a sharp, no-nonsense knock came at the door. I jolted upright, hitting my head on the low ceiling above the bed.

"What is it?" I croaked out as I rubbed my forehead.

"Up you get, Princess." Claudette's voice called, brisk and unbothered. There's a man downstairs says he needs to speak to you, urgent like."

My heart skipped a beat. Who would be asking to see me in the middle of the night? For a wild moment, my thoughts leapt to Treander, but that was impossible.

Caleb's voice echoed from the hallway, grumpy and groggy. "What's going on? Somebody better be dying."

I wrapped my blanket around my shoulders and cracked open the door. Claudette stood there, arms on her hips, looking like she'd much rather be scrubbing floors than dealing with royal drama.

Earl shuffled through the hallway, looking like he'd been dragged out of bed by a herd of stampeding sheep. "It's the middle of the night, madam," he said irritably. "Who in their right mind wants an audience at this hour? Unless they've discovered the cure to foot fungus, I suggest they wait for breakfast."

Claudette snorted. "If it were up to me, I'd have sent him packing. But he says he's family, and he's not leaving till he's seen you. Old fellow. Looks like he's wrestled a few bears in his day."

Caleb frowned, rubbing sleep from his eyes. "Family? We don't have any old men left, do we? Unless you count dad."

"Just one," I replied uneasily.

Caleb's eyebrows shot up. "You don't actually think he'd show up here, do you?"

I shrugged. "Guess we're about to find out. Can you send him up, Claudette?"

She rolled her eyes. "Fine. But if he starts any trouble, you're cleaning up the mess, not me." With that, she stomped off, muttering under her breath.

I glanced at Caleb and Earl, my nerves jangling. "Well, this should be interesting."

A short time later, heavy footsteps creaked up the stairs and a figure in a thick wool cloak appeared, moving with a kind of stubborn purpose. When he pulled down his hood, a shock of grey hair caught the candlelight.

"You!" Caleb's voice was raw. His fists clenched, and before I could even blink, vines shot from the walls.

Claudette wasn't going to be happy about the damage...

"Caleb, stop!" Earl shouted as he grabbed Caleb's arm, surprisingly quick for someone in a nightgown.

Alastair stepped into the light, his face gaunt, eyes shadowed. "It's alright. Let him be," he said, voice rough as gravel. "It's no more than I deserve."

Caleb clenched his fists so tightly that his knuckles went white. "I'll be the judge of that," he snapped, his voice shaking with fury. "You're the reason Grandma's dead."

The accusation hung heavily in the air.

"Enough, Caleb," I said, forcing my voice to stay steady even as my insides twisted. I had no love for Alastair, but I knew he wouldn't have risked showing his face after three years unless it was for something big. "Why are you here?" I asked, my gaze searching his face for any sign of the man who had once been family.

Caleb scoffed, his glare sharp enough to cut glass. "Who cares why he's here? He's got nothing to say that I want to hear." He looked like he was ready to throw a punch, every muscle in his body coiled tight.

Alastair looked like he'd aged a decade since I'd last seen him. His shoulders sagged, and the guilt in his eyes was almost painful to look at. "I came to warn you," he said, his voice rough and tired, like he hadn't slept in days.

"Warn us about what?" I asked, studying him. The last time I'd seen him, he'd handed me over to Raideron, all to put Kira on the throne. It was hard to believe that he wanted to help us now.

Alastair must've seen the wariness in my eyes. "I know what you're thinking," he said, his voice trembling. "How could I have done what I did…"

I cut him off, my words sharp. "Actually, I don't care why you betrayed me. That's just a normal Tuesday at this point. What I don't get is how you could side with Raideron after what he did to Grandma. I thought you loved her. Was any of it real?"

"I did… I still do!" he said, his voice breaking. "More than anything in this world and any other."

Caleb's anger faltered, replaced by something raw and wounded. "Then why?" he choked out. "How could you do that to her? To us?"

Alastair looked down, his hands trembling. "You have no idea the pull Raideron's magic has. It taps into your darkest thoughts, manipulates you into doing his bidding."

My temper snapped. "That's not good enough," I shot back. "We all have darkness inside us. But we don't all let it win."

Alastair nodded, his expression hollow. "I know there's nothing I can say to make it right. I'm not here to ask for forgiveness. I just want to help—if you'll let me."

"Why now?" I asked, suspicion threading through my voice.

He seemed to shrink, the weight of his shame almost physical. "After the safe house… I couldn't face any of you. But while I was gone, I learned things. Raideron's plans. I know what he's going to do next."

Caleb let out a bitter laugh. Vines crept along the walls, the air thick with the scent of earth and magic—his magic, barely under control. "Yeah, I bet you know things," he growled at Alastair.

Earl, who'd been quietly fiddling with a vial of something suspiciously purple, stepped between them, arms outstretched like he was about to break up a brawl. "Whoa, whoa, whoa! Let's not redecorate the place with vine wallpaper, Caleb." He winked, but his eyes were serious. "Let's hear the man out before we start the fireworks, yeah?"

Alastair's gaze flicked to Earl, sizing him up like he couldn't decide if Earl was a threat or just plain weird. "And you are?" he asked, voice rough.

Earl grinned, bowing with a flourish that sent a few potion bottles clinking. "Earl. Master alchemist, chaos wrangler, and—if I may be so bold—the only adult in the room who hasn't tried to sell out their grandkids to a dark lord."

Alastair's jaw clenched, but he didn't look away. "You think you know what it means to protect a family?" he said, voice low. "You have no idea what I've lost."

Earl's usual grin faded, and for once, the twinkle in his eyes was gone. "Trust me, lad, I know loss. I've bottled it, labeled it, and shelved it next to regret. But here's the thing—making more of it never fixed a single thing." His voice was gentle, but there was a warning in it.

"Just tell us why you're here already," Caleb demanded.

Alastair looked up, meeting Caleb's glare head-on. There was shame there, sure, but something stubborn too. "You have every right to hate me, Caleb. I've been a lousy grandfather. But I'm here because I want to make it right. Or at least try to."

Caleb's fists were clenched at his sides, and his voice was sharp when he spoke. "Yeah? And what does 'making it right' even mean to you?" he asked Alastair.

Alastair's eyes darkened, his posture sharpening. "Hopefully, to warn you in time. Raideron is planning to attack the day after tomorrow. He means to destroy Vail."

CHAPTER NINETEEN

REVELATIONS

Whatever I'd been expecting Alastair to say, it definitely wasn't that. Given the gravity of the situation, we'd moved down to the commons. The inn was quiet except for the four of us and Claudette, who hovered near the door to the kitchen. We sat around a small wooden table in awkward silence. The only sound was the crackle of the fire.

"What do you mean, Raideron's going to destroy Vail?" I asked Alastair, breaking the silence.

His face was grim, the lines on his weathered face seeming to deepen. "I overheard some of Raideron's soldiers talking about a new weapon that can decimate entire towns," he said, his voice low. "As soon as Germaine told me you were here, I knew I had to warn you."

That's when I noticed the shadowy figure behind Alastair. The same man I'd glimpsed earlier—tall, thin, face mostly hidden by a deep hood. All I could see was a pale jawline, a hint of stubble, and sharp, glowing eyes.

"I wish I could say it's nice to meet you, but under the circumstances, I'm not sure I can," I said to the man Germaine.

He gave a bow, somehow both polite and creepy, then shot Alastair a look and slinked back into the shadows. The way he moved, too smooth and too quiet, sent a chill down my spine.

Alastair watched him, mouth set in a grim line. "You'll have to pardon my friend," he said.

"Not the most talkative guy, is he?" I asked.

Alastair shrugged apologetically. "Well, no. But he is part demon, after all."

That landed like a bomb.

Earl went rigid. "I'm sorry, did you say demon?" His voice was still light, but there was a dangerous glint in his eyes. "Because if you brought one of those infernal creatures here, Alastair, I'm going to need a very good reason not to turn you both into frogs."

Alastair held up his hands in a placating gesture. "Germaine is half human. He's a good man... mostly."

Earl let out a long, theatrical sigh, shaking his head. "Well, this just got interesting. Next thing you know, we'll have banshees in the pantry and a basilisk in the bath." But then his gaze sharpened, all jokes gone. "What have you done, Alastair?"

Caleb's voice shot up an octave. "Can we go back to the part where demons are real? Because I feel like that should've come up before now."

I nodded in agreement, my brain spinning like a top. Demons? In Hekagia? I'd just gotten used to spellcasters and griffins, and now we were adding demons to the mix? Was there a punch card for this stuff?

"They aren't the kind of demon you're probably picturing," Alastair said as he shot a look at Germaine. "They come from the astral plane."

"So, not the fire-and-brimstone, pitchfork-waving kind?" I asked, trying to make sense of it all.

"No," Alastair said, shaking his head. "But their powers are stronger than most astral spellcasters, and let's just say their moral compass doesn't tend to point north."

Earl piped up. "And yet you brought one here?" His voice was unusually sharp, and there was a wild glint in his eyes. "I hope you at least made him check his claws at the door, Alastair."

"Germaine is not like other demons I have encountered," Alastair insisted. "He wishes to return to the astral plane, and he holds no loyalty to Raideron. In fact, he's worked as a spy against him for some time now. That's how we met."

Despite Alastair's reassurances, Germaine still gave me the creeps. But there were bigger things to worry about. I forced my voice steady, even though my nerves were strung tight as a bowstring. "Alright. Tell us what you know about Raideron's plan."

Alastair drew in a long, deliberate breath, his hands folded neatly in his lap. "It was Germaine who discovered it actually," he said. "Demons, you see, possess hearing far superior to our own." He tried for a smile, but it came out more like a grimace—like he wasn't sure he deserved to smile at all.

Earl perked up. "Oh, I've always said it's the ears you have to watch out for. Never trust a man with pointy ones, I say." He grinned, but his eyes were sharp, tracking every word.

Alastair didn't even blink at Earl's interruption. "We were in Halvenor," he began, his voice stiff, "a rather disreputable tavern on the edge of nowhere. Raideron's soldiers barged in—full of bluster, as usual. Germaine and I kept to ourselves. Or tried to, at any rate. It's difficult to be inconspicuous when your companion is half-demon."

Earl snorted. "Bet they didn't try to throw you out, though."

Alastair's lips twitched. "They did not. I suspect they feared Germaine might liquefy them if they tried."

"Is that actually something he can do?" I asked.

Caleb rolled his eyes, leaning forward with his elbows on the table. "Can we skip the horror stories and get to the point? What did the soldiers say?"

Alastair's eyes lost what little light they'd had. He nodded, clearing his throat, and when he spoke again, his words were heavy. "After a few pints of Halvenorian ale, their tongues loosened. Raideron is gathering his forces. He means to strike Vail, killing every man, woman, and child. I do not know what this new weapon is, but I assure you, it is something nefarious."

I studied Alastair's face, searching for any sign he was lying. But all I saw was regret, deep and raw. "You're sure?" I asked, my voice barely above a whisper. "Two days?"

He nodded, eyes dark and grim. "I am certain."

I turned to Earl, my throat tight. "Do you think he has the Obsidian Firestone?"

Earl's mouth tightened, silently warning me not to say too much with Alastair listening. "I'm sure we would know if Raideron had obtained the stone," he said quietly.

"But what about Kira and Ravenna? If anything's happened to them…" I shuddered involuntarily.

At the mention of Kira, Alastair's face seemed to crumple, pain etching deeper lines into his features. "How is she?" he asked, his voice barely more than a whisper.

I hesitated, but my tone softened despite myself. "Kira's doing well. She's found someone she adores, and her powers grow stronger every day."

A flicker of relief rippled across his face—a brief, unguarded moment that made him look older, more fragile. For all his mistakes, it was clear he still cared about the family he'd lost.

"I don't know if Kira will want to see you," I said quietly, "but I'll tell her that you're here."

Alastair's shoulders sagged, and he looked older than ever. "Thank you, Amira. You are… too kind."

Caleb let out a dramatic sigh. "Tell me about it," he muttered, leaning back in his chair with his arms crossed.

I took a breath, trying to push past the awkward. "There's another way you can help us."

Alastair straightened, just a little. "I'll do anything I can."

"We need to get back to the academy as fast as possible. Can you portal us there?"

Caleb groaned loud enough to earn a scolding look from Claudette. "I can't take another portal jump." He rubbed his temples, still looking a little seasick from the last time we'd been tossed through magical currents like laundry in a spin cycle.

Alastair turned to me, his brow furrowing in confusion. "Are you not able to summon your own portals?" His voice wasn't mean, just genuinely puzzled, like he couldn't quite believe I wasn't up to snuff.

My astral magic was still a mess—barely enough for a spark, let alone a full-blown portal. But no way was I admitting that to my estranged grandfather, not when I still wasn't sure if I could trust him. I just shook my head, hoping he'd let it go.

Alastair watched me for a long moment, his face shadowed and unreadable. "I see," he said at last, his voice low and a little tired. Maybe he was disappointed, or maybe he just didn't want to push. Either way, he didn't say anything else about it.

Alastair got up from his seat, moving with stiff, old-fashioned dignity. He lifted his hands in concentration, and a swirling portal bloomed open.

The air glowed with violet light, and through it, I could see the academy's front doors—solid, familiar, and impossibly far away just moments before.

"You must go quickly," Alastair said, urgency sharpening his voice. "Raideron will sense the portal any moment now."

"Thank you for telling us about his plan," I said, my gratitude genuine despite my lingering doubts about Alastair's loyalty.

"It was the least I could do," he replied, his words heavy with regret. "I have much to atone for."

Earl, who'd been quiet for once, gave a little bow, his golden robes swirling. "Well, if you ever get bored of skulking in shadows, Alastair, you're always welcome to join me for tea."

Alastair almost smiled, but it faded fast. "I fear my days of tea and leisure are long past, Master Earl."

"Won't Raideron find you now?" I asked, nodding at the swirling portal.

Alastair straightened, his old pride flickering for a moment. "Germaine will hide us. It is one of his gifts, being… what he is. Now, go. Quickly."

"Come on, Caleb," I said, turning to my brother.

Caleb hesitated, biting his lip, his eyes darting between me and the portal.

"What's wrong?"

"I'm not going with you," he said, his voice barely above a whisper.

"Don't be ridiculous. Of course you're coming with," I insisted, panic rising in my chest.

But Caleb shook his head, his jaw set in that stubborn way that meant he'd already made up his mind. "I have to go see the Hakuturi. If anyone can fix my patu, it's them. And… I need time. Losing Josiah—"

He broke off and cleared his throat gruffly. A shadow of pain crept across his face, and in that moment, he looked so much older than fifteen.

I hated it. I hated the idea of being separated again, but I could see there was no talking him out of it.

"Be careful," I whispered, pulling him into a fierce hug.

"Never," he whispered back, and I could feel his crooked smile against my shoulder.

"You're impossible," I muttered, blinking away tears.

Earl, who'd been quietly watching, gave Caleb a little wave. "Try not to get eaten by anything big and hairy. And if you do, at least take notes for me, would you?"

"No promises," Caleb replied with a grin.

With one last look at my brother, I stepped into the portal. The familiar, stomach-clenching sensation swept over me. I closed my eyes and braced for the spinning as the world shifted beneath my feet once again.

I was halfway through a yawn so big it could've unhinged my jaw when Alastair piped up. "You should leave now too," he said in a low voice.

The room felt emptier than a school cafeteria after finals—Amira and Earl had vanished through the portal so it was just me and the family traitor, marinating in awkward silence.

I rubbed my eyes, trying not to look as tired as I felt. "I think I'll wait until morning," I muttered.

Alastair's face pinched up, all tight lips and thundercloud eyebrows. He glanced at the window nervously. "Raideron is watching the portals," he said, his voice low and urgent. "He will know we've opened one. He might come to investigate."

"Great. Just what I need, Raideron popping in for a midnight snack. Maybe he'll bring cookies," I quipped.

But even I had to admit, the old man had a point. Raideron's spies were everywhere, and I'd rather not get caught napping by the world's creepiest villain.

With a groan, I started shoving my stuff into my pack. We'd barely been in Iron Mountain Village long enough for Hercules to find a decent scratching post, so it didn't take long.

Alastair was waiting for me in the hallway, hovering like a guilt trip in human form. "What now?" I grumbled.

He hesitated, then cleared his throat. "I could open another portal for you," he offered, almost like he was trying to be helpful for once. "It would be safer than traveling alone. I could… even come with you, if you'd like?"

I snorted. "Yeah, because nothing says 'safe' like traveling with the guy who sold us out to our biggest enemy. Thanks, but I'll take my chances with Hercules. At least he only bites when he's hungry."

Alastair's mouth twitched, like he wasn't sure if he should laugh or be angry at me for disrespecting him. "Suit yourself," he said, his voice suddenly wary. "Just be careful, Caleb."

For a second, I almost felt sorry for Alastair. Almost. But then I remembered everything he'd done, and the moment passed.

"Don't worry," I said, slinging my pack over my shoulder and heading for the door. "I always am."

I headed down the stairs, my boots thudding on every creaky board. The inn was quiet, except for the innkeeper and Claudette poking at the last of the embers like she was trying to keep the night alive a little longer.

The innkeeper spotted me and raised his eyebrows. "Leaving so soon, Prince Caleb?"

I flashed him a grin. "Yeah, you know how it is. Evil overlords don't defeat themselves. Besides, if I stay any longer, Hercules might eat your pillows."

That got a smile out of him.

"Can I offer you some food for your travels?" he asked, but before I could answer, Claudette zipped behind the counter and came back with a loaf of bread so fresh it was still steaming. My stomach growled so loud I thought the rafters might shake.

"You wouldn't happen to have any meat back there too… would you?" I asked innocently.

Claudette nodded and vanished into the back. She came out with a slab of mutton so big it could've fed a small army—or, more importantly, one very hungry griffin. She started to wrap it up all neat, but I waved her off. "Hercules will appreciate it as is," I said. No point in wasting good parchment on a meal that's gonna disappear in two bites.

I was halfway to the door, bread and mutton in hand, when Alastair materialized out of the shadows.

"A word before you leave, Caleb."

"Seriously? What now? You want to give me a bedtime story, or is this another guilt trip special?"

He stepped closer and shook his head. "Just a word. That's all," he said in a resigned voice.

I shifted the bread under my arm, ready to bolt if he started in on the "family legacy" speech. "Make it quick, old man. I've got a griffin to feed and a world to save."

Alastair just stood there, looking like he'd aged another ten years. His hands kind of flailed, like he was searching for words in his pockets and coming up empty. "I'm... sorry," he said, voice rough. "We never even got to know each other. That's my fault."

I didn't let him off easy. "Yeah, well, I'm glad I didn't get to know you," I shot back, my words sharp. "You're a bitter old man and you basically killed my grandma, who I did love. She's gone, and it's your fault."

He winced—like I'd actually managed to hit something under all that armor. But it was too little, too late. Amira might be a big softie—she'd probably find a way to forgive him, because that's just who she is. But me? Never.

"If I ever see you again, you won't have to worry about Raideron finding you—I'll kill you myself," I growled.

I didn't wait for him to reply. I stormed out of the inn, slamming the door so hard the windows rattled. Outside, the rain was coming down in sheets, like the sky was trying to drown me for dramatic effect. My boots squished in the mud, my cloak was already soaked, but I just kept going, fists jammed in my pockets, head down.

I tried not to think about the look on Alastair's face when I left him standing there. I should've maybe felt something—anger or relief, or at least a little satisfaction for finally telling him off. But mostly? I just felt empty. Like all the stuff I'd been carrying around inside had finally leaked out.

By the time I found Hercules, I was shivering so hard my teeth were doing Morse code. He was hunkered down under this massive old oak, feathers all puffed up like he was trying to out-brood the weather. He looked up when he saw me, those big golden eyes full of that weird, ancient griffin wisdom.

"Hey, buddy," I said, trying to sound normal. I tossed him the mutton, and he inhaled it in one bite. Then, before I could even blink, he licked my hand—rough and warm, like sandpaper, but somehow it made everything feel a little less awful. I snorted. "Yeah, yeah, I know. I'm a disaster. Don't tell anyone."

Hercules made a low, rumbly sound, then wrapped his wings

around me. Like, in a full-on griffin hug. I just stood there, letting the rain soak through my cloak, pretending it was only the weather making my face all wet.

If anyone asked, I'll blame the storm. But for a few minutes, it was just me and him, the world shut out, and I let myself breathe. Maybe I even shed a tear or two. Whatever.

Eventually, the rain eased up, and so did the tight feeling in my chest. Hercules nudged me, like, "Alright, drama queen, let's get moving." I climbed onto his back, still shaking, but it felt better. Up in the sky, wind in my face, the world spread out below us. I wasn't fixed, not even close, but at least I could keep going. And that was enough.

"Sleep now," Hercules said in that deep, rumbly voice that only I could hear in my head.

I snorted. "Yeah, right. Who just knocks out on a flying griffin? That's how you end up as a pancake on the ground, Herc."

"I won't let you fall. Sleep."

I wanted to argue—because, come on, I'm not exactly the "trust fall" type—but my eyelids felt like they had bricks tied to them. "If I wake up in a tree, I'm blaming you," I mumbled, already half asleep.

Hercules just rumbled again, warm and steady, and tucked his wings in a little tighter around me. I let myself relax, just a bit. Maybe everything was a mess, but at least my griffin had my back. And if I drooled on his feathers, well… he'd never tell.

My head still felt foggy from… well, everything. The sun hid behind a thick layer of clouds, but there was just enough light to see the Aether Woods below us—what was left of them, anyway. The trees looked like blackened skeletons, all burnt and twisted. Somewhere down there, something shrieked loud enough to make my skin crawl, and I felt Hercules tense up beneath me. He let out a deep roar and dropped down below the tree line, wings slicing through the cold morning air.

Chief Tara was already waiting for us when we landed. I had no clue how she knew we were coming—maybe Amira sent her a message, or maybe the Hakuturi had built-in radar. Either way, she stood there, tall and proud. When she bowed, her blue wings stretched out wide. "Prince Caleb," she squawked, "It has been a long time. It is good to see you again."

"Good to see you too, Chief Tara," I said.

"The world has changed since you last walked these woods." She glanced around, her gaze lingering on the empty paths and shuttered huts. "We have lost much. Raideron's shadow grows, even now."

The place was too quiet. It was weird.

I mean, I wasn't expecting a parade or anything, but I thought maybe my arrival would get a little more attention. Amira's definitely would have.

Instead, it was just me, Hercules, and Chief Tara. "So, uh… where is everybody? Did I miss the memo about a secret party?"

Chief Tara's eyes scanned the empty paths like she was counting ghosts. When she spoke, her voice was soft, but there was steel underneath. "The Hakuturi march for Vail Castle at dawn. Some are preparing, but many have already been lost."

I swallowed hard, feeling like a jerk for expecting a welcome wagon. "Sorry. I didn't know," I said quietly.

She cocked her head, birdlike and unreadable. "Why have you come, Caleb?"

I shifted, suddenly wishing I'd just gone with Amira. "Actually, I was hoping you could fix my patu. It, uh… sort of broke." I fished the splintered pieces out of my bag, holding them out like a kid showing off a failed science project. "Guess it wasn't as indestructible as advertised."

Chief Tara's eyes narrowed, her feathers bristling. "That should not have been possible. It was forged to withstand nearly anything."

"Yeah, well, emphasis on nearly," I said, trying for a grin but mostly failing. "Raideron happened."

That was all I needed to say. Her feathers puffed up and she let out a low, angry squawk—the kind that made me really glad she was on our side.

Tara didn't waste time. She turned and beckoned me to follow, her steps silent and sure. We stopped at a hut that smelled like metal and magic. The Hakuturi didn't use fire thanks to Raideron, so the forge glowed with swirling sparks of magic, like embers caught in a whirlwind.

A young Hakuturi woman worked the bellows, her massive red wings fanning the magical flames. She wore brown safety goggles that made her look like a cross between a mad scientist and a steampunk owl. She nodded at Chief Tara when we walked in, but didn't stop what she was doing.

Chief Tara let out a sharp squawk that nearly made me jump out of my boots. "Piper, this is Prince Caleb. He is in need of a sword."

I threw up my hands, nearly dropping the pieces of my patu. "Whoa, whoa, no swords for me, thanks!" I said. "I was actually hoping you could fix my patu."

Chief Tara's big black eyes blinked at me, and for a second, I thought she might actually laugh. "The last time we met, you were disappointed in my gift."

I scratched the back of my neck, trying to look anywhere but at her. "Yeah, well, turns out I was an idiot. My patu's awesome. Is there any way you can fix it?"

Piper stopped flapping her wings and let out a dramatic sigh. She wiped her hands on her soot-stained apron and yanked off her giant goggles. "Hand it over, then," she said, her voice flat and a little annoyed.

"No pressure, but my griffin's counting on me to not die, so… y'know. If you could work your magic, that'd be great."

Piper barely glanced at my patu. "I can fix this, no problem."

"For real?"

"Yes," she squawked, rolling her eyes. "But are you sure you wouldn't rather have a magical sword? Much better than a patu, in my opinion."

I grinned, shaking my head. "Nah, my patu and I go way back. Besides, swords are for people who just want to look cool. I want to kick some astral monster butt." I tried to sound all casual, but I probably just sounded like a sentimental dork.

Still, I meant it. Some things you just don't trade in, no matter how shiny the alternative.

Piper shrugged. "Suit yourself."

"So, uh, how long is this gonna take?"

Piper scooped up the busted pieces of wood and chucked them into forge. Instantly, the red-hot energy flared, and my patu—my trusty, loyal, been-through-everything-with-me patu—turned to cinders in a blink.

"What the—?!" I yelped, nearly diving in after it.

Tara blocked me with her wing. "Just wait," she clucked.

Easy for her to say—she wasn't watching her favorite weapon go up in flames. Literally.

Piper poked the ashes with a pair of giant tongs, then pulled out a jar of green sludge that looked like something I'd find under my bed after a month of not cleaning.

"What is that?" I asked, trying not to gag.

"Trust me, you don't want to know," Piper said, not even looking up. Chief Tara nodded in agreement.

So then I waited. And waited. And waited some more.

Just when I was about to give up, Piper let out a squawk that sounded like an angry chicken. Then she reached into the forge and pulled out my patu. It looked... perfect. Like it had never been broken at all! Piper handed it to me and I turned it over in my hands, half-expecting it to fall apart. But nope—it was solid, warm, and somehow even better than before.

"Thanks!" I said with a grin.

Piper just waved me off, already elbow-deep in some new project. "You're welcome. Now go away," she said.

Chief Tara ruffled her feathers and gave me that classic Hakuturi stare—serious and steady, like she could see straight through me. "I shall accompany you to the academy now." Not a question. More like a royal decree.

And let's be real, I wasn't about to argue with a seven-foot-tall bird chief.

"Uh, are you sure?" I asked, trying not to sound too eager. How cool would it be to show up at the academy with Chief Tara at my side? Maybe Naomi would even be there to see it...

Tara nodded. "It is on my way to Vail Castle."

I shot her a grin. "Well, I guess we're a team now."

She didn't answer, just started walking, feathers settling back into place. When Chief Tara decides something, you just go with it. I hustled after her, patu in hand, feeling pretty epic.

CHAPTER TWENTY

A SIREN'S PROMISE

The palace walls were carved from mother-of-pearl and veined with coral that glowed a faint blue. It was actually kind of pretty, if I ignored the fact that my lungs were starting to burn.

The Gill Draught was wearing off, and I was not about to be the first princess in history to drown in a hallway, so I powered through, sticking close to Klerope as she zipped ahead.

"You sure you know where you're going?" I snapped, not even trying to hide how done I was with this whole underwater maze. My patience was running on fumes, and every twisty, glowing hallway just made me itchier. I hated not being in control, hated feeling like a fish out of water—literally. This place was so far out of my comfort zone, it might as well have been on another planet.

Klerope shot me a look over her shoulder—sharp, bossy, the kind of look that said she enjoyed being in charge, even if she pretended otherwise. "This way—quickly!" she whispered, her voice tight. I rolled my eyes but followed her. No point arguing with someone who actually knew the layout.

Gnash swam beside me, looking about as graceful as a walrus in a tutu. "Gnash not like this place," he grumbled.

Hard to disagree with that.

"Where is everyone?" I muttered, scanning the empty halls. The place was deserted, but I could feel eyes on us.

Thalior swam up, his trident clenched tightly like he was just waiting for something to go wrong. "They're hiding," he said, his voice low and bitter. "Narissa's gotten worse since Raideron started whispering in her ear. She's crueler than ever."

One of the rebel sirens—a wiry girl with a scar that looked like it had an interesting story—nodded in agreement. "Just last week Narissa turned her own handmaiden into a tuna fish and served her for dinner. All because the poor girl forgot to curtsy."

"Great. Remind me not to forget my manners," I muttered, earning a snort from Gnash.

We rounded a corner and Klerope suddenly threw out her arm, stopping so fast that I crashed into her. "Wait," she whispered.

I heard it too—voices, echoing through the vaulted corridor, warped from the water.

Thalior peered around the gilded archway, then ducked back. "Two guards. Right outside the throne room."

I clenched my fists, frustration bubbling up. "We can't just stand here and twiddle our thumbs. If those guards spot us, we're toast."

Gnash hefted his satchel, grinning like this was the best part of his day. "Gnash smash?" he offered.

Klerope grimaced. "No. They're just doing their jobs. We need to take them out quietly—no bloodshed."

"And how exactly do you suggest we do that?" I asked, my voice full of sarcasm. "I left my bag of sleeping powder in my other jacket."

Gnash rummaged in his satchel and pulled out a handful of smooth, heavy pebbles. "Gnash bring rocks," he said, beaming like he'd just solved all the worlds problems.

"No wonder you were swimming like a drunken whale," I muttered, but I couldn't help a small smile. "You planning to knock them out with those?"

He nodded. "Gnash has good aim."

I raised an eyebrow. "Really? Because if you miss, we're all shark food."

His smile faltered and he looked down sheepishly. "Gnash try his best..."

Thalior stepped forward. "I'll do it," he said.

Klerope nodded, her trust in Thalior clear. "Do it quickly," she whispered. "We'll only get one shot."

I pressed my back to the wall, every sense on high alert. This was it—the moment that would decide if we made it to the throne room or ended up as Narissa's next seafood special.

Gnash clutched his rocks like they were treasure, his eyes wide as he looked around. "Get ready to move," I whispered to him, my voice low and sharp. "If this goes sideways, we bolt. No heroics, got it?"

He grunted in response, clearly disappointed.

Thalior crept to the corner, pebbles in hand, moving with silent, deadly precision. I held my breath, counting the seconds, every muscle tensed to run or fight. Then, with a flick of his wrist, he sent the stones flying. There was a muffled thud, a startled grunt, and then—nothing.

"All clear," Thalior called back.

Klerope let out a shaky breath, relief all over her face. "Well done, my love," she said.

I rolled my eyes at the duo, but secretly I was glad that we didn't have to fight our way out.

With the rebel sirens at our backs, we swam up to the throne room doors—massive, warped, and covered in barnacles, like the sea itself was trying to keep us out.

Klerope looked over at me, her eyes wide with a mix of nerves and hope. "Are you ready?"

I glanced back at the rebels—half of them looked like they'd barely survived puberty, let alone a coup. They were staring at me like I was supposed to have some brilliant plan. Typical.

"Ready as I'll ever be," I said. "Let's take her down."

Together, we shoved the door open.

The throne room was ridiculous—pearl walls, gold everywhere, and a floor so shiny I could see my own scowl reflected back at me. At the far end, Queen Narissa lounged on her throne like she was bored, crown gleaming, one guard feeding her sardines like she was some pampered housecat. A harpist played in the corner, the music wobbly and off-key in the water.

The harpist caught sight of us and froze, the music dying with a discordant twang. Every head in the room turned. Narissa's gaze landed on me, cold but amused.

"So, you managed to escape," she said, her voice echoing off the pearl walls. She didn't even bother to stand.

I shrugged, letting my sarcasm do the talking. "Wasn't exactly hard. You might want to invest in better locks—or at least guards who aren't asleep at the trident."

Narissa's eyes narrowed, but she didn't rise to the bait. "To be fair, it appears you had some help." She turned her glare on Klerope and Thalior, her voice sharpening. "You two will be executed for your treason."

Klerope lifted her chin, voice ringing out stronger than I'd ever heard it. "You're the one who's betrayed *us*, Narissa. By siding with Raideron, you've turned your back on siren-kind."

A shockwave rolled through the throne room—like someone had just dropped a shark in the middle of a school of guppies. I caught the flicker of doubt on the faces of Narissa's courtiers and guards—tails twitching, eyes darting, everyone suddenly realizing maybe the queen wasn't as perfect as she liked to pretend.

For a split second, Narissa's perfect icy mask cracked. But then she pulled herself together, lips curling into a sneer as she straightened her crown.

"The land dwellers have never cared about us," Narissa scoffed as she addressed the court. "Why should we care what happens to them? Raideron offered me power and I took it to help our people."

I snorted at that.

Klerope wasn't having it. Her tail lashed out, sharp and angry. "No. You did it to help yourself."

"Narissa's eyes narrowed. "So what is this, mutiny? Treason!" She waved a sharp hand at the rebel sirens fanning out behind us, forming a perimeter around her and her hulking guards.

Klerope swam right up onto the dais, bold as anything, and turned to face the whole room. Her voice rang out, clear and strong. "This isn't a mutiny. As next in line, I challenge Narissa, Queen of the Sirens. You have failed our people for the last time."

The room erupted in whispers—some sirens nodding, others looking like they might faint. I could feel the tide turning, and for the first time, real fear flashed in Narissa's eyes.

"How dare you!" she hissed, shooting up from her throne in a swirl of golden hair and angry bubbles. "After all I've done for you?"

Klerope scoffed, flicking her tail. "All you've done for me? You mean treating me like garbage my whole life?"

Narissa reached for her trident, her voice dripping with venom. "Clearly, I didn't do a good enough job putting you in your place. But don't worry, that will soon be rectified."

She lunged at Klerope, trident flashing. But Klerope was

faster—she dodged with a flick of her tail, then, with a move so smooth it looked rehearsed, she knocked the trident from Narissa's grip. It clattered to the pearl floor, spinning away.

"Is that the best you can do, Nessie? Really?" Klerope taunted.

"Don't call me that!" Narissa shrieked, diving for her trident like a spoiled kid going after a stolen toy.

But Klerope was done playing. In a blur, she pinned Narissa to the cold, polished floor with her own trident.

The queen thrashed, crown crooked, but Klerope held her fast, fierce and unyielding.

"Enough, Narissa. It is over." Klerope's voice was steady and commanding, nothing like the meek girl I'd first met.

The throne room went silent. Even the water felt like it was holding its breath. All those sirens—rebels, courtiers, guards—just stared, waiting to see if Klerope would actually finish what she started. If it were me, I'd have ended it right there. Narissa was slipperier than an oiled eel, and the palace was still crawling with loyalists. But Klerope hesitated, her trident wavering.

Just as I was about to yell at Klerope to get on with it, a sharp, familiar screech echoed through the room. The currents exploded into a chaotic swirl of bubbles. Olivia materialized out of nowhere, her red hair blazing like a warning sign.

"Took you long enough," Narissa grunted, still pinned beneath Klerope's trident.

Olivia's lips curling into a smirk. "I came as soon as I heard."

"You're too late," Klerope replied, her voice stiff but proud. "Narissa agreed to my challenge and I defeated her fairly."

Olivia's eyes flashed. "Who cares about being fair?"

In a blink, Olivia lashed out with her razor-sharp talons, forcing Klerope to scramble back. Narissa wriggled free, leaving her trident stuck in the floor.

"Hey!" I shouted, darting forward, trying to draw Olivia's attention away from Klerope.

It worked. Olivia's sneer locked onto me. She inhaled, her hair igniting with fiery light as she grew taller and taller until her head brushed the ceiling. I knew what came next: acid spit.

I whipped my tail, shooting across the throne room like a torpedo. My fingers closed around the queen's trident. It was cold, heavy, and way more intimidating up close. With a grunt, I yanked it free from the pearl tile and hurled it at Olivia.

Olivia batted the trident aside like it was a toy, her ear-splitting laugh echoing through the water. Sirens scattered in every direction, fleeing for cover as she unleashed a torrent of black venom.

The water churned with chaos. Even Narissa's guards bailed, leaving the queen to her fate.

"Would you knock that off!" Narissa shrieked, her voice going full on panic mode. "You're destroying my throne room!"

Olivia laughed again and lunged for me, but she was so big and juiced up on Raideron's magic that her movements were slow and clumsy. I darted away, circling the throne room, scanning for the trident. Without my magic or dagger, it was the only shot I had at stopping Olivia.

"Want my axe?" Gnash asked from the sidelines, hefting it like he was about to throw a tree trunk. But I could barely lift his axe, let alone swing it at a giant, rage-monster siren.

"Thanks, but I'm good," I called, just as I spotted the queen's trident on the other side of the throne room.

Olivia didn't even bother to stop me as I swam for it, she just tossed her head back and laughed. "You don't even know how to use that," she chided.

Klerope, who'd managed to back Narissa into a literal corner, shouted encouragement. "You can do it, Kira! You have royal blood. Just focus and the trident will heed your commands!"

Royal blood, huh? I gritted my teeth, squared my shoulders, and went for it. If Olivia wanted a fight, she was about to get one—Hale style.

I aimed the trident at Olivia, channeling every ounce of stubborn, reckless energy I had left. Lightning exploded from the tip, slicing through the water with a crack so loud it made everyone flinch.

The bolt slammed right into Olivia's chest. She shrieked loud enough to rattle my bones, her giant form convulsing as she shrank down. She collapsed in a heap of burned scales and that ridiculous tangle of red hair.

Narissa looked like she might faint. She whimpered, ripped the pearl crown off her head, and shoved it at Klerope with shaking hands. Klerope took it, her face unreadable, and handed it to Thalior, who bowed so deep I thought he might snap in half.

"My liege," he said, his voice echoing in the stunned silence.

I kept my trident pointed at Olivia as I swam closer. She looked disgusting. Her tail was scorched, her chest oozed blood, and her eyes were glassed over. I thought she was dead, but then she let out a pathetic little groan.

Figures. Too stubborn to die.

Olivia glared up at me, her voice scrapping like she'd swallowed sandpaper. "What… are… you… staring at?"

I tightened my grip on the trident, letting my words come out cold and flat. "Just deciding if I should put you out of your misery or not."

She wheezed—half laugh, half cough. Still too proud to beg, even with half her scales burned off.

"Fine, I guess I'll just let you suffer then." I turned my back, knowing full well that nothing would infuriate her more than being ignored—especially by me.

"Wait!" she croaked.

I smirked, turning around slowly to face her.

"I have information," she gasped, her gills fluttering weakly. "If you save me, I'll tell you what I know."

I rolled my eyes. "You'd say anything to save your own skin, Olivia." My fingers drummed impatiently on the trident shaft.

She actually managed a bitter little smile. "True," she admitted, "but I know things."

"Such as…"

"Raideron will attack soon," she wheezed.

I snorted. "Wow, thanks for the breaking news. Try harder."

Olivia rolled onto her side. I jerked the trident up, muscles tense, ready to jab if she so much as twitched the wrong way.

But she lifted a bloodied arm, weak and pitiful. "Just… trying to get comfortable," she muttered, barely more than a gurgle.

I lowered the trident a fraction, but kept my glare locked on her. "Tell me what you know, and maybe I'll consider letting you live."

She coughed again and blood leaked out the corners of her mouth. I wasn't sure she'd even make it through the conversation. Not that I cared. But I needed her to believe I could save her, just long enough to find out what she knew.

I yanked an empty vial of Gill Draught from my satchel and flicked it in front of her face, letting it catch the light. "This'll save you," I lied, voice flat. "But you talk first. Now." I kept my face blank, but inside, my nerves were buzzing like a live wire.

Olivia's eyes darted from the vial to my face, searching for any hint I was bluffing. Then her body seized in a violent spasm, and when it passed, she was left gasping, barely hanging on. She nodded, desperate.

"Spill," I snapped, holding the vial just out of her reach, covering it so she couldn't see it was empty.

"I am not Raideron's only spy," Olivia sputtered.

I tried to keep my face neutral, but my mind jumped to Savannah. "That's not news," I said, rolling my eyes. "Raideron always has spies."

"There is… one you will not expect." Olivia's eyes locked on mine, full of cruel amusement.

My heart hammered. Was she about to confirm my suspicion?

"Who is it? Tell me their name!" I barked, leaning in, the trident an inch from her chest.

Olivia's lips twisted in a faint smile. "The vial first…"

I clenched my jaw, frustration burning through me. If I gave her the vial, she'd know I was bluffing. But if I didn't, I might never get the name of the traitor. I hesitated, torn, my tail flicking in irritation.

But Olivia made the choice for me. With one last, rattling breath, her eyes fluttered shut and her body went limp, blood drifting in lazy spirals through the water.

Something in me snapped. "No, no, no—don't you dare!" I lunged forward, grabbing her by the shoulder and shaking her, hard. "You don't get to check out now!" But she was gone. Typical Olivia—always leaving a mess for someone else to clean up. I slammed the trident down into the sand, sending up a spray of grit, my chest heaving with anger. She'd screwed us over one last time, and I hated her for it.

"Enough," Klerope said gently, kneeling beside me. She pried my hands from Olivia and we watched as her lifeless body slowly drifted up through the water and vanished out into the Eastern sea.

After everything she'd done, all the chaos and pain she'd caused, it was a better ending than she deserved. But I was too wiped to care. My arms felt like lead, and my chest was tight— too tight. I couldn't breathe!

My gills burned. I clawed at my throat, trying to suck in water, but it was like breathing air again for the first time. I spun, searching for help, and spotted Gnash thrashing nearby, his eyes wild, mouth gaping.

I kicked toward Gnash and grabbed his arm to steady him. "Hang on, big guy. We're getting out of here," I said, even though my own vision was starting to blur at the edges. My chest felt like it was being squeezed in a vice, every breath harder than the last.

"Hey!" I barked, voice thin and ragged. "Klerope! The Gill Draught's wearing off."

Klerope's eyes went huge. "What can I do?"

"Surface. Now!" I croaked out.

Klerope grabbed my arm, her grip strong, and started hauling me through the grand pearl doors. I clung to Gnash, dragging him along, my tail flicking with every frantic kick.

We shot out into a vast, open space, ringed with shell-encrusted columns. Hundreds of sirens erupted into cheers as we passed, all of them vying for a look at their new queen. Thalior and the other rebels did their best to hold the crowd back, but I barely noticed. My vision was tunneling, the world going fuzzy at the edges.

Thalior's voice cut through the chaos. "My love, where are you going?" he called out to Klerope.

"We need to get Kira and Gnash back to the surface," she replied without slowing down.

Thalior gestured for another siren to take his place and hurried to Klerope's side. "I will accompany you," he said, his tone leaving no room for argument. Relief flickered across Klerope's face, even as she tried to hide it.

Gnash was barely conscious. His eyes rolled back as Thalior grabbed him and took off. I kicked hard, tail lashing behind me. The water felt thick as syrup and there was nothing but endless black shadows above us. I had to trust Klerope and Thalior to get us out before we both ended up as fish food.

"Wait!" I gasped, my words bubbling out. "The Obsidian Firestone. We can't leave without it!" I wasn't about to let us blow the whole mission at the finish line.

Klerope reached into her pouch and pulled out a big, black orb swirling with red light, handing it to me. "You mean this?"

My throat felt like it was full of sand so I didn't try to talk, but

I raised my eyebrows to show my surprise.

"It was actually pretty easy to get it away from Narissa," Klerope said as we shot for the surface, her tone way too casual for someone who'd just pulled off grand larceny. "I grabbed it off her before the guards took her to the dungeon."

With the Firestone tucked safely in my pack, I clung to Klerope as she swam us upward, fast as a barracuda. My gills burned, every breath felt like swallowing glass. I clung on to Klerope, my grip probably bruising, and kicked hard.

"We're almost there," she said, but her voice sounded a million miles away, like I was listening through a tunnel.

I forced my eyes open, but the water was so murky I couldn't see squat. The seawater stung, so I squeezed my eyes shut again, jaw clenched, and just focused on the rhythm of Klerope's swimming.

Klerope didn't let me down. We broke the surface just as my lungs screamed for air. I gasped, coughing up seawater, and spotted Gnash sputtering beside Thalior, clinging to him like a half-drowned kitten. He was alive. I was alive. We had the Obsidian Firestone. That was all that mattered.

The two star-crossed sirens dragged us the last stretch to shore. My legs felt like overcooked noodles (two days with a fishtail will do that to you) but I managed to stagger up the beach, collapsing face-first in the golden sand. I pressed my forehead to the ground, letting the heat chase away the chill of the deep. For a second, I let myself breathe. Just one second.

Of course, peace never lasts. Just as I was about to close my eyes and pretend the world didn't exist, a loud conch shell call shattered the quiet. I groaned, rolling onto my back, sand sticking to my skin, and glared at the sky. "Seriously?" I muttered. "Can't a girl catch a break?"

"What's that?" Gnash grunted, sprawled in the sand, looking like a beached manatee with a hangover.

I propped myself up on my elbows, sand sticking to my arms, and squinted into the sunlight. Ravenna was tearing down the hillside, hair flying behind her like she was leading a charge. I forced myself to my feet just as she barreled into me. We crashed backwards into the sand, laughing and gasping for breath.

"Nice to see you're not dead," I said, grinning up at her, even though my chest still burned from the swim.

Ravenna playfully punched my shoulder. "We've been waiting here for hours. What took you so long?" Her voice was sharp, but her eyes shone with relief.

I rolled over, shaking sand out of my hair, and grabbed my leather pack, which was still soggy and smelled like seaweed. "Just picking you up a present," I said, tossing Ravenna the Obsidian Firestone. "Compliments of the new siren queen."

Ravenna's eyes went wide as she spotted Klerope and Thalior in the shallows. "Thank you for returning the stone to us," she said, bowing her head in respect.

Klerope nodded back. "I am sorry that it was taken from you in the first place. Narissa should never have gotten involved with Raideron."

"Agreed," I said, "but I'm glad it meant we got to meet. Turns out you're actually pretty cool."

Klerope smiled, glancing at Thalior with a sappy look. "Will you return to Palaesar for our wedding then?" she asked me.

I shook my head and said, "As much as I'd love to party with you, there's no way I'm ever getting back in the water. I'll send you a killer gift instead."

"We wish you luck in your fight against Raideron then," Klerope replied. "We will do whatever we can to help."

With that, Klerope and Thalior slipped back into the Eastern Sea, fading into the blue. I watched them go, arms crossed, chin up, knowing that the sirens were in good hands. Maybe there could finally be peace between us. But I wasn't betting my last coin on it.

Ravenna looped her arm through mine. "Come on," she said. "The entire village is waiting for us."

"Oh, great. Can't wait to see what kind of welcome I get this time," I grumbled.

"Don't be like that," Ravenna teased. "You did what my father asked—you recovered the Obsidian Firestone. And you did it without using your astral magic."

I shrugged, trying to hide the pride bubbling up inside me. "Didn't exactly have a choice," I muttered.

But then it hit me—I'd actually done it. Faced down Olivia and the queen, and made it out the other side. No magic, just me.

Ravenna stopped and looked at me, her expression softening. "Are you alright?" she asked me as she wiped a tear from cheek.

I flashed her a lopsided grin, feeling lighter than I had in days. "Never better."

CHAPTER TWENTY-ONE

UNSTEADY GROUND

I tried not to see it as a bad omen that Alastair's portal had spat Earl and me out onto the academy lawn. It was the middle of the night, and rain hammered down on us in icy sheets, soaking me before I could even catch my breath.

"Thanks a lot, Alastair," I shouted into the rain.

Couldn't he have aimed his portal a little better... like somewhere *inside* the academy?

Earl didn't waste a second. He shook out his golden robes, water flying everywhere, and uncorked a small glass vial. "Hold still, Your Highness," he said as he tossed the potion at our feet. A shimmering barrier sprang up around us, muting the rain to a distant drumming.

I let out a shaky laugh, my teeth chattering. "Thanks, Earl," I managed.

He gave me a sideways look, his eyes twinkling behind rain-fogged spectacles. "That's what I'm here for, Amira. Someone has to keep you in one piece until your coronation."

Inside, the academy was silent—eerily so. Our wet boots echoed down the empty corridors, the sound swallowed by shadows. Every gust of wind against the windows made me jump. As I made my way to my chambers, I tried to remind myself that I'd faced worse than a dark school, but the feeling of unease stuck with me.

"Your Highness!" Aria's voice rang out shrilly, startling me. She stood in the doorway of my chambers, her hands clutching her apron as if she'd just seen a ghost.

I gasped—too late to stop the surge of magic running through me—as a fireball leapt from my fingertips, slamming into the stone above her head. The sharp scent of scorched rock filled the corridor, and shame prickled up my neck.

"Oh, Aria, I'm so sorry!" I cried out, mortified. My hands shook as I tried to steady my breathing.

Aria, to her credit, didn't even so much as flinch. She just ushered me into my room, her voice gentle but brisk. "No harm done, Your Highness. But we weren't expecting you back until tomorrow… is everything alright?"

"Plans changed," I said, trying to sound casual, but my voice came out thin. "It's nothing urgent," I added.

Aria clicked her tongue, her gaze sweeping over me. "You're drenched through," she said. "Come, let's get you out of those wet things. I'll draw a bath, and you can warm up by the fire."

I managed a tired smile. "Thank you, Aria, but I think I'd rather just get some sleep."

Aria gave me a disapproving look but didn't argue. "Very well. But at least let me get you dry." She didn't wait for an answer as she helped me peel off my sodden cloak and boots, her hands gentle and efficient.

She moved around the room with quiet purpose, lighting the hearth and setting lavender candles on the mantle. The scent of woodsmoke and flowers filled the air, and I felt some of the tension in my shoulders begin to ease. Once I was settled under a pile of blankets, Aria paused at the door. "If you need anything, just ring. I'll be nearby."

"Thank you," I murmured, already half-asleep. The warmth seeped into my bones, and exhaustion pulled me under.

But it wasn't long before I was jolted awake by a sharp, insistent banging outside my window. I lay tangled in the sheets, heart pounding, disoriented, caught between the remnants of a nightmare and the golden sunlight streaming through the curtains. The storm had passed, but the quiet felt uneasy, broken only by the relentless knocking outside my window.

I dragged myself to the balcony, rubbing my eyes and squinting into the morning light, ready with a few choice words for whoever thought it was a good idea to wake me up after the night I'd had. But as my hand closed around the doorknob, I froze. There, just beyond the glass, was a face I knew better than my own reflection.

I didn't think. I just bolted out of my bedchamber and ran to the front door—barefoot, hair wild, nightgown flapping ridiculously behind me. "Your Highness!" Aria's voice chased after me, scandalized and sharp. "What are you doing?" But I barely heard her.

All I knew was that I had to get to him. It wasn't logic. It was something deeper, like the world had narrowed to a single point, and that point was Treander, standing in the sunlight, looking so impossibly real after so many nights of missing him.

I flung open the front door and sprinted down the steps, ignoring the shocked gasps and wide-eyed stares. Let them talk. Let them see their future queen running across the lawn in her nightgown. For once, I didn't care.

Treander's eyes locked on mine just before I crashed into him. He caught me, arms strong and warm, and kissed me fiercely, like he was trying to make up for every second we'd lost.

The world spun away. I clung to him, tears stinging my eyes, and for the first time in months, I let myself believe that maybe, just maybe, things could be right again.

He pulled back then, brushing a tear from my cheek with a calloused thumb. "Are you alright?" His voice was low, a little shaky, and so full of worry it almost undid me.

"You're here," I whispered, ignoring his question, because honestly, nothing else mattered. He was standing in front of me—alive and whole, when for so long I'd been terrified that I'd lost him for good.

He smiled shyly, but with the same warmth that had always made me feel safe. "Where else would I be?" he said.

I didn't trust myself to answer. If I tried, I'd probably start crying, and I'd already made enough of a spectacle for one day. So instead, I kissed him again, pouring every ounce of relief and longing and confusion into it. Somewhere behind us, the archers let out a chorus of whoops and cheers.

Aria, who'd been trailing behind me in a flurry of shouts, finally caught up. She looked absolutely horrified, clutching my silk bathrobe like it was a shield against my lack of decorum.

"Honestly, Your Highness," she scolded, her voice wavering between outrage and concern, "this behavior is not at all becoming of a queen." She thrust the robe at me, her cheeks pink with outrage.

I tried to muster my most regal tone, but it came out more like a plea. "Aria, please go away now."

She blinked, her mouth open in protest.

"But—"

"Seriously, not now," I snapped, my patience fraying.

I watched as realization dawned on Aria's face, her eyes flitting from me to Treander. "Oh my!" she stammered, dropping into a clumsy curtsy before practically fleeing back inside.

Treander and I both burst out laughing, the sound bubbling up and breaking the tension that had been wound so tight inside me. But as the adrenaline faded, confusion crept in, curling cold and uncertain in my chest. The last time I'd seen him, he'd barely been functional, let alone able to wield a hammer.

I looked up at him, searching his face for answers I wasn't sure I wanted. "What does this mean for us?" I asked, my voice barely above a whisper.

Treander brushed a stray curl from my cheek, his eyes questioning. "What do you want it to mean?" he asked.

I hesitated, the truth heavy on my tongue. "I don't know…"

I was happy to see him, to feel his arms around me again. But that didn't erase everything that had happened, or the impossible choice that still loomed ahead of me.

Hekagian law was clear: I had to marry before my coronation. My parents expected me to choose Ajay, to unite our royal bloodlines. Treander had neither title nor fortune, just a battered bow and a band of ragtag orphans. Not that I cared about any of that, but it wasn't just about me or what I wanted.

"I need some time to think," I said finally, my voice barely above a whisper.

Treander's arms stiffened around me, as if he could anchor me there with him. "Time to think," he echoed. "I suppose that's fair. I don't come with a castle, just me and my winning personality." He tried to make it sound light, but there was something raw underneath.

"It's not that," I insisted.

"Then what is there to think about? Do you not love me anymore? Is that it?"

His question caught me off guard. "I… I'm just confused!" The words rushed out, messy but honest. "It's like my head is full of static. I can't even hear myself think."

Treander's eyes searched mine, earnest and a little desperate. "That's not what I asked, Amira. I don't care about the council or the crown or any of that. I just need to know that you still want me. That there's a chance I can fix this."

My throat tightened. "I can't deal with this right now," I cried.

I took a shaky step back, desperate for space, but Treander caught my hand. He pulled me back into his arms, holding me tight, like he was afraid I might disappear if he let go.

"You don't have to have all the answers right now," he murmured, his voice rougher than usual. "I just miss you. That's all."

I pressed my face into his shoulder, blinking hard as my fingers curled into the soft fabric of his shirt. I wanted to stay with him like that forever, to let all my worries fall away. But the knot in my chest wouldn't loosen, and I knew that the longer I held him, the harder it would be to leave.

I stepped back, letting my arms fall to my sides. Treander's hand lingered at my elbow, then slipped away.

Footsteps pounded across the courtyard, drawing my attention away from Treander. "Your Highness, Princess Kira has returned," one of the archers called to me breathlessly.

I caught a flash of Kira's blonde hair as her carriage made its way toward the academy. Even from far away, I could hear her snarky voice. "Nice nightgown, Amira!" she shouted. Then she held up a large black orb—the Obsidian Firestone.

Relief crashed over me. She was safe. The Firestone was safe.

"I have to go," I told Treander, my voice barely steady. Kira and Ravenna needed to know about Raideron's plan. Even without the Firestone, his threat to Vail was still very real.

Treander hesitated. "We'll talk soon?" he asked.

"Soon," I promised.

But as I ran to meet Kira at the gate, my eyes fell on the spot where Shani had given her life to save mine. A wave of grief washed over me, then turned to guilt as my thoughts strayed to Ajay. He was back home in Alkrimia mourning his sister and here I was, betraying my promise to him by kissing Treander.

I tried to put on a brave face for Kira and Ravenna. They were so happy, chatting away as we walked back to the academy. But once inside, the weight of everything hit me like a punch to the chest. My vision blurred at the edges as I leaned against the front door, my legs too shaky to move.

"Whoa, are you okay?" Kira's words were filled with worry. She was already at my side, steadying me before my knees could give out. Her grip was strong, and I clung to it like a lifeline.

I tried to answer her, but my throat closed up. All that came out was a shaky, "I—" before the tears started, silent and warm against my chilled skin.

Kira used the sleeve of her leather jacket to wipe my face, her voice dropping into a soothing murmur. "It's okay. You don't have to say anything. I've got you."

"I need to get out of here," I cried. "I can't be seen like this."

"Screw them all," Kira said fiercely, her eyes flashing purple.

Ravenna appeared on my other side, her presence quiet and steady. She knelt so we were eye-to-eye, her dark hair spilling over her shoulders like a curtain. "Is there anything we can do?" she asked.

"Just get me out of here. Please," I whimpered.

Without a word, Ravenna slipped her arms around me and lifted me up, careful and strong. I let my head fall against her shoulder, eyes squeezed shut. I hated feeling so small, so breakable, but I couldn't hold myself together any longer.

Ravenna carried me to my bedchamber as I went in and out of consciousness, my mind shutting down out of self-preservation. I barely remember her tucking me into bed.

When I woke, the sky outside my window was pitch black, the kind of darkness that makes you wonder if it's morning or the middle of the night. My body felt like it was made of stone, heavy and sore, like sleep had only pressed the exhaustion deeper into my bones.

Kira was curled up the chair next to my bed; knees tucked to her chest. She looked so peaceful, I almost hated to wake her. Almost.

I nudged her with my foot. "Kira, it's time to wake up."

Her eyes snapped open and she glared at me. "Seriously?" she grumbled, swatting my foot away.

In spite of everything, I smiled, just a little.

"I figured you'd appreciate the direct approach," I said with a shrug.

Kira sat up and looked around groggily. "Where's Ravenna?"

"I haven't seen her," I admitted, pulling my blanket tighter around my shoulders to block out the chill. "I just woke up."

Kira yawned, stretching her arms overhead. "Why exactly am I awake at the gods-forsaken hour?"

I glanced at the clock on my nightstand, my stomach twisting with guilt as I realized how late—or early—it actually was.

I never should have gone back to sleep without letting the others know about Raideron's plan to attack Vail, but there was nothing I could do about that now.

"I have to tell you something important, but I need you to not freak out over how I heard about it," I said nervously.

Kira arched a pale eyebrow. "What is it?"

I took a breath, searching for the right words.

"It's about Grandpa…"

Her eyes went wide. "Alastair?"

I nodded, feeling a strange mix of dread and hope twist in my stomach.

Kira's face turned a stormy mix of emotions. "What did he want?" Her voice was careful, but I could hear the edge in it.

"He came to warn us."

"Warn us about what?" Her tone sharpened, like she was already running through a dozen battle plans in her head.

I let out a long breath. "The usual. Raideron's planning to attack Vail. Alastair says he's got some kind of weapon that can wipe out an entire town."

Kira's eyebrows scrunched together like she was trying to work through a difficult puzzle. "But no weapon could do that. Aside from the Firestone anyway, and that's safe with us."

"You haven't told me how you got it yet, by the way." I felt the need to point that out. She seemed different somehow. I couldn't put my finger on how or why, but I was certain that it had something to do with her time in Wahiao.

"I got the Firestone. That's all that matters," Kira replied with a shrug. "Oh, by the way, Olivia's dead."

My mouth fell open in surprise and Kira smirked at my reaction, spinning her dagger between her fingers nonchalantly.

"Wait—Olivia's dead? Why didn't you lead with that?"

Kira rolled her eyes. "You mean while you were a puddle on the floor? Didn't seem like the right time."

I shot her a half-hearted glare.

Kira waved me off. "I'll tell you about it later. Right now, I'm more interested in what Raideron's up to. Something tells me that he's not going to stop just because he didn't get the Firestone."

"Me neither," I replied grimly. "And he plans to attack today."

Kira nodded, her eyes suddenly sharp. "Good."

"How exactly is that good?" I asked.

"We have the Obsidian Firestone and the Elemental Staff. Now Earl just needs to work his mojo and Bam, we've got ourselves a weapon to take Raideron down." She leaned back with her boots propped on the edge of my trunk and a look of satisfaction on her face.

"Why are you suddenly so optimistic?" I asked her.

Kira just shrugged, her voice light. "I've just got a good feeling. For once."

"Who are you and what have you done with my sister?" I nudged her shoulder, trying to tease a smile out of her.

It worked. She let out a low laugh and shook her head. "Don't get used to it," she grumbled.

I hesitated, the question I'd been avoiding pressed at the back of my mind.

"Are you... upset about Alastair?"

Kira stilled, her jaw twitching as she stared at the floor. For a moment, the only sound was the soft rustle of her leather jacket as she hugged it tighter around herself. She shrugged one shoulder, pretending not to care, but her eyes shone with tears.

"He still loves you," I said softly.

Kira snorted. "Did he say that?" Her tone was sharp, but there was a tremor underneath, like she wanted the answer to be yes.

"He didn't have to..."

"Whatever," she muttered, pushing herself up from the chair. "As far as I'm concerned, Alastair can rot in hell."

I watched her carefully, the air between us growing thick with everything she wasn't saying. I wanted to say something or to comfort her somehow, but I knew better than to try while she was hurting. The only person who seemed to be able to reach her then was Ravenna.

"Come on," Kira said, her voice clipped as she raked a hand through her tangled hair. "Let's go get the others. We've got bigger problems than Alastair." She didn't look at me as she strode toward the door, her boots thudding heavily against the worn rug.

I barely had time to stand before Aria swept into the room. "Oh no you don't!" she scolded, planting herself squarely in front of me, arms crossed in that way that meant she wasn't moving for anyone—not even the future queen.

"What?" I asked, trying to sound innocent, though I knew exactly what she was about to say.

Aria's eyes narrowed, and she jabbed a finger toward the wardrobe. "You are not leaving this room without being properly dressed," she insisted in a crisp tone.

Kira leaned against the doorframe, arms crossed, her smirk razor-sharp. "You'd better listen to her. Aria's got more backbone than half the council, and you know she'll win this round." The tension in her shoulders had eased just a little, but beneath all the armor, I could see she was still hurting.

Aria nodded in approval and got to work pulling out long green dress that shimmered in the sunlight. I sighed in resignation and sat down on the stood in front of my dressing table. I could see Kira's reflection in the mirror, still grinning at me.

"Shouldn't you go find Ravenna?" I asked, feeling annoyed.

Kira didn't miss a beat. "Sure. Should I find Treander too?"

"No!" I said, maybe a little too fast.

"You sure?" Her gaze pinned me, sharp as a blade.

"He can't help with this," I said, trying to sound casual, but Kira didn't buy it for a second. She just stared, arms folded, waiting for me to crack.

I fumbled for another excuse. "Besides, the archers will need their rest if there's going to be a battle."

Kira snorted, but finally pushed off the doorframe. "Whatever you say, Your Highness." She gave a dramatic, mocking curtsy, then ducked out into the hallway—just barely dodging the pillow I lobbed at her retreating back.

CHAPTER TWENTY-TWO

A SHADOW OF DOUBT

The library was awash in pale sunlight when I arrived a short time later, properly washed and dressed, thanks to Aria.

I'd always found comfort in the library, and this day was no exception. Towering shelves crammed with ancient tomes, battered spellbooks, and scrolls bound in cracked leather, rose all the way to the ceiling, making the room feel both endless and safe.

In the center of the library stood several long oak tables. At the moment, they were all buried under open books, potion vials, and half-finished notes. Kira had claimed a chair there, her boots propped on the table and a battered scroll dangling from one hand. Her eyes flicked over the words as her other hand drummed restlessly on the table.

Earl sat next Kira, rolling an empty vial between his palms, his eyes darting to the door every few seconds. "Any sign of Caleb?" I asked him.

"Not yet, I'm afraid," he replied.

"Knowing Caleb, he's probably just waiting to make a dramatic entrance," Kira added.

I peered over her shoulder at the scroll, "What's this?"

"The Elemental Scroll. Earl wants to make sure we're not about to blow ourselves up." She finally glanced up, her gaze sharp. "On the off chance you were hoping for an easy day, sorry to disappoint you. We have to bind the Obsidian Firestone to the staff before we can use it to purify the Elementals."

Both items in question sat on the table in front of us, gleaming with quiet, dangerous power. A large cauldron had been placed between them, its surface etched with runes I didn't recognize.

"Great, so what do you need from me?" I asked, bracing myself for some complicated magical ritual—probably involving something gross, like royal flesh or a tooth.

Kira squinted at the scroll, her lips pursed in concentration as she read. "Nothing," she said finally, like the word tasted weird in her mouth. "Huh. That's a first."

"Seriously? Not even a drop of blood or a lock of hair? Are you sure you're reading it right? Maybe Earl should double check."

Kira rolled her eyes. "If you want to volunteer a finger, be my guest. Otherwise it looks like you get to keep all your body parts today."

A familiar, overly confident voice rang out from the doorway. "Geeze, Amira, not everything's about you, ya know."

Kira was right, Caleb did always have to make a dramatic entrance.

"It's about time you showed up," she said teasingly.

"You try flying halfway across Nithandore on a griffin," Caleb shot back with a smile.

"How was the Hakuturi village?" I asked him.

"It was great." Caleb grinned and hefted his massive wooden club. "My patu is better than ever."

No matter how much the world changed, some things—like Caleb's knack for getting into trouble and coming out the other side grinning—would always stay the same.

"Good, you're going to need it," Kira said, her tone dry but her eyes full of that fierce spark she always got before a fight.

Caleb's grin vanished. "I know," he said solemnly. "I saw Raideron's army on my way here. They're heading straight for Vail Castle."

Kira snapped to attention. Her spine straightened and one hand curled tight around the edge of the table as she looked at Caleb. "How many soldiers?" she asked him.

"Thousands," Caleb said, his voice grim.

My mind raced, trying to process the news, but I forced myself to sound calm. "Good thing we have a plan," I said, nodding toward the Elemental Staff and the Obsidian Firestone—our last hope, gleaming between us.

"You got the Obsidian Firestone!" Caleb smiled approvingly.

Kira leaned back in her chair, a smirk tugging at her mouth.

"Told you I'd handle it," she said, her voice edged with pride. "Someone had to."

Ravenna, who'd been perched against a bookshelf across from us, shot Kira adoring look. "Wait until you hear how she did it," she said, her tone warm.

But before Ravenna could fill us in, the library door creaked open again and Savannah's pale head popped in, her eyes lighting up when she saw me. "Amira, you're back!" she squealed.

"How did you know we were in here?" Kira asked, her tone sharp and suspicious. She didn't even bother to hide it anymore.

Savannah pulled back and glared at Kira. "I heard voices. Figured it was weird, since the school's basically a ghost town now. What are you guys up to?" Her gaze drifted to the Firestone.

Kira shot me a look—the kind that said, "Don't you dare." But I couldn't bring myself to lie to Savannah.

"We have a plan to stop Raideron," I said, keeping my voice careful but honest. Kira's glare could have melted a cauldron, but I kept my eyes on Savannah.

"Really? What is it?" Savannah's eyes widened as she looked around at the contents stewed all over the table.

Kira didn't let me answer. She leaned forward, her voice flat as steel. "That's private information," she snarled.

"What is that supposed to mean?" Savannah asked, her voice thick with hurt.

"It means we don't trust you," Kira snapped back.

Savannah's gaze slid to me. "Even you?"

I froze.

Lately, everything about Savannah had started to feel off. Her nervous glances, her too-easy explanations, the way she always seemed to know more than she should. Savannah had always been a good liar, but what if it wasn't just Raideron she'd been lying to? Doubt twisted in my stomach, cold and sharp.

"Come on," I said, forcing a smile and trying to steer her toward the door. "Let's get some air."

But Savannah wouldn't budge.

"I want to know what's going on," she said in a tight voice.

"I'm sure you do," Kira scoffed from across the table.

Savannah turned to me, her eyes wide and pleading.

I was trapped. Caught between my oldest friend and my sister, both of them waiting for me to pick a side.

"I'm not getting in the middle of this again," I said, raising my hands defensively, but my words only seemed to make things worse. Savannah's jaw clenched and Kira's eyes narrowed, the air between them crackling.

Kira's voice was low and serious when she spoke. "Olivia's last words were that there's a traitor among us."

"What do you mean?" I asked, my voice unsteady.

"I mean exactly what I said," Kira replied, her gaze never leaving Savannah. "On her literal deathbed, Olivia confessed that someone at the academy is spying for Raideron."

Savannah's face twisted, pain flickering beneath her anger. "You always think the worst of me, Kira. You've never even tried to trust me. Not once."

"Trust is earned, Savannah. And you've given me nothing but reasons to doubt," Kira replied in an icy tone.

Savannah's face turned red. "You have no idea what I've been through." Her voice broke, but she continued. "What I've had to do just to stay alive." The rose bush in the corner shuddered, then exploded, petals and thorns flying like shrapnel as Savannah lost control of her magic.

Kira rolled up the Elemental Scroll and tucked it safely into her jacket, glaring at Savannah as she did it. "Get her out of here," she growled at me. "Before she ruins everything."

"But maybe I could help," Savannah tried, her voice thin and desperate.

"Or maybe you're the spy," Kira shot back.

"Enough!" I snapped, raising both hands as if I could physically hold back the storm brewing between them. "Savannah, let's talk outside. Please."

Savannah's jaw tightened angrily, but she followed me.

The door clicked shut behind us, sealing off the tension in the library. Savannah turned to me then, her eyes shining with hurt and something close to panic. "What's going on? Did I do something wrong?"

My stomach twisted. "No, of course not," I said, too quickly. I felt the lie settle in my chest.

Savannah searched my face. "Then why won't you tell me what you're doing in there?" She jerked her chin toward the library, her voice trembling. "Why am I always the last to know?"

"It's... complicated," I said, my voice sounding as lame to my own ears as it must have to her.

She let out a shaky breath. "Isn't it always with you?"

I tried to steady myself, searching for words that wouldn't make things worse. "Listen," I said, "We might have a way to defeat Raideron, but I can't talk about it. Not yet."

"Because you think I'm a spy," Savannah said in a dry tone.

I shook my head, but the denial felt thin. "Because we don't know who the spy is."

Savannah's anger flared. "Give me a break. Kira's been filling your head with all this junk about me talking to Raideron. But I told you about that as soon as I could."

She wasn't entirely wrong. She had told me why Raideron let her go. But she hadn't told me she'd be contacting him again. And she'd vanished during the academy attack...

"I want to believe you," I whispered.

"Then *do* believe me," she pleaded, her eyes glistening. She took a step closer, but I flinched, and she stopped short, her shoulders tensing.

I shook my head, unable to meet her gaze. "It's not that simple and you know it."

Savannah's posture stiffened. "It is that simple," she replied, her voice trembling with anger. "You don't trust me."

"That's not true!" I protested.

She let out a bitter laugh and wiped away the line of tears that ran down her cheek. "It is true. Some friend you are."

Savannah spun on her heel and stormed off, her footsteps echoing down the corridor as she headed for the dorms, leaving me standing there with the ache of doubt and the sting of her words.

I wanted to call after her, to tell her it was all a misunderstanding, that I believed her. But I couldn't honestly say that was true, so I let her go.

Left alone with my own thoughts, I felt their weight settle over me. I was really excelling in the relationship department lately: first Kira, then Treander, now Savannah... I was running out of people to disappoint.

I needed to move, to do anything other than stand there drowning in self-pity. Spellwork had never been my strong suit anyway, and Earl was more than capable of figuring out how to bind the Firestone and the Elemental Staff. If there was going to be a battle, at least I could try to be ready for it.

The rhythmic thud of arrows greeted me as I entered the armory. Darreon was there, his focus absolute as he loosed arrow after arrow into a battered straw dummy. For a moment, I just watched him. He was steady, unflinching, everything I wasn't.

He noticed me and paused, lowering his bow. "Your Highness, it is good to see you," he said, his voice warm but formal.

"You too," I muttered, not really in the mood for pleasantries. I hovered in the doorway, unsure whether I should disturb him.

Darreon studied me for a moment, his gaze gentle but perceptive. "Is something the matter, Your Highness?"

I tried to shrug it off, but my shoulders just slumped. "I don't know. Lately it feels like I can't do anything right."

"Is this about Treander?" he asked quietly.

I sputtered, caught off guard by how quickly he'd picked up on that. "No…" I let out a breath. "Not just Treander."

Darreon raised his eyebrows, waiting. The silence stretched, but he didn't push. Instead, he offered a small, reassuring smile and set his bow aside, the gesture careful and deliberate. "I should tell you, I know about what happened in the courtyard yesterday. Treander confided in me about it."

"He did?" My cheeks burned, and I found myself twisting the hem of my dress sleeve awkwardly.

Darreon nodded. "Yes, but I won't betray his confidence by telling you what he said. Queen or not."

I couldn't help but smile at that. Darreon's loyalty to Treander was unwavering, and give that trust was in such short supply lately, it was oddly comforting to know that some bonds still held strong.

"I wouldn't expect you to," I replied with a soft smile. "And I'm not the queen yet. Maybe I never will be."

Darreon's brow furrowed, concern creasing his usually unreadable face. "What do you mean?" he asked, crossing his arms, his posture suddenly more guarded.

I shook my head, waving him off. "It's nothing. I just have a lot on my mind." The words hung between us, heavier than I intended. The truth was, the weight of the crown—and everything it meant— felt impossible most days.

I wanted to ask Darreon how he managed to stay so steady all the time, but the question caught in my throat.

I found my thoughts circling back to Treander, as they always seemed to do. "About Treander—" I paused, suddenly unsure if I should go on. "Is he really doing better?"

Darreon's expression softened. He paused, as if weighing how much to say, then gave a gentle nod. "He has good days and bad days," he said quietly, his tone careful and kind, as if he understood how much the question cost me to ask.

"But he's himself again. How did that even happen? Last time I saw him, he was…." I hesitated, chewing my lip.

Darreon shifted uneasily.

"You don't have to tell me anything you don't want to," I said gently. "I'm just trying to understand."

He let out a slow breath, like he was weighing every word. "It happened the day after you left for Roanoke. I checked the infirmary that morning and he was gone. We searched for hours and finally found him by the stream, bow in hand, fishing like nothing had happened."

I could picture it: Treander, calm and focused, sunlight on his fiery hair, the darkness finally gone.

"That's amazing," I said, hope flickering in my chest.

Darreon's mouth tightened. "It wasn't easy. Those first days, he was drowning in guilt. He blamed himself for Ajay's sister. For not being there."

"But that's ridiculous. He had nothing to do with it!" My anger surprised me. Maybe because it was easier to be mad than to admit how much Treander's pain hurt to watch.

Darreon nodded, but his eyes didn't leave mine. "He carries more than most, Your Highness. That's just who he is."

I shook my head, trying to make sense of it all. Treander always took on everyone else's burdens, but this—this was too much, even for him.

"He seemed okay yesterday, though," I said.

Darreon's gaze dropped to his boots. "I thought maybe some hard work would help ease his mind. And it did, for a time. He laughed a little, even. But after you showed up… he had a rough night. But that's all I'll say." His tone was gentle, but there was a finality to it.

A rough night. My dropped stomach dropped. Of course he had. I'd basically dumped all my confusion on him in the courtyard and then just walked away to find Kira. Why did I always manage to say the worst possible thing at the worst possible time? I wanted to believe I was doing the right thing by being honest with him, but now all I could think about was the look on his face when I'd walked away. I hated that I'd hurt him.

Was I ever going to get things right?

I was grateful for Darreon's honesty though, and for the way he always protected Treander, even from me.

He let out a breath, and for the first time, I noticed the exhaustion in his face—the dark circles under his eyes, the way his shoulders slumped just a little. Had I asked too much of him, leaving him to hold everything together while I was gone?

"Thank you for keeping an eye on things," I said, hoping he could hear how much I meant it.

Darreon dipped into a small, respectful bow. "It's my honor, Princess. Always."

I hesitated, then forced myself to ask another question I'd been dreading. "Anything... unusual to report?"

His thick eyebrows arched. "You mean about Savannah, I presume?"

I nodded, bracing myself.

"I'm afraid I don't have much to report on that front. She mostly kept to her chambers," Darreon paused.

"I did hear that she sent her lady's maid away, though." His voice was neutral, but I could tell he was watching me closely to see how I'd react to that bit of news.

"That doesn't surprise me," I said, trying to sound unbothered, even though my mind was spinning. "Savannah grew up on Earth, like me. It's weird at first, having someone fuss over you all the time. I still haven't gotten used to it."

"Even so..." Darreon notched an arrow, his movements precise. "It's unusual. She didn't join us for a single meal either. Not once, as far as I can recall."

I tried to brush it off, telling myself maybe Savannah just didn't want to eat with the archers. They could be a lot, especially when they got rowdy. But even as I made excuses for her, the doubts kept piling up.

Darreon's last arrow thudded into the straw dummy's forehead. He allowed himself a small, satisfied smile.

"Nice shot," I said, genuinely impressed. "You make it look so easy."

He shrugged, already lowering his bow. "Did you come here in search of me, Princess?" His tone was polite, but there was a hint of curiosity underneath.

"Actually, I was hoping to get some practice in myself."

He gestured to the open space. "The room is yours. Or if you'd prefer solitude, I can take my leave."

"I don't mind if you stay," I replied. "In fact, I'd welcome your help. I'm kind of lost in here."

Darreon handed me a worn-down practice sword, the kind we usually reserved for first years. I swung it clumsily at the straw dummy, missing entirely.

"I see we have much work to do." Darreon tried to stifle a laugh as he showed me the proper way to hold the sword (like nobody had ever tried that before).

Just then, a portal shimmered open between us. Darreon was instantly alert, stepping toward me, but there was no danger—just a piece of parchment that shot out and landed in my hands.

Darreon eyed the letter warily. "Would you like some privacy?" he asked, but I had already started reading it.

My eyes flicked over the first lines, and my stomach dropped. "Actually, I think we'd better get the others," I said, my voice shaking as I folded the parchment and slipped it into the pocket of my dress. "It's a message from Raideron."

CHAPTER TWENTY-THREE

THE COST OF SECRETS

Darreon and I rushed back to the library, my heart pounding as I clutched Raideron's letter in my hand. Everyone was still there, clustered around the table.

As soon as I finished reading the letter aloud, Kira's eyes narrowed. "Don't you think that's a bit weird?" she said, her tone edged with suspicion. "Right after Savannah hears we have a plan to defeat Raideron, now suddenly he wants to 'talk'?"

I couldn't deny it—the timing was almost too perfect. Besides us, nobody else knew about our plan to free the Elementals. Who else could have tipped him off? The doubt gnawed at me, but I forced myself to stay focused.

"Raideron's giving us until sundown today. If we don't agree to meet him in Middlehaven by then, he'll march on Vail. We have bigger things to worry about right now than Savannah."

Caleb scratched the back of his neck, his eyes uncertain. "This must be some kind of trap," he said.

"Obviously, but I don't see that we have much of a choice. We have to go." I turned to Darreon, hoping for some kind of backup or at least a different perspective. "What do you think?" I asked.

Darreon looked surprised to be called on, but then he straightened, his tone careful and measured. "I am not certain I can offer much guidance, Princess. Why not consult the Guard?"

"There's not enough time," Caleb cut in, shaking his head, curls bouncing as he paced a tight circle. "If we go to the Guard, they'll drag the Council into it, and you know how long those windbags take. Vail will be toast before they even finish arguing about the agenda."

Kira snorted. "I'm with Caleb. Why waste time? We've got the Elemental Staff—" she jabbed a thumb toward the staff, her eyes glinting with reckless confidence, "—and the Firestone. Let's just go for it. Maybe we'll get lucky for once."

Earl furrowed his brow. "I wouldn't be so quick to assume it'll be that easy," he said in a low voice. His eyes were guarded with the caution of someone who's seen too many plans go bad.

Kira rolled her eyes, tossing one of her braids over her shoulder. "He doesn't even know we have the Elemental Staff," she insisted, her tone edged with hope and a hint of challenge. "We can catch him off guard."

Caleb stopped pacing, planting his patu on the floor. "He knows something," he said, worry creasing his face. "Otherwise, why would he want to meet at all?"

Ravenna, who'd been standing a little back from the rest of us, listening carefully with her arms folded, nodded sharply. "This all comes back to what, if anything, Raideron knows. Maybe it's time we stop dancing around the question and just ask Savannah what she knows."

Kira's eyes sparkled with vindication. She threw her hands up, practically bouncing in her seat. "Told you! Finally, someone's listening to me for once!"

I searched the room for support, but nobody would meet my eyes, not a one of them.

"So that's it? You all think Savannah's the spy?"

Caleb finally looked up. "It's starting to look that way. The way she disappears all the time…"

"That doesn't prove anything!" I shot back, clinging to denial.

Kira stopped pacing. "Come on Amira, Raideron contacts us the moment we have a plan. That's not coincidence—it's a leak."

Caleb straightened, tapping his patu against his boot. "Look, maybe you should just go talk to her. If she's hiding something, you'll know."

"I'm coming," Kira cut in. "If she's lying, *I'll* see it."

"No." My voice was sharper than I intended. "If you come in swinging, Savannah will shut down. I need her to talk, not feel attacked."

Kira's glare was icy. "So now I'm the problem? Fine. Go play diplomat. Just don't blame me when she stabs you in the back."

"That's not what I meant," I sighed, rubbing my forehead as the start of a migraine set in. "I just—"

I started to protest, but Ravenna stepped between us, her presence calm and commanding. "Enough. We don't have time for this. Amira, you're the only one she might talk to. Go. We'll handle things here."

Earl nodded in agreement, his eyes twinkling. "Let's not turn this into a family brawl, shall we? Kira, how about you send Raideron our reply?"

Kira huffed and snatched the parchment from Earl. "Just… be careful, okay?" she said without looking up. "I know you think Savannah would never hurt you, but people change."

I chanced a quick pat on her shoulder. "I know. I'll be fine."

Her voice softened, just a little. "I'll be right here if you need backup. Just yell."

I managed a weak smile, but my heart was pounding. What if I was wrong about Savannah? What if Kira was the only one seeing things clearly?

I hovered outside Savannah's door, my fist raised but frozen in midair. What was I even supposed to say? "Hey, are you betraying us to the villain who's been trying to kill me since forever?" My stomach twisted. She was supposed to be my best friend. I didn't want to believe Kira could be right, but I needed the truth.

I knocked. Once. Twice. Then a third time. Nothing.

The relief that washed over me was almost as strong as the dread. Maybe she wasn't in. Maybe I could just walk away and pretend none of this was happening.

But then I saw it—a flicker of purple light leaking out from under the door. My heart stuttered. Magic. I pressed my ear to the wood, desperate, and caught the faintest sound of voices. One sharp, one familiar, both too low to make out. Without thinking, I nudged the door open a crack and held my breath, hoping whoever was inside wouldn't notice me.

Savannah lounged on her bed, posture relaxed, a sly smile tugging at the corner of her mouth. In front of her, a portal glowed in the dim candlelight. At its center, Raideron's face appeared, twisted and hungry, eyes like pits of midnight. His voice was a low hiss. "What have you learned?"

Savannah let out a frustrated sigh. "They're hiding something, but I don't know what. They don't trust me anymore, not even Amira. But that just makes it more fun." Her tone was light, almost amused, as if she relished the game. It was a side of Savannah that I'd never heard in all the years I'd known her.

A chill ran through me. I wanted to burst in, to scream, to demand answers. But all I could do was listen as my best friend casually sold me out to the monster who'd ruined my life.

Raideron's eyes narrowed, his voice turning venomous. "You disappoint me, Savannah. I didn't bring you this far for excuses. I need that information."

Savannah let out a short, mocking laugh. "Relax. I'll get what you want. They're so desperate, it's almost too easy. I just need a little time to gain her trust again. Amira's always been soft."

I pressed my hand to my mouth, barely breathing. I'd come here for answers, but now that I had them, I wished I could unhear everything.

"Good, get to it. My army is in position to take Vail, and once I have the Firestone, nothing will be able to stop me. But I must know what Amira is planning."

"I'll do whatever it takes to find out," Savannah replied coldly, her hands balling into fists at her sides.

Raideron's image flickered, his mouth curling into a cruel smile. "See that you do. Otherwise, you're useless to me."

The portal snapped shut and Savannah sat back, stretching her arms overhead, looking pleased with herself. Not shaken or guilty, just… happy. She reached for a small, leatherbound journal and began scribbling, her lips curled in a satisfied smile.

And that was it. My heart broke, right there. Savannah hadn't just lied—she'd been playing both sides, feeding Raideron whatever scraps she could get. Maybe she'd been doing it all along. Maybe I'd never really known her at all.

I stumbled away, tears streaming down my face, Savannah's betrayal burning like acid in my chest. I barely made it to the library before I broke down. Kira caught me as I collapsed, her arms strong and steady. She didn't say "I told you so." She just held me while I sobbed into her shoulder.

After a while, I wiped my cheeks and glanced around at the

empty room. "Where is everyone?" I managed in a hoarse voice.

Kira's arm tightened around me. "They went after Savannah."

"Oh." The word felt small, but I couldn't help it. Everything inside me felt hollow.

"They're bringing her here," Kira said, her tone flat but her eyes sharp. "Don't worry about the Elemental Staff, Earl's got it locked up in the armory. No one's getting near it."

Shouts echoed from the corridor. The library doors crashed open and Caleb and Ravenna burst in, Savannah in tow. Her hands were bound behind her back with thick vines, and she stumbled as Caleb shoved her to the floor in front of me.

"Just let me explain!" Savannah pleaded, her voice cracking. "If you'd just give me a chance—"

Kira stepped forward, her eyes glowing dangerously. "No more chances, Savannah. You've burned through every last one."

"But—"

I cut her off, my voice shaking with anger and heartbreak. "I saw you, Savannah. I saw you talking to Raideron."

Savannah's face crumpled, but she didn't deny it. "It's not what you think," she murmured.

"It's exactly what we think. You sold us out," Kira snapped.

Savannah struggled against her bonds as tears streamed down her face. "Raideron has my parents," she stammered. "If I don't do what he says, he'll kill them. But I've only been pretending to help him. I swear, I've never told him anything that would hurt you. I would never betray you!"

Kira scoffed. "Enough. You've been caught red-handed. Nobody here believes your lies. Not anymore."

"So what happens now?" Savannah asked in a quiet whimper. "Will I be executed?"

Her wide-eyed fear nearly undid me, but ignored the sick feeling in my stomach and pressed on. "No, Savannah. I'm not Raideron. I don't execute people."

Savannah slumped back on her heels, staring out the library window. "So, what will you do with me?" she asked.

"You'll be sent to the dungeons at Vail Castle," I said quietly. "It's the only place you won't be able to contact Raideron."

She nodded, her tears falling unchecked. Her hands were still bound behind her back, and I wanted to wipe away her tears like I used to, but I knew that I couldn't. Not anymore.

With an impassioned flick of her wrist, Kira opened a portal to the cells at Vail Castle. Two guards were already waiting.

"I sent word ahead," Kira said, turning to Savannah, her voice clipped. "They're expecting you."

I knelt down next to Savannah and studied her face. All her usual bubbliness had gone, leaving a hollow, unreadable shell.

Despite everything I'd overheard, I had to give her one last chance. "Is there anything you want to say for yourself?"

"Nothing I say will matter at this point," Savannah murmured. "Just get it over with."

She didn't fight as Caleb and Ravenna lifted her to her feet, or as they led her through the portal. But as the guards locked the door to Savannah's cell, she looked up at me in defiance. "You'll regret this," she snarled right as Kira snapped the portal shut.

"I'm sorry," Kira said afterwards. "I honestly didn't want to be right."

My throat felt tight, like if I tried to speak, I'd just fall apart.

Then, a soft knock came at the door.

"Who is it?" Caleb called out, his voice rough.

"It is I," came Darreon's muffled reply.

Caleb opened the door and Darreon slipped in with Treander following close behind him. For a second, nobody said anything. The tension was so thick that you could cut it with a sword.

Caleb cleared his throat. "Uh, maybe not the best time, man."

"It's fine," I said, wiping the tears from my face.

Treander didn't hesitate. He crossed the room in three long strides, not caring about the awkwardness or the audience. His voice was low and urgent as he sat down on the couch and wrapped me in a hug. "Are you okay? I heard about Savannah."

I glanced at Darreon, who looked away, guilt flickering across his face. But honestly, I couldn't be mad at him. He'd brought the one person he knew I needed most.

"I'm fine," I said, pressing my cheek into Treander's shoulder.

Treander pulled back, his lips pressed into a thin line. "You don't have to pretend. I've seen you after a night in the stables. Trust me, you can't scare me off."

I tried to smile, but it came out as a grimace.

"Really, I'm okay," I insisted.

Treander reached out, his thumb brushing away a tear that I hadn't realized had fallen. "You don't have to be," he murmured. "Not with me."

Kira, tactful for once, cleared her throat and ushered the others towards the door. "Come on. Let's give them some space."

Caleb shot Treander a warning look that was full of brotherly concern. "We'll be just outside."

The door closed behind them, and suddenly the quiet between us felt charged. The library seemed impossibly quiet—just the faint tick of the clock, the scent of old parchment, and the distant echo of footsteps fading down the corridor. I felt strangely exposed, as if the walls themselves were watching, waiting for one of us to say something.

I shifted to the other side of the couch, out of Treander's reach, hoping it would relieve some of the tension coiling in my chest, but it didn't. My heart hammered, and I stared at my hands, twisting the edge of my silk sleeve to keep myself from falling apart.

"My apologies for barging in," Treander said, misreading the way I'd scooted away. His voice was stiff and uncertain. "I know you said you needed some time think, but after I heard what happened with Savannah, I... well... I wanted to check on you."

I looked up, meeting his eyes. "I'm glad you're here," I admitted, surprising both of us.

Treander's eyebrows shot up. "Truly?"

I nodded, feeling the knot in my chest loosen. Treander hesitated for half a second, then wrapped his arms around me in a hug that was warm and familiar. I let myself relax into him, letting the chaos fade for a minute. There was just the steady thump of his heart and the way he smelled faintly of rain and campfires.

We sat like that for a while, not talking, just breathing. I closed my eyes and tried to memorize the way his thumb traced comforting circles on my back, and the safe, quiet bubble we'd built together.

Of course, that's when Caleb knocked, his voice gentle but annoyingly practical as he cracked the door open. "Sorry to break up the cuddle-fest," he said, "but it's time."

"So, do I get to play the dashing hero again yet?" Treander cracked a crooked smile, but there was a seriousness in his eyes that undercut the joke.

My heart skipped a beat at the idea of Treander facing Raideron again. "I don't think that's a good idea," I said, my voice thick with worry.

Treander straightened, the smile fading from his face. "Why not? Haven't I proven myself in battle? Or is it that you fear I'm still broken, that Raideron's poison lingers in my veins?"

"It's not that at all," I tried to assure him, but he looked away, unconvinced. "You know what he's capable of. If Raideron turns his magic on you again…"

Treander tapped his fingers against his leg—a nervous habit I'd only seen when he was truly upset. "I know what you're about to face, and I can't just sit here polishing arrows while you walk into the lion's den."

I tried to smile, but it faltered. "If everything goes as planned, there won't be any fighting today."

Treander reached for my hands, his grip warm and steady. "Plans are for council meetings. Out there, things get messy. Let me be there. I can be of use, you'll see."

I slipped my hands from his and cupped his jaw. "I don't doubt it, Treander. But I need you here, safe. Or I won't be able to focus on anything else."

He covered my hands with his own, drawing me closer until our foreheads touched. "You ask much of me, do you know that?" His voice was rough, but there was a spark of humor in it.

Treander let out a sigh of resignation. "I'll wait here, as you wish. Just promise me you'll return. Swear it."

For just a second, a flicker of guilt tugged at me. Ajay's name echoed in the back of my mind, a reminder of what everyone expected of me. But sitting there with Treander, I knew where my heart truly was. Where it had always been.

"I promise," I whispered, letting the vow settle between us.

CHAPTER TWENTY-FOUR

MEETING IN THE MIDDLE

The road to Middlehaven stank like stale magic and sulfur. Rain had churned the ash and soot into a sticky, ankle-deep sludge that clung to my boots and made every step a battle. I was starting to think the universe had a personal vendetta against us.

Ravenna walked just ahead, every muscle tense like she was ready to take on a whole army by herself. Meanwhile, Caleb was behind me, grumbling loud enough for the whole world to hear.

"My boots are never going to recover from this mess," he complained, shooting a mournful look at his mud-caked feet.

Kira flicked rain out of her eyes and scowled. "I better not get trench foot from this."

"Tell me about it," Caleb agreed. "Your feet smell bad enough as it is," he said, earning a punch from Kira.

Darreon and Gnash flanked me, both of them silent but solid. Darreon's hand rested on the hilt of his sword, his eyes scanning the ruined landscape with a calm, unflappable focus. Gnash, on the other hand, just grinned at me—a big, reassuring, gap-toothed smile that somehow made the world feel a little less terrifying.

I'd ditched my dress for a more practical pair of wool trousers and a thick cloak that kept most of the rain out, but my real comfort was the Elemental Staff, which I clutched tightly in my hand. Earl had brought it out from its hiding place in the armory just before we'd left and placed it reverently in my hands.

"You'll need this," he'd said as he peered over his golden spectacles. "And don't let Kira's pessimism get to you. You're readier than a frog in a rainstorm." His words felt like a premonition as rain relentlessly beat down on us.

"This better be worth it," Caleb grumbled. "How do we know if Raideron will even bring the Elementals with?" Caleb's voice was half-drowned out by the storm even though he was right next to me. "Maybe he just wants to monologue at us for an hour and call it a day."

I shot him a look. "Raideron doesn't know we have the Firestone. He has no reason to think we might be able to save them. Why wouldn't he bring his greatest weapon to use against us?"

Darreon's face tightened. "So you do not believe Raideron wishes to negotiate, Your Highness?"

"Do you?" I asked him, arching an eyebrow.

He shook his head, rain dripping from the brim of his hood. His eyes narrowed as the blackened skeleton of Middlehaven came into view. "I do not," he said firmly.

My heart hammered in my chest as we entered the village, but I forced myself to keep going. I was Amira Hale, heir to the throne, and I would not let Raideron see me flinch.

Ravenna stood by my side, silent but fierce. She scanned the shadows, every muscle coiled and ready. "Stay sharp," she whispered as Gnash and Caleb slipped away to scout the area, silent as shadows.

I gripped the Elemental Staff so tightly my knuckles ached, and tried to steady my breathing. Whatever happened next, I was glad I wasn't facing it alone.

Then came an unmistakable, mocking voice. "Ah, *Little Princess,*" Raideron jeered, his voice surrounding us even though he was nowhere to be found. "So nice to see you again."

I forced myself to stand tall and shouted, "Show yourself!"

A cackle split the air. Lightning crashed down in front of us, blinding white. I staggered back, blinking away spots. When my vision cleared, Raideron stood there, draped in his tattered black cloak, four strangers at his side. They looked…wrong. Too tall, skin tinged with a sickly purple glow, eyes glazed as if they were seeing some world I couldn't. They moved in eerie unison, like puppets on invisible strings.

Raideron's lips curled into a smile that made my skin crawl. He jerked his chin at one of them—a woman with wild iron-grey hair and crimson robes. Her eyes flared, molten red, and fire blossomed in her palms.

Kira yanked out her hidden dagger and pointed it at Raideron. "So much for talking, huh?"

"Consider them my insurance policy," Raideron quipped.

"What do you want, Raideron?" I asked in a low growl.

He shrugged, as casual as a vulture circling a corpse. "Same as always. Power. Surrender, and maybe I'll even let your friends walk away from this."

"Somehow I'm not surprised," I shot back. "You've never been very original, Raideron."

His thin lips stretched into a sinister smile. "So do we have an understanding, then?" he purred, tilting his head. "You give yourself over to me and I'll tell my friends to leave yours in peace."

I met his gaze, refusing to blink. "And if I don't agree to your terms?"

Raideron let out a sharp laugh. "You know, I almost admire your stubbornness, Princess," he spat, his voice oily and cold. "But let's not pretend you have any cards left to play. I'd hate for your friends to pay for your pride."

Kira, never one to back down, shot him a wicked grin. "Oh yeah? I bet you didn't know Olivia is dead," she fired back. "And that wanna-be queen Narissa? She's locked up for good. I made sure of it."

Raideron shrugged, unfazed. "I knew the sirens would fail me. They're not exactly the brightest sea mammals in the ocean." His lips curled in a sneer, like he was already bored with us.

Kira rolled her eyes, her voice dripping with sarcasm. "And you are? Please. You're just a washed-up villain with a flair for drama."

Raideron's eyes narrowed to slits. "Watch yourself, child."

"Or what?" Kira snapped.

"Kira, enough." I tried to warn her to stop, but it was too late.

Suddenly, the old woman became animated. With a flick of her wrist, she sent a fireball screaming through the air. It hit the ground inches from us, blasting a crater in the mud and sending a shockwave through my bones. Kira fell, a strangled groan escaping her lips as she rolled to her side, clutching her ribs.

"Kira!" I screamed as panic clawed up my throat.

I lurched forward, but Raideron was faster than me. He nodded at another of the Elementals—a man in dark green robes, and the ground buckled beneath Kira. Vines, thick as my wrist and black as midnight, shot up and snaked around her.

Kira's eyes went wide. "Oh, come on—" she started, but the vines cocooned her within seconds, swallowing her up.

"Let Kira go!" Ravenna's voice cracked through the storm, sharp as her taiaha. She looked ready to tear Raideron apart with her bare hands.

Raideron didn't even bother to look at her. He just flicked his fingers, bored, like he was shooing away a fly. "The girl isn't dead, just immobilized," he said, his tone as flat as a weather report. "I'd suggest you don't test my patience further, though."

Ravenna tensed, ready to strike, but I caught her arm. "Not yet," I whispered, my voice trembling with the effort to keep my fear at bay. "We need to be smart about this."

Raideron's eyes were cold and triumphant. "Well, Princess?" he drawled, his lips curling. "Will you come quietly, or shall I give you a demonstration of what real power looks like?"

I caught movement at the edge of my vision—Caleb and Gnash, slipping back from their reconnaissance.

Caleb shook his head once, his bright with excitement. Raideron's army was still at Vail. He had no reinforcements. It was just us and him. Well, and four elemental beings, but I tried not to dwell on that part.

"How about this," I shot back. "Release the Elementals from whatever twisted spell you've got them under, and maybe we'll let *you* walk away."

Raideron blinked comically, then tipped his head back and let out a shrill laugh. "A negotiation, is it? Oh, Princess. You really haven't learned, have you? This meeting was just a courtesy. I do enjoy a little ceremony before the slaughter. Rest assured, once I'm finished here, Vail will burn."

The storm raged around us, but all I could hear was my own heartbeat and the echo of Kira's voice—defiant, furious, and muffled by thorns. I wanted to scream, but I forced myself to be still. Raideron wanted me rattled. He wanted me to break. I refused to let that happen.

"We have something you want," I said, letting the words hang.

"Is that so?" Raideron drawled. "What could you possible have that I would want?"

"The Obsidian Firestone."

Raideron sneered. "We've danced this dance before, haven't we?" he said, his voice low and dangerous. "Each time, you think you'll win. Each time, you lose a little more. Shall we see what you are willing to lose today?"

"I think I'll pass, actually." I mustered a smirk, even as my heart pounded.

Caleb and I locked eyes, just for a second. I could see the plan forming in his mind, wild and reckless and so, so Caleb.

Raideron must have sensed him though, because he spun around to face Caleb, but he was too late.

Caleb slammed his hands into the mud, and the earth answered with a vengeance. Raideron let out a startled curse as the ground liquefied beneath him, sucking him down in a swirl of magical quicksand. In a blink, he was trapped up to his chin, his arms pinned, his face twisted in pure outrage. Honestly, if I hadn't been terrified, I might've laughed.

"Not so tough when you're the one stuck, huh?" Caleb called, his voice fierce and just a little breathless. There was a wild light in his eyes, a spark I hadn't seen since before Josiah's death.

Caleb didn't waste a second. With a flick of his wrist, the vines binding Kira snapped and fell away. She tumbled out of the tangle, coughing and gasping, but alive. Caleb sprinted to her side, hauling her to her feet. Raideron thrashed, spitting threats at them, but the quicksand only tightened around him.

Kira shot Caleb a crooked grin, even as she wiped blood from her split lip. "About time. I was starting to think you'd let me rot in there."

Caleb rolled his eyes, breathless but grinning. "You? Please. We both know you'd have chewed through those vines yourself if I'd taken any longer."

I dropped to my knees beside Kira, my heart pounding so hard I could barely hear anything else. Mud instantly caked my pants, but I didn't care. "Seriously, are you okay?" I asked her.

"Never better. Let's finish this."

Adrenaline surged through me like wildfire as I raised the Elemental Staff high. The Obsidian Firestone at its tip pulsed with a deep, ominous glow. Hope sparked in my chest. Maybe this was it. Maybe we finally had a chance to beat Raideron.

But he was already clawing his way out of the quicksand, his face twisted with fury. "You think you can stop me?" he spat, his voice ragged and wild, his eyes burning with rage. "You children never learn. You're nothing but gnats, buzzing in the dark."

The Elementals drifted toward us, drawn by the power of the staff like iron to a magnet. I waved the staff at them, desperate, willing it to do something, anything. "Come on," I whispered, my voice cracking. "Please work!"

Nothing. The staff just pulsed in my hands, useless. The Elementals kept coming, their eyes empty, their movements jerky and wrong, like puppets with their strings tangled.

"It's not working!" Caleb shouted, panic cracking his voice.

"Tell us something we don't know," Kira shot back.

I tried again. Still nothing.

Across the chaos, I caught a glimpse of Ravenna waving at us. Her voice was lost in the wind, but she pointed frantically toward the spot where Raideron had been trapped only moments ago.

"Where did he go?" I asked Caleb, my voice rising.

Caleb shook his head, eyes wide. "How should I know? He's like a cockroach that never stays squished!"

A cold, unnatural wind curled through the village, setting my nerves on edge. Raideron reappeared at then, his cloak billowing like a thundercloud. But he wasn't alone. He had Gnash suspended in the air like a broken doll, his massive body limp, his head twisted at an angle that made my stomach lurch.

"No," I whispered. "No, no, no."

Kira's face went white. Caleb's fists clenched, magic flickering at his fingertips. Ravenna let out a sound I'd never heard before—a raw, animal scream that cut through the storm and made my heart splinter.

"You didn't have to do that!" I shouted, my voice cracking with fury and grief. The Elemental Staff trembled in my grip.

"Let this be a lesson, *Little Princess*," Raideron sneered, his voice echoing through the village. "You're out of your depth. And now, you get to watch everyone you love die."

I stared at Gnash, at the blood, at the way his chest didn't move. My hands shook. The staff felt heavier than ever. For a moment, I couldn't breathe. Was this how hope died—quietly, in the mud, while the villain laughed?

Gnash had been with me from the beginning. He was steady,

loyal, always ready to shield me from harm. The loss of him left a hole in our ranks, and in my heart, that nothing could fill.

Kira's hand found mine, her grip fierce, grounding me like a lightning rod. "We're not done yet," she whispered, her voice trembling but stubborn, like she could keep the world spinning by sheer force of will. "Not by a long shot."

She turned on Raideron, her voice low and lethal, every word vibrating with rage. "I will kill you," she growled. "If it's the last thing I do, I will kill you."

Raideron sneered. "Not if I kill you first." He gestured to the Elementals, and they surged towards us.

Kira turned to me, her eyes wild and desperate. "Try using the staff again," she urged.

"But it doesn't work!"

"Do it, Amira! Don't you dare give up now!"

I gritted my teeth and tried again, but the staff didn't respond to my silent plea. Magic vibrated through the staff, but I couldn't figure out how to tap into it. "This thing didn't exactly come with an instruction manual!" I shouted back.

Kira eyes darted between me and the Elementals. "Maybe... no, never mind. It's stupid," she said, biting her lip in embarrassment.

A fireball roared past my head, close enough to singe my hair. I ducked, heart hammering. "If you've got an idea, now's the time to share it!" I locked eyes with Kira, trusting her, needing her. Because if we didn't figure this out, we were all dead.

She didn't hesitate again. "Maybe if you, me, and Caleb all hold onto the staff at the same time it'll work?"

I dove to the right just as the Elemental in blue robes shot a scalding stream of water at me, narrowly missing. "It's worth a shot!" I called to Kira, breathless. "Caleb, get over here!"

Caleb was locked in a brutal dance with the green-robed Elemental, dodging a rain of thorns that sliced through the air like knives. "I'm a little busy not dying!" he shouted, but even as he said it, he hurled his patu with considerable strength. The club connected with the Elemental's head and the man crumpled to the ground.

Kira's eyes flashed with wild, stubborn light as Caleb made his way to us. "We grab the staff. All three of us," she said eagerly. "We do this together, or not at all."

Caleb nodded. "Let's end this."

We reached for the Elemental Staff together—my hand at the center, Kira's above, Caleb's below. The Obsidian Firestone pulsed as if it could sense what was coming.

"Ready?" I said, my voice firm and steady, even though my insides were shaking.

"Always." Kira squeezed my hand, her grip fierce.

Caleb, battered but grinning, wiped blood from his temple with the back of his hand. "Let's show this creep what happens when you mess with the Hales."

That was my little brother, always ready to laugh in the face of monsters.

We raised the staff together, our hands overlapping—mine trembling, Kira's steady, and Caleb's warm and sure. Magic surged through the staff. A blinding white light shot out of the Obsidian Firestone, slicing through the storm-dark air and slamming into the Elementals.

Raideron shrieked. Not his usual smug, villainous cackle though. This was raw, panicked, his voice cracking as he threw his cloak over his head. "No! It's not possible!" he howled.

The Elementals staggered in unison as the light hit them. The sickly purple color drained from their skin, swirling away like smoke in the rain. Their eyes cleared and they blinked in confusion, as if waking from a nightmare.

The woman in red looked around with uncertainty. "What is happening?" Her words trembled, but there was a spark behind them, like a fire just starting to catch.

"You're free from Raideron's spell," I said.

Her eyes snapped to Raideron. Fury twisted her features, and for a second, I thought she might incinerate him on the spot. But before she could, he turned and bolted, vanishing into the mist like a coward.

His voice echoed through the village, thin and venomous. "You have not won this day, *Little Princess*. You've only delayed the inevitable. I will have your powers. Hekagia is mine!"

Caleb snorted, rolling his eyes. "Keep telling yourself that!" he shouted into the rain.

But Raideron's laughter slithered through the valley, cold and mocking. "Beware the spy amongst you."

"Too late, Savannah's already been imprisoned," Kira said.

Raideron laughed again. Then... nothing. Silence, heavy and uneasy, settled over us.

I stared at the spot where Raideron had disappeared, unease prickling at the back of my neck. "What do you think he meant by that?" I asked the others.

Kira shrugged, but I could see the tension in her shoulders, the way her eyes darted to the shadows. "Who knows? He's probably just trying to mess with us."

"It's classic Raideron," Caleb said in agreement as he grabbed his fallen patu and wiped away the mud.

"Maybe," I muttered.

But Raideron hadn't even hesitated when Kira mentioned Savannah being locked up. The certainty in his warning sent a cold suspicion twisting in my gut, one I didn't dare voice—not yet.

CHAPTER TWENTY-FIVE

THE ELEMENTALS

Thousands of years ago, four Elementals—beings from another world—traveled to Hekagia as emissaries, hoping to share their magical teachings with the primitive humans who lived there.

Instead, they found a world ravaged by astral magic. The people of Hekagia begged the Elementals to save them from the Magi Nostrum, a sect of powerful astral spellcasters who had plagued the land for decades.

At first, the Elementals hesitated to interfere in mortal affairs. But after witnessing the devastation wrought by the Magi Nostrum, they knew they could not stand by while innocents were slaughtered. Calling upon their greatest powers, they unleashed fire tornadoes that tore through the Magi Nostrum's ranks, drowned their enemies in a massive storm, and opened the earth to swallow those who remained.

Yet some Magi Nostrum managed to escape, retreating to Shadowfell Castle. In their desperation to rid Hekagia of the Elementals, they poisoned the Southern Portal, severing the link to the Elementals home world, trapping them in Hekagia forever.

The Elementals were devastated at first, but as time passed, they accepted their fate. They even fell in love and started families, spreading their magic throughout the land.

They opened temples to teach Hekagians about elemental magic, and their numbers grew. Ballads were sung about their great deeds; stories were written that told of their triumphs over the Magi Nostrum. The Elementals became legends during their long lives.

Iskra, who had long since mastered her fire magic, was the fiercest among the Elementals. She single-handedly laid waste to many foes before finally settling down in the outskirts of Alkrimia. There she fell in love, and lived happily for many years—but Iskra was the first to feel the Magi Nostrum's wrath.

Though it took a long time to recover, the Magi Nostrum were like a parasite, impossible to get rid of unless you destroyed them all. They grew in secret, swaying others to their cause with honeyed lies. When they attacked Iskra's village, it was swift and fierce. They left none alive except for her. It was said that her cries could be heard from miles away.

Aquis, the oldest of the Elementals, preferred to spend his time in the ocean. But eventually, he too fell in love and settled down, founding Mistral. Aquis had many children and lived a good life. He even made friends with the sirens, a notoriously fickle people.

But on a cold winter's day, long after Aquis had forgotten about his old life, the Magi Nostrum crept into Mistral. Despite his skilled water magic, the Magi Nostrum slaughtered everyone but Aquis. They left him alive not as a mercy, but as revenge. If it hadn't been for Iskra showing up then, Aquis would have walked into the ocean and let the current carry him away.

Terran, the youngest of the Elementals, spent his time gardening and using his earth magic to till the rich soil of Hekagia. He was kind-hearted, caring for all creatures, large and small. He eventually learned to communicate with them, a skill he later passed down to his children. Terran was a strategist at heart and knew the Magi Nostrum would come for him. And come they did.

While the Magi Nostrum succeeded in burning his gardens to the ground, Terran had laid many traps throughout the city of Vail to keep its people safe. He made sure they were safe before joining Iskra and Aquis to seek his revenge on the Magi Nostrum.

Last of the Elementals, but not least, was Akash. His ability to glide through the air and manipulate the weather made him an outcast in Hekagia, but eventually he found his place among the people of Nithandore, high up in the mountains. He stayed there for many lifetimes.

Akash preferred to use his brawn rather than his brain, and was known to have temper tantrums that would light up the night sky with lightning. But he was good to the people of Nithandore and taught them how to mine the mountains. The village prospered for *a long time.* But eventually the Magi Nostrum found Akash as well. Their astral monsters descended on the mountain village during the night, claiming nearly everyone until Akash put an end to their terror. The other Elementals arrived too late to prevent the village's demise, but they joined Akash in his grief.

The Magi Nostrum were bent on destroying the Elementals and their lineage. One by one, their offspring were hunted down and killed. Enraged, the Elementals banded together once more to bring the Magi Nostrum down. They, along with their disciples, met at their most sacred temple—the place where they had first crossed over from their home world. But the Magi Nostrum had grown strong, drawing on evil magic from the astral plane, the likes of which even the Elementals had never faced.

The Elementals' disciples perished in the battle, leaving only them alive. Desperate, the Elementals combined their powers in one last attempt to defeat the Magi Nostrum, creating the Elemental Staff to harness their strength. But it wasn't enough.

The Magi Nostrum knew they couldn't kill the Elementals, so instead they put them into a deep slumber—one from which they would never awaken. The Magi Nostrum transformed them into statues and then razed the Elementals' temple to discourage anyone from ever trying to resurrect them.

With the Elementals out of the way, the Magi Nostrum went on to terrorize Hekagia for many years. The Elementals, not dead but not quite alive, bided their time, for they knew that a chosen few of their descendants had survived. One day, it was foretold, one would be blessed with all of their powers. She would free them from their prison—the Savior of Hekagia.

CHAPTER TWENTY-SIX

BETWEEN GRIEF AND HOPE

It's weird how the world just keeps spinning after you lose someone. Two days after Gnash's death, we gathered under an old oak tree at the academy for his memorial, the sky fittingly heavy and gray. Kira stood near his gravestone, her jaw set in that stubborn way that usually meant she was about to pick a fight. But today, she just looked lost.

Ravenna slipped her arm around Kira's shoulders, and for a long time, the two of them just clung to each other, like if they let go, they'd fall apart completely.

Caleb stood off to the side, his hands shoved deep in his pockets. When it was his turn to say something, he cleared his throat and managed, "Guess I'll finally get a word in at breakfast, huh, big guy?" It was the kind of joke Gnash would've liked.

I pressed a wildflower into the earth beside Gnash's battered axe, wiping away my tears.

As the ceremony ended and we drifted back to the school, the weight of loss stayed with us. But life, relentless as ever, refused to pause for our grief.

The return of the Elementals, for all their legendary power, brought a new kind of chaos. Mourning gave way to the strange, stumbling dance of trying to teach ancient beings how to live in a world that had long since moved on without them.

Iskra had nearly fainted when she saw the chandelier in the entrance hall. She grabbed my arm so hard I thought she'd leave a bruise and hissed, "Is that lightning trapped in glass?" Her eyes were huge, like she expected it to explode at any second.

Terran spent a solid hour poking at the wall sconces, muttering to himself about "glowing fungus" and giving them suspicious side-eye, like they might bite him if he turned his back.

Akash, meanwhile, kept glancing up at the copper pipes running along the ceiling. "If those things move, I'll blow them up. Mark my words," he grumbled, his voice all gravel and thunder.

Aquis peered at the pipes, then shrugged. "Perhaps it is simply the water's way of saying hello. All currents find their path, eventually."

It took nearly a week to bring them up to speed. Even then, I caught Terran eyeing the light switches like they were some kind of trick. By the time they were semi-acclimated—meaning they'd stopped flinching every time the lights flickered—my coronation was days away. The pressure was mounting. If we were going to defeat Raideron once and for all, it had to be soon.

I was outside in the training ring, sparring with Ravenna, when Iskra approached me. Ravenna had just deflected my fireball with a flick of her taiaha and a smirk, making it look way too easy. I was lining up another shot, determined to at least singe her sleeve, when a voice cut through the air like a flying dagger.

"So, thou art the great Savior of Hekagia?" Iskra called, her voice ringing out across the lawn like a challenge from the old days. My fireball veered off course, leaving a smoking hole in the grass and my pride in tatters.

Once Raideron's curse had faded, the Elementals magically de-aged themselves. Iskra was now a tall woman of thirty, with auburn hair that glowed like fire. Her eyes were sharp, and she looked me up and down with a shrewd, almost disappointed expression that made my cheeks burn with embarrassment.

"I don't know about all that," I muttered, suddenly wishing I could disappear into the grass. "But I am Amira Hale, if that's what you mean."

Iskra arched a brow, her lips twitching in amusement. "Does thou not prefer to be called Princess Amira?"

I shrugged awkwardly. "To be honest, I don't prefer it."

For a moment, I braced for a lecture, but Iskra's expression softened into an approving smile. "In my time, titles were earned in the forge of hardship, not handed down like trinkets. I will call you Amira, as you wish."

"Thanks… I think." I shot Ravenna a questioning look, but she just smiled at me, completely unhelpful.

"How are you feeling?" Ravenna asked her.

"Better now. Thy friend Earl is a miracle worker, though his methods would have startled the healers of my time," Iskra replied, rolling her shoulders as if testing out her new body. "Yet, I find myself restored."

"You look... better." I said, a little sheepishly.

Iskra laughed, a sound like crackling fire. "That is a kind way of putting it. I suppose I owe ye thanks for dragging me out of Raideron's pit of despair—even if your aim could use a century's practice."

I glanced at the grass where my last attempt at besting Ravenna had gone awry. "I don't think even a century would be enough to help my aim."

Iskra stepped closer to me, her gaze burning like embers. She clasped her hands behind her back, deliberate and steady. "You have much ahead of you, Amira. Saving the world is never simple, but I sense you have the mettle for it."

"I'm glad one of us thinks so," I muttered.

"I believe so too," Ravenna added. "Your training is going just fine. And I have no doubt that I leave you in capable hands." She smiled respectfully at Iskra.

Iskra inclined her head in return. Then she turned to me, her hair catching the sunlight. "Shall we?" She gestured at the training ring with a sweeping motion that felt both like a challenge and an invitation.

My stomach twisted. Sparring with an Elemental?

I glanced over at the archery field, where (of course) Treander was practicing. I could feel his gaze on me—steady, reassuring, but also expectant.

"Maybe tomorrow," I said, trying to keep my voice steady.

Iskra clasped her hands behind her back, studying me. Her posture was straight as a blade, and I knew then that I was being measured for something far more than a sparring match. "There is no place for cowardice upon the throne," she declared, her words crisp and unyielding. "In my day, a ruler who faltered in such a way would scarce last a fortnight."

Her words stung, sharp as a slap across the face.

"I'm not a coward," I protested.

Iskra's lips curled into a sly, almost predatory smile. "Then prove thyself, child. Let deeds, not words, speak thy worth."

My hands shook as I stepped into the ring, but Iskra moved with the easy confidence of someone who'd spent centuries mastering her craft. Each step she took was deliberate and her gaze never wavered.

"Art thou prepared?" she called, her voice ringing across the field, every syllable heavy with expectation.

"Ready as I'll ever be," I said under my breath.

Iskra's first volley of fireballs came at me so fast I barely managed to dodge them. I stumbled to the edge of the ring, my heart pounding in my chest. I tried to summon my own fire magic but sputtered out, just as weak and uncertain as I was.

But Iskra didn't let up. Another fireball, faster this time. I spun out of the way, but not fast enough. The flames caught my shoulder, searing through my cloak. Pain exploded down my arm, but I gritted my teeth, refusing to cry out.

Iskra laughed, the sound crackling like a bonfire. "Thou must do better than that, Amira. I shall not coddle you as others have."

Anger flared in my chest. "I have never been coddled in my life," I snapped. "And I'm just getting started."

I squared my shoulders, ignoring the pain, and let my magic rise. If I was going to survive this—if I was going to lead Hekagia—I'd have to stop running from the fire and start becoming it.

I hurled a round of fireballs at Iskra, but she spun through them like she was dancing at some ancient festival. Then she lifted her hands, and the air shimmered with heat. Flames twisted around her, swirling higher and higher until she was hidden behind a tornado of fire.

"Really?" I muttered, bracing myself. "That's just not fair."

Without warning, the tornado exploded outward. A wall of fire roared toward me. Instinct took over and I threw up a shield of water, pouring every ounce of will into it. Steam hissed and billowed as the flames crashed over me. When the smoke cleared, I was still standing—singed, but untouched.

Iskra clapped, her eyes bright with delight. "For a moment, I feared thou wouldst be reduced to cinders," she declared, her voice ringing. "Yet it seems there is hope for thee after all."

I let out a shaky breath and said, "Thanks. But next time, maybe warn me before you try to roast me alive?"

She laughed, the sound warm and wild. "If thou seeks mercy, thou art in the wrong ring, Amira." She beckoned me closer, her smile turning almost conspiratorial. "Come, let us speak awhile."

I walked beside her as we made our way back to the academy. "How did you do that fire tornado thing?" I asked, unable to hide my curiosity, or my envy.

Iskra's lips quirked. "In time, I shall teach you all that I know. But first, we must speak of the Magi Nostrum. Tell me, do they yet hold sway in this age?"

"Only Raideron. He's been after me my whole life, trying to steal my powers. He's the last of them, but he's more dangerous than all of them combined."

Iskra's expression softened, but there was a new intensity in her eyes. "I am not surprised. Jests aside, you are a rare soul, Amira. I can feel my magic running through thy veins."

My eyebrows shot up in surprise. "Your magic?"

She nodded, her eyes never leaving mine. "Our bloodlines are entwined. Thou blood is filled with elemental magic, Amira. And you shall need every spark of it to finish what we began those many centuries past."

The weight of her words settled over me. "Does this mean I'm not human?" I asked, unsure if I actually wanted to know the answer. I'd only just come to terms with not being from Earth, now I had to question if I was human at all?

"That depends on thy meaning of human," Iskra replied. "We hail from another world, yet we live as mortals do. We have loved, we have lost, we have erred and paid the price, again and again. Is that not the very heart of humanity?"

Maybe Iskra was right. Maybe it didn't matter where I was born. Maybe what mattered was how I lived. I definitely felt human enough, with all my faults.

"Can you help us defeat Raideron?" I asked her.

Iskra's lips pressed into a thin line. "Raideron is a foe most worthy. He shall not fall easily, nor by half-measures."

I let out a dry laugh. "Tell me about it. We've tried... several times, actually. But he always manages to survive."

Iskra's eyes blazed with a sudden intensity. "Come," she said. "There is something you must see."

I followed Iskra, my nerves prickling. "Where are we going?" I asked, though I had a feeling I already knew. Somehow, we always ended up in the library.

Caleb was there, hunched over a sprawling genealogy chart at the table, his shoulders tense, eyes fixed on the tangled lines of ancestry. He barely glanced up as I entered. Across from him, Earl and Aquis were locked in a heated, whispered debate. On the couch, Kira and Ravenna sat side-by-side, but their bodies were turned away from each other, a silent rift between them.

Without a word, Iskra selected the thickest book from the pile on the table—a tome so heavy it looked like it could anchor a ship—and pressed it into my hands.

"What's this?" I asked, my voice small in the hush.

Iskra's gaze was gentle, but there was a weight behind it. "Can thou read what is written?" she asked, hope flickering in her eyes.

I traced the looping script with my finger. The letters were beautiful, but they might as well have chicken scratch. "No, sorry," I admitted, shame prickling at my cheeks.

Iskra's disappointment was brief; she waved it away with a flick of her hand. "Tis alright, not many people can, aside from me. This tome recounts the history of the first astral spellcasters. Through its pages, we have gleaned how Raideron amassed his power, and, how he might yet be undone."

My heart raced with excitement, but the room was heavy with something else. My stomach twisted with dread.

"What's wrong? Isn't this what we've been waiting for? A way to take Raideron down?"

Earl cleared his throat, rolling his spectacles between his fingers. "Ah, if only life were as simple as a recipe for exploding ink, Your Highness." He tried for a grin, but it faltered. "It's not that simple, I'm afraid."

My excitement faded. "Why not?"

"Because–"

"Because you have to close the rift to the astral plane," Kira cut him off. "Meaning all astral spellcasters in Hekagia will lose their powers forever. Including me."

My mind spun as Iskra laid out the plan. It was almost too simple. Raideron had survived every attempt to kill him because he'd found a way to draw power from the astral plane, a rift between worlds. The spell Iskra wanted me to use would seal the rift forever, cutting Raideron off from its power, along with every other astral spellcaster in Hekagia.

"You can't do this!" Kira's voice cracked, raw with fury and fear. "You have no right!" Magic flickered at her fingertips, purple and wild.

Earl cleared his throat. "Well, technically, she does. It's in the job description; Queen: must make impossible decisions, look good in a crown, and occasionally doom her friends to a life of mediocrity."

"She isn't queen yet," Kira shot back, her voice dropping to a dangerous growl.

"Kira, be reasonable," Ravenna said quietly, her tone gentle but firm, trying to anchor her. But Kira was already on her feet.

She crossed the room in three furious strides and ripped the spellbook from my hands. "What gives you the right to decide this for all astral spellcasters?"

I took a step back, my heart pounding. "Kira, I haven't decided anything," I said, trying to keep my voice calm.

"So you're not going to do it then?" she demanded.

"I didn't say that either."

Kira shoved the spellbook back at me, her tears falling fast. "You might be the queen soon, but that doesn't give you the right to play God with our lives." Then she stormed out of the library, the door slamming behind her like a thunderclap.

I stood there, frozen, the spellbook heavy in my arms. I looked to Ravenna, desperate for someone to tell me what to do, to tell me I wasn't a monster for even considering it. But Ravenna stood off to the side, her face shadowed with worry for Kira.

"I'll go try to calm her down," she said softly, and slipped out of the library without another word.

Sunlight streamed through the library windows, painting golden stripes across the room and making the dust motes dance. But the mood in the room was anything but light.

"What do you think about all this?" I asked Caleb as I plopped into an open chair next to him.

He didn't look up from his book. "I'm not sure I get an opinion on this one, Amira. It's not my powers on the line." His tone was flat, but his jaw was tense.

"Well, if you want my advice," Earl piped up, "I'd say we all run away and open a bakery. Less drama, more pastries. But, ah, I suppose that's not very helpful right now."

His voice softened, the joke fading. "Whatever you decide, Amira, just make sure it's your choice. Not the council's, not Kira's. Yours."

I opened my mouth to answer, but the library doors banged open so hard I yelped instead. Terran and Akash swept in, sunlight glinting off their ancient clothes. They looked like they'd just stepped out of a legend—or maybe a museum.

Caleb's whole face lit up when he spotted Terran. He tried to play it cool, but he kind of looked like a golden retriever seeing another dog at the park.

Terran's voice rumbled, deep and steady, like rocks grinding together. "Hello, Prince Caleb. How are you this afternoon?"

Caleb tried to sound casual, but his voice cracked. "Hey, Terran. Uh, things are... wild, I guess."

Akash cleared his throat loudly in annoyance. The sound reminded me of car tires crunching over the gravel road to our farm in Michigan. It was both soothing and grating at the same time. "Can we move this along?" he huffed, arms crossed, foot tapping like he had somewhere better to be.

I straightened, hugging the spellbook to my chest a shield. "Move what along?" I asked nervously.

Iskra scowled at Akash, then turned to me. "The spell to close the rift requires more power than thou hast ever wielded. It will require much effort, but can be done."

I bristled, hugging the book to my chest. "But I haven't even decided if I'm going to do it," I protested, my voice rising. "You're all acting like this is already set in stone."

Akash snorted. "Destiny doesn't wait for you to make up your mind, Princess."

"There's got to be another way!"

"There's isn't," Iskra replied, her voice firm. "You need not do this alone, Amira. But you must be ready."

Akash slammed his fist on the table, making the spellbook jump in my lap. "Enough dithering," he snapped, his words sharp as broken glass. "There's no decision to make. Raideron must be destroyed, and this is the only way. We begin training at dawn."

"But my coronation is in six days," I pointed out. "I'll never be ready in time."

Iskra pursed her lips, her eyes thoughtful and steady. She always looked like she was weighing the fate of the world—and I suppose this time she was.

"It will be difficult, but not impossible," she said, her words rolling out slowly. "Thou must reckon with what you are willing to lose, though. Despite what Akash proclaims, Master Earl is correct: the choice is yours alone."

And just like that, Grandma Ana's letter made sense. Somehow, she'd known that it would come to this. I just hope she'd been right; that those who love me will understand, no matter what I decide. But I couldn't imagine Kira ever forgiving me for taking away her magic.

I pressed my palms to my eyes, exhaustion washing over me. "I need some time to think."

"There is no time," Akash replied, his tone as rigid as stone.

I met his stare, refusing to back down. "Then we'll have to make time," I shot back. "I'm not about to let anyone rush me into this decision. Not with what's at stake."

Akash looked like he wanted to argue, but Iskra placed a steady hand on his arm. "Peace, Akash," she said. "Let the child breathe. We shall gather again on the morrow, when thy heart is ready to decide."

A single day to make such a monumental decision didn't seem like nearly enough time, but I nodded in agreement anyway. If that's all the time I had, then I would just have to make the most of it.

CHAPTER TWENTY-SEVEN

THE ULTIMATUM

As I left the library, the sunlight felt almost mocking—too bright, too cheerful for the storm inside my head. I wandered the halls, hoping I'd find Kira somewhere, but her bedchamber was empty, and the training room was just as deserted. So I dragged myself back to my own room and collapsed onto my bed, the spellbook still clutched to my chest.

I was so tired I could barely move, but my mind wouldn't stop spinning. Thoughts blurred together, leaking into each other like watercolors left out in the rain. Every time I tried to focus, the decision loomed over me—close the rift, save the world, maybe destroy Kira's magic forever.

I stared up at the swirling pattern on my ceiling, letting my mind drift. The shapes twisted and danced, refusing to settle into anything familiar.

Hours must have passed. Eventually, I reached for the spellbook Iskra had given me, flipping through the pages with numb fingers. Most of it was unreadable to me, the script looping and foreign. But here and there, I caught glimpses of something that made my heart soar—my grandma Ana's handwriting, scrawled in the margins.

She'd written in the same language as the book, her notes curling around the ancient spells. I traced her words with my fingertip, wishing I could talk to her one more time. Why hadn't she just told me everything three years ago? Maybe she'd known I wouldn't have understood, not back then—not when I was still so new to Hekagia and magic. I guess I'd never get the chance to ask her now. All I could do was hope she'd been right—that when the time came, I'd know what to do, and that the people I loved would understand. Even if it broke their hearts.

The only thought I could hold onto, the one that surprised me most, was how much I needed my mom. I hadn't let myself think that in years. But when everything felt hopeless, all I wanted was for her to wrap me up and tell me it would be okay, like she used to when I was little.

I could see Vail castle through my window, way off in the distance, glowing faintly. I changed into my riding clothes and slipped out to the stables. Of course, Treander was there, brushing down a restless bay.

He glanced over his shoulder and flashed that crooked, too-bright grin. "Well, well. If it isn't the Queen of Sneaking Out. You know, most people knock before invading a man's midnight horse therapy."

"Sorry. I just... needed air. And maybe someone to talk to."

Treander set aside the brush with a nod. "Lucky for you, I am an expert in both breathing and conversation. Also, I make an excellent midnight snack, if you enjoy stale oats and questionable apples."

I laughed, but the ache in my chest didn't ease. "You ever wish you could just run away from all of it?"

He leaned against the stall, his arms crossed. "All the time. But then I remember I'd have to leave you behind, and, well—" He shrugged, cocky but sincere. "I'm not that brave."

"You're ridiculous," I said, rolling my eyes.

He grinned. "Yes, but you love me for it. Or at least, I hope you do." His cheeks went red, but he didn't look away.

I cleared my throat, my voice turning more serious. "I'm going to Vail Castle... please, don't try to stop me."

He studied me for a long moment, the torchlight catching in his russet hair. Then, with a little bow, he stepped aside. "Stop you? Not even if the stars themselves commanded it. But let me accompany you. The roads aren't safe this time of night."

I wanted to argue, to insist I could handle myself, but the truth was, I was grateful for his offer. The others would have a fit if they knew what I was up to, but maybe they'd forgive me if Treander was with me. I nodded and shot him a grateful smile.

He saddled his stallion with a flourish, then helped me up, his hands lingering just a moment longer than necessary. We rode in silence, the only sounds the steady clop of hooves and the distant call of a nightbird.

I hadn't realized how close Treander was until I felt his chest pressed against my back, the warmth of him bleeding through his shirt. I hadn't bothered with a cloak—too stubborn and desperate to get away. There was barely any space between us, and I could feel the tension in his body, the way he shifted, clearing his throat like he was about to speak but thought better of it.

"Is everything okay?" I asked, glancing back at him.

He hesitated, then gave me a coy smile. "I confess, I've never been so glad for a midnight ride. There's a certain magic to it, don't you think? The world asleep, just you and me and the road ahead...."

The dull moonlight caught on the silvered leaves of the whisperwood trees, making the whole path shimmer like it was dusted with magic. I tried to play it cool, even as my pulse hammered.

"Well, I sort of had to. I'd have probably ended up in a ditch somewhere if you weren't here to steer us."

Treander leaned in, his breath warm against the back of my neck. "Is that truly the only reason you let me come along?" His lips brushed my ear, and my brain just... fizzled. For once, I had nothing clever to say.

He chuckled, a deep, rumbling sound that vibrated through his chest. "Your Highness, it is unlike you to be without speech."

"Don't get used to it," I managed, my voice embarrassingly breathless.

He laughed again, softer this time, and the sound eased something tight inside me. Then he shifted, freeing one arm from the reins and wrapping it around my waist, pulling me closer. I let myself lean into him, letting the tension of the day melt away.

"Can I ask what prompted this late-night adventure?" he murmured, his voice gentle but edged with curiosity.

I sighed, letting my head rest against his chest. "Oh, you know. The usual. I have to make a decision that could change the fate of everyone in Hekagia. No pressure or anything."

He stiffened behind me, his hand tightening just a little. "You mean your coronation?" His voice had that careful note, like he was bracing for bad news.

"No, it's not that," I said quickly, trying to reassure him.

He relaxed, the tension draining from his body as he exhaled. "Is it anything I can help with?" he asked.

"Not this time."

He was quiet for a moment, then squeezed me gently. "Then I hope you find what—or who—you're searching for at the castle."

"It's my mom," I replied, just as softly. "I really need to talk to my mom." The words sounded childish, even to. Almost eighteen, future queen, and still needing my mother. I was glad that Treander couldn't see my face turn red.

But his voice was almost wistful when he spoke. "I remember my mother only a little," he said. "It's more of a feeling than a memory. Just… knowing I was safe, like nothing in all of Hekagia could hurt me. I haven't felt that way in a long time." He hesitated, then nudged my shoulder with his chin. "Not until I met you, anyway."

His words sent my heart racing again. Why did he have to be so charming? I wanted to say something back, anything, but my throat closed up.

Treander squeezed my hand in reassurance. "You don't have to say anything," he murmured, his voice barely above a whisper. "I understand. Sometimes you just need someone to tell you it's all going to be okay."

If we'd been in a car instead of on horseback, I would have leaned over and kissed him right then. But I wasn't about to risk falling off a horse and breaking my neck, so I waited until we finally reached Vail Castle, just as the sky began to pale with dawn.

The castle stood in front of us, its towers silhouetted against the first streaks of sunrise, lanterns glowing in the windows like sleepy fireflies. The scent of damp earth and wildflowers clung to the morning air, mixing with the woodsmoke that drifted from the castle chimneys. Somewhere in the distance, a bell tolled the hour, echoing across the dew-soaked lawn.

Treander swung down first, boots landing with a soft thud on the mossy stones. He turned to help me dismount, his hand warm and steady in mine. My legs were stiff, but I barely noticed.

He started to lead the horse toward the stables, but I reached out and caught his sleeve. He turned, concern flickering in his green eyes. "What's the matter, Your Highness?"

I kissed him fiercely. Treander dropped the reins, his arms locking around me. My heart hammered so loudly I was sure the castle workers could hear it, but I didn't care. For a few seconds, nothing existed except the two of us.

But reality crept back in, as it always does. Treander pulled away, though I could see the effort it took him. His breath was ragged, his eyes searching mine like he was trying to memorize every detail.

"Amira," he said, his voice raw. He almost never used my real name, and never like that. I knew I was in trouble then.

He pressed my wrists to his chest, holding me close. "I can't do this anymore," he said, pain flickering across his face. "I can't keep pretending I'm fine sharing you with another man. And I can't keep waiting for you to choose one of us."

His words cut deep. Anger and longing welled up inside me. "It's not that simple and you know it," I said, swallowing hard.

"But it is," Treander insisted, his voice trembling but fierce. "I love you, Amira. And I know you love me back. That's the only thing that matters to me." His eyes searched mine, stubborn and hopeful.

I yanked my wrists free, frustration flaring. "And what would you have me do?" I demanded. "Give up the throne for you?"

He shook his head, russet hair falling into his eyes, and for a second, he looked every bit the reckless, impossible boy I'd fallen for. "Hekagian law says you must be wed before your coronation. It does not say to whom." His voice was low, but there was a spark of mischief underneath.

My heart thudded unevenly in anticipation.

"What are you saying?" I asked him breathlessly.

His face lit up in a lopsided grin.

"Marry me."

The words echoed in my mind, impossible and undeniable.

I stared at him, stunned, as the heavy door of Vail Castle creaked open behind me. Someone was coming, but I couldn't take my eyes off Treander.

"You… you're serious?"

Treander's eyes were locked on mine—steady and unwavering, like he'd already made his choice and was just waiting for me to catch up.

"I would not have asked if I wasn't certain. I cannot imagine my life without you in it. Not anymore."

"My parents would never allow it," I said, shaking my head. The words came out sharp, the weight of expectation pressing down on me like iron shackles.

Treander exhaled in frustration, but his voice was gentle. "Parents be damned."

"Spoken like someone who doesn't have parents to worry about." The words slipped out before I could stop them, though I instantly wished that I could take them back.

His eyes went wide, hurt flashing across his face. For a second, the only sound was the wind rattling the banners that hung above the castle gate.

"I didn't mean—" I started, but the words were already out there, and I knew I couldn't take them back.

Treander let out a laugh, but it was sharp and hollow, nothing like his usual easy grin. "That was cruel, Amira. Even for you." His voice was quiet, but it stung more than if he'd shouted.

I crossed my arms, hugging myself. "What's that supposed to mean?"

"Did you ever even think about how I felt, watching you with Ajay all summer, pretending it didn't gut me every time?"

"You're the one who told me to be with him!"

"I know!" he said, louder. "But only for the sake of the realm. Not because I wanted to. I thought—"

He broke off, his eyes dropping to the ground. "I thought you'd choose me."

The silence stretched between us, thick with unsaid words. The wind stirred the leaves in the courtyard, and somewhere behind us, the castle door creaked again.

"I'm sorry," I whispered, reaching for his hand, desperate to close the distance between us, to take back everything I'd said and everything I hadn't.

But Treander stepped back, just out of reach, and shook his head. "No. Not this time." His voice was rough, and there was a finality to it that made my heart lurch.

"Please," I murmured, my voice barely more than a breath. But he just waved me off, jaw set, eyes shining with something fierce and wounded.

He drew a shaky breath, then said, "Either marry me... or let me go."

The words slammed into me, knocking the breath right out of my lungs. "I—" I started, but the words tangled up and died. My heart was pounding so loud I was sure Treander could hear it. I was stuck—caught between what I wanted and what everyone else expected.

And then...

"Amira!" My mother's voice cracked across the courtyard like a whip. Because of course she'd pick this exact moment to show up and ruin everything.

She stood at the top of the castle steps—back straight, eyes blazing. "What on earth do you think you're doing?" she demanded, her gaze slicing through me. "You're making a scene."

I turned back to Treander, but he was already swinging up onto his horse. Panic made my heart race.

"Treander, wait—please don't go!" My voice came out small, desperate, barely louder than the wind.

He paused, just for a moment, then glanced over his shoulder at me. His voice was rough, but steady. "I've said all I can, Amira. I hope you find what you're looking for." He didn't look back again.

I stood there, numb, watching him ride away. My body felt hollow—like someone had scooped everything out of me and left nothing but cold.

"Enough of this nonsense, Amira," my mother snapped, her voice sharp and controlled. She marched down the steps, her heels clicking like a metronome of doom.

I turned slowly, blinking hard, trying to keep it together. Her eyes met mine, and for a moment, her stern expression faltered. The anger faded, replaced by something softer.

She hesitated, then draped her cloak around my shoulders, her hands surprisingly gentle. "Are you alright?" she asked, her voice lower now, as if she could sense I was about to shatter.

I didn't answer. I just stood there, shivering, fists clenched in the folds of her cloak.

She studied me shrewdly, her gaze searching mine. "What are you doing out here? It's freezing."

"Treander asked me to marry him." My voice was low in shocked disbelief.

She let out a long sigh, rubbing her temples like she was getting bad news from the doctor's office. "And what did you say?"

"I didn't say anything." My cheeks burned with shame.

"So you've still not decided then?" Her tone was clipped, but there was a tremor beneath it.

"Well, I..." I trailed off, the words dissolving on my tongue. That's when I really looked at her. Her face was gaunt, almost hollow. Her blonde hair had turned silver and there was something worrisome about the way she stood, like a strong wind might blow her over.

Suddenly, Treander's ultimatum felt a million miles away. All I could see was my mom, fragile and trembling, and the panic that spiked in my chest had nothing to do with romance.

"What's wrong with you?" I asked her bluntly.

This time, she didn't dodge the question. Instead, her whole posture shifted. Her shoulders sagged, and she reached for my hands, her fingers cold and shaking. "Come with me," she said softly, guiding me toward the castle. "We need to talk."

I let her lead me, my mind reeling. Treander's words echoed somewhere in the back of my head, but right then, all I could think was: Please, not her. Not now.

CHAPTER TWENTY-EIGHT

SECOND CHANCES

My mother collapsed as we crossed the castle's threshold. One second, she was regal and composed, chin up like nothing could touch her. The next, she crumpled, right there on the marble floor.

"Mom!" My voice cracked as I dropped to the floor, catching her before she could hit her head. Her skin was freezing—like a snowstorm in Michigan level freezing. Her pulse barely fluttered under my fingers.

I pressed my hands to her cheeks, desperate, trying to will my fire magic to do something. But all I got was a weak spark and a sick feeling in my stomach.

Madame Galena appeared then, her robes swirling around her like she'd materialized out of thin air. She knelt beside us, her usual calm replaced by fear. "Your Highness…" Her voice was soft, almost apologetic, as she took in the sight of my mother's limp body in my lap.

"What's wrong with her?" I whimpered, my throat tight.

Galena's hands were gentle as she checked my mother's pulse, her brow furrowing. I saw the shine of tears in her eyes, but she blinked them away. "I don't know," she said, her voice barely above a whisper. "She's been getting weaker ever since she came back from Shadowfell Castle. Raideron's handiwork, I'd wager."

"Then fix her!" My words came out sharp, desperate. "You're the best healer in Hekagia—please, Galena, do something!"

Galena shook her head, her shoulders sagging. "We've tried everything," she said, her voice heavy. "Every healer, every potion, every spell I know. Nothing's worked. She's… she's slipping away, Your Highness. I'm so sorry."

I stared down at my mother, willing her to open her eyes, to squeeze my hand, to say something snarky about me making a scene. But she just lay there, so still and small, and I felt the world tilt under me. I'd never felt so powerless in my life.

"But she was fine," I said, but even as the words left my lips, I knew they weren't true. I'd seen the signs. The way her skin had lost its glow, the stiffness in her movements. She'd been in pain, and she hadn't told me.

Madame Galena rose slowly, her face shadowed and tired. "She's been holding on for your coronation, Your Highness. But she's running out of time."

I swallowed hard. "Does my dad know?"

Galena nodded, guilt flickering across her face. "He knows. He's been trying to be strong for you and Caleb."

"And Caleb? Does he know too?" My voice cracked on my brother's name. I couldn't imagine him finding out like this.

Before Galena could answer, heavy footsteps echoed across the entrance hall. My dad appeared, looking like he hadn't slept in days. His face was ashen, eyes rimmed with exhaustion. "No," he said, coming to a stop beside me. "Caleb doesn't know."

He bent down and scooped my mother into his arms, cradling her against his chest. She stirred, just barely, her hand brushing his shoulder like she recognized the comfort of his touch.

I watched them, my heart aching. My father—always so composed, so unbreakable—looked suddenly lost, holding her like something that was precious and already half gone. The reality of the situation crashed over me.

"How could you keep this from me?" I demanded as we made our way to the infirmary.

Dad didn't look at me. His jaw was tight, and I could see the pain etched in every line of his face, like he was holding himself together by sheer will.

"It was your mother's wish," he said, his voice thick. "She didn't want you to worry. She wanted you to focus on the coronation."

I let out a wry laugh, but it came out as a choked, ugly sound. "Why would she want that?" I asked. "Why would she want me to pretend everything was fine when she's—" My voice cracked, and I bit back the rest.

Dad shrugged one shoulder and repositioned my mother in his arms. "Because she knew you, Amira. She knew you'd drop everything to try and save her."

"Of course I would!" I snapped, my voice rising, raw and desperate. "She's my mother. I would do anything to help her."

Dad shook his head, his voice grave and final. "There is no cure, Amira. Her mind, body, and soul have been altered by whatever Raideron did to her. You must have noticed the changes in her over the last year?"

The signs had been there all along. Her decline—both mental and physical—hadn't been sudden. It had happened slowly and subtly, the kind of thing you only see clearly when it's too late. I just hadn't let myself see it. Some stubborn, childish part of me still believed my parents were unbreakable. That no matter what happened, they'd always be there.

So I ignored the warning signs. The way her voice had gotten sharper, her temper quicker to flare. The way she hovered, questioning every decision I made. I'd told myself it was just stress, or fear, or the weight of everything we'd been through. But now, looking back, I saw it for what it was. It was desperation. A woman trying to hold together the pieces of a life shattered by something dark and unseen, fighting to keep us safe even as she was falling apart herself.

"There has to be something we can do," I insisted.

Dad shook his head, his eyes full of helplessness. "I wish there was, Amira. I really do…"

"What about Earl?" I asked, desperation making my voice rise. "He's got all kinds of tonics and cures, maybe there's something you haven't tried yet."

But the look on Dad's face told me everything. Of course they'd already gone to Earl. Of course they'd tried everything. Which meant Earl had kept this from me, too.

My stomach twisted, anger and betrayal rising up in my chest. "So everyone's just been lying to me?" I snapped. "Why does everyone feel the need to protect me? That's all anyone's ever done my whole life. Even the people who claim to love me."

Dad flinched like I'd slapped him. "I'm sorry, Amira," he said quietly. "For everything." He lowered himself onto the cot and gently laid my mother down beside him, brushing a stray strand of silver hair from her face. His shoulders were slumped, his eyes hollow with exhaustion.

"It's okay," I said, my anger draining away as I looked at Dad. He just looked so tired, so defeated. "None of this is your fault."

"I suppose it's mine then." My mother's words were so soft I almost missed them. Her eyes fluttered open, unfocused, searching for me.

I froze. I didn't know what to say, so I said nothing at all.

"Hush, Lilliana," Dad murmured, his hand trembling as he brushed her hair back from her forehead. "You need to rest." His voice was gentle, but I could hear the fear underneath.

She smiled weakly, her fingers curling around his sleeve, clinging to him like he was the only thing anchoring her to this world.

"He's right," I said, dropping to my knees next to her. The stone floor was freezing, but I barely felt it. "None of that matters right now. The only thing that matters is getting you better."

Her gaze drifted to me, and for just a moment, I saw her—the real her. The artist, the mother, the Royal. The woman who used to sing while she painted, who could make me laugh even when the world was falling apart. I grabbed her hand, holding it tight in both of mine. "I'm not giving up on you. I won't. I promise."

"Amira, we talked about this—"

"No, *you* talked," I shot back at my dad. "Now it's my turn. I will find a way to save her. No matter what."

Mom's face pinched with worry. She tried to push herself up, but Dad gently pressed her back against the pillow. "Enough, Amira! You're upsetting your mother." His voice was rough, but I could see his hands shaking.

"It's alright," she whispered, her voice thin but somehow still soothing, like when I was little and she'd chase away my nightmares with a song. "I'm well enough. Let me speak to her alone."

Dad hesitated, jaw clenched, a silent battle flickering in his eyes. For a second, I thought he'd refuse. He looked like he wanted to wrap us both up and never let go. But then his shoulders sagged, and he nodded, defeated. Without another word, he slipped out, closing the door behind him with a soft click.

Mom turned her gaze to me, her blue eyes tired but still so familiar. "Don't be angry at your father," she said quietly. "He was only doing what I asked."

"Why didn't you tell me?" I asked her, my voice trembling.

She sighed, her breath rattling in her chest. "Maybe it was selfish, but I wanted you to remember me how I was. Not like this. Not a shell of who I used to be."

"So what was your plan?" My voice came out raw and shaky. "To just… die without even telling me you were sick? Like that would've made it easier for me?" I blinked hard, refusing to let the tears fall. I wanted to be angry, but all I felt was scared.

She flinched, but didn't look away. "I thought that maybe if you didn't see it happening, it wouldn't be so hard."

"Well, you were wrong." I swallowed, the ache in my chest twisting sharper.

She let out a breath. It was a tiny, tired sound. "It would not be the first time that I have been wrong." She reached for my hands. Her fingers were cold, but her grip was steady. And just like that, I was a little kid again, clinging to her hand, wishing she could make everything okay.

Then she managed a faint, knowing smile. "Treander's proposal was very sweet. I didn't realize he cared for you so deeply."

Heat rushed to my cheeks. "You heard all that?"

She nodded, her smile growing just a little.

I shook my head, trying to push the memory away. "Well, it doesn't matter. I can't even think about that right now."

Mom tilted her head, giving me that sharp, assessing look that made me feel like she could see straight through me.

"This is the other reason I didn't tell you I was sick," she said. "You can't put your life on hold for me, Amira. Your coronation is only a matter of days away. It's time to decide."

"I don't know if I'm ready," I whispered.

Mom squeezed my hand, her grip weak but determined. "You are ready, Amira. You just haven't let yourself believe it yet." Her voice was gentle, but there was steel underneath, like she was daring me to argue.

I looked up and met her eyes. For a second, the whole world, the crown, the council, Treander's voice in my head, all the impossible choices, faded away. All I saw was my mom: tired, yes, but still fighting.

"So you won't be disappointed in me if I don't marry Ajay?" My voice trembled, the question raw and childish, but I needed to hear her say it. I needed to know I wasn't letting her down.

She didn't even hesitate. "Of course not," she said, her voice steady as ever. "That was Raideron's curse talking, not me. I trust you, Amira. I trust you to make the right decision for yourself and for Hekagia." She squeezed my hand again.

It was like I could finally breathe. She was right. Deep down, I already knew what I needed to do. The path ahead was still terrifying, and I knew the choices I made would shape more than just my own future. But with her hand in mine, I felt steady. Like maybe I could actually do this.

Mom watched me for a moment, her eyes soft. "So you've decided then?" she asked quietly, her voice full of hope and pride.

I nodded, and even though my hands were shaking, I managed a smile. "Yeah. I have," I said. "But only because of you."

She sighed in relief, the lines around her eyes softening. "I did nothing but tell you what you already knew, Amira."

I almost laughed, but it came out as a watery snort. "You did what you always do, Mom. You were there for me when I needed you most." I leaned down and pressed a kiss to her hand. For a second, I just stayed there, breathing her in, wishing I could bottle this moment and keep it forever.

I turned to go, but mom's voice caught me at the door. "Amira, one favor," she said, her words trembling. "Please don't tell Caleb. I want to tell him myself."

I hesitated, worry gnawing at me. "Soon?" I asked, needing to be sure. "You promise?"

She nodded, her eyelids already drooping, exhaustion pulling her under. "Soon," she whispered, and I could hear the promise in her voice, even as she drifted toward sleep.

I lingered in the doorway for a minute, watching her, and then slipped out. I'd meant to go straight back to the academy, but I barely made it past the main corridor before a soldier intercepted me—breathless, armor clanking, helmet askew like he'd sprinted the whole way just to find me.

"Your Highness," he gasped, bowing so low I thought his helmet might actually roll off and clatter down the stairs. "One of the prisoners is asking for you."

I didn't have to ask which one.

I followed the soldier to the dungeons; they were just as dark and gloomy as I remembered, though the dust and cobwebs had been cleared away. Last time I'd descended into their depths I'd been running from Raideron. This time it was on my own terms.

Savannah was in the first cell, curled up on a threadbare mat. Her blonde hair hung in tangled clumps around her face, streaked with grime. Dirt clung to the tatters of her dress. She looked so small, so lost—nothing like the girl I'd once called my best friend. The Savannah I remembered was all sunlight and daisies. We'd laughed together, cried together, fought side by side. But she'd lied to me. And now that lie sat between us, thick as iron.

She looked up as I approached, her eyes wide and glassy. "Amira?" Her voice was barely more than a whisper. "You actually came?"

I crossed my arms, trying to keep my face blank. "You asked for me, so here I am. What do you want?"

Savannah pushed herself upright, wincing as she moved. She tried to smile, but it faltered. "I wasn't sure you'd come, after everything."

"What do you want?" I asked again, my voice turning cold.

She flinched, her fingers twisting in the hem of her ruined dress. "I deserve that. "I just…" She broke off, searching my face. But I stood motionless, giving nothing away.

Savannah let out a shaky breath, her shoulders curling in. "I never meant to hurt you, Amira. I swear. Raideron has my parents. He said if I didn't help him, he'd—" Her voice broke, and she pressed her fist to her mouth, fighting tears.

I stared at her through the bars, my hands curling into fists at my sides. Anger and sadness twisted inside me, sharp and tangled. "You could have told me," I said, my voice tight. "You could have trusted me."

Savannah let out a bitter laugh. "I wanted to, Amira. I swear I did. But every time I tried, I'd see his face in my head, hear what he'd do if I messed up. I thought if I played along, I could keep everyone safe. I thought I could fix it before you ever found out."

"Well, I did find out," I whispered, my throat burning. "And I don't know what hurts more—the betrayal, or the fact that part of me still wants to believe you were ever really my friend."

Savannah's head snapped up, her voice suddenly fierce. "I am your friend," she insisted, her words tumbling out in a rush.

"Please, let me prove it! I have information about Raideron. Something that can help you stop him!"

I narrowed my eyes, searching her face for any sign she was lying. "How do I know this isn't just another trick?"

She swallowed hard, her hands gripping the bars so tight her knuckles went white. "I know I don't deserve your trust," she said, her voice trembling. "But I'm telling the truth, I promise. I wouldn't lie to you. Not about this."

I wanted to be angry. Anger was simple. It gave me something to hold onto, something to shield myself with.

But beneath it, doubt gnawed at me. Could she still be the friend I'd loved like a sister? I didn't know. And that uncertainty hurt worse than anything else I was feeling.

"I don't think I'll ever be able to trust you again," I said quietly. "But I'm willing to hear you out."

Savannah let out a shaky exhale, her whole body seeming to straighten, hope flickering in her eyes for the first time. "You won't regret this, Amira. I swear."

"I'd better not," I warned, my voice sharp.

She nodded, brushing the last of her tears away with the back of her hand. When she spoke, her voice was steadier, more focused. "I found the rift to the astral plane."

I froze. Of all the things she could have said, that was the last one I'd expected. My mind spun, trying to catch up. "Where? How?"

Savannah's expression darkened, shadows flickering across her face. "Shadowfell Castle," she said quietly. "I had a lot of time to explore while I was locked up there. The rift's hidden deep in the dungeons, behind a sealed door."

A warning bell went off in my head.

"Then how did you get inside?" I asked, my voice sharp, every instinct screaming at me not to trust too easily—not again.

Her gaze dropped to the floor for a moment before meeting mine again. "There was a guard," she said slowly. "He wasn't loyal to Raideron, not fully. I think he pitied me. Or maybe he just wanted to see what would happen."

She swallowed, her throat working as if the words themselves were hard to get out. "He gave me the key. Told me Raideron was tampering with things no one should touch."

A chill crept down my spine.

Savannah hugged her arms around herself, shrinking into the thin blanket on her cot. "I didn't understand it at first," she said, her voice low. "But when I stepped inside... it wasn't just a room. It felt alive." She shivered, her eyes darting to the shadows in the corners of her cell as if she half-expected them to move.

"There were symbols etched into the walls—ancient ones, older than anything I've ever seen." She hesitated, squeezing her eyes shut for a second before forcing herself to go on. "There was a tear. Like someone had dragged a jagged blade through the fabric of the world. It just hung there, pulsing."

"The rift," I said breathlessly.

Savannah nodded, her eyes haunted and far away. "I saw a wasteland—full of twisted, broken creatures I can't even begin to describe. And the sky..." Her voice faltered, and for a second, she looked like a little girl again, lost and scared. "It wasn't a sky at all. Just endless shadows. Shifting. Watching. Like it knew I was there."

I swallowed, trying to steady myself, my fingers tightening around the cold iron bars. "Savannah... do you think you could get us back to that room?"

A flicker of determination crossed her face. "I can," she said, her jaw set. "I know every secret passage in that castle. I spent enough time hiding and running to learn them all. If you need to get there, I can show you the way."

I hesitated, not wanting to get too hopeful. "Do you still have the key?" I asked, watching her closely.

"No," she admitted, her tone sly. "But I know where it is."

CHAPTER TWENTY-NINE

SACRFICE AND SALVATION

It was midday, sunlight streaming through the tall windows and casting shifting patterns across the floor. The library was already buzzing with the energy of the day, but the real storm was brewing between Kira and Savannah.

Kira's eyes narrowed, purple sparks snapping at her fingertips. "What is she doing here?" she demanded, her voice low and dangerous. "She should be locked up in the dungeon, not strutting around like she owns the place."

Savannah rolled her eyes. "Relax, Kira. I'm not here for a reunion. I'm here to save your butt—again. You're welcome, by the way."

"Yeah right," Kira snorted. "The last time you 'helped,' you nearly got us all killed. Sorry if I'm not rolling out the red carpet for you."

I stepped between them, arms outstretched. "Enough! Both of you. We don't have time for another one of your showdowns. There are bigger things at stake." I shot Kira a look, silently begging her to let it go, just this once.

She opened her mouth to object, but at that moment, the door banged open and Caleb strolled in, hands shoved deep in his pockets, curls wild and eyes still half-asleep. He took one look at the scene and groaned.

"Great. Just what we need, another showdown before breakfast." He flopped into a chair, patu clattering against the table, and started peeling an orange like he was watching a particularly dramatic play.

Earl shuffled in behind Caleb, trailing the scent of burnt sage and pickled onions. His golden robes swished around his ankles, and he paused in the doorway, surveying the room with a twinkle in his eye and a lopsided, knowing smile. He raised both hands, palms out, as if calming a roomful of startled pixies.

"Now, now, let's not boil over before the kettle's even on," Earl said, his voice warm and gravelly, like he'd spent the morning arguing with a stubborn cauldron. "There's enough tension in here to curdle my best healing salve."

He ambled further into the room. "Now then, what's this about urgent information and saving the world before teatime?"

Savannah drew a breath, meeting Kira's glare with a level stare. "I found the rift to the astral plane. If you want to stop Raideron, you need me."

Even Earl fell silent at that.

For a moment, the only sound was the faint crackling of the fireplace and the distant echo of footsteps in the corridor beyond the library. Then Caleb broke the silence. "Wait—are you serious? You actually found it?"

"I know a secret way into Shadowfell Castle. And I know how to get us to the rift," Savannah confirmed with a nod.

A spark of excitement flickered in Earl's eyes. He leaned forward, elbows on the table. "If what you're saying is true, Savannah, this could be the chance we've been waiting for. The universe does love a bit of symmetry. Perhaps it's finally time for the scales to tip in our favor."

Everyone looked thrilled. Well, everyone except Kira.

She turned to me, her voice tight. "So you're really going to do it? Close the rift?"

I met her gaze, my heart in my throat, wishing she could see how much this was tearing me up inside. "There's no other way to defeat Raideron. I have to do this."

She swiped at her eyes with the sleeve of her battered leather jacket. "I know you do," she muttered, her voice rough. "But that doesn't mean I have to like it."

The idea of sacrificing astral magic just seemed too big, too permanent, and way too much for a seventeen-year-old who still forgot to eat breakfast. But that's how it always seemed to go: the universe tossing impossible choices in my lap and expecting me to just deal with it.

But I looked around at my friends and felt the tension in my shoulders ease. For the first time in ages, hope flickered throughout the library. We had a way to finally defeat Raideron once and for all, even if it wasn't a perfect solution.

Kira's voice was tight as cleared her throat and turned to Savannah. "Alright. Let's hear everything you know."

Savannah sank into a velvet armchair, her gaze drifting to the window as if she could see the castle from here. "The magical barrier around Shadowfell Castle is gone. Raideron can't keep it up anymore, so that's one problem out of the way."

Kira rolled her eyes. "We already knew that."

"Did you know there's a secret passage in the dungeons? One that leads out past the castle walls and into the forest?"

Kira's jaw tightened, clearly hating that Savannah had information she didn't.

Savannah continued, her voice low and determined. "We can get inside Shadowfell Castle no problem. But reaching the rift won't be easy."

Caleb leaned forward, elbows on his knees, curiosity and nerves mixing in his tone. "Why not? What's waiting for us?

"After losing the Elementals, Raideron is even more paranoid than usual. It's going to take a miracle to get the key."

"Where is the key?" Caleb asked.

Savannah hesitated, nervously tucking a strand of short blonde hair behind her ear.

"Spit it out already," Kira chided her.

"Raideron has it," Savannah said with a sigh. "He found out that one of the guard's let me see the rift. Now he keeps the key on him at all times."

Kira shot Savannah a look. "You could've led with that."

Caleb groaned, running a hand through his hair. "Great. So what's the plan—ask him nicely? Or do we just hope he leaves it lying around?"

Kira's eyes narrowed and she gave a decisive nod. "I can do it," she said, her voice determined.

I shook my head, cutting her off before she could say more. "No. Absolutely not."

She rolled her eyes, defiant as ever. "I'll shadow walk. He won't even know I'm there."

"That's insanely risky, Kira."

Kira's eyes blazed. "So is sitting here doing nothing. If we want to stop Raideron, we have to take risks."

Akash's gravelly voice rumbled through the room as he stormed into the library. "I'm with Kira. It's time to take the fight to Raideron."

"Hush," Iskra chided, gliding into the room behind Akash.

We quickly filled them in on the plan. They listened intently, asking questions and adding what they knew about Shadowfell Castle's defenses. When Savannah got to the part about the rift, Iskra raised a hand, commanding silence.

"Amira, it shall fall to you to seal the rift. Mark me well—it shall not be a simple task." She turned, her gaze steady and ancient, yet her words clear. "You must summon forth every shred of power within you, for no less than that will close the breach."

I let out a frustrated sigh, rubbing my temples. "We've been through this. There's no way I can master my powers in time."

Iskra's eyes flashed. "There is no choice. Should you falter, the rift will gape wide, and Raideron—may his name be cursed—shall remain unconquered. His armies will sweep across Hekagia like a plague, and thy reign shall perish before it begins. Steel thyself, child. Destiny waits for none, and the hour is upon us."

I didn't really know what to say to that, but I was saved from having to figure it out by a familiar voice at the doorway. "Then we better get started."

Yasmine's posture was confident, her dark hair pulled back in a long, neat braid. The last time I'd seen her, she'd been weighed down by grief, but now there was a quiet strength in her eyes—a steadiness that I was happy to see had returned.

I caught myself before launching into a hug, remembering how much she disliked it. Instead, I offered her a grateful smile and a small, respectful nod. "What are you doing here? I thought you'd sworn this place off for good."

Yasmine's lips twitched in a rare, dry smile. "I did. But apparently, you're a lost cause without me." She nodded once, a gesture that was both a greeting and a challenge.

I let out a laugh, feeling the tension in my shoulders ease. "You're not wrong."

Yasmine's eyes softened just a fraction. "Then come," she said, her voice gentle but insistent. "There's no time to waste."

As I fell into step beside her, my mind slipped back to my mother, wasting away in the castle infirmary. Yasmine was right. There was no time to lose. Maybe, just maybe, if I could defeat Raideron, the curse on her would be broken. That small spark of hope was enough to keep me going.

I took my place in the training ring, bracing myself for Yasmine's attack. She stood across from me, arms loose at her sides, her expression unreadable. Thick strands of astral magic flowed from her palms, winding their way toward me.

"Summon an astral shield to block me," she instructed, her tone calm but expectant.

I closed my eyes, reaching for the well of power inside me. But astral magic was still the slipperiest of all my abilities—never quite there when I needed it. I tried to focus, willing the shield to form, but nothing happened.

Yasmine's spell struck me square in the chest, knocking me backward into the training dummy behind me. I landed hard, the breath rushing from my lungs. She tittered in disapproval. "Did you even try that time?"

"Yes," I snapped, rubbing my bruised knee as I pushed myself upright. "I'm doing my best."

"No, you aren't," she snapped back with a disapproving look. "You are distracted. What is the matter?"

"Nothing," I muttered, avoiding her eyes, suddenly fascinated by the chalk lines in the grass that were meant to show me where to stand. Not that they helped me any.

Yasmine crossed her arms, her tone turning firm. "I cannot do my job if you are unfocused. Tell me what is bothering you."

I hesitated, but then relented. "It's Treander. He left the academy last night. I don't think he's coming back."

Yasmine's face softened. "Why would he do that?" she asked, her tone a bit gentler.

"It's a long story," I said, my thoughts drifting back to the moment Treander had asked me to marry him—and how I'd let the moment slip away. "I think I really blew it."

Yasmine was quiet for a moment, her eyes steady on mine.

"You're allowed to make mistakes, Amira," she said, her voice low and even. "But you're not allowed to let them stop you. Not today." She didn't offer comfort in the way others might, but the steadiness in her gaze was a silent promise that she'd help me find my footing again, no matter how many times I fell.

"Alright," I said, letting a mischievous note creep into my voice, "your turn. What exactly happened in Alkrimia?"

Yasmine blinked, caught off guard. "What do you mean?"

I grinned, refusing to let her off the hook. "The Yasmine I know would never say anything even resembling that mushy. You met someone, didn't you?"

Yasmine's cheeks turned a faint shade of pink. She cleared her throat, suddenly all business. "That's... none of your business, Amira."

I couldn't help but laugh at her clear discomfort. "Come on. Who is it?"

Yasmine let out a sharp huff, hands on her hips in annoyance. "Can we please return to your training? There is much at stake."

"Not until you tell me who it is," I insisted, shaking my head with mock seriousness.

Yasmine hesitated, her eyes darting away for a moment before she met my gaze. There was a flicker of uncertainty in her usually steady expression. "It's... Ajay," she said at last.

The revelation stunned me into silence.

"But you don't have to worry," she added quickly, "It is obviously unrequited. He cares for you, not me."

The vulnerability in her voice surprised me. Yasmine, who always seemed so unflappable, was... nervous. She shifted her weight, crossing her arms in front of her chest like a shield.

"How did this happen?" I asked, trying not to spook her.

Yasmine gave a small, helpless shrug. "How does such a thing ever happen? The journey to Alkrimia was long. We shared many talks and found comfort in our shared grief. He is a kind soul."

I hesitated. "Do... do you love him?"

Yasmine looked at me for a long moment, searching my face, then finally nodded. "I am sorry," she whispered. "I know it's foolish."

I shook my head, offering her a gentle, understanding smile. "It's not foolish, Yasmine. Not at all."

She let out the breath she'd been holding, her posture relaxing just a fraction. "Thank you," she said, her tone clipped but sincere. "Now, if you're done prying into my personal life, can we get back to your training? There's still a world to save."

I wrinkled my forehead in surprise, and confusion. "That's it? You don't want to fight or something? You know my family wants me to marry him, right?"

Yasmine's brow furrowed, and she looked wounded. "I would never harm you, Amira," she said, her voice quiet but firm. "And as I said, Ajay does not care for me. Not in that way. He will marry you."

But I could see the pain flicker in her eyes, and I doubted she believed her own words. Yasmine was remarkable, and Ajay would be a fool not to see it.

Still, I knew she was right. Ajay would marry me, even if his heart belonged elsewhere. But how many of us would have to sacrifice our happiness for the sake of Hekagia? I thought of Treander, of Yasmine, of myself, each of us tangled in the web of duty and expectation, forced to set aside what we truly wanted for the realm. There had to be a better way.

I wandered the corridors alone that night, lost in silent contemplation. The academy was shrouded in hush; everyone else had long since gone to bed. Shadows pooled in the corners, stretching long and thin beneath the flickering lights.

Treander's absence had carved a hollow ache in my chest, one that pulsed with every reminder of him—reminders that seemed to linger everywhere I turned. His laughter still seemed to echo in the alcoves, and I half-expected to see him leaning against a doorway, arms crossed playfully, waiting for me. I replayed our last conversation over and over, knowing what I would do if I had the chance to redo it.

In that moment, I vowed that if I managed to actually close the rift and defeat Raideron, I would find Treander, tell him the truth, and hope that, despite everything, he still wanted me.

If I managed to defeat Raideron…

CHAPTER THIRTY

THE RECKONING

The next few days blurred together in a haze of training and exhaustion. Every muscle in my body ached from sparring with Yasmine and the Elementals, and my mind was a tangled mess of ancient spells. Even sleep offered no escape. My dreams were crowded with fire, shadows, and the faces of everyone we'd lost.

Two days before my coronation, I woke to Aria's gentle knock at my door. The sky outside was still that pale, uncertain gray, and the castle was quiet except for the distant clatter of servants getting ready for the festivities. Aria slipped in, her voice apologetic but steady: "Pardon me, but Iskra is asking for you in the library, Your Highness."

I groaned, sitting up slowly. Every muscle protested, and my head throbbed. I made a mental note to track down Earl and beg for one of his tonics.

Aria helped me dress, her hands gentle as she worked through the tangles in my hair. She'd laid out a gown—a shimmering violet silk thing, fit for a princess—but I shook my head. "Not today," I said, reaching for my battered riding clothes instead. "I need to be able to move."

She didn't argue, just nodded and started braiding my hair into two tight plaits, her fingers quick and sure. As she worked, I fastened my gemstone locket around my neck, pressing it into my palm for reassurance. It glowed softly, a reminder of the magic it once held.

I paused, letting the familiar weight of the locket ground me. So much had changed since it had first showed up on my doorstep—a mysterious gift from a grandmother I barely remembered. But I wasn't the same lost girl anymore, uncertain of where I belonged. I was the future queen, a descendant of legends, and the one who would decide the fate of an entire world.

As I made my way through the academy's winding corridors, I listened to the excited murmurs. The air was thick with anticipation. Even though the coronation would be held at Vail Castle, the academy had become ground zero for preparations. Sunlight poured through the tall windows, catching on silver-threaded banners and wildflowers from Nithandore. Ribbons in royal violet and gold hung from the rafters, waiting to be bundled and sent off for the ceremony. Somewhere down the hall, the scent of fresh bread and honey cakes drifted from the kitchens, making my stomach twist with a mix of nerves and hunger.

I passed a group of pages wrestling with a gilded mirror nearly twice their height, their laughter echoing off the walls. In the next alcove, two seamstresses knelt over a heap of velvet and lace, arguing in hushed voices about the final touches for the coronation gown. Even the guards—usually so stiff and unreadable—stood a little taller, their uniforms pressed to perfection, pride flickering in their eyes as I passed them.

But beneath the surface, I could feel the tension humming through the halls. Everyone knew that the coronation was more than a ceremony. It was a promise, a hope that, with a new queen, Hekagia might finally find peace. And that hope rested, impossibly, on my shoulders.

The library doors stood open, and I caught the low hum of voices inside—Iskra's, calm and steady as ever, and Earl's, already deep conversation with Caleb over some ancient spellbook.

Iskra looked up as I entered. "Good, you are here," she said, motioning for me to join her at the table. "We have much to discuss, and not nearly enough time."

I slid into the seat next to her, feeling the familiar prickle of magic in the air—a subtle charge that seemed to hum just beneath my skin whenever the Elementals were near. The Elemental Staff rested on the table between us, the Obsidian Fire Stone still affixed to it, pulsing faintly.

"What is the Elemental Staff doing here?" I asked, glancing between Iskra and Earl.

Iskra's expression was impassive, but there was a seriousness in her voice. "I have watched you these past days, Amira. Thy skills do improve, yet thou hast not mastered astral magic. And thy water magic leaves something to be desired." She paused, her gaze softening as she searched for the right words. "You are progressing well, but there is still much for you to learn."

I let out a sigh, slumping back in my chair. "Tell me something I don't know."

Earl leaned forward, nodding toward the green gemstone around my neck. "We believe the Elemental Staff can help you harness your powers, much like your locket did. It will amplify your abilities, maybe even enough to close the rift."

I frowned, studying the staff. "But how?"

Iskra's eyes lingered on the staff, her fingers tracing the ancient runes carved along its length. "The Elemental Staff is more than a mere symbol of power, Amira," she began, her voice low and steady, the cadence of another age still clinging to her words. "It is a conduit—a vessel for the combined magic of all four Elementals, and now, for yours as well."

She turned the staff so the Obsidian Fire Stone caught the light, its surface swirling with embers. "To wield it, you must do more than simply hold it. You must open thyself to it. Let it draw out the magic in your blood. The staff shall amplify what lies within you, but it will test thee as well. Should you resist the staff, it will resist you in turn."

I swallowed hard, and then asked, "Where do I even start?"

Iskra nodded approvingly. "First you must ground yourself. Feel the earth beneath your feet, the air in your lungs, the warmth of your fire, and the flow of water in your veins. Imagine your magic as threads of light, weaving from your heart, mind, and soul, and then pour it all into the staff." She demonstrated, her hands hovering just over the Elemental Staff, her eyes shut in concentration. The staff began to glow with a warm light.

"When you feel the staff pulse in rhythm to your heartbeat, speak the words of the spell. The staff shall do the rest. But only if you are honest with it—and with yourself."

Earl spoke up then. "The staff will magnify your weaknesses, Amira. If you let fear, or doubt, take hold, its magic will become wild and dangerous. You must trust in yourself."

Iskra nodded, her gaze intent. "Let the staff become an extension of thy will. Picture the rift as a wound upon the world, and thy magic as the healing balm. Pour all that you are into the staff—thy hope, courage, and love for this realm. Only then shall the staff's true power reveal itself to you."

She placed her hand over mine, the staff warm between our palms. "You are the bridge between the old world and the new, Amira. The staff will not lead thee astray, so long as you lead with your heart."

I stared down at the staff. 'Lead with your heart'.

As if that had ever been simple.

Caleb cleared his throat. "Hey, you know you're not doing this alone, right?" His voice was steady, his eyes full of steely resolve. "Kira and I—we're going with you. No matter what happens in that chamber, we'll be right beside you."

Kira nodded, her eyes fierce. "You couldn't keep us away if you tried."

Savannah stepped forward, her voice steady. "Me too. I know I haven't always been the friend you deserved, but I'm here now, and I'm not letting you face this without me."

"Don't forget about me," Ravenna added. "I'll be at your side too, Amira. Whatever comes, we will face it together."

I looked at each of them—Caleb's determined gaze, Kira's unwavering loyalty, Savannah's quiet resolve, Ravenna's steady love—and felt a surge of gratitude so fierce it nearly undid me.

"Thank you," I managed, my voice thick with emotion. "I don't know what I did to deserve family like you, but I'm glad you're here. I couldn't do this without you."

Kira grinned, bumping my shoulder. "Good. Because you're stuck with us."

A ripple of laughter broke the tension.

Kira's eyes met mine—that spark of the warrior I'd always known shining through. "So," she said, her voice low and electric with anticipation, "are you ready to finally take down Raideron?"

I straightened, meeting her gaze. "I am now," I said, my voice clear and certain.

I glanced down at the Elemental Staff, feeling the weight of it in my hands. For the first time in what felt like ages, the fear that had gnawed at me gave way to something steadier: resolve.

Kira's grin widened, satisfaction flickering in her eyes. "That's what I wanted to hear."

We didn't dare risk a portal to Zarandore. Raideron would have sensed us the moment we arrived. Instead, we trusted Caleb's shortcut: a winding, half-forgotten trail he'd found on his travels, skirting the edge of the Aether Woods and promising to save us a day's journey. Even so, the path cut straight through the ravine where Treander and I had first met. With every step, memories seeped in: the echo of his laughter, the way his face lit up in the firelight, his hand finding mine in the dark…

I forced myself to focus on the task ahead. Defeating Raideron was all that mattered now. But the ache of Treander's absence gnawed at me, sharper than I wanted to admit. It would have been a comfort to have the archers with us, and to see his steady presence at my side. Yet I knew, deep down, that it would have also been a distraction. I told myself that was why he'd chosen to stay away, that he understood what was at stake as well as I did.

The others walked ahead, their voices low and determined, but I lingered at the back, letting the memories wash over me.

As we got closer to the border of Zarandore, dark clouds started to churn overhead, blotting out the sun and casting the world in a perpetual twilight. The ever-present gloom cast by Raideron's evil had settled over the valley like a living thing, seeping into the very roots of the plants that grew there. Their petals curled in on themselves as if recoiling from some unseen poison. The air was thick with the scent of damp moss and something sharper—an undercurrent of magic gone wrong, the lingering stain of Raideron's presence there.

By the time we reached the edge of the forest that surrounded Shadowfell Castle, our group had fallen silent. Even Caleb's usual jokes had faded, replaced by a wary tension that crackled like static. Each of us kept a hand close to our weapons, eyes darting to every shifting shadow, as if expecting some monstrous creature to lunge from the darkness at any moment.

Ahead, the castle loomed—half-shrouded in mist, its towers jutting up like broken teeth against the storm-dark sky. Somewhere inside, Raideron waited. I tightened my grip on the Elemental

Staff, feeling its warmth pulse through my palm, a reminder of what we'd come to do, and everything we stood to lose if we failed.

We moved through the forest as one, hearts pounding, until Savannah raised her hand to stop us. Her voice was low, almost a whisper. "There it is." She pointed to a stone sewer grate half-hidden beneath a tangle of thorny vines. "The entrance to the castle dungeons."

Caleb stepped forward with a smirk. "Stand back," he said, rolling his shoulders. "I've got this." He strode ahead, his hands raised toward the vines. Sunlight shot out from his fingertips and the thorny mass recoiled, shriveling into ash and revealing the stone grate beneath.

I let out a low whistle. "Since when can you do that?"

Caleb shot me a look, all swagger. "You're not the only descendant of the Elementals, you know." The grin he gave me was so smug I had to resist the urge to punch him.

Savannah motioned for us to keep moving, her focus already back on the task at hand.

The sewers were exactly what you'd expect: dark, dank, and absolutely disgusting. The stench of waste hung thick in the air, so overpowering I had to fight the urge to gag as we waded through shallow pools of murky water. I did my best not to think about what might be floating in it.

"You're certain this leads to the dungeons?" Ravenna asked, her voice muffled behind a scrap of cloth pressed to her nose.

Savannah didn't slow. "Positive. I found it not long after Raideron locked me up."

"Then why didn't you use it to escape?" Kira asked, her voice thick with suspicion.

Savannah's jaw tightened. "Because he has my parents. If I'd have run, he'd have made them pay for it."

Kira didn't respond. Maybe Savannah's answer was enough for her, or maybe she just didn't want to risk breathing in the stench any more than necessary.

"If we're lucky, the guards won't have found the entrance yet" Savannah said, glancing back at us.

Caleb groaned. "What part of this is lucky, exactly?"

"We're almost there," Savannah replied, rolling her eyes.

The narrow tunnel curved ahead, disappearing into shadow. A

sudden clatter echoed from the darkness and everyone froze.

Ravenna stepped forward, her voice calm and unwavering. "Stay behind me. If it's a guard, I'll handle it."

We crept forward, each step deliberate, the silence broken only by the drip of water and the squelch of our boots. The tunnel widened, revealing a rusted iron grate hanging crookedly from its hinges. Beyond it, a faint torchlight flickered against damp stone.

Savannah crouched beside the grate, inspecting it. "This is it. This will lead us straight into the lower cells."

Ravenna leaned over her shoulder. "And the guards?"

Savannah looked up, her expression grim. "We'll have to be quick. If they spot us, we'll have only seconds before they alert Raideron."

Caleb let out a resigned sigh. "Lucky us," he grumbled.

With a low groan of rusted metal, Savannah pushed the grate aside. The opening was just wide enough to crawl through. One-by-one, we slipped into the narrow corridor.

Ravenna drew her taiaha, her stance protective. "Stay close to me," she whispered.

I tensed, ready for a fight, but the corridor was empty, not a guard in sight. Maybe that should have been relieving, but it made me even more anxious. My heart raced with anticipation.

Savannah led us down a steep, spiraling stairwell carved from ancient stone. The air grew cooler as we descended, the pungent scent of rot and rust burning my nose—but it was still better than the sewers.

At the bottom, the stairwell opened into a narrow corridor lined with iron doors. Each one was heavy and scarred, their surfaces mottled with age and neglect. Torchlight flickered from drooping wall sconces, casting an eerie glow that made the shadows seem to shift and breathe.

"This is it," Savannah said, her body convulsing in a shiver.

"Which door is it?" Ravenna asked, her voice low but urgent.

Savannah hesitated, scanning the row of iron doors. "Third from the left. But it won't matter unless we get the key."

"I'll handle that," Kira said, stepping forward.

I caught her arm, worry tightening my voice. "Are you sure you want to do this? You haven't shadow-walked in a long time."

Kira met my gaze, her eyes flashing with that stubborn, wild light I knew so well. "I can do it. Just be ready. It won't take Raideron long to figure out that the key is missing."

She took a deep breath and her form began to blur at the edges, shadows curling around her like a second skin. She smiled at me, defiant and unafraid. "Don't worry, big sis. I'll be back before you can start to panic."

But it was too late, my nerves were already frayed. I paced the corridor, my footsteps falling deftly on the warn-down stones.

Savannah hovered nearby, hugging herself so tightly it looked like she was trying to hold her own bones together. Her eyes flicked to the shadows in the corners and her breath kept catching every time a distant drip echoed down the corridor. She looked like she wanted to disappear, but there was nowhere to go—not in Raideron's dungeon. I couldn't even image how hard it must have been for her to be back in the castle after having been imprisoned there for so long.

Still, when she caught me watching her, Savannah straightened up and tried to force a smile. "She'll be fine, Amira," she said, but her voice was shaky, and I could tell she was just saying it for my sake. "Kira's done this a million times. She's basically made of shadows." She tried to laugh, but it came out thin and nervous, and she glanced at the spot where Kira had vanished, her arms tightening around herself again.

I nodded, but the knot in my stomach only tightened. The silence that followed was thick, broken only by the faint scurrying of rats and the echo of our own breathing. I leaned against the damp wall, trying to steady my nerves, but every creak of old stone sounded like a warning.

Caleb paced the dingy corridor, his fingers drumming a frantic rhythm on his patu. "She should have been back by now," he muttered.

"She's only been gone a few minutes." Ravenna's voice was calm, but her hand never left the hilt of her taiaha. "Shadow walking takes time, and precision. Trust her."

Savannah stood near the stairwell, her eyes darting between the shadows. "I don't like this... it's too quiet. There should have been guards posted here."

Caleb stopped pacing. "You think something's up? Because I swear, if this is another one of Raideron's traps—"

A sudden gust of cold air swept through the corridor, snuffing out nearly all the torches. Caleb's hand tightened on his patu, Ravenna shifted her stance, and Savannah pressed herself against the wall, eyes wide with fear.

From the darkness, came a whisper—cocky, breathless, and unmistakably Kira: "Got it."

Kira stepped into the dim light, her face pale but her grin pure adrenaline. She twirled a silver key on her finger, then tossed it once in the air before catching it. "Miss me?"

Caleb let out a shaky laugh that tried to cover how nervous he was. "Show-off. You took long enough."

Kira shot him a smirk. "You try shadow-walking past three guards and nabbing a tiny key from Raideron's pocket. I deserve a medal for my heroic efforts."

Ravenna crossed the space and planted a quick, proud kiss on Kira's cheek. "You did brilliantly," she murmured.

Kira's face softened when Ravenna brushed her cheek, but the moment passed in a blink. Kira squared her shoulders, the familiar stubborn set to her jaw returning. She turned back to the door, the iron key glinting in her hand. My heart thudded in my chest as she knelt in front of the lock. The key scraped against the ancient metal, and for a second, I thought it might refuse her. Then, with a shudder that seemed to vibrate through the stones beneath my boots, the lock gave way.

The door groaned, a long, aching sound that echoed down the corridor and made the hairs on my arms stand up. I caught a whiff of stale dungeon air. Kira glanced over her shoulder, her eyes meeting mine for just a heartbeat before she pushed the door wider. The hinges shrieked in protest, and deep crimson light spilled out, swallowing the torchlight.

A wave of dread crashed over me, so strong it nearly buckled my knees. My eyes were drawn immediately to the rift. It hovered in the center of the chamber, a jagged wound torn through the world itself. Beyond it stretched a world that defied my darkest nightmares: a Martian-like wasteland, crawling with creatures. But this wasn't Mars. It was something older. Something wrong.

Raideron stood in front of the rift, his cloak rippling in the unnatural wind that poured from the breach. His eyes gleamed with something between triumph and madness.

He spread his arms, voice low and reverent. "You feel it, don't you?" he murmured, as if we were sharing a secret. "The power of the astral plane."

The rift pulsed, casting flickering shadows across the chamber. The ground beneath our feet trembled.

Savannah stood frozen beside me, her face ashen. "You—" she started, but Raideron cut her off with a cold, cruel smile.

"I must admit," he said, his tone dripping with mockery, "I didn't expect you to come crawling back through the sewers. Brave. Foolish. Predictable." He let the words hang in the air, savoring them.

Then, with a theatrical sweep of his cloak, he stepped aside. Behind him stood a slight young girl, cloaked in midnight blue. She reached up with steady fingers, the same ones that had braided my hair countless times, and pulled back her hood.

My heart plummeted.

"Aria?" I whispered, disbelief tightening my throat. "How could you?"

Her eyes met mine. There was no guilt in them. No regret. Just a quiet, unreadable calm.

"I had no choice," she said softly.

Raideron's laugh was high-pitched and venomous. "Oh, she had a choice. She simply made the right one."

I took a shaky step toward Aria, my voice cracking with betrayal. "I trusted you. You were my friend."

Aria's gaze didn't waver. "I know," she said, her words slicing through me like glass. "That's what made it so easy."

Savannah's voice trembled with fury and heartbreak as she turned on Raideron. "You manipulated her," she snapped. "Just like you did to me. You ruin everything you touch."

Raideron tilted his head, his voice curling into that slow, unsettling drawl. "Speaking of manipulation... I have a few other guests to introduce." His smile was pure malice.

From the shadows behind him, two figures emerged.

Savannah gasped, the sound raw and desperate.

Her parents stepped into the light, their faces drained of color, eyes vacant and unseeing. Shackles hung from their wrists, and every movement was stiff and unnatural. It was unmistakable: Raideron had bound them with the same dark magic he'd used to enslave the Elementals, leaving them trapped in a living nightmare, present but powerless to act on their own will.

Savannah surged forward instinctively, but I caught her arm. "Wait," I said, my voice ringing with warning.

Her eyes were wide with desperation, pleading. "But they're right there! Amira, please—"

"I know," I said, keeping my voice steady for her sake, even as my heart pounded. "But something's wrong. Look at them."

Savannah's parents stood motionless, their bodies rigid.

"What did you do to them?" I demanded.

"Do you want to know the truth, Princess?" Raideron sneered. "It was that fool Horatious. He thought he was clever, thought he could control the power of the staff. But he was nothing but a greedy child playing with things he didn't understand. The others before him only cracked the door to the astral plane. Horatious, in his arrogance, tore it wide open. He didn't just create a Standing Portal—he created the rift."

I felt the chill of his words settle over me, but I refused to look away. My hands tightened on the Elemental Staff.

Raideron's eyes glittered with malice as he turned his gaze on Savannah's parents, their bodies rigid and unnatural. "Horatious deserved his end." Raideron spat, his voice rising, echoing off the stone. "It was a sad, human death, brought down by the very sickness he unleashed. But his failure is my inheritance. The rift is mine now. Mine to command, mine to use. And I will use it, Amira. I will use it until this world breaks."

Savannah's parents began to convulse; their faces contorted in silent agony. They didn't even have the will to scream. I could feel magic in the air, thick and suffocating, as if the rift itself was feeding on their pain. My stomach twisted at the sight.

"Stop it!" I shouted, my voice cracking with fury. But Raideron only laughed, the sound sharp and merciless.

"Stop?" he echoed, his voice mocking. "Why should I stop? This is the price of defiance. This is the fate of anyone who stands in my way."

Raideron's laughter filled the chamber, drowning out my own desperate thoughts. This was not a man who could be reasoned with. This was a monster who would burn the world to ashes just to see the light die in our eyes.

"Please," Savannah whimpered, her hands trembling as she covered her face, her whole body shaking with grief and rage.

Raideron tilted his head, savoring her desperation. "Please?" he repeated, his tone dripping with false sympathy. "I might be persuaded to release them…" He let the words hang, savoring the power he held over us all.

Savannah stood frozen, her eyes locked on her parents. The chains around their wrists glinted in the red light of the rift. They didn't speak; they just stared at her with hollow eyes.

Raideron watched her with a predator's patience, his voice dropping to a sinister whisper. "Go ahead, Savannah. Save them. I won't stop you. Be the hero you've always wanted to be."

Savannah didn't move. Her voice, when it came, was barely more than a whisper, trembling with fear and hope. "What do you want?"

Raideron's smile widened, slow and terrible, his eyes glittering with cruel delight. "A trade," he purred, savoring the word.

Savannah's brow furrowed, confusion and dread etched on her face. "A trade?" she echoed, her voice cracking.

He turned slightly, eyes flickering towards me. "Hand over Amira and I will release your parents."

The chamber fell silent.

"And then?" Savannah asked him, refusing to look up from the floor. 'What happens to Amira?"

Raideron shrugged, as if discussing the weather. "Then I will kill Amira and steal her powers." He said it so nonchalantly that I didn't know whether to scream or laugh.

Savannah's breath hitched, shallow and rapid. Panic and longing twisted her features. "There has to be another way," she pleaded, her voice splintering under the weight of the choice.

Raideron's gaze softened, almost pitying, as he shook his head. "There isn't," he replied, his tone final. "It's time to choose, once and for all. Your parents… or the girl."

Caleb clenched his jaw, his knuckles turning white around his patu. "What makes you think the rest of us will just let you take her?" He demanded, his voice was low and dangerous.

I reached out, placing a steadying hand on Caleb's shoulder. "This is Savannah's choice to make," I said quietly, my voice trembling but resolute. The moment of truth had come.

Savannah's lips parted, but no words came out. I could see the war inside her—love and loyalty tearing her in two. It was a feeling I was all too familiar with.

Kira placed a comforting hand on Savannah's shoulder to steady her, surprising us all. "Savannah," she said, "if Raideron gets control of Amira's powers, it won't just be your parents who suffer. It'll be everyone. He'll burn the whole world down."

Savannah's mother reached out, eyes pleading. "Savannah…"

Tears spilled down Savannah's cheeks as she shook her head. "I can't lose them," she whispered, her voice breaking.

The chamber seemed to hold its breath. Even the rift's unnatural wind seemed to pause, waiting.

Savannah squeezed her eyes shut, shoulders shaking. In that moment, she looked so small—just a scared kid caught between impossible choices.

Then she looked up, tears streaking her cheeks, her jaw set. She turned away from her parents, facing Raideron head-on. Her voice wavered, but didn't break. "I won't give you Amira." She wiped her face, standing a little taller.

Raideron's smile faltered, just for a moment. The flickering red light from the rift carved deep shadows across his face, distorting his features so he looked like a creature born from the rift itself. "So be it," he said coldly.

The rift pulsed, violently. The ground shuddered beneath us, the air thickening with a pressure that made my ears ring. Savannah's parents collapsed where they stood, their bodies hitting the stone floor with a sickening thud.

Savannah let out a strangled sob and dropped to her knees. "No… no, no, no," her voice was raw, torn from somewhere deep inside. She reached for them, but the earth betrayed her as cracks spiderwebbed across the stone floor, glowing with the same crimson light that bled from the rift.

The stones split open wide, until a gaping chasm opened. Savannah's parents, lifeless, slid toward the edge. She lunged forward, desperate to save them, but the ground gave way beneath them and their bodies vanished into the depths below.

"No!" she screamed, her voice shattering in the chaos.

Kira spun on Raideron, her eyes blazing with magic. "You'll regret that!"

Raideron stood calm amid the chaos, untouched by the devastation he'd unleashed. "I told you," he said, his voice rising above the roar of the rift, "I will have Amira's powers."

He raised a hand toward the rift, and the crimson light surged, casting the chamber in a hellish glow. "I've called an old friend from the astral plane to help me," he announced.

An ear-splitting roar erupted from the core of the rift. The chamber shook. Dust and debris rained from the ceiling. Then, from the heart of the rift, a shadow emerged.

It was massive, its form shifting and indistinct, as if made of smoke and shadow. Eyes like burning coals blinked open across its body, and long, clawed limbs unfurled from the void, scraping the stone with a sound that made my blood run cold.

The Timeless One.

Raideron's smile was like poison. "You remember it, don't you?" he purred, his voice curling around me like smoke. "It remembers you, too."

A shiver ripped through me, cold and sharp as a blade.

The Timeless One slithered forward and Raideron laughed, wild and high, like he'd already won.

But lost in his own madness, he didn't see Savannah push herself up from the ground. She staggered forward, every step fueled by something raw and broken inside her.

"I will kill you," Savannah snarled, her voice ragged and trembling but full of resolve.

Raideron laughed, tossing his head back, utterly unbothered. "I'd enjoy seeing you try, little traitor." His words dripped with venom, but Savannah didn't flinch. She stood there, battered and furious, her grief burning so bright it felt like it might set the whole world on fire.

Then she lunged at him, rage twisting her features. "You've taken everything from me!" she screamed, her voice breaking.

Raideron flicked his wrist, conjuring a wall of darkness that sent her flying. She hit the ground hard.

Ravenna growled, feet planted wide. "Get behind me, Amira!" She charged at Raideron, her taiaha gleaming.

Kira vanished—literally—her form dissolving into shadow. She reappeared behind the Timeless One, her hands crackling with astral magic. "Come on, ugly," she taunted, her voice tight with adrenaline. "Let's see if you can keep up." She hurled a bolt of purple energy, her magic wild and beautiful.

I squeezed my eyes shut, remembering Iskra's words: "Find the pain. Let it rise." So I did. I reached past the fear, past the confusion, and found the ache Raideron had left in me—the ache he'd left in all of us. The stolen lives. The broken families. The scorched lands. I let it burn through me.

Roots pressed into the earth beneath my boots as I drew strength from the land itself. The Elemental Staff thrummed in my grasp, its warmth pulsing up my arm, alive and restless.

I steadied my breath, feeling the world shift around me—a wild wind whipped my hair across my face, sparks leapt and danced in the gloom, and the ground shivered, cracks racing outward as water shimmered over the stones. Fire curled along my skin, fierce but gentle, as the Obsidian Fire Stone blazed to life, casting molten light across the chaos.

Through the chaos, Raideron's eyes found mine. Everything else fell away—the roaring rift, the clash of magic and steel. It was just us, suspended in this one inevitable moment.

I leveled the staff at Raideron, pouring every ounce of will into it, urging the staff to cleanse the world of his poison. "It's time," I whispered, and the staff obeyed.

A surge of magical energy burst from the staff—a blinding beam made of all the elements; all wrapped in shimmering astral light. It roared through the chamber like a living storm, unstoppable and pure.

The blast struck the Timeless One first.

Its smoky form writhed, limbs curling inward. It let out a an other-worldly scream as it was dragged backwards into the rift. It lashed out at the last moment and grabbed onto Aria, dragging her kicking and screaming into the astral plane.

But the power of the staff didn't stop there. It rippled across the rift, weaving golden strands of magic through its jagged edges. The rift shuddered, closing slowly, like a wound beginning to heal.

Then the beam finally hit Raideron.

He screamed—not in pain, but in fury—as the beam engulfed him. "No!" he bellowed. "This world is mine!"

The rift pulsed one last time, then collapsed inward with a thunderous crack, sealing itself shut. Raideron vanished within it, and for a heartbeat, the world itself seemed to exhale. The air cleared. The crimson glow of the rift faded, replaced by the gentle flicker of torchlight.

Savannah dropped to her knees; her whole body wracked with sobs. Her shoulders shook, and the sound of her grief echoed through the ruined chamber. Ravena lowered her taiaha and stepped back, giving Savannah space, her expression unreadable but her stance protective.

Kira emerged from the shadows, her blade still drawn, eyes sharp and restless. She scanned the room until her gaze landed on Caleb. He stood frozen, mouth slightly open, staring at me like he was seeing me for the first time.

The Elemental Staff was still warm in my grip, the magic inside me slowly settling.

But just as I managed to take a breath, the castle itself groaned, a deep sound that vibrated in my bones.

A tremor rippled through the stone beneath our feet. The walls of Shadowfell Castle shuddered, and the ceiling above us cracked with a roar that drowned out everything else. Chunks of stone broke free, plummeting like meteors.

I threw myself against the nearest column, arms over my head as debris rained down. Dust filled the air, stinging my eyes.

"It's time to go!" Kira's voice cut through the chaos, sharp and urgent. With a flick of her wrist, a swirling portal burst open, casting purple light across the rubble-strewn chamber.

Ravenna hauled Savannah to her feet. "You cannot stay here," she said, her voice firm but kind. "Your parents wouldn't want that for you."

Savannah hesitated, eyes wide and lost, but then she let Ravenna guide her through the portal.

Caleb grabbed my arm. "Come on, Amira!"

We sprinted for the portal together, dodging falling stones. Behind us, Shadowfell Castle groaned and collapsed inward, the sound echoing like thunder. We stepped through the portal and left the ruins of Shadowfell Castle behind forever.

CHAPTER THIRTY-ONE

A FUTURE OF OUR OWN MAKING

I slept longer that night than I had in years, sinking deeply into the soft mattress. And for a few blissful minutes after I woke up, I just lay there, tangled in the sheets, letting the quiet wrap around me. No alarms, no urgent knocks, no one demanding I save the world before breakfast.

But then the silence settled around me, becoming thick and unfamiliar. Aria would normally have been there by now, bustling around, coaxing the flames in the fireplace to life. Instead, the room felt hollow. She was gone—like so many others. The sting of her betrayal still burned, but it was her absence that hurt the most.

I rolled out of bed, shivering as my feet hit the stone tiles. With a flick of my wrist, I lit the fire myself. But I used too much magic and too little finesse, and the flames flared up, singing my nightgown. "Smooth, Amira," I muttered. "Future queen of Hekagia, can't even light a fire without nearly burning the place down."

With the fire sorted (kind of), I turned my attentions to my closet, where a row of dresses stared back at me like a jury. What does one wear to tell the Golden Council that the world's worst villain is finally gone?

I settled on a long-sleeved blue velvet dress, something regal but not too fussy. My fingers fumbled with the buttons and laces. Aria always made it look so easy, her hands quick and sure, chattering away about the latest castle gossip while she tied ribbons and fastened clasps. I cursed under my breath, trying to remember the order of things, embarrassed by how much I'd come to rely on her.

My hair was the worst of it. I glared at my reflection, at the wild tumble of curls that refused to be tamed. I twisted and pinned, recalling the way Aria would coax each lock into place, murmuring encouragements and silly jokes about "royal ringlets." My own attempts were clumsy, and more than once I had to start over, tears stinging my eyes.

When I finally managed something that resembled an updo, I stepped back and took a shaky breath. I hardly recognized the woman staring back at me. The softness of childhood had faded from my features, replaced by sharper angles and the faint scars of battle. My posture had changed, too—shoulders squared, chin lifted, back straight in a way that would make my mother proud.

I looked older and stronger. Like someone who had survived.

A knock sounded at the door—Caleb, with his usual lack of patience. He barged in, curls sticking up in every direction, grinning like he'd just won a bet.

"You ready, Your Majesty?" he teased.

Before I could answer, Kira came up behind him. She leaned against the doorframe, arms crossed, eyebrow arched. "You planning to stare at yourself all day, or are we actually going to do this?" Her voice was sharp, but there was a softness in her eyes, a silent promise that she had my back, no matter what.

I squared my shoulders, wiped my eyes, and forced myself to smile. Today, we would face the council. Today, we would tell them that Raideron was gone, that the war was over, that my coronation would go on as planned.

Tomorrow, I would stand before them as their queen.

The Great Hall buzzed with excitement. Dignitaries from every corner of Hekagia jostled for seats at the long wooden table, their voices rising and falling in a dozen accents. I scanned the crowd, picking out the familiar faces that anchored me: Earl, resplendent in his golden alchemist's robes, caught my eye and gave me a reassuring wink. Across from him, Sir Webley was already nodding off, his page—poor kid—frantically elbowing him awake every time his chin hit his chest.

In the back, the Elementals sat together, a little apart from the rest. Iskra's fiery hair was impossible to miss, and she watched the proceedings with arms crossed, her gaze sharp and wary. Beside her, Terran looked like he'd rather be outside digging in the gardens, while Aquis and Akash whispered to each other, their expressions unreadable.

Front and center, Caleb sat with the other newly minted members of the Golden Guard. He looked like he was trying to stay serious, but the pride in his eyes was unmistakable.

I caught his gaze and he gave me a thumbs-up, mouthing, "You got this." I tried to believe him.

Sir Adley's voice sliced through the chatter, sharp as a sword. "So it is true then—Raideron is finally gone?" The room fell silent, every eye turning to me.

I nodded, forcing myself to meet his gaze. "He's gone."

Sir Adley leaned forward, his dark eyes narrowing. "And you're sure this time?"

"We're sure," Caleb said before I could answer, his voice ringing with the kind of confidence only he could pull off. He sat up straighter, shoulders squared, daring anyone to argue.

The hall erupted—cheers, laughter, even a few tears. But Sir Adley didn't join in. He stayed seated, arms folded, lips pressed into a thin line.

"You've spun us quite the magnificent tale," he said, his voice dripping with skepticism. "But how long until those of us with astral magic lose our powers?"

Earl stood, his movements slow and deliberate—probably because he'd just sat on his own spectacles again. "It's been over a day, and not a single spellcaster has lost their powers," he said cheerfully. "No one's turned into a frog or a pumpkin, either. After conferring with the Elementals, we are convinced that closing the rift has had no affect on astral magic in Hekagia."

Lord Adley scoffed, his cheeks flushing. "And I'm expected to just take your word for it? A disgraced alchemist and a couple of children?"

Earl's eyes flashed dangerously. "You will watch your tone when you speak of the future queen."

A rumble of agreement swept through the hall—chairs scraping, voices murmuring. Lord Adley wilted as he sank back in his seat, glowering.

Then a man from the Nithandore delegation, a spellcaster with sharp cheekbones and hair cropped close to his skull, stood up.

"And what of the Southern Portal?" he asked, his voice cool and precise.

I frowned, puzzled. "What about it?"

Lord Adley let out a huff, loud enough for everyone to hear. "She doesn't even know what's happening in her own castle!"

Earl huffed. "Her Highness has been a tad busy as of late, wouldn't you say? Saving the world, keeping me from turning the kitchens into a frog sanctuary, and—oh yes—dealing with portals that now open at random. Even odder, the castle staff have reported seeing flashes of unfamiliar places through it."

He turned to the room, his voice carrying. "But for the real answer, let's ask someone who actually knows what they're talking about." Earl gestured grandly toward Iskra, knocking over his satchel of potions in the process. "Iskra, if you please…"

Iskra rose with effortless grace and addressed the council. "Over the centuries, the Magi Nostrum's foulness has polluted all of Hekagia, even the Standing Portals," she said, her voice commanding attention. "Yet now, with the rift sealed and Raideron defeated, the Southern Portal cleansed itself."

"What does that mean, exactly?" I asked.

Iskra's eyes flicked to the other Elementals, and I caught a hint of longing in her expression. "The Southern Portal can once again be used to travel to other worlds." Her words hung in the air, heavy with possibility.

Lord Adley let out a theatrical sigh, slumping back in his chair. "Splendid. So it's just a matter of time until we're invaded again."

Earl shook his head, his patience thinning. "Let's not dwell on that now. We have a coronation to prepare for tomorrow." He shot me a quick, reassuring smile, but I could see the worry lurking behind it.

Master Frederick, who'd been quietly fidgeting with the cuffs of his golden robe, cleared his throat with a sound like a rusty hinge. "There is still one matter to settle…" His eyes darted to me, then to the council, then back to me again.

My heart skipped a beat.

"Amira must be wed before she can be crowned queen," he reminded the council before turning back to me. "Will there be a royal wedding today?" His voice was gentle, but the question landed like a stone in my stomach.

I forced a smile, sidestepping as gracefully as I could. "Trust that the coronation will happen as planned tomorrow," I said, hoping my voice sounded more confident than I felt.

The mood in the room shifted instantly. The same people who'd been cheering for me moments before now eyed me with suspicion, as if I'd suddenly grown a second head.

"It's not that we don't trust you, Your Highness," Master Frederick replied carefully, his words tiptoeing around the tension. "But it is the law, after all…"

"I understand," I replied, my voice as firm as I could make it.

And then, as if on cue, (but I swear it wasn't) Kira burst into the Great Hall, her eyes wide with alarm. "Amira, Caleb, come quick!" she shouted, her voice echoing off the stone walls. Before anyone could stop me, I was on my feet, heart pounding, ready for whatever disaster my little sister had just dragged in with her.

I tore after Kira, my heart thudding so hard I could feel it in my throat. Kira refused to answer any of my questions except to toss a cryptic, "Just hurry up, Amira!" over her shoulder.

Caleb, for once, wasn't cracking jokes. He just kept glancing at me with wide, excited eyes, like he was in on some secret and dying to spill.

Can't I catch a break? I thought, half-exasperated, half-laughing at the absurdity. I'd just defeated an evil overlord who'd terrorized the world for centuries. Surely that should have earned me a day off?

We turned the corner toward the ballroom, which should have been bustling with servants preparing for the coronation. Instead, the hallways were strangely empty.

"Where is everyone?" I hissed at Kira, but she just shot me a sly, sideways grin.

"You'll see…" she said, her voice dripping with mischief. She shoved open the heavy ballroom doors and practically pushed me inside.

I braced myself for disaster. Instead, my knees nearly buckled as the room exploded into a chorus of "Happy Birthday!"

Balloons bobbed from every corner, and a giant "18" banner

hung from the rafters, glittering in the candlelight.

Kira turned to me with a devilish grin. "Happy birthday."

My friends and family filled the room. My parents sat together on a small couch, hands entwined, both smiling at me. My mother still looked pale, but there was a spark in her eyes I hadn't seen in years, and it made my heart ache with relief.

Ravenna and Yasmine stood off to the side, both wearing paper party hats—clearly Kira's handiwork. Ravenna looked like she'd rather be facing down a monster than wearing a hat shaped like a cupcake, while Yasmine just rolled her eyes and muttered something under her breath about "royal indignities."

I turned to Kira, still stunned. "Where did you get the decorations?" I asked.

She just smirked, crossing her arms. "I've got my sources," she said, her eyes sparkling with mischief and pride.

The crowd parted, and Savannah approached. Her eyes were heavy with grief, but she managed a small smile. "Do you like it?" she asked, gesturing around the room.

"I love it," I replied, pulling her into a tight hug.

Over Savannah's shoulder, I caught Yasmine glancing longingly at a man standing near the window, his back to us —Ajay.

He looked lost in thought, his posture stiff, hands clasped behind him.

"Hang on a second," I whispered to Savannah, squeezing her hand before weaving through the crowd. Without thinking, I grabbed Yasmine's hand and pulled her with me, stopping in front of Ajay.

He turned, startled, his soft brown eyes widening when he saw us together. "Your Highness," he said, his voice formal but gentle as he took my free hand. "It is good to see you again."

"Ajay, I have to tell you something," I began, my voice trembling just a little.

Yasmine shrank back, her hand slipping from mine. "Perhaps I should give you two a moment alone," she whispered, already turning away.

"No—stay," I insisted, catching her wrist. "Please."

Yasmine's eyes searched my face, desperate for understanding. "Why are you doing this?" she asked.

"Because you both deserve to be happy... together."

Yasmine gasped, her breath catching, while Ajay's eyes went wide with disbelief. "Your Highness…" he stammered, struggling to find his words. "Please be assured that I will do my duty and marry you tomorrow, if that is what you wish."

I met his gaze, holding it. "Is that what you wish?" I asked.

Ajay's silence said everything. He looked at Yasmine, then at me. He didn't have to say a word; I could see the truth in his eyes.

Ajay cleared his throat, his voice barely above a whisper. "I… care for you, Amira. I always will." His words were careful, measured, like he was afraid of breaking something fragile between us. "But I think we both know it's not the kind of love that lasts a lifetime."

I squeezed his hands gently, feeling the finality settle between us. "I care for you too, Ajay. You've been a good friend—a better friend than I deserved, at times. But that's all we are. Friends."

He let out a slow breath, his shoulders relaxing as if he'd been holding them tense for months.

I glanced at Yasmine, who stood frozen, her hands twisting in the fabric of her dress. "Do you love her?" I asked Ajay.

Ajay's eyes flicked to Yasmine, and for the first time that night, he really looked at her. "Yes," he whispered, the word trembling in the air between them. "I do."

Yasmine's eyes widened, shining with hope, as if the future had suddenly opened in front of her—uncertain, but full of possibilities. She looked at me, her voice trembling, thick with emotion. "Thank you, Amira. For… for this."

I felt my own voice shake as I replied, "No, thank you. For always being there when I needed you. This time, it's my turn to be there for you."

Ajay reached for Yasmine's hand, his touch tentative. "If you'll have me," he said, his voice barely more than a breath.

Yasmine laughed and nodded, her cheeks flushed with relief. "I think I'd like that," she whispered.

I stepped back, letting them have their moment. For the first time in as long as I could remember, I wasn't just the future queen, or the girl caught between duty and desire. I was just Amira— choosing happiness, and letting others do the same.

Kira staggered over, her hair streaked with sweat and her cheeks flushed from dancing with Ravenna. She looked lighter than I'd ever seen her, practically glowing with mischief.

"You look like you're about to cry, birthday girl," she teased, nudging me with her elbow. "Don't worry, I'm not done embarrassing you yet."

I groaned, but couldn't help grinning. "Kira, if you set off fireworks indoors again, I swear—"

She cut me off. "No pyrotechnics this time. But I do have one more surprise." Her voice rang out above the laughter and music, and suddenly the ballroom doors swung open.

The archers marched in, uniforms crisp, faces shining with pride. At the front was Treander. My heart stuttered. He looked... different. His russet hair was neatly combed, and he wore a suit that made him look every inch the king he could be. But it was his eyes—those fierce, unwavering green eyes—that made the world slow to a crawl. The crowd faded away as he crossed the room, gaze locked on mine.

He stopped in front of me and bowed, but there was a crooked smile tugging at his lips. "Your Highness," he said, his voice low and warm, with that hint of teasing that always made my knees weak. "Permission to cut in?"

I didn't care about the whispers or the stares. I threw my arms around him, breathless with relief. "You came," I murmured, my voice trembling.

Treander's arms wrapped around me, steady and sure. "Of course I did. I was a fool to have ever left in the first place." His words were barely more than a whisper, but they were everything I needed to hear.

I shook my head, tears stinging my eyes. "I should never have let you go."

He squeezed my hand, his thumb tracing circles over my knuckles. "We never did get that dance..." he murmured.

It was true. The last time we'd been in this room together, Raideron had ruined it. He'd stolen that moment, and many others, from us.

He led me to the center of the ballroom, and as the music swelled, he spun me into a waltz. I wasn't sure how he'd learned to dance so well—growing up with a band of orphans didn't exactly lend itself to ballroom etiquette—but he moved as if he belonged there, as if this moment had always been meant for us. With every step, my heart soared higher.

When the music faded, Treander brushed a stray tear from my cheek, then leaned in and kissed me softly, his hand cupping my face. But he pulled away too soon, leaving my heart pounding with anticipation.

"What's wrong?" I asked him.

He dropped to one knee, that boyish grin lighting up his face. The crowd gasped, holding its breath. Treander pulled out a small velvet box, his hands shaking slightly.

"I'd like to do this properly," he said, his voice full of hope and passion. "Amira Hale, will you marry me?"

I knelt down in front of him, not hesitating for a single second. "Of course," I said, my own voice shaky but certain.

The ballroom erupted into cheers, the sound echoing around us as joy and relief washed over me.

In that moment, I was exactly where I was meant to be—surrounded by friends, family, and the man I loved, choosing my own future at last.

CHAPTER THIRTY-THREE

A CORONATION TO REMEMBER

Sunlight poured through the dining hall windows, striping the floor in gold. The whole room was transformed—banners everywhere, wildflowers in every color, and so much food it looked like the kitchen had exploded. Pancakes, bacon, pastries, berries, cocoa. It was like something out of a fairy tale, except it was real, and it was for me. I almost didn't want to step inside. I was supposed to be queen today, but just then, I felt like a little kid again.

Dad was already at the table, shoveling pancakes into his mouth like he was in a contest. He was trying to get Mom to sit down, but she was fussing over a bowl of strawberries, her cheeks pink, her eyes bright. She looked... happy. *Really* happy. I hadn't seen her like that in ages, not since before Raideron's curse. Seeing her like that, I was certain it had been broken.

"Mom... did you do all this?"

She laughed, and it was the best sound in the world—light and free, like she'd finally remembered how. "Of course I did. You only turn eighteen—and become queen—once."

Caleb grinned at me, waving his fork. "You should've seen her, Amira. Up before dawn, chasing me out of the kitchen. I tried to help, but apparently, I'm a hazard."

Kira slid into her chair, still in her slippers, smirking. "That's because you set the oven on fire. Twice."

I sat down between them with a smile. "It's a miracle the castle is still standing," I teased Caleb, nudging him with my elbow.

Mom came around and kissed my forehead, her hand lingering on my cheek. "I wanted to give you one last birthday breakfast as my little girl," she said, and I almost lost it right there.

"Wait—does that mean you won't do this for us every year?" Caleb asked, pretending to be outraged as he stuffed another bite in his mouth.

I watched him, feeling this weird ache of nostalgia. "This is just like my sixteenth birthday," I said. "Well, maybe a bit grander. But probably just as much food."

Dad laughed from the end of the table, pouring cocoa. "You should've seen your mom scrambling, trying to find places for all the dishes. Pancakes on the windowsill, bacon cooling on the porch..."

Mom shook her head, laughing. "I remember Caleb sneaking toast before I could even get it on the table."

I shot Caleb a mock glare. "I guess that's why there was none left for me."

He grinned, mouth full. "Hey, you snooze, you lose."

"If I remember right, I was too busy being freaked out by Kira shadow walking in my room like a supernatural stalker," I said, shooting a look in her direction.

Kira shrugged, totally unbothered. "The toast *was* good. I took some when no one was looking."

We all stared at her, then burst out laughing. For that moment, everything felt perfect, like the world had finally given us a break. I looked around the table at my parents, at Kira and Caleb, realizing that this was what I'd been fighting for. Family. Love. The chance to just be... me.

A few hours later, I stood in front of a floor-length mirror in my dressing room, barely breathing as Kira fumbled with the last few buttons on my coronation dress. The gown was ridiculous—silk that pooled around my feet, adorned with pearls and diamonds that caught the sunlight. I looked like someone out of a storybook, not a girl who'd spent most of her life on a farm.

Kira wouldn't meet my eye in the mirror, and I could feel her anxiousness radiating off her in waves. She was always so steady, so sure, but today she looked as lost as I felt. Naomi, who'd stepped in to help after Aria was gone, gave Kira a gentle smile and took over, her fingers quick and practiced.

The door creaked, and Savannah slipped in, so quiet I almost missed her. She hovered near the doorway, arms wrapped around herself, her eyes rimmed red. I knew that look—grief, raw and fresh, the kind that never really goes away. But when our eyes met in the mirror, she managed a real smile, small but honest.

"Wow, Amira," Savannah said softly, her voice a little shaky, "You look incredible."

I turned, reaching for her hand. "I'm so glad you're here. I know it's not easy."

She squeezed my fingers, her smile growing a bit stronger. "I wouldn't miss this for anything."

Naomi finished with the last button on my dress and gave me a quick, approving nod before slipping out, quiet as a mouse. Suddenly it was just the three of us, standing together.

But Kira was quiet. Too quiet.

She was usually the one making jokes or rolling her eyes at the whole "princess" thing, but now she just focused on my hair, her brow furrowed as she tried to tame my wild curls.

"Cat got your tongue?" I teased, watching her in the mirror, hoping to coax out a smile.

She hesitated, then finally spoke, her voice low and careful. "Don't take this the wrong way, but I still think you're a little crazy for getting married so young." She tried to smile, but I could see the worry behind it as she gently combed my hair.

I laughed, but it came out a little shaky, and then winced as she tugged a knot too hard. "Ow! Careful, Kira."

"Stay still or it'll only get worse," she scolded.

I caught her eyes in the mirror and shrugged. "I suppose it is a bit crazy," I admitted. "But it also makes so much sense."

Kira nodded, her lips quirking. "You had to get married to be queen, I know. But I kind of thought you'd abolish the rule—if for no other reason than to drive Sir Adley to an early grave."

I tried to hold back my laughter, but failed, which made Kira sigh and start all over on the updo she was attempting. "I did consider it," I confessed. "But I'm not marrying Treander because of some outdated law. I'm marrying him because I can't imagine spending another day without him. He's my best friend."

"Hey, watch it," Savannah piped up, her voice teasing. "*I'm* your best friend."

Kira made a gagging face in the mirror. "I know what you mean, though," she said, her lips quirking into a smile.

After a moment, Savannah glanced between us and offered a gentle smile. "I should let you two finish getting ready," she said quietly. "I'll see you out there, Amira." She squeezed my hand one last time before slipping out.

Kira and I stood in front of the mirror, her hands still lingering in my hair. Then she took a deep breath, her expression turning serious. "I have to tell you something."

"You can tell me anything," I said, my voice soft and sincere.

She nodded, her eyes flickering with uncertainty. "After the coronation, Ravenna and I are going back to her village." The words tumbled out of her in a rush.

"For how long?" I asked, a knot forming in my stomach.

Kira hesitated, biting her lip. "I… I'm not sure," she admitted. There was an eager longing in her eyes—a hope that made me happy for her, even as sadness welled up inside me at the thought of losing her.

"Are you not happy here?" I asked quietly.

She shook her head quickly. "It's not that," she said, her voice strained. "I can't explain it, but Wahiao Village just feels like… home. I want to learn their ways, and learn how to control my astral magic, now that I know I won't lose it." She hesitated, searching my face. "I hope you understand."

A pang of sadness twisted in my chest, but I forced myself to nod. "I do. I'll miss you, but I want you to be happy. And maybe when I see you next, you can teach me a thing or two about controlling my magic."

"Deal. But don't think you're off the hook for writing letters. I expect weekly updates, *Your Majesty*."

I laughed, blinking back tears. "It's a promise."

The Great Lawn looked like something out of a fairy tale—or maybe one of those cheesy romance movies Kira always pretended to hate but secretly loved.

Caleb had outdone himself: the archway he'd woven from vines and wild roses stood at the center of a large wooden platform. Rows and rows of white chairs with gold ribbons stretched across the grass, and everywhere I looked, there were faces—friends, family, villagers from every corner of Hekagia. Even the Hakuturi had come, their feathers gleaming bright. Chief Tara caught my eye and gave me a proud nod that made my heart squeeze.

I tried to breathe, but my chest felt tight. I was eighteen, and somehow, I was about to become queen. And get married. And not trip over my own feet in front of the entire kingdom.

No pressure.

Luckily, Treander stood beside me under the arch, his hand warm in mine, keeping me steady. He looked... wow. His black and gold suit made him look older, more regal. But he wore the same boyish grin as always, the one that made my heart melt. He squeezed my hand, his thumb tracing circles over my knuckles. "You look beautiful," he whispered, his voice just for me.

I grinned, full of nerves and happiness. "You clean up pretty well yourself," I whispered back, my voice shaking a little. I couldn't stop staring at him—at the way his green eyes sparkled, at the dimple that appeared when he smiled. For a second, I almost forgot about the crowd.

But then the officiant's voice rang out, pulling me back to reality. "We are gathered here to witness the union of Amira Hale and Treander of Nithandore, to celebrate the dawn of a new era for Hekagia..."

My heart hammered so loudly I was sure everyone could hear it. When it was time for vows, my voice caught, but Treander's steady gaze anchored me. "I promise to stand by your side, in peace and in chaos, forever," I managed, my words barely more than a whisper.

Treander grinned at me, squeezing my hand so gently it made my heart ache. "And I promise to always have your back, even when you're being stubborn—which is most of the time."

The crowd burst into laughter, and for a second, all my nerves and tension melted away. The officiant's voice rang out, steady and sure: "By the power vested in me by the Golden Council, I now declare you husband and wife."

Treander leaned in, and as our lips met, the world exploded in cheers. The whole kingdom was celebrating with us, but in that moment, it was just me and him. He cupped my face, his thumb brushing my cheek. Only then did I realize I was crying.

"Are you okay?" he asked, his eyes suddenly worried.

"I am now," I whispered before kissing him again.

Before I could even catch my breath, Caeli and her little brother Sam came up to the platform, both of them beaming. Caeli held out the crown that Iron Mountain Village had made for me—gold and diamonds sparkling so brightly it almost hurt to look at. My legs shook as I knelt so she could place it on my head. She set the crown gently among my curls, her eyes wide with awe and pride.

Sam grinned up at me, his voice ringing out, "You look like a real queen now!" I laughed, pulling them both into a hug, trying not to cry all over again.

Then I stood and turned to face the sea of faces—my people, my family, my friends. The weight of the crown settled on my head, heavy and real. I took a breath, feeling the sunlight on my face, the banners of Hekagia fluttering gold above the crowd.

"My first act as queen," I announced, my voice clear and strong (even though my hands were shaking), "is to put an end to the rule that a royal must be wed in order to take the throne."

A hush fell. I saw surprise, curiosity, even a little anger, flicker across the crowd. But I kept going, my gaze finding Ajay and Yasmine in the front row, their hands clasped together. "I am lucky that I stand here today, marrying for love rather than duty. But I will not force that choice on anyone else."

"That's ridiculous!" came a lone shout from the crowd.

"That, is progress," I said firmly, my voice ringing out across the crowd. "Which is what we need now, if Hekagia is to thrive. We need to forge a new path forward."

Applause erupted—first a few hands, then the entire crowd rose to their feet in celebration.

My mother's face was full of pride. She looked a bit paler than she had in the morning, but I didn't have long to dwell on it before I was swept away by a flurry of attendants and well-wishers.

Long tables stretched out under the stars, groaning with roasted meats, vegetables, and pies that made my mouth water. The air was thick with the scent of spices and something sweet—maybe hope, maybe just cinnamon. Music drifted everywhere, and villagers and nobles alike danced under the glow of fireflies and a thousand enchanted candles. Laughter and conversation floated through the night, and for the first time in forever, the castle sparkled with celebration instead of worry.

Caleb, never one to miss an opportunity to embarrass me, stood on a chair and raised his glass. "To Amira and Treander—may their reign be long, and their arguments short!"

The table erupted into laughter, and I couldn't help but join in, my heart so full it felt like it might burst. And for a few glorious days, everything was perfect.

CHAPTER THIRTY- FOUR

LETTING GO

It was three days later when a loud knock shattered the quiet of our bedchamber. Treander groaned, rolling over, his hair a wild mess as he started to get up. But before he could even reach the door, Caleb burst in—sweaty, breathless, and wild-eyed.

"Caleb!" I yelped, clutching the blanket to my chest. "What do you think you're doing?"

He didn't even pause to catch his breath. "It's Mom. Come quick."

Those four words shattered everything.

I scrambled out of bed, barely remembering to grab my robe, and followed Caleb down the corridor, my mind racing with every possible fear.

When we reached my parents room, the world seemed to slow. Dad and Kira were already there, sitting on either side of my mother. Madame Galena stood nearby, her eyes full of sorrow. The room felt too small, the air too heavy.

Just days before, my mother had seemed almost herself again—her tan skin glowing, her laughter echoing through the halls. Now she looked... wrong. Her skin was ashen, her eyes sunken and ringed with bruised shadows. Each breath she took was shallow and ragged, her chest barely moving beneath the thin blanket.

"What happened?" I asked, my voice cracking.

My father shook his head, his face crumpling as he tried not to cry. "I found her like this when I woke up."

"But she was doing so well..." I whispered.

Caleb eased himself onto the edge of the bed and gently wrapped his fingers around our mother's hand. At his touch, her eyelids fluttered open, just a little. For a moment, I saw a spark of recognition—just enough to make my heart ache. I hurried to her side, kneeling so close I could feel the chill of her skin.

When she saw us, she managed a small, trembling smile. Dad sat down beside her, his shoulders slumped with grief. The hollow look on his face told me, without words, that there would be no miraculous recovery this time.

With what little strength she had left, my mother reached out, drawing Caleb and me into her arms. Her breath was thin and rasping, each word a struggle.

"I am so proud of you both," she whispered, her voice barely more than a sigh. "I hope you know that."

I nodded, unable to speak past the lump in my throat. Tears streamed down Caleb's cheeks, soaking into the bedspread as he clung to her hand. Dad brushed a stray lock of hair from her forehead and pressed a gentle kiss to her brow.

My mother drew in one last, rattling breath. Then, with a soft exhale, she was gone.

The days after my mother's death blurred together, each one heavy and gray, like the sky before a storm. The royal funeral was everything it was supposed to be—regal, somber, full of tradition and ancient words. But all I could focus on was the ache in my chest as we laid her to rest in the castle graveyard, beneath a canopy of ancient trees. She was entombed beside my birth parents, and I found myself drawn to that quiet place, whispering words I wished any of them could hear. I kept thinking, if I just sat there long enough, maybe I'd feel her hand on my shoulder, or hear her voice telling me it would all be okay. But the only answer was the wind in the branches.

Kira and Ravenna postponed their journey after Mom died. Their presence was a quiet anchor in the storm of loss, and I clung to it more than I'd ever admit. But as the months slipped by, I could see the restlessness growing in Kira's eyes—a longing for the adventure she'd put on hold for my sake. She tried to hide it, but I knew her all too well.

One morning over breakfast, I finally said what we'd both been avoiding. The words felt like pebbles in my mouth, but I forced them out anyway. "It's time," I told her gently, my voice steadier than I felt. "You've delayed for long enough."

Kira's brow creased with worry, and for a second, I thought she might argue.

"Are you sure?" she asked finally, her voice trembling.

I nodded, even though my heart felt heavy. "I'm sure."

I couldn't keep her from her destiny any longer, no matter how much I wanted her and Ravenna to stay with me.

They left the next day.

Ravenna left me with a promise to write soon and a warm hug that smelled of wildflowers.

Then Kira hugged me fiercely, her animal-skinned cloak wrapped around her like armor. "I'm only a portal away," she promised.

"You better believe I'll be coming for a visit soon," I said, forcing a smile. "Wahiao sounds like a great honeymoon spot."

Kira laughed, the sound bright and familiar. "Just keep it PG around me, please."

As Kira pulled away, I caught Treander's gaze over her shoulder. My cheeks flushed, and my heart skipped a beat at the sight of his green eyes shining with love—a small, steady light in the midst of so much change.

But the world didn't stop shifting just because I wanted it to. Even as I tried to hold on to the people who mattered most, life kept moving forward, tugging us in different directions.

Letting go of Kira was hard, but I told myself it was just one more change, one more piece of growing up. I thought maybe, just maybe, things would settle for a while. But I should have known better.

Grief has a way of echoing through a house, and sometimes it pushes people to find their own way to heal.

My father was the next to find his own path.

He came to me and Caleb six months after my mother's passing, his eyes shadowed with grief. "I'm going home," he said quietly, his voice thin and tired.

Neither of us were surprised. Since my mother's death, he'd become a ghost of himself—drifting through the castle halls, lost in memories. I couldn't blame him for wanting to return to something familiar, to the quiet rhythm of his hobby farm, where the earth might offer him a kind of solace that none of us could.

What *did* surprise me, was Earl deciding to go with him.

"I had never planned to return to Hekagia," Earl said to me as we stood before the Southern Portal, a glowing gateway to Earth. "I only came back to help you stop Raideron. Now my job is done."

I couldn't explain it, but Earl's leaving cut me deeply, like losing another piece of the world I'd fought so hard to save. I hugged him tightly, knowing that I might never see him again.

He tried to lighten the moment, flashing a crooked grin. "And I miss my little beach hut, the crash of the waves. Even my flamingos." He winked, but there was a bittersweetness in his eyes.

So it was that I said goodbye twice more.

But in that moment, I realized that even as everything shifted around me, some things, like the people who loved me, would always be with me, no matter how far apart we were.

After the portal's light faded and the echo of their footsteps disappeared, I stood in the empty hall for a long time, feeling the silence settle around me. It was strange how the castle could feel so full one moment and so hollow the next. I pressed my palm to the cool stone wall, half-expecting to hear Earl's laughter drifting down the corridor, or to see my father's muddy boots by the door. But there was only quiet, and the distant sound of rain against the windows.

I knew I should be used to goodbyes, but each one left a new ache, a new empty space I didn't know how to fill. I wondered if this was what adulthood really meant—not just making decisions and wearing crowns, but learning how to let go, again and again, and still finding the courage to move forward.

CHAPTER THIRTY-FIVE

A CALL FROM BEYOND THE PORTAL

Though my life was happy with Treander, the castle felt emptier than ever. My father's laughter no longer echoed down the corridors, and the scent of his morning coffee—always too strong, always a little burnt—had long since faded from the kitchens. I even missed Kira's biting sense of humor (usually at my expense).

I missed my family every day, and I knew Caleb did too, though he hardly spoke of them anymore. In fact, he withdrew further into himself as the weeks went by.

Savannah, however, remained a steadfast companion to me, quickly becoming a beacon of light within the castle despite dealing with her own losses. There was no way that I could ever make up for the loss of her parents, but I tried to be there for her the best that I could. We visited every day, healing the wounds of our past together.

It was a gray spring morning, a little over a year after my coronation, when the message arrived. I was in the throne room, reviewing the latest reports from the Nithandorian villages, when the Southern Portal suddenly flared to life.

Caleb rushed to my side, his patu raised, ready to strike, but I waved him back. The portal's magic was different now—cleansed, Iskra had said, open to worlds beyond our own. Despite Sit Adley's worry, it hadn't caused us any trouble... yet.

Still, I felt a prickle of unease as the swirling light tossed out a burnt scroll, which floated gently to the floor at my feet.

I picked it up, my heart pounding. The seal was unfamiliar: a sigil of a tree with roots that spiraled into stars. I broke it open and read the message aloud.

*"To the rulers and defenders of Hekagia,
Our world is in peril. Shadow creatures have crossed to our lands, and our magic is failing. We beg for aid from those who have faced this darkness and prevailed. Please come. The fate of many worlds depends on you."*

~The people of Lucidium

Caleb's face was pale, but his eyes burned with something fierce and restless. I knew that look. He'd been drifting since our mother's passing. He needed purpose, and here it was, calling to him from beyond a portal.

That night, I found him in the stables, brushing Hercules' golden feathers. The griffin nuzzled his shoulder, sensing his unease. "The Golden Guard is putting together a team to go to Lucidium," he said, his eyes still on Hercules.

"You're going," I said quietly. It wasn't a question.

Caleb shrugged. "They need help. And I can't stay here anymore. Not after everything that's happened."

"You don't have to explain. I understand. But promise me you'll come back."

He managed a crooked smile. "You know me. I always find my way home."

The next morning, the Golden Guard assembled in the throne room—an elite band of warriors, their armor gleaming in the early light. Master Sadiki stood at their head, his golden robes shining, a look of grim determination on his face. Hercules pawed the floor, eager for adventure.

Naomi was there too, clutching Caleb tightly like she was afraid to let him go. It was a sweet moment, but I was definitely going to tease him about it relentlessly. Because that's what siblings are for.

But when it was my turn, I just hugged Caleb tightly, fighting back my own tears. "Give them hope, little brother. And bring back plenty of stories for me."

He squeezed my hand. "I will. And Amira, take good care of Hekagia."

They stepped through the Southern Portal, its light swallowing them one by one. Caleb turned at the last moment, raising his hand in farewell. Then he was gone, and the portal faded to a gentle shimmer.

The world felt impossibly large, and for the first time, I understood what it meant to be part of something greater than myself. Our story wasn't ending, it was only changing, spreading out across worlds.

As the sun set over the rolling hills of Hekagia, I stood beside Treander on the palace balcony, our hands entwined. Below us, the kingdom stretched out in a patchwork of golden fields and bustling villages, the air alive with the promise of peace.

Behind us, two paintings hung side by side. The first was of my birth parents, their faces gentle and proud, watching over me as they always had in spirit. The second was of my mother, Lilliana—her eyes bright with wisdom and kindness, her presence a quiet strength that I carried with me every day. Together, their images formed a tapestry of love and legacy, guiding me in each decision I made.

I squeezed Treander's hand, feeling the warmth of his steady presence. I thought of all the choices, the losses, and the battles that had brought me to this place. There had been a time when I doubted my place in Hekagia, when the weight of destiny felt too heavy to bear. But now, as I looked out over the kingdom I had fought to protect, I understood that this is where it had always been leading me to. Even when I hadn't wanted the responsibility, Hekagia had been waiting for me to claim it.

This was my home, my family, my destiny—and I would rule it with all the courage and love in my heart. I placed my hands over my growing belly, content in the certainty that Hekagia's future was brighter than ever, and that the House of Hale would endure.

THE END

Made in the USA
Coppell, TX
16 January 2026